FR
SECRETS

BILL
WARNOCK

A Coronet book

First published in Australia and New Zealand in 1997
by Hodder Headline Australia Pty Limited
(A member of the Hodder Headline Group)
10-16 South Street, Rydalmere NSW 2116

**National Library of Australia
Cataloguing-in-Publication data**

Warnock, William.
Frozen secrets.

ISBN 0 7336 0454 4.

1. Japan. Rikugun. Kantögun. Butai, Dai 731 – Fiction.
2. World War, 1939–1945 – Japan – Fiction.
3. Biological warfare – Japan – Fiction. I. Title.

A823.3

Cover design by Steve Miller/Snapper Graphics
Printed in Australia by McPherson's Printing Group

For Kylie and Adam

With special thanks in Tokyo to
Robert Whymant and Rod O'Brien:
Robert who first led me to the story
and generously helped me with research,
and Rod for providing a hospitable base.
In Australia my thanks to Spencer Geroff,
Tom Hungerford, John McIlwraith and
my dear wife Diana for their generous
encouragement and invaluable criticism.

A special tribute is due to Japanese journalist
and novelist Seiichi Morimura, who
demonstrated great moral and physical courage
by publishing, in Tokyo 1986, his exposé
of Section 731 and the camp at Harbin,
The Devil's Gluttony (Kappa Novels).

Duchess: I know death hath ten thousand several doors
For men to take their exits; and 'tis found
They go on such strange geometrical hinges,
You may open them both ways.

John Webster,
The Duchess of Malfi, act 4, scene 2

At Mii's gate, the frozen bell was tolled:
Its shivering resonance increased the cold.

Issa

Interview no. 11, Kurumitzawa Tsuji, Kobe:

Kurumitzawa: 'But, you must understand, we didn't
regard the logs as human beings.'
Kaizei: 'Logs?'
Kurumitzawa: *Maruta.* "Logs of wood". That's what
we called the prisoners.'
Kaizei: 'Why are you willing to speak about
this now?'
Kurumitzawa: 'It has been troubling me more,
recently. The bad dreams have begun
again. I am an old man. I suppose I'd
just like to meet my Maker with this
off my conscience.'

Chapter 1

Like a wounded man buckling at the knees, the blue Datsun lurched left then, sickeningly, right. It came within a paint-thickness of the car in the outside lane, then swung back. The threatened driver looked alarmed. The man in the Datsun did not notice. He stared blindly ahead.

Here, along the edge of Tokyo Bay, where the freeway strode across the docks at rooftop level, all four lanes were banked up with peak-hour, homeward bound traffic. It snailed along westwards a few metres at a time, stopping and starting like some creature choking in its own lethal waste.

A dark pillow of swollen clouds pressed down on the city as though to suffocate it. Columns of rain thick as silver wire drove like spears at the windscreen.

Terrible feelings of fear and panic were mushrooming in the mind of the man driving the blue Datsun. A minute before, his teeth had been chattering with a depthless cold. Now he could feel a napalm sweat breaking on his brow. He wound down his window and pushed his arm out. A pleasing chill of rain cooled the burning skin on the back of his hand. He wiped the drops against his feverish brow and the back of his neck. Must get off the road, he thought. Have to get off the road.

He looked in his mirror. As far back as he could see there were cars. In his mind he saw himself slumped behind the wheel unable to move, with the line of cars locked behind him forever, thousands of stalled drivers honking and pressing their angry faces against his car windows. He had to get off the road.

His mouth tasted of lead. His joints felt as though they were being welded with a blowtorch. An intense white light of pain had begun to pulse in his head. He had a sense of disbelief. It could not be happening to him. He had followed all the correct procedures. There couldn't have been an error.

The stalled traffic began to move forward. Frantically, he accelerated and slewed left, charging into a too-small space in the centre lane. Blasting his horn in angry protest, a Toyota driver stood on his brake to avoid a collision. He shouted something, his face a mask of fury.

The man in the blue Datsun began to vomit. As his car began to slice sideways through the left-hand traffic lanes more horns started protesting. The car hit the wall of the freeway. For twenty metres it scraped along the concrete, the sound of rending metal adding to the din. Inside the steel cocoon of the car the man began to scream with pain.

His insides were turning to fire. No, it can't be happening, he pleaded silently. Not to me. I followed all the procedures.

A steep exit ramp opened to the left. The Datsun swung downwards in a mad roller-coaster dive to the docklands below. It shot across a narrow street missing by inches a delivery boy on a bicycle and being missed, in turn, by a giant semi-jinker freezer truck. The truck sped on, its horn blaring. The Datsun smashed over a pavement, leapt into the air and fetched up against the steel fence of a wharfside warehouse.

The light hurt his eyes terribly. Frantically, he unbuckled himself. Too late. His bladder and bowels voided. He sobbed with humiliation. He forced open the door and fell out of the car into the overflowing gutter. The laser-bright pain seemed to split his head into a thousand fragments. His last conscious thought was, not to me . . . not to me . . .

Chapter 2

For two days Ransome stayed in the neutral, no-man's-land of his hotel room, waiting for the telephone to ring.

Out there someplace Kaizei was on the run, changing addresses daily. In his letter (the joy and astonishment of it—a call for help from the friend he had believed dead!) Kaizei had said that he would make contact as soon as he could.

A silent, time-lapse film of Tokyo projected onto the double-glass walls of Ransome's room: skyscapes, cloud effects, rain, planes grooving in and out above the distant airport—day–night, day–night.

Beyond the vertical bars of the crowding office towers, the lunatic city escaped in all directions under the lowering winter sky. There was no end to it, no margin. It simply dissolved at the dirty yellow rim where the chemicals finally absorbed all the light.

Once, on the furthest horizon, a snow-covered Fuji appeared, clad in the palest wash colours, only to disappear once more like some neurotic ghost.

Call, damn you!

On several occasions he was tempted to telephone Reiko, but decided against it. Once, he dialled the number but hung up before the tone began to sound. How would she react to his being in Tokyo? He hadn't told her he was coming. It had all happened in such a rush.

He thought about her, re-running scenes from their

time together. Lying on his bed, his breath quickened at the memory of her, the blood swelling in his veins. Reiko. Conjuring her lovely face; images of flesh; the texture of her skin; her black waterfall of hair catching the light.

He should never have let her go. He should have come after her. The truth was, had it not been for Kaizei's call he would still be in the States waiting for her to make contact. It had been three months since her mother had died and she had returned to Japan to be with her father; three months and not one word. Maybe he was already history. He stared at her number written in his address book. He should make the call.

In the end, he put it off, rationalising: there will be time after Kaizei makes contact.

Ransome began to worry about Kaizei. Had he, like a drowning man briefly glimpsed in surf, surfaced from out of the past only to sink down once more to the silence of the deep?

* * *

The waiting ended at ten-thirty on the second evening. As soon as Ransome left the bathroom, he noticed the envelope that had been slipped under his door. He had been showering, so had not heard if anyone had knocked. Naked, he went straight to the door and yanked it open. No Kaizei. No hotel bellboy. The long passage-way was empty. It was a plain, sealed envelope and inside, a typed note and crude sketch map. The note read: 'Interview. Hotel Lotus, room 8. Tsuchin-kaikan, 2-Aci-Cho, Shinjuku. 11 p.m. See you. K.'

The map showed a street intersection with a cross marking the position of the hotel.

What the hell was going on? Why hadn't Kaizei called?

Ransome checked his watch. He had less than half an hour and no idea where Shinjuku was. He dressed quickly, hauled his battered video camera from its case and checked the power pack. Fully charged.

Chaos reigned in the hotel foyer. He worked his way through crowds of businessmen, a bus-load of newly arrived German tourists complete with Tyrolean hats and lederhosen, a hysterical group of formally dressed wedding guests and swarming staff.

A biting wind whipped the canopy above the entrance. Ransome thought of going back for something warmer to wear, but there was no time. He showed the map to the tall, uniformed doorman and told him he was in a hurry. A cab drew up. Ransome climbed into the front seat. The doorman spoke rapidly to the cab driver, who gave the map a brief glance then gunned the motor. The taxi shot away from the hotel with a protesting squeal of rubber.

Apart from the fact that he gave off hostility like body odour, the driver reminded Ransome of Kaizei. He was young, with the same unkempt hair to his shoulders; the earrings, the no-tomorrow attitude to driving. With racing driver changes, screeching brakes, blaring horn and a stream of savage curses, he propelled the battered Toyota through the surreal maze of Tokyo.

Ransome decided on phlegmatism.

What would Kaizei be like, all these years after that day when luck had run out for both of them? In his letter he had said nothing about himself, had told only about the extraordinary story he had uncovered.

The city seemed to have no logic. Freeways began and ended; streets ran at all angles. Ransome lost all sense of direction as the driver wrenched the cab from one street, one district, one built-up area to another.

'Shinjuku,' said the driver finally. He slowed to walking pace in a main street jammed with cars and people.

Downtown Shinjuku was lit brighter than day. The walls of the buildings seemed to be fashioned from neon into one gigantic, seamless graffiti. Ransome's eyes sought the reassurance of his own language: 'Coca-Cola',

'Las Vegas', 'Frisco Girls', 'Explicit Sex'. Like Hollywood Boulevard or Times Square, restaurants, delicatessens, boutiques, porno movie-houses and fun parlours lined both sides of the street.

The cab stopped. The driver pointed. 'Rotus,' he said.

Directly opposite, a side street ran at right angles from where they had stopped. A few yards into the badly-lit entrance Ransome could read the vertical, flashing pink neon sign that proclaimed in Japanese and English, 'Hotel Lotus'.

He paid the fare. The cab catapulted away through a too-narrow break in the traffic.

The night air was armoured with ice. Ransome shivered, settled the familiar heft of his camera bag on his shoulder, and ran the gauntlet of the main street.

Tsuchin-kaikan was one of those furtive streets you find at the arse-end of any city, offering discreet hotels and dubious nightclubs by night, tattooing parlours and pawnshops by day. Low, narrow buildings, none more than four storeys, crowded the street. Rubbish bins and bags of refuse spilled from blank doorways. Cars were parked halfway up on the narrow pavements on both sides of the street.

Knots of people were gathered in front of various buildings. A group of black American sailors draped with girls in mini-skirts shouted their way into the night. As Ransome approached the entrance to the hotel, he found himself being stared at with baleful curiosity.

A young woman wearing a black micro dress with remarkable decolletage approached him. He shook his head and looked around. No sign of Kaizei.

There is a particular shocking-pink neon that equates with tawdriness. The winking sign of the Hotel Lotus clearly indicated that it was the kind of hotel one rented by the hour.

Inside the Lotus, the roseate theme of the neon sign

was repeated. The wallpaper, the counter, the banisters . . . even the overhead light was pink.

The hotel had seen better times. The paintwork was faded, chipped and shabby with fingermarks and grease stains. The rose-patterned carpet was showing its warp.

To one side of the foyer there was a narrow, chipped counter with a modern telephone console. Immediately ahead, a flight of stairs rose steeply.

Ransome caught sight of himself in a mirror; the *gaijin* with the broken nose and bony face looked nervous.

The place seemed deserted. He moved so that he could see into the room that opened behind the counter. Empty. On the counter, a bellpush. He pressed it. There was no sound. A minute ticked by. No-one appeared. He headed for the stairs.

Suddenly, from above, a derisive snort of woman's laughter and a volley of high-pitched words. There came a rapid clacking of heels. Silver slippers, trim ankles, then the voluptuous body of a girl came into view. She looked to be about sixteen—pretty in a pouty, tart's way. Behind her was a fat, balding man of about sixty.

By her tone, she was angry with her companion. She was craning backwards, the better to hurl her abuse at him. She did not see Ransome at first. When she turned, her words stopped as though she had been gagged. She stared at him with frank approval, then smiled and said something in rapid Japanese. He smiled back and shrugged to show that he did not understand.

With a look of intense interest, she pointed to his camera. 'Films?' she asked. He nodded.

She made a loud, approving remark and immediately leaned back against the banister. With one hand she pulled her skirt up on her thigh. She flung back her head, raised her other arm high and, with showbiz extravagance, assumed a pin-up pose complete with neon smile.

'Film star,' she said, then dissolved into wild laughter

at her own splendid joke. Ransome found himself laughing with her. The parody was perfect.

The fat man arrived at the foot of the stairs. Ransome saw that his face was badly scarred. He said something to the girl. It sounded petulant. She laughed at him derisively. He grabbed her arm, glared at Ransome, and hurried her out through the foyer. As she was propelled into the night, the girl looked back and showed Ransome a pink, lascivious tongue. Long after she was gone from sight, her laughter resounded.

Ransome made his way up the worn stairs. The carpet stopped at the first-floor level. He spotted the first room number halfway along the passageway: room number two. A few yards further on he came to number three, then, without having found another door with a number on it, ran into a dead end. From the street outside he heard the sound of car horns.

Back the way he came, past the top of the stairs. Numbers five, six, and seven . . . The next door had something written on it in red. He tried it. It opened onto the fire escape stairs. There was a bad smell of drains.

Round a corner. Room number eight was directly before him at the end of the passageway. The door was closed.

Ransome looked back. No-one in sight. He listened. The uncanny silence in the hotel suggested that he might be the only person in it. His instincts were signalling danger. His nerves were pinging like radar receivers.

He knocked quietly. No sound came from inside. He listened with his ear close to the door. Nothing. He knocked again, louder this time. Still no answer. He tried the door handle. It turned under his hand. Apprehension bloomed within him like a cancer. Had something happened to Kaizei?

The door swung open.

Inside the room, the lights were blazing. Like the rest

of the Hotel Lotus, the room was entirely pink: the walls, the bedcovers, the curtains.

Carefully, he edged his way inside. Apart from its colour, it was unremarkable: a circular double bed, two bedside lights, an easychair by the curtained window, a dressing-table of hideous design topped by a large round mirror; on the ceiling, directly above the bed, another mirror. In the corner, a television set was on, its sound-less image tumbling over sickeningly.

Ransome allowed his breath to escape slowly. His mouth felt dry. He took a couple of quick deep breaths to steady his nerves. His watch showed 11.05 p.m. Where was Kaizei? He had never been late in his life. Was he waiting outside someplace?

He crossed to the window and drew aside the curtains. The window afforded a view of the hotel's entrance. Carefully, he studied the faces of the people he could see in the street. No Kaizei.

Pink light flooded alluringly from the partly open bathroom door. He was going to have to go in there. Ransome felt the same fearful apprehension he had known as a kid growing up in the country, facing the nightly journey through the rustling and shadowed garden to the outside lavatory.

Nervously, he checked the door behind him. He laid his camera bag on the bed and approached the open door sensing that there was something terrible in that room.

He swung the door back.

A blast of chill air struck him. The floor was flooded with water. Standing upright in the corner of the room was a half-transparent column as tall as a coffin.

It took a moment to register. Ice.

From within the block of ice an arm stuck out. It was clad in the sleeve of a blue business suit. The hand was clenched in a rictus of agony. Jammed between the fingers there was an envelope.

Kaizei? Oh, don't let it be him!

Revulsion crowded. His first instinct was to run. He took a grip of himself. He moved closer, his eye following the frozen arm under the surface of the ice.

Behind the melting barrier he could see the distorted face of a man who seemed to be eternally, soundlessly screaming for help.

Chapter 3

The shock of seeing the frozen man was overcome by a flooding relief. It was not Kaizei.

Ransome became conscious of his racing pulse. What the hell was going on? Get out of this!

He steadied his breathing, went back through the bedroom to the door and looked out into the passageway. No-one in sight. He closed the door and locked it, then returned to the bathroom.

He stared at the face of the dead man. In his long journalist's career in the killing fields of South-East Asia, Africa and the Middle East, he had seen hundreds, perhaps thousands of corpses, but he had never lost his revulsion at the sight of death—the stillness, the waste of it. But some died easier than others. Judging by the agonised expression, this poor devil had met his end horribly.

As far as Ransome could tell through the thick carapace of ice, the dead man was fully dressed. He appeared to be about sixty, maybe older.

He studied the corpse in its icy coffin. Who was he? Kaizei's interviewee? How long had he been here? Had the man been frozen to death, or had he died from other causes and then been frozen and dumped in this sleazy hotel room?

Get out! Go!

The envelope beguiled. Gingerly, he tugged it loose from between the fingers of the icy hand. His own surname was written on it in bold red ink brushstrokes.

'Christ!' he said out loud, mind racing.

Inside was a single sheet of paper with some Japanese characters, also in red, brushed onto it. Ransome stuffed the note and envelope into his jacket pocket.

As he grabbed his camera bag from the bed, heading for the door, he heard a brief squeal of brakes from the street below. He crossed to the window and pulled aside the curtain. In the street, directly in front of the entrance, two cars were emptying of men, some of them in uniform.

Ransome bolted into the passageway.

There were three of them in the narrow space: two in uniform, one in plain clothes. Afterwards he became certain they had been waiting for him.

The nearest uniform caught him in an expert headlock. Ransome struggled briefly. The others joined in. He went to the ground, hard. Something smashed against his shoulder. A boot sunk into his ribs. He stopped struggling and tried to make himself as small as possible, curling his legs up and protecting his head with his arms.

His left arm was twisted painfully behind his back. He was dragged to his feet, two men holding him, half-up on his toes, in a professional and painful grip. He found himself face-to-face with a tall, round-faced young man with a crew cut.

The man searched him expertly, running his hands roughly over Ransome's body and legs. He jerked open his jacket. From the inside pocket, he took Ransome's wallet. He studied the passport for a long time. He handed it to one of his colleagues, who leafed through it interestedly. Next, Ransome's outside pocket. Crewcut found the note and the envelope. His eyes widened slightly when he read the note. He looked directly at Ransome, hostile now. He shouted a question.

'I don't speak Japanese,' Ransome said.

The man shouted once more, his angry face within inches of Ransome's.

Ransome shrugged, meeting the man's gaze.

Crewcut slapped him hard across the face. The blow brought tears to his eyes.

'Fuck you, George,' said Ransome, furious.

The crew cut man hit him again.

'Sideways,' Ransome said.

Crewcut may have understood, or not. He stared hot-eyed at Ransome for a moment then said something curtly to his companions. He opened the door of room eight and went inside.

Ransome was frogmarched painfully along the passageway then shoved down the stairs. There were two other police on the last flight of steps. As he was pushed past them, one of them tripped him. He fell against the pink wooden banister, hurting his knee.

A third police car was now parked by the entrance of the Lotus. Ransome was shoved into the back seat. The uniformed men who had assisted his descent crushed in on either side of him. The one on his left held his wrist up in front of Ransome. A pair of handcuffs dangled from it. Obligingly, Ransome held out his hand. The handcuffs were snapped on.

For fifteen minutes the car sat in the street, surrounded by a milling crowd of spectators. Dark-eyed faces pressed close enough to smear the glass. The two policemen and the driver talked and laughed together, ignoring the attention.

Ransome decided that until he found someone who could speak English he would say nothing. He wondered what had happened to his camera. It was too much of a coincidence that the police had arrived when they did. Someone had tipped them off about the body. He and Kaizei had been set up. He felt a sense of dread about his friend. What had happened to him?

There was much activity. The two other police cars left, minutes apart. An ambulance arrived, bulldozing its way through the ever-growing crowd, its two-tone klaxon howling.

The apparent urgency seemed misplaced. The victim was in no hurry. All that could happen now was that he might thaw out.

A uniformed policeman cleared a path between the hotel and the car. Crewcut came bustling out. He looked in through the rear window at Ransome as though to assure himself he was still there. The driver started the motor and Crewcut slid in beside him on the front seat. He said something to his companions, who laughed loudly.

The driver switched on the siren. The car charged at the crowd, which parted like a panic-stricken school of fish. It slammed into the main street at speed, fish-tailing slightly.

The kaleidoscope of city lights blurred as the black Toyota charged through the night. Ransome felt oddly exhilarated. It had been too long since anything interesting had happened to him.

* * *

Freak show. Shinjuku Central Police Station at one-thirty in the morning was brightly lit, ugly, dirty and dangerous.

The noise ebbed and flowed: a babble of voices, shouts, screams, sobbing, wild laughter, the constant banging of steel doors. Wild-haired punks, outraged pimps, brazen prostitutes, drunks and crazies came and went—some willingly, some under duress, some injured and bleeding. The place reminded Ransome of a front-line casualty clearing station.

Violence was everywhere. It was as though the multi-storeyed, red-brick building was a fortress, with the police and the criminals conducting their war right there in the main office.

He observed all this in small grabs as he was led back

and forth through various sections of the headquarters. Since he had been hustled upstairs from the underground parking area, he had been strip-searched, fingerprinted and photographed. His possessions had been listed, receipted and taken from him. Apart from being questioned, briefly, by a sour-faced and monosyllabic woman police clerk who spoke limited English and who gave up almost at once, no-one had spoken to him.

Finally he was taken to sit in a first-floor office behind a steel desk, attached to it by handcuffs. The office was spartan: the desk, a metal filing cabinet, a clothes stand behind the door. A young policeman, starched and creased to military perfection, sat on a straight-backed chair by the door, watching him suspiciously as though, by some trick, he might vanish.

According to the clock on the wall it was 1.40 a.m. when two uniformed men arrived. The handcuffs were removed from the leg of the desk. He was ordered to stand. The handcuffs were transferred to the wrist of one of the police.

A moment later the crew cut policeman came into the office. The uniformed men came to attention. Crewcut removed his jacket and hung it carefully on the stand. He snapped his fingers impatiently. One of the uniformed police proffered a piece of paper attached to a clipboard. Crewcut signed. He jerked his head towards Ransome.

Ransome was marched down three flights of concrete stairs, through a steel door, and into a glaring white-painted passageway. He was now two floors below ground level. The place smelled of vomit, urine and disinfectant.

There was much shouting. Several police in the passageway were struggling with two prisoners. They were bundled into a cell. As he passed the open door, Ransome caught a glimpse of a club flailing.

The cell to which Ransome was taken was tiled, morgue-white and lit bright as day. There were four bunks, the two top ones occupied. As the policemen entered, the occupants sat up slowly to observe what was happening.

One policeman held Ransome's arms from behind while the other stripped off his trouser belt. He then pointed to Ransome's shoes and snapped his fingers. Ransome slipped them off and handed them to him.

The policeman took them in one hand. With the other, he held up his baton in front of Ransome's face. For a moment, looking into the man's impenetrable brown eyes, Ransome wondered if the two policemen were going to start in on him. The man turned away.

The gesture was, apparently, a warning to behave. A moment later they were gone. From somewhere outside the cell there came faint sounds: cries, the sound of fighting. The tiled walls distorted the sounds, made them echo strangely.

Ransome found himself being regarded with frank contempt.

The men could have been brothers. They had the same cropped heads, the same thickset muscular build that comes only from long hours of working out with heavy weights. Save for a breechclout, both were naked. Their upper bodies were covered entirely by intricate tattoos. The taller of the two was missing the little finger of his left hand. *Yakuza*. He had read someplace that mutilations were the honourable payment in flesh for some failure or error by a gang member.

The other man's hands were intact. He looked balefully at Ransome and said to his companion, 'Ransome-san.' They both laughed derisively.

Ransome stared at them. Christ, how many people knew he was in Tokyo? The two went on staring fixedly at him as though to imprint his face on their minds.

After a time, the man leaned forward and spoke again. He seemed to be reciting a phrase learned by heart. 'Warning, Ransome-san,' he said. 'You not leave Japan, you die like man in hotel. Understand?'

Ransome said nothing, staring into the man's bleak eyes, wondering who was so determined to suppress Kaizei's story that they were prepared to kill for it.

Chapter 4

In the bright light of a wintry morning the sterile office on the first floor of the Shinjuku police head-quarters looked marginally less intimidating. At least on this visit he was not handcuffed to the desk. Through the steel mesh set into the window, presumably there to prevent detainees hurling themselves onto the pavement below, Ransome could see the early morning traffic swishing past on a rain-soaked, elevated freeway. The leafless branches of whip-thin trees planted along the edges of the concrete were flailing in the icy wind.

The fat uniformed officer who had brought him up from the cells lounged with his back to the door, from time to time yawning extravagantly.

Ransome felt grubby and desperately tired. He had slept hardly at all. The night had passed with a numbing slowness, its progress a complex catalogue of sounds: cries of fear, of pain, of laughter from beyond the cell door, the snuffles and farts of his cell-mates.

Most of the night he had lain staring at the white tiled walls wondering how it must be to serve a life term in such a place.

It had helped to think of Reiko. Remembered kisses, remembered moments, a palisade of erotic thoughts drawn up to lock out the ugly present.

Reiko. Garret had seen her first, that day on the university tennis courts. 'Did you spot her?' he had said, nodding towards the lone woman two courts away practising her serve. He had whistled silently in admiration. 'Totally gorgeous.'

Ransome hadn't paid that much attention. Garret thought they were all gorgeous. Under the skipped tennis cap and behind the sunglasses, there hadn't been much to see, and she served laughably.

An hour later, by coincidence, he had seen her in the coffee shop. She had been by herself, reading a book, a coffee going cold on the table before her.

'Didn't your partner turn up?' he had said.

'I won't need a partner until I can serve properly,' she had replied, looking at him directly. 'I'd be too embarrassed.' She had smiled at him. Garret was right; she was lovely.

Ransome remembered the strange, disembodied feeling he had experienced. He had often thought about the ideal woman you were supposed to see across a crowded room, meet on a tram, pass on a street corner. In that first moment he had felt certain she was the one.

'May I join you?'

She had inclined her head, considering, then invited him to sit. She had put her book down. She had been reading Koestler.

Suddenly his guard sprang to attention. A man entered the room, a lean fellow of middle height. Ransome judged him to be in his early thirties.

He was dressed in an elegant dark-grey, single-button suit. He wore a blue shirt and a dark-green and blue striped tie. A gold bar held the tie in place. There were gold cufflinks at the sleeves, a white handkerchief in the breast pocket. The look was that of a prosperous lawyer.

The man sat down opposite Ransome. He put the file he was carrying foursquare on the desk before him. There was a sense of economy about his movements:

no wasted motion, no fidgeting. He looked at Ransome for the first time, weighing him up with a frank gaze. He had remarkable eyes—dark and lustrous. For a long moment they held Ransome in an odd, time-stopping way. The eyes dominated a bony face, the face of an athlete who has been on a razor's edge of fitness for one year too many.

'Have you been given anything to eat?' The accent was heavy, the words spoken as though they were being read from an advanced Linguaphone guide.

The hunger that had been insidiously clawing at Ransome's vitals since he had wakened suddenly came into focus. He shook his head, feeling slightly faint.

The man gave a little grimace of annoyance, as though he were a host at a dinner party witnessing the bad manners of a family member. He issued a rapid order, then returned his gaze to Ransome. 'Tea or coffee?'

'Coffee, please, black.'

The request became an order. The uniformed man, now at ramrod attention bowed his head, quickly. '*Hai!*' he said, then he was gone, closing the door behind him carefully.

'It may take awhile.' There was a hint of an apologetic smile. 'We are not equipped to supply breakfasts.' He opened a drawer and pulled out a small writing pad which he laid on the desk before him.

'Uto,' he said. 'Inspector Uto.'

He opened the file. Ransome saw that it contained his passport. From his inside pocket Uto took a gold pen. He laid it down beside the pad and leaned forward. The eyes encompassed Ransome without rancour.

'Why are you in Japan, Mr Ransome?'

Ransome did not want to make trouble either for himself or Kaizei. He had already decided that he would say as little as possible. He would answer questions truthfully or say nothing.

'As you would know from my passport,' Ransome gestured towards the file, 'I'm a journalist. I'm here on an assignment.'

'What is the nature of your assignment?'

'I'm assisting a Japanese colleague of mine.'

'Mr Kaizei.'

Ransome wondered how he knew about Kaizei. Had they arrested him, too? There was no point in denying it. He nodded.

'The nature of the assignment?'

'That's confidential,' Ransome said.

Uto's eyes seemed to become metallic. 'Let me remind you that we are dealing with a murder here, one in which you are implicated. I insist on knowing what this is about.'

Ransome wondered what his rights were—if he had any. He said, 'I can only tell you what happened at the hotel.'

Uto sat back and stared at him. His eyes were hostile. 'Mr Ransome, you realise that a lack of cooperation can result in your instant arrest and subsequent deportation. Your "confidential" assignment will not then take place. Is that what you want?' The voice had a blade in it.

'I don't know Japanese law,' Ransome said. 'Am I entitled to a lawyer?'

'A foreign journalist who is refusing to answer questions about a murder?' Uto seemed incredulous. 'You are entitled to nothing.'

Ransome said, 'I wasn't aware, Inspector, that you were running a police state in Japan. The outside world will be interested to learn about that.'

Uto went dangerously still. They stared at each other for a time. At length, the policeman seemed to take a decision. His expression relaxed. 'You had your camera with you,' he said. 'You were there to interview someone?' His tone had become neutral.

Ransome felt relieved. He nodded. 'Yes.'

'Someone who had information?'

'I believe so.' How much does this policeman really know? he wondered.

'Was the dead man the one you were supposed to interview?'

'I don't know. Maybe.'

Uto considered the implications of that answer for a time. 'Did you know the dead man?'

Ransome shook his head. 'No.'

'Do you know anything about him?'

'No.'

'Did Kaizei know him?'

'He set up the interview.'

'He was supposed to be there, wasn't he?'

Ransome considered the question. There was no reason to deny it. 'Yes. He didn't turn up.'

Uto said, 'You wonder how I know about Mr Kaizei and about your meeting?' From the bottom of the slim sheaf of papers in the file, he took the note and envelope Ransome had found clutched in the dead man's hand. He studied the envelope. 'Addressed to you in English,' he said.

Ransome said nothing.

'You read Japanese?'

'No.'

Uto smoothed the crumpled note and held it up to Ransome. 'So you don't know what this says?'

'No, but I thought it might tell me something when I had it translated.'

'Where did you find it?'

Ransome held his fist towards the policeman. He pointed to the space between his first and second finger. 'Jammed into the hand of the dead man.'

Uto was silent for a moment, his face still. 'Did you think Mr Kaizei left it for you?'

'No, it's not his style. Anyway, he would have written it in English. He knows I don't speak Japanese.'

Uto turned the paper around and studied it for a time. Without looking up: 'Have you any idea how much danger you are in?'

Ransome shrugged to show he didn't have an answer.

Uto gave a small snort of disbelief. 'Are you so naive, Mr Ransome? Surely Mr Kaizei told you something about the nature of your assignment?'

'I know what it's about.'

'So you know it involves some danger?'

'Yes.'

'Including murder?'

'No.'

The inspector looked irritated. 'There has been a killing and you, and probably your partner, were in the room of the hotel where it happened. That is all I know. I need to know more. That is the reason you are here.'

At that moment there was a knock at the door. The uniformed policeman came into the room. He was carrying a white plastic tray. Upon it there were several small bowls containing meat, vegetables, rice and little pastry-covered rolls. There were chopsticks. Two white plastic cups were half-filled with black coffee; the rest had spilled. Uto pointed at the tray and spoke sharply. The policeman left the room in a hurry.

While he was gone Uto sat silently, his face set in a mask as though he were listening to inner voices.

The piquant smells from the tray caused Ransome to salivate.

The fat policeman returned carrying some tissues. He mopped up the spilled coffee. He set the tray in front of Ransome, placed the second cup of coffee in front of Uto and left. Uto gestured that Ransome should eat.

As he picked up his chopsticks, Ransome said, 'You're not suggesting I had anything to do with it?'

Uto raised his eyebrows, questioningly.

'Christ, the man was set in a block of ice! How am I supposed to have done that?'

Uto looked at him without expression.

As their eyes met, Ransome felt as though his mind was being swept for lies. But there was no hostility in the look. He wasn't being accused—not of murder. Aware of Uto watching him, he began to eat. The food was delicious.

'You touched the body?'

Ransome shook his head. Once more he saw the anguished face behind the wall of ice.

Uto studied a pale blue paper in his file. 'The preliminary autopsy shows that the old man may have been frozen to death or frozen after he was dead. They cannot tell how long he had been dead. It depends what freezing method was used. We'll know more later today.'

Uto put the blue document back into the file. He stood up and walked to the window. He stood looking out at the rain. 'There are signs that the old man may have been tortured before he died.'

Tortured? Ransome felt a frisson of disgust.

After a time, Uto turned back and sat down. 'Last night,' now businesslike. 'Were you badly treated by the police?'

Ransome wondered what to say. Was the inspector a police public affairs man worried about a foreigner making a complaint? He shrugged, non-committal.

Uto looked troubled and unhappy. 'I really need to know what is going on here,' he said. A muscle on his face flickered briefly.

He watched Ransome eat for a time. 'You handle chopsticks well, Mr Ransome, but then you've lived in Asia for long periods, have you not.' It was not a question. He would have learned as much from a brief study of Ransome's heavily stamped passport. Ransome had a feeling the policeman knew a great deal about him.

Uto reached across his desk and took one of the small pastry-covered rolls. He popped it neatly into his mouth. 'No, I don't for a moment think you murdered the old man, Mr Ransome. But somebody did. Do you know who? Was it your partner, Mr Kaizei?' He sipped at his coffee, watching Ransome over the rim of the plastic cup.

Ransome said, 'Anyone less likely to murder someone, I can't imagine.'

Uto nodded thoughtfully. He gave the impression he was listening not only to Ransome's words but to the layers of meaning that might underlie them. 'The most surprising things will turn a man into a murderer, Mr Ransome. Tension, pressure, blackmail, fear. Are any of these things likely to be affecting your partner right now? Has he been under threat?'

'I'd stake my life he had nothing to do with it.'

'You *are* staking your life, Mr Ransome, make no mistake about that.' Uto aligned the note dead centre on his desk, looking across it as though he were aiming a gun-sight at Ransome's chest. He gestured towards the ornate red script. 'It says here that unless you and Mr Kaizei end your . . .' pausing as he summoned up the right word in translation, 'nosiness, you will certainly follow the dead man.' He gave a small puzzled shrug.

Christ, everyone in Tokyo seemed to know he was here. Whoever had killed the old man in the hotel room knew, the thugs in the cell downstairs knew—and they all wanted him out of the place. Had Kaizei told the dead man his name? Had he disclosed that it was an American journalist who was coming to film the interview? Had the man revealed what he knew under torture?

Uto stared across the desk, challenging now. 'Now that someone has been killed, Mr Ransome, do you intend to go on pursuing your story?'

Ransome put down the chopsticks and sipped at the coffee. It was strong and cold. 'If Kaizei wants to go on with it, yes. I've promised him I will help.'

Uto suddenly looked very tired. 'I've often wondered about what it must be like to be a journalist: finding things out about people, digging up scandal. In your case Mr Ransome, as a war correspondent, watching many people die. Is your story important enough that people must die for it?'

The question struck Ransome a low blow. He had often questioned his role as a journalist. He had often wondered why he had been prepared to film the brutality of men, women and children dying by fire, bullet or bomb. Always—save the once when he'd had to fight for his life—he had been the passive observer, taking not the slightest action to alter the grim reality he was recording.

'Inspector Uto,' feeling the need for the title—there was a distancing factor in formality—'I make only one judgment about the jobs I do: is the story worth doing or not? No professional journalist would fail to do a worthwhile job because of what might happen afterwards. I don't suppose policemen do either.'

Uto acknowledged the crack with a slight lift of his eyebrows.

'I think this assignment is worth doing.' Ransome knew he sounded defensive.

Uto weighed him up in silence. After a time he said, 'I think, Mr Ransome, you have been involved in what you Americans call a "frame-up". Apparently we,' grimacing here, 'that is, the local police, were told that you would be in the hotel and that there would be a dead man there. An anonymous telephone call,' watching keenly to see how Ransome reacted to this revelation.

Ransome gave a weak smile. From the first moment in that tawdry hotel it had smelled like a set-up.

'Someone is extremely anxious that you and your colleague Kaizei should not go on with this investigation of yours. The same person was possibly responsible for the death of the old man. I need to know who and why.'

'If it's of any use, Inspector,' Ransome said, 'the two men in my cell last night knew who I was. They made the same threats as were in that note.'

'What men?'

'Two prisoners. Young guys, covered in tattoos, one with a finger missing.'

'When did you see them last?' Uto looked as if he had been slapped.

'An hour ago. They were in the cell when I left to come up here.'

The policeman jumped to his feet and hurried from the room.

Ransome sat staring out the window thinking through the implications. Could these two thugs be the killers? he wondered. Maybe arrested at the same time? And what had happened to Kaizei? Where was he? Was he in a cell somewhere? It wasn't like him to fail to turn up. And if he had arrived at the rendezvous before Ransome, he would never have gone without leaving some kind of warning. Not Kaizei. Not his style.

Ten minutes passed before the inspector came back. Uto's face was grim. He stood behind the desk and leafed through the file.

'Secrets, Mr Ransome,' he said. 'All societies are full of them. I suspect you must be about to reveal one that may embarrass some very powerful people.' He looked at Ransome with a strange expression on his face. 'About those two prisoners. You must be mistaken. They keep the most careful arrest records here. According to station reports, no men like those you describe were arrested last night. And there is no record that you shared a cell with anyone.'

He doesn't believe it either, Ransome thought. He said, 'Yeah, sure. I confess. I just made them up. I was lonely.'

Chapter 5

The two policemen sitting on guard just inside the front entrance watched blankly as Ransome and McGregor left. Their expressions were those of men who know for certain that everyone is guilty.

Outside, it was freezing cold. A thin, icy sleet slanted into their faces. McGregor put up an umbrella. They stood close together under it.

Ransome breathed the cold air, gratefully. He said, 'Sorry about this. The police found your number in my address book. I had planned to call you socially, not to get me out of jail.'

McGregor said, 'Typical of you, Ransome. You're only in the place five minutes and you're where the shit's flying.' The Edinburgh brogue was still as thick as treacle. 'Jesus! Murder, nights in salubrious Shinjuku jail—the whole catastrophe.' He was impressed.

'It hasn't been boring,' Ransome said.

'Come on, I jagged a parking space. That's some kind of miracle in this town.' McGregor grabbed Ransome's arm and, holding him under the spread of his large umbrella, led off along the street.

The streets were bleak. Pedestrians leaned into the rain and skipped from one sheltered place to the next.

As they walked, they began to hear distorted sounds of screamed exhortations, answered by loud, disciplined chanting. Near a major intersection, the noise became deafening. It filled up the spaces between the buildings and drowned out the noise of the traffic on the overhead expressway.

The procession was a huge and orderly affair, headed by two sound trucks festooned with red and black banners and covered by protective mesh. From inside the cabins the leaders—young, tough-looking men—took turns in shouting slogans through their booming amplification systems.

A senior police officer walked in front of the marchers. He wielded a riot baton as though it were a swagger stick. At the crossing, the lights changed to red. The police officer halted the march. There, a dozen policemen were organising the traffic flow to accommodate the demonstration. Pedestrians were not permitted to cross.

'You have a better quality of rabble in Japan,' Ransome said, amused. 'They wait for the lights to change.'

'That's what scares me about the bastards,' McGregor said.

The lights turned green. The procession set off once more. There were several hundred marchers, all in lockstep, each with his arms around the waist of the man in front, walking six abreast in squads of about a hundred. The leaders of the squads carried banners covered in signs. Every hundred yards another sound truck sustained the marchers with ear-shattering slogans. All were men, almost all of them dressed in the salaryman's ubiquitous grey or blue suit with a sober tie, but there was a sprinkling of workers in overalls. Every marcher wore a white headband bearing red and black characters and the Rising Sun flag. They chanted as they marched.

'Who are these guys?' Ransome asked.

'Right-wing extremists. The kind of crazies who say the capitulation in 1945 was a betrayal of the Japanese people by the army and the navy; that the Japanese people never surrendered. You cannot believe how many of them there are in this country.'

Ransome eyed the banners. 'What are they on about?'

'They're urging everyone back to the disciplined ways of patriotism,' said McGregor with heavy sarcasm.

'A well-organised vocal minority?'

McGregor shook his head, looking sober, 'Oh, they're much more dangerous than that. It's a very heavy political scene here at the moment. The government's caught up in a big scandal, the Right are pushing for power. The place is likely to go up in flames any minute. It's a dicey situation. Luckily, the Prime Minister may be a card-carrying crook, but he has stamina. Unlike the bee, which stings and dies, Norimura stings and lives on.'

The next change of traffic lights split the procession in two. As the marchers halfway back were held up, their cries to their departing comrades sounded mournful.

McGregor said, 'It's a lively town at the moment. All this political stuff plus a *yakuza* gang war. One of the *yakuza* heavies was shot down last night in Osaka. His girlfriend's in intensive care. Tit for tat for another two killings the week before. It's unusual. They might be head cases, these people, but they don't usually shoot each other in the streets.'

'Connected with this political thing?' Ransome said.

'Good question,' McGregor grimaced, thoughtfully. 'Could be. There's a lot of nationalist feeling among the *yakuza*.'

The lights changed. The police beckoned the marchers forward and, at last, the procession passed from sight. The slogans and chanting gradually faded under the traffic's roar.

They had been held up by the march for nearly ten minutes. Ransome could feel the rain soaking his trouser legs. His shoes had not been designed for wet weather.

They crossed under the expressway and walked into the narrow streets of Kabuki-cho, lined with eating houses and gift shops. There were few people about.

Gloomy shopkeepers stood in front of their shops and market stalls. McGregor led him around several corners and finally turned into a narrow alleyway. An ancient Jaguar was parked up on the pavement with two wheels on the road. The passenger side was within inches of the yellow concrete wall of a house.

McGregor became still. 'Listen,' he said. From somewhere beyond the high wall there came the plucked, hesitant sound of a harp. 'Samisen,' McGregor said, his round face transformed by a gentle smile. For a few moments they stood together listening to the dulcet sound of the lovely music. 'This shitheap of a city is full of beautiful moments.' He unlocked the car, manoeuvred his considerable bulk into the driving seat and reversed the car sharply, clear of the wall.

Ransome climbed in. The car was warm inside. Immediately he felt better. He was with a friend. The nightmare of the previous night, of being a captive in a strange land, began to recede.

'A man's a lunatic to have a car in Tokyo,' said McGregor. He let out the clutch and began to drive confidently through a twisting maze of backstreets so narrow that two cars could not pass unless one mounted the pavement.

'Alright, while I take our lives in my hands in this traffic, you be the entertainment. How come I suddenly get a call from the police telling me you're in the slammer?'

How much to tell? He could not risk revealing too much. McGregor was a working journalist and, as Ransome recalled from their days in South-East Asia, a notably tough-minded one. To McGregor a secret was something you kept only long enough to get it on the front page. Anything he considered newsworthy was potential copy.

Ransome decided to keep it simple and tell no more

than he needed to. 'You remember KT? Kaizei?' he said.

'Katie?' McGregor said, shaking his head in sorrow. 'Your madskull mate, the poor bastard. Sure, I remember him.'

'I'm here to do an assignment with him.'

'*On* him?' misunderstanding.

'No, *with* him.'

'You're kidding me.' McGregor looked astonished. 'I thought he'd bought it in Kampuchea.'

'So did I, until he wrote me,' Ransome said.

McGregor punched his steering wheel. 'How about that!' He laughed, joyfully.

Ransome told McGregor about his feelings when Kaizei's letter had come out of the blue.

'He might have told somebody. His name's still on the "Missing in Action" honour board at the Foreign Correspondents' Club. What's the assignment?' McGregor had the look of someone smelling a story.

'Something heavy he's been working on.' Ransome avoided complications and details. He told McGregor only that he had arranged to meet Kaizei and that a dead man had been found at the rendezvous.

'Dead bodies in hotels. What the hell are you two up to?'

Ransome said, 'I'll know more when I finally catch up with Kaizei.'

'Was he there last night?'

Ransome shook his head. 'He was supposed to be, but he didn't show. I think he's in a bit of bother.'

'Bother? What kind of bother? A gang war story? *Yakuza*, that kind of stuff?' McGregor sounded envious.

'Something like that.' Ransome tried not to think of what might have happened to his friend.

McGregor neatly manoeuvred his way through a six-way interchange, caught a 'go' sign and swung into a side street, narrowly missing a motorcyclist. They were now in a pleasant inner-city area that reminded Ransome of Paris or Eastside New York.

'Akasaka,' McGregor announced. 'A *gaijin* ghetto. The rents kill you, but there's no place else worth staying.'

'My hotel's here someplace.'

'What's it called?'

'The Prince.'

McGregor made a mock-impressed face. 'A rich journalist, yet.' He drove the car underneath a narrow apartment building. 'How'd a decent cup of coffee go?'

The apartment occupied the top half of the building. As McGregor opened the door he called out, 'Su?'

There was no reply. Ransome caught a fleeting expression on McGregor's flushed face: part embarrassment, part annoyance. 'She must have gone into the newsroom,' he said. 'She's got a big project on. She's there a lot these days. I work mostly at home. You'll have to meet her another time. You'll love her. She's gorgeous.' He spoke with an odd lack of conviction.

McGregor was notoriously successful with women. There had always been a pretty Vietnamese woman around, or one of the myriad journalist camp followers fresh from England, Australia or the States. Ransome wondered what was wrong with his present relationship.

'Kick off your shoes,' McGregor said, slipping off his own. He put Ransome's wet shoes and socks on top of a radiator in the tiny hallway. He went through to the kitchen and began to make coffee. 'Look around.'

McGregor and Su appeared to live well. The apartment was small, but the white walls and the sparse furniture gave an impression of space. In the comfortable sitting room there was a fine Art Deco sideboard and a matched pair of ladderback chairs. Adorning the walls was a set of Japanese ideographs that appeared to be very old. There were several exquisite pieces of pottery displayed on a low table.

Ransome remembered that McGregor had always been an odd mixture. In Vietnam he had been one of the hard players, doing crazy things to get stories and even crazier things off duty. The more he drank, the wilder he became. His wildness sat oddly with his passion for antiques and pottery. He had bought good pieces on Saigon's black market and, with great care, shipped them back to his parents in Scotland. Once, in the beer garden of the Club Sportif, he had shown Ransome a pot he claimed was over a thousand years old. He had spent five thousand dollars on it.

They swapped autobiographies. Ransome drank coffee and McGregor had three scotches in quick succession. He drank with an odd amalgam of gluttony and guilt. He would toy with each drink for several minutes before finally succumbing and sinking it with a single, embarrassed swallow. McGregor told him how he had landed a London bureau job with the London *Sunday Times* after Saigon fell. 'For six years it bored the crap out of me. Then I wangled some freelance work and came to Tokyo. Best thing that ever happened to me.' He sounded somewhat defensive.

A month after he had arrived in Tokyo he had met Suroko, 'the one woman for me'. She was a fellow journalist. They had met in the Foreign Correspondents' Club and again, two days later, at a party thrown by an American advertising man. She had moved into his flat that night. They had been together ever since. Four years. 'Wait till you see her,' McGregor said. 'Bloody lovely.'

A key sounded in the lock. McGregor sprang to his feet. 'That's her now.' He sounded relieved.

From the moment he saw them together, Ransome was aware of a space between them. There was a lack of spontaneity in their hug of greeting. These two people were going through the motions.

Suroko was, in fact, pretty rather than gorgeous. Her
face was very typically Japanese. Ransome felt as though
he had seen her before. Then he made the connection—
her curving nose and high-domed brow came straight
from one of Utamaro's paintings. Her night-black hair
hung down in a smooth bob. Her complexion was as
flawless as porcelain. She barely came up to Ransome's
breastbone, but was so neatly proportioned that she
seemed taller than she was. When they shook hands, her
grip was firm.

'How do you do, Mr Ransome,' she said, her voice
treating the consonants with meticulous care. 'Robbie
has told me so much about you that is admiring.' Her
smile was reserved.

'Admirable,' said McGregor, smiling doubtfully at her.

'Call me Jack,' said Ransome. 'Please.'

'Are you just leaving?' she seemed disappointed.
'Won't you stay for lunch?'

McGregor said, 'He's expecting an urgent phone call.'

'What a pity,' Suroko said. 'I hope we will meet again.'
She sounded as if she meant it.

Ransome liked her. 'I do, too,' he said, smiling at her.

'Did you really spend the night in prison?' She looked
concerned, like a hostess whose guest has been insulted
by another.

Ransome nodded.

'Did our police treat you badly?' the journalist's curiosity showing on her face.

'Been treated worse,' Ransome said, smiling. And he
had. A Vietnamese military cell once, a misunderstanding. He'd carried rifle-butt bruises on his back for
months. He said, 'But they might not be so friendly if
you were guilty'.

He wondered how much to tell them. He had omitted
to tell McGregor about the two *yakuza* who had
mysteriously disappeared from the police arrest records

overnight. But there was no point involving his saviour in something ugly and possibly dangerous. He decided to say nothing about that.

'I would like to write story about going to prison,' she said. She gave a little giggle. 'First I must commit crime.'

* * *

'Great girl,' Ransome said as McGregor walked him down into the street.

'Yes, she is.' McGregor sounded wistful.

Two blocks brought them to a main street that ran alongside the gardens of the Detached Palace. At the foot of the hill, Ransome's hotel rose up from behind the expressway in a pale sweep of concrete and glass.

'How long are you staying?'

'As long as it takes,' Ransome said. 'Sorry to drag you into this.'

'Most interesting thing that's happened to me for too long. If you need any help, call me.'

'I will,' said Ransome.

'I mean it,' McGregor said. 'I'm bored shitless writing endless stories about the faltering Japanese economy. Not everyone's lucky enough to find themselves in the middle of a murder. I hope your pal turns up—and in one piece.'

Ransome said nothing.

They parted at the end of the driveway that ran up to the entrance of the hotel.

'One final thing,' McGregor said as they shook hands. He grinned at Ransome. 'Probably no-one's said it yet, but—welcome to Japan.'

Chapter 6

The phone was purring when Ransome entered his hotel room. Kaizei—it had to be! He snatched up the handpiece.

'Hurro Loundeyes,' the voice said.

'Man,' said Ransome. 'Oh, man, it's good to hear you.' Kaizei's mock Japanese accent brought a rush of affectionate memories to the surface, together with a depthless feeling of relief.

Kaizei said, 'Great to have you here, Jack.'

'You okay?' Ransome said. 'I was worried sick you'd been arrested last night. Where did you get to?'

'Last night?' Kaizei sounded puzzled. 'Arrested? What are you talking about?'

'At the hotel . . . the Lotus. Even as he spoke, Ransome felt the chill beginning in the pit of his stomach.

'What Lotus Hotel?' There was alarm in Kaizei's voice. He was making the same connection.

'You sent me that note, right? To meet there for the interview?' Thinking: the note was *typed*. Oh Christ, he'd fallen for it.

'I didn't send you a note. I didn't even know you were in Japan. When did you get here? Last night?'

'I've been here for two days, three counting today.'

'Come on! I've been calling you on the hour for the past two days,' Kaizei said. 'Last night I called three times. I assumed you had been delayed.' He sounded agitated. 'They just kept saying you hadn't checked in yet.'

'Hadn't checked in? That's bullshit! I've called the desk

a dozen times asking if you had phoned. Late last night I had a note pushed under my door. I just assumed it was from you. It was signed "K". I fell for it. I finished up in the slammer accused of murder.'

'Murder?'

'When I arrived at the hotel some guy had been murdered and the police tipped off. They were waiting.'

'Murdered? Who was murdered?' Kaizei's voice was quiet.

Ransome said, 'I don't know the name. An old man. When I was released by the police this morning, he still hadn't been identified. And whoever did it left a note warning us to lay off. Naming us both.'

'Jesus Christ.' Kaizei sounded sick. 'Pick you up outside the front in ten minutes, okay?' The phone clicked off.

Ransome paused for a moment considering whether to take his camera gear along, but decided against it. He had worked with Kaizei often enough to know that he gave specific briefings. He grabbed a jacket and left the room.

As the lift sped silently down from the twenty-fourth floor, he thought about the implications of last night. Why had the desk been telling Kaizei he hadn't checked in yet? Why had he been told there had been no calls?

He caught his reflection in the mirror of the elevator. The face that looked back had deep shadows under the eyes. You're getting too long in the tooth for this stuff, Ransome thought.

At reception he asked a series of questions of the desk captain, and the man went off to check. He returned, smiling professionally. No, there had been no calls save the one that had just been put through. No, it was not possible that the switch operators would have wrongly advised callers that he had not checked in. There must be some mistake. Was he sure his caller rang the correct hotel? Very sorry, cannot help.

Someone had separated Kaizei from him very neatly indeed.

In the vast foyer, a slick pianist was playing 'The Lady is a Tramp' on the white grand. A doorman saluted him. He went out through the sliding glass doors.

The wind whipped him in the face. He buttoned up his jacket against the chill. There was no sign of his friend. He moved a little way from the entrance, walking back and forth to keep the blood circulating.

A constant flow of cars drove up the hill to the entrance of the Prince. Ransome looked in vain for Kaizei among them. The occupants—venerable older men, some of them accompanied by beautiful women; elegant young businessmen; lone women in chauffeur-driven limousines—were bowed out of their cars into the building by a team of bellboys.

In Kampuchea Death was a Lady. That month she had been especially busy. Ransome had last seen Kaizei in a paddy field in Kampuchea, the day their survivors' luck had finally run out. They had both bought it in the same fire-fight.

Eight days later, when he had talked his way out of hospital, he had found Kaizei posted as 'missing, believed killed'. Journalists were dying faster than hope that year, but he had not believed it of Kaizei. Ransome had begun looking for his friend that day, but there was so much confusion, so many people being killed that all medical trails were hopelessly trampled.

He had quizzed the helicopter pilots who had flown the grim circuits and bumps that day, hauling out the wounded; the medical orderlies who played God every day on the triage, sorting the wounded into categories of 'saveable' and 'hopeless'; the base hospital where, in theory, records were kept. Who had shipped him out? Who had tended his wounds? Who had seen him arrive at a hospital? Following up Kaizei's trail had become an obsession. It went on for months, without result. It was as though his friend had been wiped off the bomb-scarred and bloodied face of the Kampuchean earth. Everyone remembered and no-one remembered.

He'd had it reported to him, variously, that Kaizei had lost a leg, an arm, two legs, died of a gut-shot, died of loss of blood. Each person he had spoken to was either certain that Kaizei had been sent on some place further back or equally adamant that he had never got that far.

He had asked everyone he'd met, had spent days dealing with bureaucrats, nights checking medical lists; he had phoned Kaizei's colleagues, his countrymen, his news bureau. No-one knew. No-one could remember. Few could have cared less. For the locals, the loss of one more foreign journalist was of no account. For the other Western journalists, talk of Kaizei's demise—the legendary Kaizei whose life was notably charmed—was an unwelcome reminder of their own mortality. They preferred not to discuss it. Behind their sympathetic words Ransome heard the true, unspoken descant of their relief: it had been someone else who had bought it.

Ransome had been finally obliged to believe Kaizei was dead when, one drunken night during some self-determined rest and resuscitation in Bangkok, a journalist from the London *Sunday Times* had told him that she had heard Kaizei had been shipped out to Saigon aboard an American transport. There he had died of his wounds. It was hearsay and therefore, to his deepest journalistic instincts, entirely unsatisfactory, but Ransome had been inclined to believe her. She had had a fling with Kaizei, too. She had known he and Kaizei were close friends. He had judged that she cared enough about both of them not to pass on lightly such a piece of bad news.

So, his friend, companion, saviour was dead. It had been too late then for mourning. The cathartic celebration of grief was lost to him. Since that time there had been only a sense of loss, of let-down. Then, after all the years, had come his letter that had been the circuit-breaker for the terminal boredom of travelogues and promotional documentaries. Now, in a few minutes, they would be reunited.

Still no sign of Kaizei. He checked his watch, worried that he might have missed him, or misunderstood the message. Tokyo lay beyond the screen of pine trees and dark hedges of daphne that surrounded the hotel, its limitless skyline blurred by a low mist. The traffic on the elevated expressway at the foot of the hill swished by.

Suddenly, above the traffic noise, there came a sound like tearing calico. A gleaming motorcycle surged up the drive. The rider, dressed in black leather, was a science fiction creature, his face obscured by the wrap-around visor of his helmet.

The motorcycle drew up immediately in front of Ransome. The rider straightened up and flicked back his dark visor. The eskimo face, the acne-scarred cheeks, the face creased by a gap-toothed smile. Kaizei! KT. Katie to his friends.

'Howdy, Loundeyes,' said Kaizei, in passable American.

Ransome grabbed him around the shoulders in a bearhug. 'For a dead man, you feel very substantial,' he said, smiling in disbelief at the sight of Kaizei. All that desperate searching for his friend had been a nightmare—not real, imagined. KT was here, and alive.

But it was a different Kaizei. The smile cut out like a faulty circuit. He seemed anxious. Ransome was taken aback; he had never seen Kaizei look worried about anything.

Kaizei said, 'What did the hotel say about my calls?'

'Their records show no calls, save for the one you just made.'

'Shit!' Kaizei was grey-faced. He looked around sharply. 'Anyone follow you?' he asked.

It hadn't occurred to Ransome to check. 'I don't know.'

'Let's get our tits out of here. Climb aboard.' Kaizei dropped his visor and revved the engine.

Ransome mounted the pillion. The bike took off around the courtyard of the hotel. Clinging to Kaizei's shoulders, he leaned into the tight curve. They shot down the driveway to the street. Kaizei paused for a moment, picked a gap, then slammed into the traffic.

*   *   *

The Rappongi district is split in two by an elevated rail track. The track straddles the centre of what was once a wide tree-lined avenue. On either side of this dense curtain of steel, traffic surges ceaselessly. Both sides of the track are occupied by foreign powers.

The Rappongi is *gaijin* country. The pavements are jammed with tourists. The smart shops, cinemas, coffee shops and boutiques, the little art galleries, foreign language bookshops, international restaurants, bars selling imported beers, and high-price bordellos all cater for their Western tastes. English is spoken here.

Behind the main drag lies a warren of narrow streets lined with expensive apartment buildings and elegant houses discreet behind high walls, affordable only for business tycoons or diplomats. Some brilliantly designed glass and steel buildings house advertising agencies, architects' offices and computer bureaus.

In the older streets above the narrow shops there are lofts which have become fashionable. The rents are astronomical. In one of these, Kaizei was staying with a young woman called Eiko: Nakasone Eiko. They had been students together. Now she worked as a high-class whore. Not that she worked much. There was a Japanese-speaking American diplomat who paid the rent, and there was a film producer from Toho Films whose open credit card helped with her clothing expenses and spending money.

Eiko wore yellow dungarees and a bow tied in her hair.

She looked about fifteen, which was about fifteen years younger than her age, and she was model-girl beautiful. There was a high gloss about her that suggested she spent a great deal of time pampering herself.

She greeted Ransome with interest and very limited English. Kaizei had told her about him. When they arrived she kissed both Kaizei and Ransome with enthusiasm and immediately opened a bottle of Krug champagne.

'Her lovers have excellent taste,' Kaizei said. 'Krug is the only thing she drinks.'

'You always did choose your accommodation with care,' said Ransome. 'Here's to us.'

The three raised a toast and drank.

'It's great to see you again, Jack,' Kaizei said.

His face was alive with excitement. Ransome recognised the expression; he'd seen it on Kaizei's face half a hundred times before. It was the heady exhilaration of being back in action, a combination of fear and joy when the bullets are flying and you feel both immortal and frightened out of your wits. He had felt it himself.

'And thanks for coming.' He topped up Ransome's glass. 'As you now know all too well, we have ourselves a story!'

Ransome looked at his old friend with wonder. The years that had elapsed since they had last seen each other on that bloody morning in a Kampuchean paddy field had suddenly compressed into a moment. It was as if their conversation had been interrupted only the day before.

Much about Kaizei remained the same: the hair tied in a queue, the three earrings in his left ear and the stylish, if somewhat offbeat, clothes. But much was different. Kaizei had gone through South-East Asia apparently unscathed, always managing to look about eighteen years of age. Now he had aged. His face was thinner and deeply lined. Old pain marked his face like a shadow. Most obviously, he now limped badly.

Eiko finished her champagne, said something to Kaizei and disappeared into the bedroom.

'She's going to leave us in peace,' he said.

A few minutes later Eiko came back wearing a full-length mink coat and matching hat. She smiled in friendly fashion at Ransome, kissed Kaizei and left, clattering on spike heels down the passageway towards the lift.

Kaizei closed the door. His face became sober. 'Tell me about last night.'

Ransome gave him the story to the last detail. 'It has to be our interviewee, doesn't it?'

Kaizei nodded, his face a mask of worry. 'I'm afraid so. I got him to agree to talk on camera just a few days ago. Then you didn't turn up—or that's what I thought—and I had to keep him on the boil. Two nights ago I called him and there was no answer. I went to his place. He'd gone. I thought maybe he'd been scared off.'

'The police say the man was tortured.'

Kaizei stared at him, his face registering an expression of disgust. He sat with his eyes closed, silent for a long time. 'Otabe Eiji, his name was—if it *is* the man I organised to interview—a very bright, tough-minded man who knew what he was doing. He was a top scientist.'

Ransome asked, 'Did you tell him my name?'

'No, but I was dumb enough to tell him that there was an American cameraman flying in to do the filming. There can only be so many American journalists coming in on any given day. They must have picked you up when you came into the airport.'

'They'd need access to passenger lists. Somebody must have some clout.'

'Somebody has,' Kaizei said. 'They isolate me from you by blocking my calls. They set you up in a murder.'

'There's more.' Ransome told him about Uto's questioning and the threat by the two *yakuza* who had been in his cell.

Kaizei was startled by this. 'There must be police involvement.'

'Sounds that way,' Ransome said. 'Soon after I told the inspector about the *yakuza*, he ordered my release. Strange guy. He was obviously very pissed off about the other police. I got the impression he felt he was being screwed.'

'You tell him why you're here?'

'No.'

Kaizei said, 'You and I, my friend, are in a very heavy scene. It's a nasty story. There have been pressures on right from the beginning, so I've been keeping my head down, interviewing under false names, changing addresses. I've been lucky. I've been away for years so no-one knows what I look like.'

'Still no photos?'

Kaizei made a sceptical face. 'None that I'm aware of.'

'Your crazy superstition paid off.' Ransome laughed. In all the time he had known Kaizei, he'd had a total aversion to having his photograph taken. Ransome had once seen him pay a journalist a hundred dollars for a roll of film containing a casual picture of him taken in a Saigon bar.

'Early on, somebody began getting at my contacts. At first it was harassment—phone calls, interviewees warned off, that kind of thing—but lately things have become very ugly.' Kaizei smiled a brief, grim smile. 'A couple of weeks ago, just after an interview in Kobe, I must have gotten careless. Somebody tracked me. A truck ran me off the road, wrecked my car. I was lucky. I got out. At first I didn't connect. Then a couple of days ago—the day I thought you were arriving—somebody fire-bombed my flat.'

Ransome said, 'Tell me what it all means.'

Kaizei filled their glasses. He took a sip and raised his eyebrows in appreciation. 'Always hide in the homes of rich women,' he said. His face became serious. 'About six months ago I came back to Japan. I went back to Hokkaido. My home town: Hakodate. I hadn't seen my parents for years. I was just picking up the pieces.' He paused. 'I began writing a story about my father's war. He had served in the navy. This led to the idea of writing a series of articles about war veterans. Then my father introduced me to an old family friend of his—Mr Aoyama, an amateur historian. I was asking him how the war had changed his life, that kind of thing. Halfway through the interview, he suddenly said, "There's something terrible I want to tell you about." It came out of the blue. He's got religion. One of those . . .' Kaizei searched for the word.

'Born-agains?' Ransome hazarded.

'Something like that,' said Kaizei. 'He seemed to want to get it off his chest. Confession, or expiation or something. During the war he was an army doctor specialising in administration. He told me that he'd served in a special secret unit, Section 731, which was involved with some . . .' Kaizei made a distasteful face, 'medical experiments on prisoners. He'd been sitting on the secret for over forty years. When he finished, I knew the story was the biggest thing I'd ever struck.'

'So why call me?' Ransome said.

Kaizei smiled ruefully. 'It cried out for television. I couldn't persuade any of the cameramen I knew in Japan to shoot the footage for me. Some of the people I asked thought it was too hot. Others thought that I should let sleeping dogs lie. Some who were willing at first would mysteriously lose interest. The word got around very fast. After a time, nobody wanted to know.' He shrugged. 'So, I thought of you. I suppose the obvious answer is I wanted to work with you again. I knew you didn't scare easily. In fact, I knew you didn't scare at all.'

'The dead man—what connection was he to your historian?'

'Otabe was another ex-member of Section 731. It was Mr Aoyama who told me about him. Aoyama keeps a very low profile, but he's been doing a lot of research on the Section, tracing ex-members for me. He's set up interviews all over the place, but always his name stays out of it. He's scared stiff.'

'Has he been threatened?' Ransome asked.

'Not so far. Mostly, he gives me the names, I make the contacts. A couple of guys he trusts, he's written to. Apart from them, nobody knows about him.' Kaizei grimaced. 'I'm fairly certain it's Otabe they've killed. A fascinating character. He kept hinting at "some much worse crime".'

Ransome thought about the frozen man in that too-bright hotel bathroom. 'You're in deep shit, Katie, aren't you?'

Kaizei made a rueful face.

'The car wreck—is that where you copped the limp?'

Kaizei smiled. 'No, that was something else.' He pulled up his trouser leg and rolled down a red sock. From the knee down, his leg was artificial.

'Jesus Christ.' Ransome was horrified at the sight of the elegantly moulded plastic-and-aluminium contraption. 'Just from the knee down?' hoping it wasn't worse.

'Just from the knee down,' Kaizei said. He patted the limb. 'Latest state of the art.' There was pain and regret on his face. 'It's not too bad. Just took awhile to get used to the idea, that's all.' He looked rueful. 'Doesn't exactly improve your sex appeal.'

'You buy that the day I saw you last?'

'Tell you about it, some day.' Kaizei rolled up the sock and pulled down his trouser leg.

Ransome was shaken. He did not press the point.

Kaizei poured the last of the champagne into their glasses.

'Your Mr Aoyama,' Ransome said, 'he can't yet know about the dead man.'

Kaizei made a wry face. 'I'll have to tell him. Not that I think it'll stop him. He's become obsessed with this thing. It's like a crusade for him. But Jack, it's not your crusade. I had thought maybe you could come in for maybe a week or so, get some interview footage then ship straight out. No danger. But now somebody knows you're here and why,' shaking his head in frustration, 'you'd better go back to the States, Lansome.'

Ransome laughed. 'Come on, I've only just got here!'

Kaizei laughed too. 'I remember you saying exactly that on our first night in Kampuchea.' He knew that Ransome was going to stay. 'It's going to be interesting, my friend.'

'Isn't it,' Ransome said. He looked around the elegant apartment. 'At least you're hiding out in style. How long have you been here?'

'A few days. But I'm planning to move someplace else tomorrow. I don't want to implicate Eiko; she knows nothing about all this. You and I are both going to have to be moving targets.'

'How come your contact knows so much?'

Kaizei limped into the kitchen. He came back with another bottle of champagne. 'Let me tell you about the remarkable Mr Aoyama and his story.' He filled Ransome's glass and poured a drink for himself. 'You'll be so glad you came.'

There was a look on his face that Ransome had never seen before—that of a man who had seen something appalling.

Chapter 7

'Aoyama served in the medical corps. He was called up in 1937 and worked as a doctor in the Manchurian invasion; logistics mainly, behind the lines stuff: casualty clearing, hospitalisation, the provision of medical supplies, that kind of thing. He was apparently very good at it.

'In 1938 he was transferred to a special section based in Harbin. He told me he had been amazed by the scale of the place. He says, and I don't know that he's not exaggerating, that there were 2600 medical staff there, all volunteers. The security was absolute. He had never heard a single mention of Section 731 in his previous army medical corps days.

'He quickly learned that the original project had been about germ warfare—the development of the bubonic plague as a weapon to use against the Americans. Some of that was in the transcripts I sent you.'

Ransome nodded.

'But gradually Aoyama discovered it was about more things than simply germ warfare. The Section had mushroomed. A vast bureaucracy had grown up around various other programs, all involving the use of thousands of prisoners of war. The medical staff, all volunteer doctors, had been drawn by the prospect of being able to conduct any experiment they could conceive on human guineapigs.'

Ransome felt a chill forming in the deepest part of him. The few documents Kaizei had sent him had disturbed him; now a whole dreadful design was coming into focus.

He looked at his friend. Kaizei was Japanese. What could he be thinking of as he told this story about his own countrymen? Ransome had never really thought of Kaizei in terms of his nationality before. He was simply a friend, a good man to know in a tight corner.

Kaizei continued. 'Aoyama was given a job as head of the medical records office. It was all classified work, very secret. He dealt with the daily logistics of allocating the prisoners of war to be used for experimentation. He remembers it as a very difficult job since he had to deal with the claims of the heads of the various specialist sections as they competed for . . .' here Kaizei shook his head in disbelief, 'scarce resources.' He gave an odd, distracted smile. 'There were never enough organs to go around. The doctors apparently lobbied and manoeuvred like bureaucrats.'

He looked out of the window and was silent for a time. Suddenly he asked, 'Who was that German the Jews hanged for war crimes?'

'Eichmann,' Ransome said.

'Yeah, Eichmann. Aoyama often mentions him. He likens himself to him. Didn't Eichmann claim he was only following orders?'

Ransome nodded.

Kaizei said, 'For Aoyama, at first, it had simply been a job. But towards the middle of the war, disgust had set in. He knew what was going on—all of it. He talks about the great struggle of conscience that seized him. He got religious. In his view, that was what saved his sanity. At war's end everyone working in the Section was forced to take an oath of lifetime secrecy. So, for all those years he's buried it inside.'

'It must eat you up, something like that,' Ransome said.

'Not everyone,' said Kaizei. 'I've met several of his

comrades who haven't given it a thought. It's funny—
what seemed to trigger him off when we first talked was
my mention of the Pol Pot horrors. Remember that day?'
Kaizei shook his head and took a deep breath.

Ransome remembered all too vividly the mass graves;
the bare, bloodstained rooms; the iron beds and the elec-
trodes and the rows of photographs of the victims—the
proof of thoroughness in the search for ideological
purity. Kaizei and he had been unable to speak for days
after that ghastly revelation.

Kaizei said, 'A few minutes after I mentioned Pol Pot,
he suddenly wanted to talk about the camp at Harbin.
Then the floodgates opened. I couldn't believe what I was
hearing. I'm not sure I do even now.'

'Maybe it's bullshit,' Ransome tried to play the devil's
advocate. 'Maybe he's exaggerating. Maybe he's gone
round the twist.' But, already, he knew it was true.

Kaizei shrugged and went on. 'I stayed around for
several days. He needed to talk about it. He'd been
writing it down for years. He has it all in files and note-
books, like a good bureaucrat should. He gave me a few
names of men he had served with. I began by seeking
them out. Without mentioning his name, I'd drop in on
them without warning. Some of them refused to speak
about the unit, some became angry, a few violent. But
others, hearing that the secret was out, were so relieved,
and it all came spilling out. Some of them would give me
the names of ex-Section members they had kept in touch
with. I finished up talking to half a dozen of them.'

'It didn't take long for the word to get about,' Kaizei
said. 'Some of the more hostile ones were ex-Section
members who meet for annual reunions.'

'You'd think they'd hide in shame, wouldn't you?'
Ransome said.

'No accounting for taste. Somebody's been active,
trying to keep this thing under wraps, lately. Several

ex-members I spoke to told me they'd been warned that if they spoke to me they would pay a deadly price for breaking their oath.'

Something was nagging at Ransome.

'I don't get it. A guy is tortured, then frozen to death because he's got some connection with a World War II war crime?' Ransome was watching Kaizei carefully, not wanting him to misunderstand his doubts. 'The world forgives war crimes very quickly. Shit, we were doing deals with that animal Pol Pot in six months.'

Kaizei said, 'That's what is worrying me.' He shook his head. 'There's politics in there someplace, but I don't know how it fits together. It seems that some very important people don't want this thing to come out. I've had "friendly" unofficial warnings by various authorities that I was treading on dangerous, un-Japanese ground. Until my car was wrecked, the police were harassing me— picking me up on bullshit charges of speeding, running red lights, that kind of thing. I was charged with drunken driving once. Lucky I had a decent lawyer.' He looked troubled.

'You guys must play your politics very hard,' Ransome said.

'We do. *They* do.' Kaizei stood up and limped to the window. 'There's a lot more to it than I've found out so far.' He grinned suddenly, remembering something. 'Oh, you'll love this. One of the newspapers, who had never bought my stuff, ever, suddenly wanted me to go to Angola. A television network suddenly needed me in Beirut.' Kaizei grinned. ' "We need good strong front-line stuff," the man said, "like you did in Vietnam." '

Ransome laughed. 'Please get your arse shot off.'

'Exactly,' Kaizei said, his face suddenly dark. 'I listened politely and declined. Then the stakes went up. After they bombed my flat I took off and have kept moving ever since.'

'When do we talk to Aoyama?'

Kaizei looked unhappy. 'He won't go on camera.'

'If he has all the facts, he could be our best interview.'

'Yeah, I know. But either he's frightened because he knows too much or he feels some strange kind of loyalty to his senior officers. So far I haven't been able to persuade him.' Seeing Ransome's disappointment, he said, 'And he is a friend of my father's, so I can't press him too much. But I'll keep trying. Anyhow, we've got work to do. I've organised a lot of interviews. You ready, willing and able?'

Ransome nodded. But he was troubled. People being tortured and killed now for something that went all the way back to World War II? What sort of country was this? What kind of people were these? Something was out of joint. He said, 'I hope we don't get anyone else killed.'

Kaizei stared at him, but said nothing.

Chapter 8

After two days of extraordinary suffering, the man in the blue Datsun died.

On the day of the accident he had been taken to the nearest hospital. Preliminary diagnosis failed to establish the cause of his illness. The extreme symptoms led doctors in casualty to believe that he could be suffering from some contagious disease. He was placed in an isolation ward.

Later that evening, after he had been examined by five doctors, including a specialist in epidemiology, he was transferred to the Tokyo area infectious diseases hospital located on the small island off Funabashi. There the victim was nursed under the strictest barrier conditions.

Health authorities, aided by the local police, began a discreet inquiry. The man was identified as Harada Matsui. He was twenty-nine years of age and unmarried. He had graduated in biochemistry from Tokyo University. His academic background had been brilliant. At the time of his death he had been employed as a laboratory assistant with a food company.

Harada did not recover consciousness. His death was timed at 9.37 p.m. on the second day after his admission to hospital. With the utmost care, a post-mortem was conducted. Several hours later the body was hastily burned. No public announcement was made. His parents, who were tracked down to a northern prefecture, were subsequently notified that he had died of 'causes unknown'.

The food company laboratory was closed down and rigorously 'swept' by a Department of Health team. The laboratory assistants who had worked alongside the man were screened. None of them displayed any abnormal functions. Four days after the man's death, after some discreet pressure from the government's Department of Trade, the laboratory was given a clean bill of health. Normal business was resumed the following day.

A routine report of the matter was automatically passed on to the Prime Minister's Department. There, the Special Intelligence Unit examined the report for possible political implications. The committee judged the matter serious enough to warrant ongoing attention. A senior officer from the Department of Health was coopted to the unit and given a watching brief.

Chapter 9

Kaizei and Ransome travelled by *shinkansen* to Nagasaki, Kobe, Kagoshima and Otake to talk to four ex-Section members.

The last thing they wanted was to endanger any of these men, so, from the first, they established patterns of evasion: changing taxis, getting off trains at stations short of their real destinations, returning hire cars to different depots—always one eye over their shoulder, always checking rear-vision mirrors, always watching their backs.

Kaizei could seek the anonymity of the shoal. It was harder for Ransome. He had a high-profile problem: *gaijin*, red hair, his bulk and height. The freezing weather helped; it gave him a reason for wearing scarves around his face and a variety of headgear: parka hoods, hats, sunglasses.

Twice in that first journey out of Tokyo, Kaizei organised overnight stays for them both with sympathetic friends, but in the end they decided that the more Ransome associated with other Europeans, the less obvious he was. He would stay in tourist hotels, one or two days only.

The ex-Section member in Kagoshima had agreed to speak, but when they arrived his wife would not let them in. She told Kaizei he had been warned in a phone call not to talk about his wartime experiences. She wanted to know why. Kaizei told her nothing.

The other three had been willing.

* * *

Ransome sighted through the lens to a face crinkled with age: Uezono Kaoji, retired railway employee, Nagasaki.

Uezono had a half-grown beard. He told them it was a disguise. Since he had agreed to speak he had come to believe he would be in danger. 'There are many right-wing groups,' he said, 'and the Liberal Democratic Party is behind them.'

Kaizei put his questions in both Japanese and English, then simultaneously translated the answers. Uezono spoke in a detached voice, as if reciting something he had once heard, of fragmentation bomb experiments done on prisoners, of experiments with poison gases, of lethal injections. 'We worked with tabon—a nerve gas. A drop the size of the head of a pin on a man's eyeball caused epileptic fits in ten seconds—death within a minute. I didn't like working with the stuff. It was too dangerous.'

Ransome entered his detached observer's mode, distanced from it all by the camera. He framed Kaizei looking intense as he asked the questions. Ransome wondered, What's going on in his head as he translates this stuff; hearing these horrors from one of his countrymen?

The image of Uezono once more, in closer focus this time. Ransome listened to his piping voice.

Kaizei translated: 'You can't say I was a bad man. It was war. The Japanese way is to obey a superior. We do not act as individuals. We Japanese can do any evil when we are in groups. A war is like being drunk—the worst excesses can be forgiven and forgotten next morning.'

* * *

In a cake shop in Otake, a seaside town just beyond Hiroshima, they interviewed the proprietor, Satomo Shohei, a little man with glutton's food stains on his tie, his cheeks blown out with fat as though inflated from within.

He told them he had been recruited falsely into the Young Technicians Corps. He said, 'We were mostly boys who had not gained high enough marks to get into medical school. They said that when we had done some years as technicians our studies would give us the status to become doctors. It was all lies. They just wanted us to do the dirty work.'

Kaizei: 'Dirty work?'

Satomo: (after a long pause, thinking through his reply) 'The doctors didn't get personally involved in all the things that were done in there.' He closed his eyes and took a deep breath. 'They were experimenting, using prisoners of war as guinea pigs.'

Kaizei: 'What sort of experiments?'

Satomo looked uncomfortable, moving in his chair, ill at ease.

Satomo: 'Various experiments. Cholera, plague, typhus—that kind of thing. Our job was mainly vivisection—collecting organs for the various teams doing the experiments.'

Kaizei: 'What did they do with them?'

Satomo: 'Various tests, post-mortem analysis . . .' He began to look around wildly, as though anxious to avoid Kaizei's eye. 'There was a room . . . where they kept all the bits . . .' his breathing was broken like that of a defeated runner, '. . . organs, heads . . .'

Watching Satomo's face through the lens, Ransome was fascinated. The man's eyes were popping with astonishment, as if he could not believe he was saying these things. He was being delivered of a demon.

At the end of the interview Satomo said, 'In a war you obey orders. We were only kids. They betrayed us more than we could ever betray them. They marked us for life.'

* * *

Extract of interview, Kentaro Tashiri, Kobe.

Kentaro: 'I was responsible for at least one thousand vivisections, although I didn't cut up the logs myself, but

I was present. Sometimes there were no anaesthetics. They screamed and screamed, but we didn't regard the logs as human beings. They were lumps of meat on a chopping block.'

Kentaro was the proprietor of a print shop. In the window of his shop there was a single print, vivid against a black mount. It was of a great gold and black bird of prey searching for victims, hanging like an axe over a frozen, snow-covered landscape. Kaizei told him that the artist was Hiroshige, a famous 19th century court painter. The pitiless look of the predator reminded Ransome of the faces of the men they had been interviewing; these old functionaries who claimed they had only been following orders.

After the interview, Ransome bought the print.

* * *

Such ordinary faces. Such ordinary men.

The interviews of those who were present, who took part in these unspeakable things, who witnessed what went on and who now wished to exculpate, excuse, excise, excommunicate themselves from their shared and secret past, shook Ransome more profoundly than he had ever been shaken before.

How could they be so unmarked, Ransome wondered, after what they had witnessed? After what they had caused to happen?

After seeing the evidence of the Pol Pot holocaust, Ransome had come to think of horror as an incurable cancer. Carbon date the psyche of someone who has known horror and, no matter how long ago it happened, the evidence of it will show up like the diseased bone of some prehistoric cave dweller.

But where was the evidence of horror on these faces? As they reflected that distant holocaust, some looked anxious, some expressed regret, but for Ransome it was not enough. It seemed to him that most of them looked unscathed as if, like latter-day Dorian Greys, they had made some pact with the Devil.

* * *

They didn't talk much on the train trip home.

Kaizei seemed to have shrunk. It was as if the truths he had been hearing with every interview were eating him from within.

As the train raced across the Kanto Plain back to Tokyo, Ransome broke the silence. 'When did you cop the steel foot?' he asked.

Kaizei said, 'The last time we saw each other.'

'I didn't see you get hit.'

'You fell first,' Kaizei said. 'I saw you go down about five yards from me. I thought we were both gone. I got cut down by some small-arms fire. One of the medics put a tourniquet on my leg. A few minutes later the position was overrun. I was lucky. I crawled into a clump of bamboo. I knew if they found a journalist there they would give me a hard time. I blacked out. A couple of hours later the paddy was retaken. I'd lost a lot of blood. They used coconut milk to transfuse me, then shipped me out on the back of a wagon. I finished up being evacuated by helicopter a couple of days later. What about you?'

Ransome said, 'Looked worse than it was. Flesh wound. The bullet went right through. No permanent damage, except for an interesting scar,' thinking, how would I have felt if I'd lost a limb? He went on, 'But how come you disappeared? There was no trace of you. Nobody knew where you were, or what happened to you.' He told Kaizei something of his year-long search.

'It's funny,' Kaizei said. 'You spent all your time looking for me. Me, I just assumed you were dead. I'm sorry. I must have left my optimism back there someplace.' He smiled wanly. 'I finished up in a Kampuchean hospital. It was chaos. The wounded were coming in hundreds a day.' He shook his head, looking sick. 'They took this off,' making a chopping motion with the edge of his hand at the knee of his steel leg. 'Suddenly I was walking wounded—crutch assisted. I stayed in Phoc Luang for a few weeks then, as soon as I could get around, I caught a lift on a transport down to Ben Hua.'

To the north, snow-clad Fuji swung past. A small provincial station went by in a blur. The sound of the wheels changed note as the *shinkansen* switched tracks.

Kaizei spoke in a low voice as though talking to himself. 'The thought of being maimed, like all those other poor bastards you and I saw over the years, was too much. Somehow it always seemed to me that either I was immortal or, if I stopped one, I'd get it right between the eyes. Nice and clean. Snap!' He snapped his fingers. 'Just like that. Shows you how wrong you can be. I assumed you'd taken a fall and that didn't help. Bought a ticket out to Bangkok and kept on going all the way to Paris. I didn't bother to tell the bureau, didn't want to talk to anyone. I freaked out for awhile. Been in there too long, I suppose.'

Kaizei looked at Ransome with a troubled expression. He poured himself another beer. 'I had a bit of a breakdown there,' looking embarrassed. 'Spent six months in a clinic shouting rather a lot and sometimes not talking at all. It's hard to remember. When they let me out, I went to Switzerland and had this thing fitted. Life is less painful if you're not a Kampuchean peasant.'

Ransome said, 'You had a rough time.'

Kaizei looked at him. 'Yes,' he said.

'When did you discover I was alive?'

Kaizei laughed. 'It must have been fate. One day in Sapporo I'm in a doctor's surgery and I pick up an English-language edition of *Time*. There's a review of *No Man's Land* with a picture of you looking very pleased with yourself. I was so embarrassed, I couldn't bring myself to get in touch with you. I felt as if I'd deserted a pal in a tight corner.' Kaizei shrugged. 'Then I found this excuse.' He grimaced, sceptical now. 'Maybe I should have left you in peace.'

Ransome said, meaning it, 'Maybe we should both leave this thing in peace.'

'I can't,' Kaizei said simply. He shook his head as though shaking off a bad dream. '*Maruta*,' he said, spitting out the word. 'Men regarded as having no more feelings than logs of wood. Those doctors would claim they were working in the interest of science. Jesus, it's hard to believe! And yet we war correspondents watch terrible things in the interest of reporting the so-called truth. Are we so different?'

Ransome said, 'Of course we are! We're all curious, but some kids tear the wings off flies. That's not just curiosity, Katie, that's something else.'

Kaizei said, 'I've been thinking a lot about this. If you start off with an elitist, fascist notion like *bushido*, there's a historic inevitability to all the rotten things that follow. The truth is that we Japanese, as a group, hold everyone else in contempt. In Vietnam, being Japanese was a plus for me. We weren't part of it. I wasn't involved emotionally in any way. With this thing, the further we go,' he managed an apologetic smile, 'the more Japanese I feel— and the more uncomfortable I feel.'

Poor bastard, Ransome thought. In him, the interviews had stirred up ancient, sour and unspoken thoughts and feelings. He had grown up conditioned to hate the Japanese. His mother had never been able to deal with the war. If something about Japan came on television, she would switch it off. If there were a travel article about Japan she would quickly turn the page. There was no such country as Japan. No such race as the Japanese. They had cost her everything.

For Ransome, her faceless concept of them—the 'Japs',

the 'Nips'—didn't apply to Kaizei. He was just a colleague who always seemed to be where the action was, a laughing, nerveless young man shooting his pictures under fire or hammering away on a typewriter someplace back behind the lines.

Kaizei. A few times they had found themselves in the same army vehicle heading to or from some fire-fight. On a couple of occasions they'd had a drink together. Sometimes their paths wouldn't cross for weeks on end. By the processes of time, chemistry and mutual respect they had become friends.

Later, as the *shinkansen* neared Tokyo, Kaizei asked out of the blue, 'Why have you never spoken to me about your father's death?'

Ransome became evasive. 'It never came up.' He was thinking, Kaizei's father was my father's mortal enemy. The difference was that Kaizei's father had come home safe from the war.

'You didn't ever know him, did you.'

'No, I was conceived on a weekend pass.' At times Ransome had thought that romantic. It had always seemed strange, not knowing his father. Other times the idea of his father had been an ache like a missing limb.

Kaizei fell silent.

Ransome was thinking, if we could distil the essence of our fathers and our mothers and know only that about them, then maybe they would all be heroic. His father's essence was that of a hero, a legend. He had seen him only as a black and white image narrating the introduction to the half a dozen newsreels he had shot in the Philippines. A fit, good-looking fellow—much better looking than me, Ransome thought—with red hair like his own; the same smiling man in the wedding photograph that had stood on his mother's dressing table until the day she died: Sam Ransome, war photographer.

'You said he died in one of our prison camps,' Kaizei edged warily onto the minefield.

My father didn't die, Ransome thought, he became somehow immortal in the footage he shot. In recent years, every compilation film about World War II had used one or more of his images: the wounded soldiers in the pouring rain, the fire-fights, the strain on those young faces made old by the nearness of suffering and death.

'It's history, pal. He was in the wrong place at the wrong time.' What was the point of telling Kaizei the truth—that his father had died on a pointless, punitive death march in Bataan? Few had survived and he had not been one of them. There were some things best left unsaid.

Ueno Station. They hurried through the crowds, walked two blocks, then caught a taxi. Ten blocks on, not having spoken a word, they changed taxis. Kaizei watched out of the back window to check if they were being followed. Near the Meiji shrine they stopped and had coffee in a crowded *kissaten* on stylish Omote-Sando Avenue.

'Did you tell those guys about the dead man in the hotel room?' Ransome said.

Kaizei shook his head. 'But I told them all, right at the beginning, that I was under threat and that they would be, too. I warned them not to tell anyone they had spoken to us. They got the message.'

'Now what?'

'I need to go north to see Aoyama. Last night on the phone he told me that he'd run down a couple more ex-members of the Section for me, including some officers.'

'You want me there?'

Kaizei said, 'No, I need to protect Aoyama. You, Loundeyes, are hard to miss. Red-haired *gaijin* stick out like dog's balls in this place. It might take the heat off you a bit if you just acted the tourist for awhile. I'll be gone all day tomorrow. Catch up with this girlfriend of yours, why don't you?' He gave a lewd waggle of eyebrows. Kaizei had always been impressed by Ransome's success with women.

A day on his own. Kaizei was right—it was time to contact Reiko. 'I might just do that,' Ransome said.

He went into a cubicle in the bathroom of the coffee shop and unloaded cassettes from his camera. He put them into the padded postage bag he had brought along. Each day he had been posting off the taped interviews to his friend Martin Garrett in San Diego, who would see that they were stored in a safe place.

Back in the coffee shop they made arrangements to meet as soon as Kaizei returned.

Ransome left first. As the taxi pulled away from the curb, he looked back through the rear window. Kaizei was standing outside the coffee shop looking around carefully, with the alert manner of a bodyguard making sure his charge was not being followed. One advantage of being a war correspondent, Ransome thought, the danger tends to come from in front.

Chapter 10

The vaulted Ekō-in temple stadium amplified the excited roar of the crowd as the wrestlers hurled themselves at each other with explosive force. The young Hawaiian, Muritasuma, easily the bigger of the two and fighting savagely, quickly propelled his opponent from the sanded ring. The loser sprawled ignominiously over the rice bales of straw that offered a soft landing for the fighters.

There was wild cheering. The air filled with articles of clothing, cushions and whatever other objects of admiration that came to the hands of the adoring fans.

In the VIP box nearest the ring, among a group of young men in dark suits, a cabinet minister laughed and applauded loudly, making it obvious that he was pleased by the victory. An American with him said, 'I know that fucker from Nam. He's a loose cannon.' He swallowed a bowl of sake, which was immediately refilled by a pretty hostess.

'I've told you. I don't want them taken out yet.' The cabinet minister was smiling and bowing to some people in a nearby box. 'Some of the things they are uncovering are of great interest to me. Whatever we think of these nosy journalists, they are good at research. They are uncovering some fascinating things. I want to know what they come up with. *Then* I'll deal with them.' He made a victorious gesture at the winning wrestler as the man left the ring. The big Hawaiian bowed and moved on.

'My friends have invested a lot in you and your

political future,' said the American. 'Those two dig enough dirt on you right now and you could be political history. My friends would not like that. They would not like that at all.'

The cabinet minister sipped at his bowl of sake. 'We will keep the pressure on, but allow them to continue.'

'I say, take them both out now.'

'And I say, this is Japan. This is my territory. I decide when we deal with them. Is that clearly understood?' There was no mistaking the ice in the cabinet minister's voice.

The American said nothing. The cabinet minister continued to react theatrically to the excitement around him, the populist politician working the crowd, aware that his every gesture was being read by a large number of people in the stadium.

To the cheers and whistles of the crowd, the next two combatants entered the ring.

Chapter 11

The streetlights were on. The wind was seeking out things to break. The knife-edged tower of the Prince sliced upwards into the underbelly of a black cloud. The first swollen drops of icy rain were leaking out. Staff hurried from the hotel bearing armfuls of umbrellas to protect clients from the oncoming downpour.

Ransome quickened his steps up the double-track driveway towards the hotel entrance. He hadn't advised the desk that he was coming, but hoped, with luck, that he could identify himself, pick up the personal effects he had left in his room, and be gone in a few minutes.

A tall, well-dressed young man with an Elvis Presley quiff of hair falling forward on his forehead was standing on the pathway. As Ransome approached, he smiled. Ransome automatically smiled back.

The young man stepped in front of him. He said, 'Mr Ransome? You are invited to accept invitation to have important conversation. You have five seconds to make up your mind.'

The English was carefully articulated, but it took a moment for the man's words to take meaning. Ransome's attention was preoccupied by the discreetly held handgun pointing directly at his navel.

There were three of them. As well as the good-looking young man there was another whom Ransome could now see out of the corner of his eye, looming behind him. A third man, older than the others, was standing by the open door of a black Mercedes which formed the third wall of the trap. The driveway was busy with people coming and going from the hotel, but no-one seemed to notice the tableau.

Ransome's mind came out of neutral. 'Who wants to talk to me this badly?'

Without taking his eyes off Ransome, the young man opened the car's rear door. 'One . . .' he said.

He looked about eighteen. Ransome said, 'What happens *after* I have this important conversation?'

The young man opened the door wider. He was smiling once more, showing perfect even white teeth. 'Two . . .' he said. A slight motion of the foresight. The gun seemed to grow in size.

He won't mind using that thing, Ransome thought. In fact, he'll enjoy it.

'Please get in car.'

It seemed sensible, at that moment, to comply.

The young man slid in behind him. The driver was already behind the wheel. The other man came in through the opposite door, wedging Ransome between them with a crush of heavy overcoats and shoulders. The two young men grinned at each other across Ransome. They seemed relieved that things had gone so smoothly.

'Very sensible,' the young man said, his grin wider and more gleaming than before.

He likes the way he looks when he smiles, Ransome thought. He said, 'I bet all the girls succumb to your charms.'

The young man stared at Ransome for a moment as though trying to gauge the weight of the remark, then he gave a little high-pitched laugh. 'Yes,' the young man said, 'they do.' He said something to his companion, who laughed loudly.

The car eased silently away down the driveway. Already the gun was out of sight. The car was oppressively hot. The driver edged his way into the traffic.

'Sorry, you must wear this.' He handed Ransome what appeared to be a black silk handkerchief. Opened out, it proved to be a bag with drawstrings. Ransome stared at it for a moment, not wanting to recognise its function.

It had been a long time since he had been obliged to wear a blindfold: the last occasion, all those years ago, when he had gone into North Vietnamese controlled territory. He had felt exhilarated that day, standing nervously next to the jeep by the side of the jungle road waiting for his contact to show.

Ransome shook his head. 'You don't need that. It won't make any difference. I don't know Toyko well enough to know where I am anyway.'

The young man took the gun from his pocket and held it flat in the palm of his hand in front of Ransome's face as though it were something to be considered by a detached observer. 'It is necessary.' Pearly teeth glinted once more.

Here we go again, Ransome thought, feeling annoyed. He took a last look around. At that moment the rain started. Outside the darkened glass of the car, people scattered like chickens. The driver started the windscreen wipers.

Ransome took the silk bag in two hands, noting the time on his wristwatch as he did so: 5.10 p.m. He pulled the bag over his head. The light was blotted out as though he had been anaesthetised.

* * *

The car stopped at last. At a guess, the trip had taken forty minutes. The two on either side of him had made desultory conversation, occasionally laughing at each other's jokes. The young man had not spoken English again.

The air in the silk bag was warm and damp from his own breath. He wanted to rip the thing off.

When the doors were opened there was salt in the

wind, the smells of docks and fish. In the distance, the hoot of a ship's siren. No way of telling where they had brought him, or of finding the place again. The car had twisted and turned half a hundred times.

He was pulled out of the car, someone's hand on his head to stop him bumping the top of the door. Consideration, Ransome thought. Maybe they don't mean to kill me.

Two of them guided him, a hand on each elbow. The driver must have stayed with the car.

Cool, blown rain brushing the backs of his hands. It had been the same on that historic day, being met by the Vietnamese soldiers, slight as boys in their black pyjamas, and being led blindfold over the ditch into the maze of jungle paths that fringed the paddies, cool rain falling. On later trips, once they trusted him, the blindfolds had been dispensed with.

Up a flight of steps. Through a sliding glass door. Across a tiled floor. A lift rising slowly upwards. Then carpet underfoot. Into a room with several people in it.

Their chatter ended as he was pushed into the room. He heard the young man say something. There was a nervous laugh. Through another door.

The front edge of a chair was pushed against the back of his legs. He sat down. Felt for the arms: polished wood. His foot kicked something: the leg of a table. He reached forward. He was sitting at a smooth-topped table or desk.

There was silence, but he could sense other people present. Then, at the far end of the room, two people began to talk; a harsh voice dominated.

'*Hai!*' someone said in a frightened voice.

Somebody left the room. After a time someone entered.

For the next ten minutes Ransome heard people come and go. The conversations were sometimes low and intense; from time to time there was anger in the dominant voice, a hectoring quality.

A pause in the activity. 'Take off the mask,' the young man said from behind him.

The sudden light hurt Ransome's eyes. At the opposite end of a long table sat a group of three men in shirt-sleeves. In the centre was a frog-faced fellow of about sixty. He had a shock of white hair so thick it looked like an ill-fitting wig. The hair contrasted with the single black eyebrow that slashed squarely across his pale face. His nose was flat, like that of a tent boxer.

The other two men were bigger and much younger. Ransome guessed that one of them was a son; he shared the unfortunate squat features and single eyebrow of the older man. The third was lean and effete looking; the face below cropped hair was gaunt as an addict's, the eyes hidden by mirror glasses. On the table in front of them lay a pile of envelopes.

Ransome looked around. His two abductors stood behind him with their backs to a door.

'Is this the guy who wants to have the important conversation?' Ransome said.

The young man looked anxious. 'Do not speak,' he said.

The older man said something to his henchmen, who laughed. Then he spoke to the young man, who answered quickly.

Ransome checked his watch: 5.58 p.m. Through the window that framed the three men at the head of the table, he could see cranes floodlit by orange lights. Between warehouse buildings, the darker shape of a passing ship showed against the gleaming waters of the harbour. It could have been any part of the docks. There were no especially noticeable landmarks from which he might get a fix.

Four men in shiny business suits came into the room.

They walked to the frog-faced man and bowed to him. He nodded back, coolly. One by one they handed envelopes to him. He put them, unopened, on the pile before him. There was a brief conversation, then the four bowed their way out of the room.

Mirrorglasses rose and went to the door behind Ransome. After a moment he returned, leaving the door open behind him. He resumed his seat at the end of the table.

Into the room came a powerfully built young man, maybe eighteen or twenty. He was wearing brightly coloured punk clothes. His hair was dyed red and cut in mohawk style. He was scared stiff. He stumbled slightly as he made his way the length of the room to stand near the three men.

Mirrorglasses said something to him. The punk's eyes widened. He seemed to shrink in stature. *'Hai!'* he said. He bowed deeply, his hands clasped in front of him, his back parallel to the floor. In that position he spoke for a long time in a guttural voice as though explaining something and apologising. The three considered him without speaking.

The punk straightened up. His face was bleached by fear. He took two white handkerchiefs from his pocket and put them on the table, side by side. He slipped off his bile-green jacket and carefully hung it over the back of a chair. He was wearing a string T-shirt without sleeves. His weightlifter's arms were entirely covered in elaborate tattoos. There was a sheath in his belt at the small of his back. From it he drew a knife. He laid it on one of the handkerchiefs. He bowed to Frogface and sat down.

Ransome knew what was going to happen. He felt his mouth dry and his stomach muscles cringe.

Don't do it!

It was all over very quickly. The punk spread his hand

flat on the second handkerchief, palm down. He laid the edge of the knifeblade on his little finger. He took a deep breath, then, with a great shout, he sliced through the flesh and bone in one savage sweep. The shout changed key into an animal cry of anguish.

His face distorted. Veins stood out like twigs against the flesh of his neck and shoulders. The knife clattered onto the polished surface of the table. With his good hand the young man grabbed the other handkerchief and wound it around his maimed fist. He pressed it against his chest.

Ransome's breath whistled past the taste of gall in his throat.

The punk sat motionless for maybe half a minute, then, with a great effort of will, he folded the edges of the handkerchief over the severed finger as though it were a parcel. He picked it up and struggled to his feet. He offered it to Frogface, who had watched the whole performance with obvious admiration.

Frogface stood up. He took the grisly gift and bowed to the young man. Mirrorglasses led the young man slowly from the room, supporting him with his arm.

Ransome felt his stomach muscles unclench. A tide of bile subsided.

A moment later Mirrorglasses returned and resumed his seat. He said something that made the old man laugh.

Frogface began to speak, staring at Ransome with blank eyes.

The young man translated. 'He says the boy made a small mistake. As you have seen, he was obliged to pay for that mistake. He says you are making a mistake. He says that you are interfering in Japanese things that are not the business of foreigners. He says you are making a much bigger mistake than the stupid punk with the dyed hair. The price you will have to pay is much higher.'

Frogface continued. As he did so he slid the handkerchief in front of Mirrorglasses and jerked his head towards Ransome. The man rose and walked the length of the table. He put the bloodied offering in front of Ransome, unwrapped it and went back to his seat.

Ransome glanced down. The finger looked small and shrunken. He noticed that the nail was rimmed with grease.

The young man translated once more. 'He says if he wanted to kill you now he could do so. But because you are guest you will get a chance that would never be given to a Japanese. He says give up your investigation or you will be found and killed. He says do not think you can ignore this warning. You will have seen how easy it was to bring you here.'

Frogface suddenly stood up. Looking directly at Ransome he shouted in a loud snarling voice, 'Understand!'

It was no time for debate. Ransome nodded.

The black bag came back down over his head.

* * *

The car tyres loudly protested the fast u-turn in the driveway of the Prince Hotel.

Ransome dragged off the blindfold, frantically tearing at the strings that had been tied at the back. By the time he had it off, the Mercedes was already at the bottom of the driveway. The red brakelights came on, then showed intermittently as the driver tried to force his way into the implacable wall of traffic.

Ransome hunted his pockets looking for a pen to write down the car's plate number. In his left-hand jacket pocket, a handkerchief. He pulled it out. Not his.

The handkerchief felt damp in his hand. Something hard wrapped inside. 'Oh, shit!' Ransome said, disgust welling.

The blood looked black under the streetlights. The

Mercedes was gone, swallowed up in the traffic.

Holding the grisly parcel in his hand, he began to walk up the driveway. As he passed a rubbish bin, he dropped the bloody handkerchief into it.

So, this was the way the local thugs demonstrated the advantages of not making mistakes. Ransome had to admit that, as a method of communication, it wonderfully concentrated the mind.

Chapter 12

He was in a runaway taxi. The streets of Tokyo looked like a neon-lit river. The taxi was being driven by Kaizei. Then, in a too-bright, garish bathroom there was a young punk with a knife. He cut off his own steel and plastic leg and became an old man wearing a mask of ice over his face. The old man's screams ran on and on.

The telephone.

Ransome sat up in bed grabbing the handpiece. A telephonist, in perfect English, read a message: a Mr McGregor had rung, had asked him to call back.

He hung up and leaned back, thinking about the night before. He felt his flesh quiver as he thought about the young punk.

He had to stop this. It was a day off—his day to call Reiko.

In his address book she was listed under her married name. He had scribbled her Tokyo phone number along-side her San Diego address. He made the call.

The dial tone buzzed a dozen times before someone answered.

'*Mushi mushi.*' The high-pitched voice of an older woman.

Enunciating clearly, Ransome said, 'May I speak with Mrs Reiko Hauser please?'

There was a rush of Japanese.

He felt foolish. 'I'm sorry, I do not speak Japanese.'

Another barrage of words, then the voice said, 'Very

sorry.' A silence. The connection did not appear to be broken. He hung on. There was a long wait.

'Can I help you, please?' A man's voice, dark-toned and authoritative. Reiko's father, perhaps?

Again he apologised for his lack of the language.

'I have a little English,' said the voice.

'My name is Ransome. I would like to speak to Mrs Hauser, Reiko Hauser, if that is possible.'

There was a pause. Ransome felt intimidated, like an unwelcome guest. 'That is the right number?'

'My daughter?' said the man. The tone was cool. 'Are you friend of Reiko?'

'Yes, I knew her in San Diego.' Knew her? Jesus!

Another long pause. 'Please leave your phone number. I will tell her you called.'

Her father was acting the watchdog. Ransome had no choice. He would have to hope she would respond. 'Thank you,' he said. 'You are very kind.' He gave the number of his new hotel. The phone went dead.

* * *

He stood dripping on the carpet beside the bed, dabbing himself dry with the towel he had snatched on the way to answering the phone. It had to be her. Had to be.

'Jack?'

The sound of her voice! He said, 'Hello, Reiko.'

'What are you doing in Tokyo?' Incredulous.

'Hoping to see you. An assignment came up out of the blue. I jumped at the chance to be here.' He was aware of how pathetic it sounded. He should have come three months ago.

'Oh, it's so good to hear your voice.' She sounded excited. Pleased. Perhaps it was still there for her, after all. 'When did you arrive?'

'A few days ago . . . but I've been out of Tokyo.' Thinking, I should have called. 'I was worried you wouldn't get my message. Your father sounded deeply suspicious.'

Her distinctive, joyful laugh sounded, causing an ache of longing.

'He thought you must be a friend of Willy's—or even Willy disguising his voice.'

Ransome said, 'No wonder he was cool.'

'Since Willy, my father is unimpressed with foreign callers asking for me. I don't think he really wanted to tell me that you'd called, Jack,' she said. 'I'm so glad you did.'

'I badly need to see you,' Ransome said.

She paused. 'Do you think that's wise?' A despairing note sounded in her voice.

A silence hung. 'Are you alright?' Ransome asked.

'Yes, Jack, I'm alright.' Her voice was unconvincing, something veiled and reserved in its tone. She said, 'You can't begin to know how bad it's been here for me . . . and the kids.' She sounded close to tears. 'I've missed you so much.'

He should have followed her here months ago. As on so many occasions in the past, he had failed to listen to his instincts.

He said, 'I didn't know whether to write again or wait until you had sorted out your life here.' His words sounded lame.

'I'm sorry,' said Reiko, 'I should have replied. I loved getting your letters. They were lovely. Things have just been very difficult.'

It should never have been about letters, Ransome thought. If he'd acted, it would never have been necessary to write.

'How long are you going to be in Japan?'

'For awhile,' he said, thinking: as long as it takes to see you, to find out where we stand. 'I have my first day off today. Are you free?'

The question implied: is there someone else? Surely here in Japan there would be a suitable match for a beautiful divorcee?

There had never been a shortage of admirers. She had once told him of the nine formal offers of marriage she had had as a young music student, and of her parents' embarrassment as she had rejected them one by one. 'Very suitable matches,' she had said, smiling. 'Businessmen, doctors, lawyers ... But all of them assumed I would give up my career.'

She gave a little groan of frustration. 'Jack, I want to see you, too, but today I can't. And not tonight. I have to prepare dinner for my father's business colleagues. He thinks my role in life is to replace my mother as his official hostess.' She sounded cynical.

'What about right now?' Lust taking hold of him. The thought of spending the morning here in this room with her!

The sexual possibilities were not lost on her. They had shared a few hotel rooms in their time. From the beginning of their affair she had delighted him with her sexual spontaneity.

'It's a lovely idea but ...' she hesitated. 'Jack, it's very difficult here for me. I'm not sure things can work out between us.'

'You just said you missed me,' Ransome said, fighting off dismay.

'Oh, don't misunderstand,' Reiko said. 'If only you could know how much I want to see you!' Her voice trembled. 'It's just so terribly complicated, that's all.'

He said nothing. He could see her face. Taste her.

A jetliner cut a downward groove in the lead grey sky over distant Narita.

'I'll be there in an hour,' she said.

'I'll meet you in the foyer,' Ransome replied, aware that his voice was hoarse.

He waited for her to disengage, then slowly hung up, trying to interpret the contrary signals.

Reiko. A few flash-frames of remembered flesh stirred

his blood. He felt the damp of his skin cooling in the airconditioning.

She had been the one great thing that had happened to him after he had finally returned home.

After Saigon fell he had spent six miserable months in Bangkok, trying unsuccessfully to settle in a city that the war, coupled with R and R, had turned into a cesspit.

Inevitably, boredom had set in; he had needed the fix of action. He had followed the wars: some time in Africa, some time in the Philippines and the Middle East, free-lancing for the networks. But hunting down the action had not proved to be enough. He realised that the Asia wars had been the high point of his life: conflicts in which he had cared about the fighters of both sides. Seeing people at their best and worst had changed him. He had come to view the fortitude of his own country-men and their enemies with awe. Nothing would ever be the same again.

When he had returned to the States at a low personal ebb, he had accepted a network contract to make half-a-dozen documentaries of his choice. Martin Garrett had been generous. He had enjoyed the company of old friends. Their energy and optimism had embraced him, and yet he had felt like a stranger, so long had he been away. True, there had been the rush that came from the success of his documentary and the fifteen minutes of fame that it had brought him but, in spite of that, his life had seemed curiously empty.

Then, one day, Reiko happened, a chance encounter on a university tennis court.

It was as if she had been meant to happen. He had been there just in time to pick up the pieces of her dis-astrous marriage to Willy.

Willy. That prick. He had once threatened to change Ransome's mind about Reiko, but the one time they met, he had backed off.

She had met Willy while studying at the Munich Conservatorium. Their marriage had been convenient: she the lonely and vulnerable student, he the senior lecturer in composition, tall, handsome and well connected in music circles.

But Willy had been a problem from the first day. By the time they came to America their marriage was over. He had serially screwed his female students at the school of music, slept with her Japanese friends with whom she played tennis at university, drunk too much and occasionally knocked her about.

She had stuck out her marriage for seven years, mainly for the sake of the children, but also because she was too proud (and too realistic) to leave America and go back to her family. It was only when the beatings became a habit that she moved out.

Reiko. Their wild and thrilling affair had made him hope she would stay and start a new life with him in California, or anywhere. But then everything fell apart. Her mother died. Her father's plea for her to return to Japan made her confused and unhappy. The hurt of her broken marriage had been greater than Ransome had realised. 'I need to sort out my life,' she had said on the night before she left. But later, clinging to him in the black hours before the dawn, she had added, 'I'll be back. You cannot know how important you are to me.'

Farewelling her at the airport, watching her disappear into the departure lounge with the two excited children, he had been oddly confident that she was committed to a life with him. That was before her silence had begun to knaw at his optimism.

Maybe all that had happened between them was not a dream. Was it possible, he wondered, that she would come back into his life again?

He should have come with her.

* * *

She arrived early. When he came out of the lift, she was already by the reception desk, about to call his room. She turned and saw him. She was just as he remembered: the wide clear eyes, the shattering smile of greeting.

'You look wonderful,' he said. He wanted to kiss the extravagant mouth, taste her breath on his tongue, touch once more the incredible softness of her skin.

'You too.' She seemed shaken. She closed her eyes for a moment. 'I'm taken by surprise, Jack. I haven't composed myself for you.'

'Me neither.' He caught her hands, made to kiss her.

She hung back, laughing. 'Suddenly I'm shy,' she said, glancing about the foyer. 'Isn't that ridiculous! It's very public and women don't kiss publicly in Japan.'

'Is that right?' Ransome said.

Reiko reached up and kissed him lightly on the mouth. It was like closing a high-voltage circuit. 'You cannot believe how much I've missed you,' she said.

'Let me look at you.' Still holding her hands, he gazed at her. He had never seen her so elegantly dressed. She had always been stylish but the sleek clothes she was wearing now were clearly expensive: a superb ankle-length black fur coat and knee-high leather boots. Her hair had grown longer since he had last seen her. It spilled out from under a jaunty peaked cap.

She released her hands as though embarrassed. 'It's Yassie's birthday in a few days,' she said. 'I promised them I'd take them shopping this morning—so I have the kids with me,' this with a rueful smile. 'I hope you're not going to hate that.'

He followed her gaze. The children, dressed in red parkas, were watching from a table a few yards away. They looked towards him with curiosity and no little apprehension.

The kids. So that was what her restraint was about. Ransome crossed to them and squatted down to their level. Katsuki and Yasuko had inherited their parents' good looks. Both were taller than he remembered. Their clothes were formal and neat, not like the casual gear of the tanned urchins he had known. They looked at him as though he were a stranger.

'Hello, you guys,' he said. 'Nice to see you again,' and offered to shake hands.

They stared doubtfully at him.

Reiko said, 'Say hello to Jack.'

'Hello, Jack,' they chorused in obedient unison, but as they shook hands, their eyes were grave and guarded.

It had been like that when he first met them: the initial reserve of children caught up in an ugly family situation. In time they had become friends with him. He was going to have to win them over again.

He stood. Reiko was staring at him. They drank each other in, oblivious of the children, of the place and of the people around them. The last moment he had seen her now fused seamlessly with the present.

Ransome said, 'Nothing has changed for me, Reiko. I was hoping I could persuade you to come back with me.'

'Nothing has changed?'

He shook his head.

She continued to stare at him in silence, as though unable to comprehend him being there.

'It's ulterior motive time,' he said. He grinned at her. 'I wonder if the kids would like to see the view from my room.'

She laughed lightly. 'I know I would. It *is* very public here,' smiling a distracting conspirator's smile at him.

He said, 'I took the precaution of having room service deliver a celebratory bottle of champagne for us. I'll just order some lemonade and cakes for the kids.'

In the lift, she took his hand, her grip almost painfully tight. His urge to hold her was overwhelming.

There was less opportunity for them to be close than

they had hoped. The children's reserve quickly evaporated. They wanted their mother to point out the various parts of Tokyo that could be seen from the twenty-fourth floor: the city's clone of the Eiffel Tower and the Imperial Palace, half lost in a low mist; close under them, the Detached Palace and its gardens; and away to the South West, the harbour where it met the Sumida River. Katsuji wanted to operate his camera. Both took turns at looking through the lens and adjusting the focus.

Standing close, brushing fingertips, entering each other's space—it was agonising.

While the kids played and ate their cakes, Ransome and Reiko talked their way down the bottle, trying to pick up the threads.

There was a new dimension to her. Behind her obvious pleasure at being with him, a shadow. The plight of the children bothered her badly.

Reiko said, 'It's not that they have forgotten how to be Japanese. They have never learned. Being bilingual hasn't helped much. They're suffering from my disease, Jack,' she gave him a rueful look, 'suspended halfway between two different worlds. I think it's actually worse for them than for me. At school they get all kinds of abuse. The other children call them "*hen-Japa*"—strange Japanese. They're completely bewildered. It's as though all three of us come from some alien race.

'But at least they don't have to deal with my father. It's been a running battle ever since we came back from America. My father is displeased with his daughter,' this, wryly. 'He wants me to live in Japan, to settle here and marry again, this time to a Japanese. I've told him I can't live in Japan, and under no circumstances will I marry a Japanese man.' She laughed. 'He just can't believe I would defy his authority.'

She sipped her champagne.

'I've been away too long. I laugh in the wrong places,

speak when I'm supposed to shut up,' looking unhappy. 'We have this proverb: "Hammer down the nail that sticks out." My father is determined to hammer me down. He likes my cleverness, but resents my foreignness. He can't stand me arguing with him instead of meekly agreeing. He doesn't even like me questioning him. When his business friends are around, I don't always remember to use *keigo*, the very polite form of address. He claims that it makes him lose face. He keeps talking about how we must keep our Japanese identity. I ask him what's so fragile about it that it needs constant defining, reinforcing and repair. He talks about "purity" and "pride". I tell him not to worry, I'm not going to rot the flimsy fabric of Japanese society single-handed.' She laughed sourly, shaking her head in frustration.

She took his hand in hers, tracing the tips of the fingers of her other hand down the length of the tendons, feeling Ransome's skin as though she were blind. 'I don't know what to do, Jack. I don't know whether to keep trying harder to be Japanese, or to escape.'

Ransome said, 'Escape. Escape with me.'

'I wish it were that easy,' she said.

* * *

It was time for her to go.

Reiko crouched down beside the children and whispered in their ears. 'They have a request,' she said, smiling at him.

The pair looked nervously at Ransome. Yasuko took his hand and said, 'Will you take us to the zoo, please?'

'What a marvellous idea!' Ransome said. Looking at Reiko's lovely face, he thought, it's going to be alright.

She said, 'Are you really brave enough to come to the zoo with these two devils?'

'Oh, Mom,' said Katsuji, sounding like any embarrassed Californian kid.

Yassie said, 'They have a panda there.'

'Can't wait,' Ransome said. 'I've never seen a panda.'

'He's a big bear from China,' said Katsuji.

'And he's black and white and doesn't make love to his wife,' Yasuko said.

They had their only private moment together as the children ran from the room to press the button to summon the lift.

'I'm glad about the zoo,' he said.

'You're not the only one with ulterior motives.'

Suddenly she was in his arms. There was a frantic quality to her kisses. Her soft, yielding mouth, the perfumed breath, the flicker of tongues, the promise of more. Then the moment was over; the children's voices approaching along the passageway prised them apart.

Waiting for Reiko was a white, chauffeur-driven Rolls Royce. An amiable-looking middle-aged chauffeur sprang out and opened the rear doors for them, bowing deferentially. He wore a smart uniform complete with peaked cap, leggings and rows of silver buttons.

Was Reiko rich? Money was not something they had ever spoken about. He had assumed something vaguely middle-class—after all, her parents had to be wealthy enough to have sent Reiko to Europe for several years to study music—but she had seldom spoken about her family; she had told him only that her father was an engineer.

For the chauffeur's benefit, they restricted themselves to shaking hands.

Ransome said, 'I'll call you the moment I'm free.'

She looked at him steadily, then gave a little nod, as though making up her mind about something.

'Soon,' she said, squeezing his hand. 'Please.'

As the Rolls drove off, she smiled at him through the rear window. The children waved cheerfully.

Chapter 13

On the way to Aoyama's *ryokan* in Ikebukuro, Ransome told Kaizei about being abducted by the *yakuza*.

Kaizei stared at Ransome white-faced. 'Jesus Christ. I can't believe how lucky you were.'

'That was the impression I came away with,' Ransome said.

'They give you any idea who they were?'

'Not a clue.'

Kaizei was silent for a time. 'You'd better get out, Jack. You're a sitting duck.'

'I'll be fine,' Ransome said, making lewd eyebrows, 'if I can just break this madcap habit of smiling at hand-some young strangers.'

'You're crazy, you bastard,' Kaizei said, laughing.

'You're the one who needs to be careful,' Ransome was serious now. 'They've botched two attempts on you. Next time your luck might run out.'

They both knew that Kaizei would not have escaped alive.

* * *

A scared-looking old man peered through the narrow opening. Aoyama: the secret reef of gold, the anonymous keeper of the knowledge. He had agreed to come from the north to be interviewed.

The door closed. Ransome heard the chain being slipped.

On the way to meeting him, Kaizei had taken special

precautions. They had changed taxis twice, doubled back by underground. Only when he was totally convinced they were not being followed, did they head for this faceless Tokyo hotel, Aoyama's hideout.

'*Konnichi wa!*' the old man said, smiling warmly at Kaizei. The smile did not overcome the strain written upon his face. He bowed, then shook hands with Kaizei, who made the introductions.

Aoyama looked at Ransome with curiosity, then bowed. His handshake was frail. Cool skin, thin as paper. He wore a neat pinstripe suit, a white shirt and a sober tie.

So this was the man who had first cracked open the serpent's egg. He looked harmless enough—a compact, nuggetty little fellow with thick bifocal spectacles that magnified his eyes hugely and made him squint as though he were regarding Ransome through the wrong end of a telescope. There was a shock of cropped white hair standing straight up.

For several minutes Kaizei and Aoyama talked rapidly together. Ransome noted the respect with which Kaizei treated him, his body language as deferential as that of an admiring son.

Kaizei said, 'He has decided that since you are brave enough to be here helping me uncover this crime he is now willing to be filmed. That's a breakthrough.'

Aoyama was listening keenly as though he understood English well enough to follow the conversation. He smiled at Ransome.

As Ransome set up his camera, Aoyama drew several files from a suitcase on his bed. He stacked them neatly on the desk before him. His movements were precise. When he flicked through the files, Ransome noted their rule–column orderliness. 'Ask him where he got all this,' he said.

'I already have,' Kaizei said. 'When the Section was

pulled out of Harbin, he thought he might have some defensive leverage if he managed to keep copies of certain secret files. Call it insurance.'

'Like being in bed with an unexploded bomb.'

'Yeah,' Kaizei said. 'And my friend knows it. Some of it is more recent—data he's collected in the past couple of years. He's developed an obsession about setting the record straight.'

Aoyama gave a tight smile.

They began the interview. The questions and answers were in Japanese but, since there was time, Kaizei translated as they went.

Aoyama spoke briefly of his recruitment, then of his administrative problems: of the logistics of how prisoners who had survived one experiment could best be used for the next. 'Before a vivisection,' he said, 'there was always the problem of reconciling the claims of the various teams for the organs.' The bureaucrat's problem. The very matter-of-factness of his evidence gave it a relentless force.

They were at the heart of the matter: facts, figures, statistics, records of experiments, the number of prisoners, the numbers of soldiers and guards. Aoyama, with his passion for detail, had sat in the middle of the horror observing the pitiless machine as it gobbled up three thousand men. His medical degree combined with his meticulous nature made him the perfect choice as bookkeeper to the Section.

From his own memories, from his subsequent research, from the conversations he had had with other Section members whom he had persuaded to talk, he knew a great deal of the total story. He told them of how, two months before the end of the war, a group of Russian prisoners had broken out of their cells.

'They were all shot down in the compound—maybe forty or fifty of them.'

'Where did they come from, the prisoners?' Kaizei asked. 'Were they all serving soldiers?'

'Some of them were. But most came to us through the *Kempei Tai*,' Aoyama said. 'They sent us any Chinese and Russians who were thought to be spies or saboteurs, as well as any Chinese and Koreans who were suspected of anti-Japanese activities. Communists, some recalcitrant Chinese who had been recruited into our army, a few Americans—there was never a shortage of *maruta*.'

Hearing the translation, Ransome said, 'Americans? Did he say Americans?'

Kaizei repeated the question. Aoyama nodded.

'Jesus.' This had not come up before.

Kaizei questioned him closely about this. Aoyama insisted that there had been American, British and Australian prisoners used in tests.

'How did they come to be in Harbin?' Ransome was shaken.

Kaizei repeated the question. Aoyama answered, 'Not Harbin. One of the programs was on tropical diseases. Tests were carried out on prisoners of war in the islands: New Guinea, Singapore and Indonesia.'

Kaizei pressed on, leading the man through the interview one careful question after another. Aoyama had been an industrious, hard-working officer. 'One of my duties was responsibility for printing the results of the experiments—dozens of them, hundreds of them. I read them all. A lot of people around today make a good living from the information they derived in Harbin.' He looked contemptuous.

As Kaizei and Ransome listened, the suffering of the prisoners, the callousness with which they were treated, appalled them.

Aoyama said, 'March 1945 was an especially intense time for us. General Ishii came back on orders from General Staff. He had been relieved of his post in 1942 for squandering funds. But they needed him. They had determined to launch an all-out bacteriological attack on the enemy. Things were going badly for Japan all over the Pacific, but the fear of war with the Russians was doubly great. I saw orders specifying that we would drop bombs charged with plague fleas on areas where the attack was expected to come from: Khabarovsk and Vorishilov. There was a second plan, to spray key areas with bacteria.

'There was tremendous pressure on us in administration. Ishii ordered the Section and all its branches to increase the rat population to three million so that the plague-infected fleas would have sufficient hosts. Rat nurseries had to be built. Refrigerators for storing the plague bacilli had to be commandeered and modified. The manufacture of the ceramic bombs had to be stepped up. New units had to be trained in handling the weapons. It was a nightmare. But we worked night and day.

'Everything was ready to go very quickly. We sat waiting for the order to go. The command never came. On August 9th, when the Russians launched their offensive, panic set in. The general ordered that all research documentation should go back to Japan. Other specified documents were to be destroyed at once. The command personnel decided that not a single log was to be left alive and that all installations that might give any idea of what the Section had been doing were to be destroyed.

'I saw the minutes of that plan. The annihilation of the prisoners was to be handled by a special unit recruited from Ishii's fellow townsmen and commanded by one of his brothers. Ishii baulked. He ordered that everyone should take part in the killings. That way we all would share responsibility for it. So I was part of what happened next.'

At this point Aoyama became silent for a long time.

When he began to speak again, his voice was no more than a whisper.

'I'd never been in the compound where the prisoners were kept. Not many of the garrison had. When we entered, the wounded were being finished off with pistols. It was a slaughterhouse. There were bloodstained corpses in the corridors and in the cells. The faces of the corpses were distorted by convulsions. Potassium cyanide had been put into their food. They had died terribly. Those of the *maruta* who had had a presentiment of death and refused to eat that day were machine-gunned through the judas holes set in their cell doors.

'We had to drag out the bodies. Eight pits had been dug in the inner courtyard. There were fires blazing around the bodies. The smoke that rose had a sickening stench. But it was soon obvious that the pits were not enough.

'It went on all through the night. Searchlights were playing over the scene. There were some of our soldiers in the pits separating the flesh from the bones. The bones were crushed to dust in a special machine. The rest was doused in petrol and burned.

'I couldn't stand it. I managed to get away from that terrible place. I worked on burning documents. Bonfires of them. Details of the biological warfare attacks on the Chinese, details of experiments that had gone wrong and the lists of murdered logs all went to the flames.

'A huge contingent of soldiers was dismantling the laboratories and the cells. They had terrible trouble with those. Finally, they blew them apart with fifty-kilogram bombs, one to a cell. All the tissue samples were thrown into the Sun Hua River. In a few days, most of the evidence had been covered over. It was as if the camp had never been there.

'My office was taken up with organising transport. Another nightmare, but the general had the support of command and by August 16th (here he referred to one of his meticulous files) we were on trains heading for the Korean border. By the 18th, we had shipped out for Japan.'

Aoyama slumped back in his chair, deathly pale. He seemed to sleep for a minute, or so. Kaizei completed the translation. Ransome switched off the camera. After several minutes of complete silence, Aoyama opened his eyes and nodded to Kaizei. They resumed.

'We were all worried about what was going to happen to us. The command issued us all with an ampoule of potassium cyanide, "just in case". That made us even more worried. About a dozen men took them. The shame of it all was too much for them. Then, as we were about to board the ship, the Section was lined up and the officers, men and civilians who were attached to the Section were sworn to do three things. We were sworn to lifelong secrecy about all we had seen. We were to swear that we would not enter public or government office. And, finally, we were to swear that we would not maintain contact with each other.'

Aoyama looked disgusted and said, 'We all swore, of course, but not ever to see one's comrades again? Most of us ignored that subsequently. I have kept in touch with scores of the Section men over the years. And as for not holding public, or government office—what a joke! There are plenty of them who have gone on to become rich and powerful. Thirty years we kept the secret for them. All of us have suffered!'

Suddenly he stood up, shaking his head. He seemed overwhelmed with exhaustion. He muttered something to Kaizei.

Kaizei said, 'He wants to end it there. He's flying back north this afternoon.'

Ransome checked his watch. They had been with the old man for three hours. He said, 'Ask him if he knows what the dead man meant when he said something about there being a much worse crime.'

Kaizei hesitated then asked the question.

Aoyama seemed suddenly frightened. He spoke in an agitated manner for several minutes to Kaizei, then, with a series of dismissive gestures, made it obvious that he wanted them to leave.

Later, going down in the tiny lift, Ransome asked what he had said.

'I'm not sure what he meant.' Kaizei seemed puzzled. 'He said, "There's more, much more",' concentrating on remembering the exact words. '"You are only at the beginning."'

'Can that mean that something went on after the war?'

'He wouldn't explain. He said, "Keep asking the questions and you'll come to know the real horror of it all."' Kaizei stared at Ransome as the lift doors opened. 'The "real horror"? What in God's name can he mean?'

Chapter 14

From the Kyoto, he rang McGregor.

He picked up on the first tone. 'Christ, I was hoping you'd call. I tried to reach you at the Prince but they didn't know where you'd gone.' He sounded agitated. 'I need to see you, pal. There's something weird going on.'

Ransome said. 'I moved to the Kyoto. Come over.' He gave him the address.

'Half an hour,' McGregor said.

Ransome hung up. The phone gave a little secondary trill of sound. Ransome stared at it. Christ, he thought, it's bugged. He put the handpiece down, thinking, the room too? Or was he just being paranoid? He picked it up and unscrewed the earpiece. Nothing he could see. Surely nobody could have set up a bug so fast? He'd only been there two nights. But he decided to assume that his hunch was right and act accordingly.

McGregor arrived looking worried and breathing unhealthily, as though he had been running.

Ransome offered him a drink.

'Whisky if you've got it.'

McGregor gulped down the first generous measure. Ransome refilled his glass and waited, curious to learn what this was about.

McGregor slumped back on the divan, his gut swelling in front of him. He looked soft and old. 'What are you up to, Jack?' There was an accusatory tone in his voice.

'Hang on a minute.' Ransome stood up and crossed to

the console by his bed. He turned on the radio and twirled the dial until he found some rock music. He turned up the volume.

McGregor watched him, wide-eyed. 'You're having me on,' he said.

'Paranoia time,' said Ransome.

McGregor's face lit up at this, the journalist rallying. 'Goodness,' he said, grinning, 'what have we here?'

'You said "something weird" was going on?'

'The dead man in that hotel,' McGregor said. 'Tell me what that's all about.'

'What's the problem?'

McGregor stared at his glass as though hypnotised by it. 'Suroko could lose her job, is the problem.' With an effort, he tore his gaze away, looking directly at Ransome. 'After you'd gone, I filled her in on what I knew: me getting the police call to identify you at the jail, what you told me about finding a body, Kaizei not turning up, you spending the night in jail. So she, being a good journalist,' drinking down the second whisky, 'when she gets to her newsroom, she checks. Surprise, surprise, she finds nothing has appeared in any newspaper about a dead man in a Shinjuku hotel. And her television newsroom— which illustrious organisation, by the way, has made shock horror sensationalism into an art form—appears to know nothing of this curious affair.

'She smells a story and follows up. She calls her police contact, and, believe me, she has very good police contacts. Her contact knows nothing but promises to find out and ring her back. After a couple of hours he calls back and says there is no report of a body in a hotel in Shinjuku. "It didn't happen," the man says. "Your information must be wrong." She makes another couple of calls. No dice. No-one is talking.'

McGregor looked at his empty glass. Ransome made no

move to fill it. He encouraged further talk with a questioning silence.

McGregor went on. 'Now comes the good bit. Late afternoon, she gets a call to see the news director, A nasty wee toe rag called Akai. He tells her she is getting herself into trouble by harassing the police about some crazy story being put about by a dubious friend of her husband—namely you, Jack. He says this person—you—is mixed up with undesirable elements, especially one renegade Japanese journalist who is wanted by the police for unspecified crimes. Akai tells her to lay off. There is no story. When she protests that her source is impeccable, things start getting even more interesting.

'Akai says, "By helping this American journalist you may be causing harm to the national interests of Japan. You are in danger of being regarded as a traitor." Heavy stuff! When she asks him what he means, he stalls. Su reckons he didn't know what was going on, but had simply been ordered to get her to lay off.

'She starts to argue that it might be a great story for Mr Akai's beloved television station. He gets heavy. She is reminded very bluntly that her position as one of the few on-camera women journalists in this great modern state is only a trial arrangement.' McGregor looked sour. 'It's been a "trial arrangement" for three fucking years, notwithstanding she's the best in the business by a mile.'

Ransome said nothing.

'By now, she's one very puzzled, intrigued and worried lady. But stupid,' said McGregor, 'Suroko, is not. So she undertakes to drop the subject. Then Akai turns the screw a touch further. He tells her that the less she and I have to do with you, the better. You'll be pleased to hear he described you and Kaizei as "trouble-makers". Does that sound familiar?'

Ransome laughed. It was a phrase that had been used

about him several times in Vietnam, particularly after each of his visits behind Vietcong lines.

McGregor said, 'For someone who's just arrived in the place, my friend, you are not a popular person.'

'Seems not,' Ransome said. He made a decision about McGregor. 'Look, I didn't ever intend to get you into this, but it seems like you're involved whether I like it or not. So let me tell you what I know. If, after you've heard what it's about, you want to steer clear, fine. I don't want you or Suroko compromised or put at risk in any way. But if you want to be part of it, maybe there'll be a story in it for you.'

McGregor looked pleased. 'Thanks. But how about you telling both of us together? Come and dine with us. Our place is not . . .' here, he pointed at the ceiling, mouthed the word 'bugged' and burst out laughing. McGregor was enjoying himself.

* * *

'Kaizei turned up.'

McGregor, now resplendent in a kimono, stopped stirring the fish soup. 'In one piece?'

'Well, two pieces, if you count his metal and plastic foot. Apart from that, alive and kicking.'

'A metal foot? Jesus!' McGregor sucked his breath through his teeth in horrified reaction to the idea of being maimed. 'The poor bugger. When did that happen?'

'The day I saw him last in Kampuchea.'

Ransome gave him a potted version of Kaizei's history, his disappearance after the fire-fight that had taken both of them out of the war correspondence business. 'He was out to lunch for awhile. He hasn't published a single piece in a couple of years. He had just decided to start again when he ran into the story we're working on now.'

By unspoken agreement, they left discussion about the real issue until Suroko arrived, which she did half an hour later. As she came through the door, kicking off her rubber ankle boots and peeling off a heavy coat, the sight of Ransome seemed to surprise her.

McGregor said hastily, 'Jack's agreed to fill us in on what's happening.'

'Good,' she said, managing a bright smile. Ransome gained the impression she was not all that pleased to see him there. She looked worried and drawn. The hug she gave McGregor was perfunctory. 'I need a drink,' she said, going into their bedroom.

McGregor refilled their glasses and poured a scotch for Suroko.

Moments later she reappeared clad in a cotton kimono matching his. 'You are a dangerous man to know, Jack,' she said.

'Mac told me. I'm sorry I got you involved,' Ransome said. 'I thought the least I could do was tell you what I know.'

And over an excellent dinner he did.

Su proved to be a brilliant cook. She served bean curd soup served with sake, *soba* served with *mirin*, a sweet liqueur, followed by raw fish and pickled vegetables washed down, surprisingly, with a good Australian chardonnay. She had listened in complete silence, deeply troubled by what she was hearing. 'How horrible,' she said, her voice very quiet. 'No wonder they do not wish people to know this.'

'Who are "they"? that's the question,' McGregor said. 'They must be powerful. Otherwise how in God's name have they managed to keep it under wraps for more than forty-five years?'

'I don't know how they've kept it quiet all this time, but I know they're motivated by fear of prosecution for war crimes,' Ransome said. 'All the ones we've talked to have been waiting for the midnight knock on the door. By keeping their oath they thought they were safe.'

'Maybe they were right,' McGregor said. 'As soon as the story starts to come out, people start getting knocked off. That kind of thing gives oath-keeping a good name.'

'Look, I had no idea when I came that it was going to turn nasty—at least not this nasty,' Ransome said, feeling embarrassed now. 'Frankly, I'm sorry I dragged you into it and I think the two of you should have nothing further to do with it, or with me.'

'Nonsense,' McGregor said, 'it's a story that must be told.'

Suroko flashed him a brief, preoccupied smile. 'Mac,' she said, putting her hand over his. 'I can't touch this. If I do—or you do—I will lose my job. Jack's right. We shouldn't have anything to do with it at all.'

'Or with him?' McGregor looked at her steadily. She met his eye with equal force. 'He's a friend, for Christ's sake.'

Ransome cut through the impending quarrel. 'Suroko's right, Mac. You've been very kind and helpful, but after tonight I'm going to stay right out of your way. There's no way I want Suroko to risk losing her job—or worse.'

McGregor stared at them both in turn, biting his lip. Then he nodded, accepting the truth of it. 'What about you, Jack? You know, it's not going to be like Nam. You could be a neutral there, just another journalist recording a war. In this country, a *gaijin* covering a story like this— a lot of people, even ones who weren't involved, are going to think of you as a deadly enemy.'

Chapter 15

Patrol Officer Harada Uneido yawned mightily. Several times in the past ten minutes the stifling overheated air in the car had almost overwhelmed him. He glanced at his watch: seven a.m. It had been a long night.

His driver, Sato Tudaro, echoed the action with an exaggerated yawn of his own. Leaning back from the steering wheel to the full stretch of his arms, he shook his head like a dog worrying its prey. Their eyes met briefly. As one, they burst out laughing. They were both thinking the same thing.

'Ten more minutes,' Harada said.

'I know.' Sato slowed the car. There was no point in running into a problem right now. Problems belonged to the next shift.

They cruised quietly through the empty streets, neither talking, thinking only of their waiting beds. They had been on night shift now for three weeks out of their six-week tour of duty. Both of them were already sick of it.

To their left, the high blocks of run-down apartment buildings were replaced by the marshalling yards that stretched to the edge of the fishing wharves two hundred metres away. The road dipped. Seen from close to eye level, the parallel rail tracks seemed to fuse into a floor of steel.

Some railway workers were walking along the track. They were bent forward into the teeth of the wind as if they were skating on the glinting surface. Beyond, gulls wheeled, white against arctic grey.

'Five minutes,' Harada said contentedly. They were passing a high mesh fence in front of an enormous rusting shed that was in the process of being dismantled. The metal cladding had been removed from one end, showing a skeleton of girders inside.

Sato slowed the car abruptly. 'Is that smoke?'

A hundred metres ahead, from the top of one of the tall steel doors of the shed, there rose a thin plume of black smoke. Harada made a small grimace of annoyance. Their uneventful night had been wrecked. He had half a mind to drive on and do nothing. 'Best we take a look,' he said.

Sato accelerated, looking for an entrance. 'Call the fire service?'

Harada shook his head. 'Best check it first.'

They flew past the high chainlink for a quarter of a mile before they found an open gate where a single rusting rail track crossed the street and entered the yard of the abandoned building.

Sato hit eighty as they raced back along the tracks, fenceposts blurring. Already the thin reed of smoke was thicker and darker. They both clenched their teeth as he bumped diagonally over a dozen rail tracks at speed. Ten metres from the building he braked hard.

Out of the car, fast, the wind catching at them with freezing talons as they ran. The great door was hung on tracks black with grease. It slid sideways with surprising ease.

The building inside was vast. A mezzanine deck traversed the rear half. The space under the deck was thick with smoke. A draught-borne column of it was being sucked out high above their heads. Opening the door had broken the symmetry of the column. The black smoke wavered as though it had lost its way.

Fifty metres away, in the middle of the ground floor, a car was burning, flames leaping through the rear windscreen. Two yellow-clad men, who appeared to be wearing helmets and boots, were standing near it. As soon as Harada and Sato appeared, the two began to run towards the far end of the building.

'Stop!' Drawing their pistols, Harada and Sato ran after them. The two men quickly disappeared into the smoke. Harada stopped at the burning car. The heat was intense.

Sato, young and fit, ran on hard after the men. Under the mezzanine he was quickly enveloped in smoke. He slowed. Breathing was becoming difficult. He took a last deep breath and plunged into the gloom. Above the low roar of flames there came the sound of metal clanging.

Within a few metres, he came to a steel door. There was no door handle. It had been locked from the other side. Quickly he searched along the wall in either direction. There was no other exit. Choking now, he turned and ran back through the pall, back to where he could hear Harada shouting for help.

In spite of the intense heat, Harada had managed to open the rear door of the burning car. Crouching low, with his hat held in front of his face as a shield, he was dragging something one-handed from the car, something in flames.

When Sato came close he could see that it was the body of a man. Both policemen burned their hands seriously getting the body out of the car because the bottom half of the man was shrouded in what remained of a melting green garbage bag.

Chapter 16

They drove to the house up a straight driveway between fields entirely covered in white plastic. It was new-looking; a neat, two-storey brick building with a blue tiled roof and asbestos sidings on the upper floor. It appeared deserted. The front door was open. No-one answered their knocks or Kaizei's loud shouts. Kaizei took a quick look inside, but the house was empty.

To one side there was a small shed. Everything in it was neat and orderly: tools all arranged on a shadow board, bags of produce and fertiliser in neat stacks. A blue utility stood in one corner. There was a small bench saw. Someone had been cutting wood recently; the smell of bruised pine hung in the air. Along the length of the outside wall of the shed, covered in a red tarpaulin, was a head-high stack of cut firewood.

Beyond, there was a long, low, glass greenhouse. They looked for their man in there. Hundred of pots with seedlings filled the table-high racks. To one side there was a shelf packed with potted red poppies and young rose bushes. The greenhouse was deserted.

Kaizei limped away to the far end and disappeared behind some greenery. Ransome went back outside. After the warmth of the potting shed the keen north wind cut through to his skin. He shivered and buttoned up his padded jacket.

The farm was a narrow L-shaped property bounded half-a-mile away by the curve of a *shinkansen* track. It lay on a narrow strip of flat farmland wedged between two

parallel ranges of low hills. To the west, the wooded
shoulders of the slopes had been partly cleared. Upon
them grew a grove of pines. A little temple was perched
on the summit of the nearest peak.

In the hour's drive from Nagoya, they had passed a
dozen such temples, and not a mile from where he now
stood, Ransome saw a giant yellow ferroconcrete statue
of some Buddhist deity standing guard above a tiny
village.

On the adjacent farm, which seemed to be the only
one sharing the little valley, he could see rows of green-
houses. The black earth was half obscured by the long
strips of white plastic sheeting that kept the frost from
the crops; market garden vegetables, carrots and toma-
toes. A couple of black and white cows grazed on the
slope of an emerald field. A bright pink blanket hung out
of the upstairs window of the farmhouse. There was no-
one in sight.

Kaizei reappeared. 'Not a sign. He might be up there.'

Behind them, rising above the house, was a steep slope.
Most of it was a dense, dark tangle of trees, but a strip
had been cleared and neatly terraced with a mosaic of
grey granite boulders.

Ransome picked up his camera from the car. They
ducked through the three-strand fence and began to walk
between the low tents of white plastic sheeting. Under it
were hundreds of staked and pruned rose bushes. They
climbed halfway up the slope. There was a trellis for
climbing flowers, an orchard of persimmon and orange
trees. Higher still, parallel rows of clipped and manicured
tea bushes ran up to the summit of the hill where they
followed the contours of the topmost slopes like a green
maze. There was no sign of their man.

Kaizei stopped and looked back. He was breathing
heavily. In spite of the cold, sweat was glistening on his
brow. His artificial foot must have made the climb

agonising, but he had not complained, climbing doggedly on.

'That looks like him,' he said.

From their position they could see someone working at the furthest part of the field, close under the rail track: a distant, lone figure crouched down between the rows. The light caught the white plastic, making the field look like a frozen pond of ice.

They set off down the hill. Above them, the wind sang in the wires of an electric power cable that strode across the valley on giant steel legs and climbed the hills beyond, heading for a range of distant mountains, the north slopes of which were dusted with snow.

The man they had come to see kept on working. If he had seen them, he gave no sign. Ransome wondered if he tended this enormous crop by himself.

His name was Sakurai Koji. He had been a biochemist serving in Section 731; that was as much as they knew about him. Ransome wondered what his reaction would be to having his past cast up to him like a corpse from the depths of the sea. But Sakurai knew they were coming and why. He shared a mutual friend with Mr Aoyama. This friend had told Aoyama that Sakurai had come to much regret his part in the work of the Section. Aoyama had written to him asking if he would see Kaizei. He had agreed to cooperate.

As they approached they could see that Sakurai was spraying chemicals onto the rose bushes, wearing a mask and thick gloves. They were within a few metres of him before he acknowledged their presence. He stopped his work, put the spraygun into a bucket, and slowly stripped off his mask and gloves, looking at them in silence.

Sakurai and Kaizei bowed politely. Kaizei introduced Ransome. Sakurai bowed to Ransome, flashing him a distracted smile that revealed a mouthful of steel teeth. They shook hands. The eyes were old and shrewd. He was a small man with a head that seemed too big for his wiry, almost frail body. He wore neat blue dungarees and a peaked cap with a Japanese advertising logotype written on its brim.

Kaizei spoke to him at some length. After a time, the man shook his head regretfully.

'He's agreed to talk,' Kaizei said, 'but he won't be filmed.'

Ransome said, 'Tell him I can keep his face out of it if he's worried.'

Kaizei smiled. 'He's not. He says he's too old to be frightened. It's just that he would be embarrassed being interviewed on film.'

'Has he been threatened?'

'He hasn't said so, but Mr Aoyama warned him it could be dangerous.'

Ransome looked at the old man with respect. 'Ask him if he minds me taking pictures of him going about his work—long shots only.'

This time the old man looked thoughtful for a moment, then he nodded and laughed a high nervous laugh. He said something to Kaizei.

'He says, "Alright, why not?"'

Ransome smiled his thanks at the old man.

Sakurai picked up a bucket in which were various gardening tools and began to lead them back towards the house. He did not speak on the way, nor until the interview began, but he seemed comfortable in his silence. It was as though his solitude had extinguished the need for dialogue.

The old man made tea for his guests. His movements were neat and methodical. Everything seemed to have a place. The house gleamed with cleanliness. He motioned them to be seated, poured the pale green tea, then sat down opposite them, watching with interest as Kaizei set up his tape-recorder. Kaizei began his questioning.

For the next hour Sakurai spoke quietly in a measured and thoughtful way. He thought out careful answers to Kaizei's occasional questions, but essentially the interview became a monologue. Kaizei translated as he spoke. Ransome gained the impression the old man might have been delivering a prepared speech. They stopped halfway when the tape had to be changed.

'In 1936 I graduated from the Tokyo University as a doctor. I gained high honours in chemistry in which subject I found myself particularly interested. I was married to the young woman my family had deemed suitable and she immediately became pregnant. A fellow student of mine, Mr Imuri, told me of a special army medical section that was being set up to do medical research. He had joined and encouraged me to do so. My family were not well off, so if I was obliged to become a general practitioner it might be years before I could work in a laboratory situation, which was my first love. He assured me that I would have the opportunity to do original research. I jumped at the chance.

'My friend, who was very well connected, told me later that he had been asked by the authorities to help with recruiting among the outstanding students of that year. He put my name forward and, a week or so later, I was interviewed by some army medical corps officers at the Tokyo Medical Institute.

'There were three officers present. They did not give me their names, but I found out later that the senior officer was General Ishii. The interview was very straightforward. I was asked if I had any special interests in original medical research. I told them I was keen to work in areas of blood chemistry: on the nature of blood, cures for blood diseases and disorders, and so on.

'A few weeks later I received a letter saying that my application for admission into the medical corps had been accepted and I was to report to the Shinagawa

Barracks on such and such a date. I had, by this time, given up hope of acceptance and was arranging to take a post in a country hospital. I was overjoyed. I duly arrived at Shinagawa and, after a brief period of training, was commissioned as a lieutenant and immediately shipped to Harbin.

'It was stressed to us recruits that the work we would do was classified top secret. We were not allowed to speak to anyone about our work, nor our research interests. I remember I travelled to Manchuria by boat and train with about a dozen officers. Not one of them spoke about their destination to the others, but all of them turned out to be volunteers for the program. We arrived there in March of 1937.

'We were amazed by the scale of the operation at Harbin. There were several hundred doctors and other medical personnel there by then. I believe the total rose as high as two and a half thousand at the height of the Section's work.

'I entered into my work with enthusiasm. Scientifically, it was a perfect setup. Instead of having to try out one's theories on animals for years, we could go straight to trying them out on humans to see if they worked. All through my officer training period I had been making notes on the various theories about blood-related matters that I wished to put to the test. I conducted various experiments, some of which gave promise of important breakthroughs.

'My work did, of course, have a particular military significance since so many soldiers died from loss of blood. The powers-that-be must have liked what I was doing. They asked me to head a group whose purpose was to find blood plasma substitutes, especially those that might save lives in the combat areas, where blood plasma was always in short supply.

'It was an exciting challenge. I was at first dedicated to

what I was doing. I saw it as a vital development that would finally lead to saving the lives of soldiers and civilians and have considerable post-war value. I was the leader of the group and must take the responsibility for everything that happened.'

At this point in his monologue, Ransome observed, Sakurai began to speak more and more slowly. It was as though he were dragging each word clear of some glutinous swamp in his mind.

'Not all of my group were research scientists of the first flight. Indeed, some were downright unscientific. They did not seem to care about the sufferings that were inflicted on the prisoners as they tried one crackpot scheme after another.'

Sakurai stopped for a long time at this point. He was having difficulty composing himself.

'I remember the agony of one prisoner particularly. He was a Russian—a young man, very fit and healthy when we began. The prisoners were well fed and kept in good health before they were used in the trials. It was important, as you would understand, that the results were not skewed by negative health factors. I had not liked the concept that was put forward by my colleague, but his theory could only be proved by scientific test. We replaced the prisoner's blood with horse blood. He died in great agony.'

As Sakurai spoke, tears began to flow down his face.

'I was haunted by that man's cries, particularly. Why him, I don't know; there were many who died as badly. Some of my own theories resulted in deaths almost as horrible.'

Sakurai took a deep breath, wiped the tears from his cheeks impatiently. He straightened his shoulders and went on.

'It was about that time I received from my wife a letter containing a photograph of my son. I had never seen the child, who was born after I left for Manchuria. Somehow my child and the young Russian became mixed up in my mind. I realised then that no matter how my fellows regarded the prisoners, I could only see them as men like us. It occurred to me that although, in my heart, I believed the work I was doing could produce important results that might benefit mankind, I could not justify the effects the experiments had on these poor devils. I understood for the first time that the single-minded pursuit of a scientific theory can result in evil acts. And I knew that I was caught up in terrible matters.

'The members of the various medical disciplines tended to stick together, but I knew of other work that was going on there which was even more terrible than that in which I was involved. I began to feel ill, constantly—a kind of nausea that made it difficult for me to work. I knew that I could not go on at Harbin. I decided that *seppuku* was the only honourable way out. I tidied up my personal affairs, wrote a farewell to my parents, and then, suddenly, the Russians were coming.' Here Sakurai laughed, shaking his head in disbelief. 'We had been a secret organisation, but the secret that had been kept from us was that we were losing the war.

'My memories of that ignominious retreat—we were carried along by a wave of shame and fear—are jumbled now. All I know is that when I came home and the war ended I knew that I would be hunted down and would pay on the scaffold for my crimes against humanity.

'Although I tried to settle into a normal life, it was impossible. My lovely wife and the son I had never seen until that moment seemed too pure, too decent for me to corrupt with my presence. I felt unclean and judged myself unworthy of them. I judged it better that I leave my family quickly, before they became used to me and depended upon me. I knew that any day, the occupying army would discover the secrets of Harbin

and they would come for me. And so I left without a
word. They were in reasonable circumstances and
would not starve.

'I wandered around Japan for ten years, working
enough to eat, helping with charities and war relief and
generally trying to expiate the crimes I had been part of.
I did not change my name. I did not really attempt to
hide, although, in truth, I was on the run.

'About fifteen years ago I came here. I worked for the
old man who owned this property for several years. It was
a market garden then. He grew vegetables for Nagoya. His
whole family had died in Tokyo during a fire-bombing
raid when he, his wife and two children had been visiting
her parents. When he died, there was no-one else and he
left the land to me.

'I thought this a sign that I should settle down. I work
hard. I have found there is a market for roses and
poppies, so I can make a comfortable living. I send
money anonymously to my wife and child.' Sakurai
smiled, sadly. 'Of course, it cannot last. Some day the
authorities will come and the past will catch up with me.
Working with the flowers has brought me a kind of
peace. But, that aside, there are few moments when I
cannot hear the cries of that young man.'

The old man lapsed into silence. His face became still,
as though he were listening to a voice inside his head.

Kaizei asked Sakurai something. Turning to Ransome
he said, 'I've asked him why he agreed to meet us.'

The answer was spoken with fervent intensity. 'I agreed
to this interview only because I wanted the opportunity
to tell young scientists that no matter how promising
and important the discovery they seek may seem, they
must never forget their humanity, as I once did.'

He rose and, without a word, walked upstairs. After a
few minutes he returned carrying a manilla envelope.
From it he took a small photo album. He sat down at the

end of the divan and opened it at the beginning. Ransome craned forward to look.

The collection began with some poorly focussed photographs of himself as a young medical doctor. There was a wedding photograph showing Sakurai in formal clothes with a young wife in a kimono. She was short—barely coming up to his shoulder—stocky and pretty. They were both smiling with an awkward fixed expression. There followed some sharp, well-composed shots of the same young woman seen in a tiny garden in the company of an older couple, presumably his or her parents. On the next page, there was a posed studio picture of the same woman in smart street clothes, in her arms a baby boy smiling widely at the camera. Sakurai stared at it for a long time. He began to sob, quietly.

Ransome and Kaizei caught each other's gaze, but made no move.

The old man said something in a whisper to Kaizei.

Kaizei was close to tears when he translated for Ransome. 'He just said that his son will be over fifty years of age this year. He only saw him once, briefly, in 1945.'

When the old man turned the page at last, Ransome saw several shots of him as a young man in uniform. He was posed variously in front of some large buildings: sometimes alone, sometimes with other officers. There was one shot of him in a white coat in a laboratory. He was posed holding a test tube containing a dark liquid. The man said something to Kaizei.

Barely able to conceal his excitement, Kaizei said, 'The camp at Harbin. I've never seen a single photograph taken there.'

There followed several pictures of groups of soldiers smiling at the camera. One shot showed two enormous sumo wrestlers facing off on a low wooden platform surrounded by hundreds of cheering men in uniform. The pictures ended. There followed only some blank pages.

Sakurai turned to the back of the album. He took from an envelope two faded photographs. He handed the first one to Kaizei, and said something.

'The top brass, Section 731,' Kaizei said, disbelief in his voice.

After studying the photograph, he handed it to Ransome, who stared, fascinated by the ordinariness of the men in the picture. He spotted Sakurai at once, sitting to attention, second from the right in the front row. He was one of a group of eight officers, all in full uniform. They surrounded an aristocratic-looking officer of obvious high rank.

Sakurai pointed himself out to Kaizei, who nodded, then pointed to the senior officer. 'Ishii,' Sakurai said.

'Sweet Christ,' Kaizei said, in English. 'Aoyama told me he thought that all official photographs were destroyed. A picture of Ishii and his staff officers! This is unbelievable.' He took the photograph from Ransome and turned it over. On the back was pencilled in a date—Something written in Japanese. Kaizei translated: 'Harbin, July, 1942.'

Kaizei asked to see the second photograph. He held it so that Ransome could study it. The shot had obviously been taken at the same session, either a few minutes before or after the posed photograph. The officers were at ease and appeared to be laughing and joking together. Several of them carried their hats in their hands. The General was caught half-turned around, addressing a remark to someone in the back row. The young Lieutenant Sakurai was speaking to the officer on his left, a smile on his face.

Kaizei began to ask questions, which he translated as he went.

Sakurai: 'I had almost forgotten these pictures existed.'

Kaizei: 'Who were these officers?'

Sakurai: 'The section heads who were in charge of the various programs.'

Kaizei: 'Can you remember their names?'

Sakurai: 'Yes.'

Kaizei pointed to the officer in the top left of the picture.

Sakurai: 'Kanaka.'

Kaizei wrote the name down.

Kaizei: 'What work did he do?'

Sakurai: 'Germ warfare. He was working on the plague bacillus program with,' he pointed to the next man, 'Osatko.' (His finger moved faster now, to each man in turn.) 'Hamada, drugs . . . Obe, surgical techniques . . . Yonoi . . . he was administration—third in command.'

Sakurai hesitated. He tapped the face of the next man impatiently. Clearly, he could not remember the names of the remaining men.

Sakurai: 'I can't remember his name, but I do remember he worked on pain thresholds . . . ah . . . ah . . . No, it's no use!'

Sakurai moved his finger to the faces of the remaining officers, but it seemed his memory had seized. He shook his head in frustration.

Kaizei: 'Try to remember.'

Sakurai: (pointing to a dark-haired man on General Ishii's left) 'He's called . . . (a grimace of frustration) No, the name won't come . . . but I remember he ran the experiments to do with the effect of low temperatures on performance.' His finger moved. 'This man . . . Was it Watanabe? He worked on tropical diseases.'

The old man sat back, looking despairing. 'I'm getting too old to remember such things. I'm sorry. Their names are so familiar to me, but they simply won't come into my head. It was so long ago and there were so many programs.'

Abruptly, he rose. He crossed to the kitchen sink and stared out the window at the valley beyond. 'I have said enough. All that is history now. What's done is done.'

Ransome said, 'Could you ask him if I can take some shots?'

Kaizei closed the photograph album and went to Sakurai. He handed him the album and spoke to him quietly. The old man did not reply. Kaizei looked at Ransome and shrugged.

Sakurai walked outside. They followed him. Ransome switched on the camera, picking up shots of the old man entering the greenhouse. He followed him as he walked along the narrow corridor between the ranks of flowers. Sakurai stopped, turned and stared at them, a lone figure surrounded by a blood-red moat of poppies. He put his hand up in front of his face. Ransome stopped filming at once. The man said something to Kaizei, turned on his heel and walked away from them without another word.

Ransome said, 'That's it?'

Kaizei nodded.

As they got into the car, Sakurai appeared by the far end of the greenhouse. He stood staring over towards the distant mountains.

Ransome was moved by the sight of the troubled old man standing alone in the mournful beauty of that ordered winter landscape. Behind Sakurai the parallel slopes of the valley climbed gradually upwards. Near the horizon, the stony ramparts paled from black to grey, as if losing their substance, until they were insubstantial enough to be swallowed by the mist. On each peak there was a television tower. In the furthest distance there rose a mountain with ice and snow mantling its black shoulders.

The old rosegrower did not move, nor look towards them.

Ransome said, 'Do you think he's alright?'

Kaizei said, 'I think our man is hearing cries from the past.'

Chapter 17

'*Satyr tragopan*,' Ransome said, reading the legend. 'What a wonderful bird!'

'What a funny name!' Yassie said. The kids laughed gaily. The elegant fowl paced the floor of its cage, its vivid grey and red plumage ruffling in the keen wind. Hanging onto Ransome's hands, the two children steered him towards the next cage. He caught Reiko's eye. She had been watching him, smiling.

The visit to the zoo was proving to be fun for all of them. Although it was cold, the weather had been kind; they had not needed their umbrellas. Apart from the seemingly endless queue to see the panda (holding hands urgently in the privacy of the crush), Ueno Zoo was uncrowded enough for them to see all the exhibits easily.

They had admired the panda. They had marvelled at the bulk of the gorilla in his winter quarters. They had eaten ice-creams and hot dogs and ridden on the overhead railway. At the zoo's shop, Ransome had bought them each an English-language book on bears, 'to keep your English up to speed'.

Reiko had stayed close, and from time to time would touch his hand. The children's presence merely added to the sexual tension between them.

* * *

'Are you sure you want me to meet him?' Ransome said.

'Yes,' emphatically. 'I want him to see that not all Western men are bastards.'

They were silent in the Rolls, content to look at each

other and hold hands. Yasuko slept on her mother's lap
and Katsuji, finally silenced by exhaustion, watched the
city slip past, his nose pressed to the window.

They came to a leafy suburb that had the air of a diplomatic quarter: glimpses of imposing houses locked
behind high walls. The Rolls swung into a gravelled
driveway through tall, wrought-iron gates. Ransome
looked back. A man in gardening clothes swung the gate
shut behind them. Under the high stone wall, half-
hidden by tall, bamboo-wrapped trees, another gardener
was raking leaves.

'We're home,' Reiko said.

The car swung around a circular drive. A patch of manicured lawn framed a striking piece of black steel sculpture. To one side of the driveway there was a fence hung
with a dark-leafed creeper. It ended in a grove of bamboo
growing by a corner of the imposing two-storey stone
house.

The house had an air of permanence about it: solid,
beautifully proportioned, quite old. There were wrought-
iron screens over the windows.

The chauffeur jumped out and ran round to open the
door on Reiko's side. They all got out of the car, the children looking worn out. She spoke to them in Japanese
and they went off around the side of the house. 'He'll be
in his potting shed,' she said. 'He has a passion for
gardenias.'

The chauffeur went back behind the wheel. The car
crunched away beyond the house and swung into an
open bay in a discreet four-car garage half hidden by a
screen of beech trees.

'Thank you,' she said, leading him to the front door.
'It was wonderful of you to come. The kids like you very
much.' She looked back towards the garden. 'And so do
I.' She kissed Ransome very deliberately. The kiss lasted
a long time. Her mouth opened on his, their tongues

touched; he felt weightless, aware of her cool fingers tracing his cheekbone. 'I've been wanting to do that all day,' she said, breathless.

Ransome took a deep breath. 'Can we be together, soon?'

Reiko nodded, 'Very soon.'

A gardener came into view wheeling a barrow filled with leaves. She opened the front door. 'I will tell my father you are here.'

'He does know I'm coming?'

'I said I might bring you.' She grinned at him. 'He may be a bit stiff with you, but I know you'll be diplomatic. He's not impressed with me having Western male friends.'

'From what you've told me about Willy's habits, I can't blame him.'

They entered a hallway which contained only a black lacquer table upon which was a blue ceramic bowl containing a single gardenia. To one side was a painted screen. Over the three panels, Portuguese soldiers rode caparisoned horses through an idyllic Japanese countryside on their way to the Shogun's palace. On the centre screen, by the gates outside the palace, retainers readied presents for the *gaijin* invaders. On the right-hand screen, inside the palace, the Shogun was listening to music played by his geishas.

'What a lovely thing,' Ransome said, arrested by the beauty of it.

'Yes,' Reiko said. 'My father collects antiques.'

She led him through to a large room overlooking a walled garden. Ransome's eye was drawn outside by the spare beauty of the sculptured trees, artfully placed rocks and the play of light on a tiny lake.

The room was a careful balance of Japanese and Western furniture and artefacts. In one corner there was a grand piano, and beside it, resting on its stand, Reiko's cello. On the walls some Japanese paintings and scrolls hung comfortably alongside some European Impressionist paintings. On a black bamboo frame there hung a duck-egg blue silk kimono patterned with golden bamboo leaves. It looked fragile, as though it might disintegrate in a puff of wind. On every surface there were ceramics and pieces of sculpture. The floors were strewn with antique Chinese carpets.

In spite of the crowding treasures, the room looked comfortable and lived in. There was a pile of magazines on a coffee table, a television set in the corner.

So this is her background, he thought.

Reiko crossed to a sideboard. 'Drink?'

'Please.'

She poured a scotch and handed it to him. 'I won't be long.' She walked out into the garden, and he watched her as she went down the side lawn and entered a small glasshouse.

Ransome walked about the room looking at the paintings and the ceramics. One of the paintings was a Cezanne; another, a Van Gogh. Not copies: originals. Discovering that, he laughed out loud. This was serious wealth.

He went behind the piano to look more closely at an ornate samurai sword. The scabbard was hung on a frame attached to the wall. He gripped the long handle and felt the serrations, lovingly fashioned by some long-dead craftsman. The blade eased silkily out and back.

On top of the grand piano there were a dozen or so silver-framed photographs. One was of Reiko as a child, posing sweetly in a sailor suit, with what appeared to be her mother and father. Another showed her at about age sixteen. Already her beauty was in full flower. Except that her face had developed more definition and character, she had changed little since that time—here Ransome did a rough calculation—maybe twenty years ago.

The largest portrait was of Reiko's late mother, a handsome rather than beautiful woman. She looked to be in her sixties. The resemblance between mother and daughter was clear.

Two wedding photographs. One was presumably Reiko's grandparents, judging by the sepia tone and the old-fashioned clothes. In the other, the young girl in the traditional bridal gown could have been Reiko. The handsome young man looked stiff and proud in formal tails and top hat.

In the crowd of other photographs—there were several of Katsuji and Yasuko—the only one not in a silver frame took his attention. It was of two army officers.

Ransome picked it up and studied it. It was no more than a snap taken in available light against the sunstruck wall of a white building. It was yellowing with age. He recognised the taller of the two men from the wedding photograph: Reiko's father. He stood to attention, very straight and confident, looking directly into the lens. His uniform was splendid, set off by a gleaming belt and sword. His shoulder insignia, and that on his cap, appeared to denote a high rank.

The other man was younger looking and several inches shorter. His uniform was darker and plainer and he appeared to carry a lesser rank. He held his hat in his hand down by his side. His face was thin with prominent cheekbones. Ransome wondered who the man was.

At that moment Reiko came back into the room, accompanied by an older version of the high-ranking officer in the picture. Ransome put down the photograph.

'Jack,' Reiko said, 'this is my father.'

He was a strongly-built man with a thick crop of iron-grey hair. The heavy eyebrows were still jet black, and dominated a pale face deeply creased with lines that fanned outwards from a wide and subtle mouth. He was wearing gardening clothes: a battered tweed jacket over a roll-neck pullover and grey slacks.

'Mr Takanichi, how do you do?' Ransome offered his hand.

Takanichi shook hands and bowed slightly.

'Mr Ransome,' he said. His gaze was guarded, as though he were being introduced to someone he did not quite trust.

There was an awkward silence. At that moment the two children ran in from the garden. They came and stood close to Ransome. Yasuko took his hand and said, 'Grandfather has ducks in his pond.'

Takanichi looked puzzled for a moment, perhaps not quite understanding the English as spoken by his grandchildren, then he laughed. He looked at the two children with great fondness. Their friendliness to Ransome seemed to thaw him. Speaking carefully, he said, 'My daughter tells me you were kind enough to take my grandchildren to the zoo. It is many years since I have been there.'

The effort at sociability seemed to exhaust him. There was an awkward silence. Reiko looked nervous.

Takanichi said, 'Please sit down, Mr Ransome.'

Ransome sat down on a chair facing the garden, Takanichi sat opposite. Reiko crossed to the sideboard and began to pour drinks. She said, 'I told my father about your work in Vietnam.'

'You are here as journalist?' said Takanichi. The unspoken question was: are you here because of my daughter?

He answered carefully. 'Yes. A friend of mine, a Japanese journalist, has asked me to film some interviews for him.'

Reiko handed her father his drink and sat down opposite him.

'What kind of interviews?' Takanichi asked.

Ransome felt suddenly awkward about this. 'Historical. It's about World War II.'

Takanichi raised his eyebrows slightly. He sipped his scotch. 'Is this your first visit in Japan?'

Ransome nodded. 'Yes.'

Reiko said something to her father in Japanese. Takanichi looked at him with fresh interest. 'You are interested in Japanese culture?'

'I told him about your liking his Portuguese screen,' Reiko explained.

'I've been admiring your collection. It's wonderful.'

Takanichi rose suddenly. 'Come, I will show you.' He seemed relieved at having something to talk about.

For the next half hour he walked Ransome around several rooms on the ground floor of the spacious house. He spoke authoritatively of Old Kutani ware, of Ninsei, and Kenzan, Old Imari and Kakiemon. He persuaded Ransome to hold the ceramics in his hands, to feel the glazes of pieces, some of which he claimed were three hundred years old.

At length they walked in the garden. Takanichi showed off a dozen fine contemporary metal sculptures scattered through the grounds. 'We have a great culture in our country, Mr Ransome,' Takanichi said. 'I think it is a pity my daughter has been corrupted by living outside Japan.'

'But surely she now has the advantage of being able to understand two cultures,' Ransome said.

'She is in danger of finding herself stateless, without any cultural roots at all.' There was curtness in his tone. He gave the impression of a man unused to being contradicted.

He led Ransome into his potting shed. 'Gardenias, Mr Ransome. My passion.' The small glasshouse was filled with hundreds of pots of gardenias at various stages of development. The warm air was heavy with the beautiful perfume. 'In the right environment, things grow to their full beauty. Outside it, they never achieve their potential.' He removed a tiny leaf that showed a brown edge.

'I believe that people should stay strictly within their own culture, accepting those standards willingly.'

'Surely there is great strength in hybridisation?' Ransome said.

Takanichi shook his head dismissively, as though slightly annoyed by the superficiality of the remark.

Pressing the point, Ransome said, 'I think it inevitable that cultures will merge and the boundaries blur. That's been the lesson of history.'

Takanichi flashed a sharp look. 'Then I hope it will happen long after my time. Nothing good can come of it. Look at the disaster of Reiko's marriage. She can neither be happy in your world, nor ours,' he said, not without bitterness.

Ransome said, 'When I look at Reiko I see someone who has successfully bridged the gap between our cultures, and when I look at your beautiful and highly intelligent grandchildren I see great hope for the future.'

The man looked thoughtfully at Ransome. 'Reiko has told me a great deal about you. I am beginning to understand what she was talking about. But that does not change how I feel.' He stopped, facing Ransome now, not hostile but wanting to be understood. 'I must tell you that I would hate to see my daughter become involved with another Westerner, including you, Mr Ransome.'

He walked out of the potting shed, leaving Ransome shaken. Please be diplomatic, she had said. Jesus, he thought, I've wrecked it, in spades.

Chapter 18

McGregor said, 'There's a guy wants to meet you.'
'Who is he?'

'Someone called Cord. An American. Said he'd heard you were in Tokyo.'

'Cord? Never heard of him. Did you tell him I was here?'

'No way,' McGregor said.

'What's it about, did he say?'

'No, but he asked me to introduce you to him. He must know who you are. He wants to talk to both of us. Said it was urgent and that he's only in Japan for a few days. What are you doing for lunch today?'

Cord? Ransome thought. How interesting that someone he had never heard of should know he was in Tokyo. But why not? Everyone else seemed to know.

'Alright, I'll come in.'

'About twelve-thirty,' McGregor said. He gave Ransome directions and rang off.

* * *

At the Foreign Correspondents' Club, McGregor greeted him warmly. 'I've organised temporary membership for you. There's a form to sign.'

He took Ransome down one floor to the administrative office on the nineteenth floor of the Yurachko building. Ransome produced his dog-eared United States Journalists' Association membership card and signed up. He now had full privileges and could buy meals and drinks. Back upstairs he bought twenty thousand yen's worth of club chits from the reception desk.

Ransome said, 'Let's go meet this Mr Cord.'

* * *

Harry Cord was one of those open-faced Boston Irish who can dominate a room by their sheer energy. In his case, his height and bulk helped. He looked like a former footballer who was being slowly overwhelmed by the good life.

He was maybe fifty; the fair hair was beginning to thin. Ruddy, sunburned skin spoke of recent time spent in a hotter climate. There were freckles as big as ten cent pieces on the backs of his huge hands. The handshake wasn't competitive, but underlying the firm grip was the promise of immense physical strength. The eyes were bright blue and set deep within his fleshy face. They harboured an expression that made Ransome think they might have witnessed too many nasty things.

Lunch began with small talk. Cord was familiar with Ransome's front-line news reports on network television news; had seen the documentary, had read the reviews. Although curious about the man, Ransome was content to let the conversation run.

Cord began to question McGregor about his views of the Japanese economy. What were labour relations like? How did an exporting nation crack the closed Japanese market?

'You don't,' McGregor said. 'They'll pay lip service to the balance of payments problem, but frankly there's no way they are going to allow competition here. They've got their own domestic market tied up. They can charge anything they like here—and do. The profits they make here go to subsidise the dumping of their exports at discount prices. Market share's what they're about and they are determined to be *itchiban*—number one—in all the major categories of world trade. For them, business is the moral equivalent of war. They tried to beat the West in a war and lost. But they're going to win the peace and, believe me, they'll succeed, by fair means or foul.'

'What kind of foul plays do you mean?' Cord asked.

'You name it, they're doing it. The old cartels—the *zaibatsu*—were broken down by law after World War II, but they're alive and well. They're supposed to be illegal, but now they call them "trade associations", or some such euphemism, and carry on as before. They dominate the market. There are secret government subsidies for research and development paid out of gambling levies. They block imports with bullshit quality control regulations. They maintain a false value on the yen.

'You complain about their methods and they'll deny it. You prove they are lying and they say: very sorry, we'll change our ways; we'll cut out the collusion, or the dumping, or the blocking of imports. But all they do is change the window-dressing. The effect is always the same. Japanese manufacture is protected, overseas rivals are put out of business.'

McGregor was in full flight. It occurred to Ransome that, for someone who professed to love Japan and chose to live and work there, not to mention being in love with a Japanese woman, his views of Japanese business methods were remarkably cynical, even venomous. He wondered if the undercurrent he had picked up between McGregor and Suroko had anything to do with this bitter viewpoint.

'This is great stuff,' Cord said. 'And that's the reason I wanted to speak with both of you. Let me fill you in on my background. I'm basically a financial writer, or rather I was. I've got me a major new client: an American semi-government agency with special interest in the matter of American–Japanese economic relations, particularly our exports.'

Here Cord paused to reach into his wallet and hand them each a business card. Ransome read 'Worldtrade Inc., Special consultant: Dr Harold V. Cord'. There was an address at the World Trade Centre, New York. The message was repeated in Japanese on the back of the card. A Tokyo telephone number had been added, written in a bold and sloping hand.

Cord said, 'The US trading record with these people is very bad. Frankly, they're pissing on us. We can't sell them the time of day. I need, and I need it very badly, inside evidence of some of the malpractices that you've just been talking about.'

McGregor's eyes were bright. 'What sort of evidence do you want?'

Cord said, 'Inside dopester stuff but specifically, television documentary material. We're planning a series of programs ostensibly exploring the Japanese economic miracle. Provisional title: "Japan Inc.".'

He directed his attention at Ransome. 'I need television because I have a propaganda job to do. We need to tell this story to the widest possible audience before we start lobbying Washington for protection through changes in our import–export rules with the Japanese.' He put his wallet back into his inside pocket. 'Anyone use another beer?'

As they waited for the drinks, Cord said, 'There are some things you haven't mentioned, Mac, but you probably know about them anyway. Some of our manufacturers have gone into joint-venture agreements with Japanese companies. Now they're finding products identical to their copyright machinery and technology coming back into the States under another name and at half the price. Only the names have been changed to protect the guilty. But of course, they claim it's all the result of original Japanese research. You might even fall for that line if they didn't incorporate the original fucking design faults! We need evidence that the copyright has been ripped off. And there's another area: computers. We're way ahead of the world at this time, but we know that our industry's been targeted by the Japanese government. That worries the Christ out of us. We recently have had reason to believe that they're actively involved in industrial espionage, stealing some of our latest technology.'

Cord sat back and studied them both. 'So, what do you say, gentlemen? Are you interested?'

McGregor looked at Ransome.

'The pay's good,' Cord said.

'It's right up your alley, Mac,' Ransome said.

'Yes, I'm interested,' McGregor said. 'When do you need the material?'

'There's a Senate inquiry coming up in Washington in a few weeks time. We must have the first program to air before then. So, I'm afraid we've got a very short deadline. We must begin immediately.'

'Pity,' said Ransome, 'it sounds interesting.'

'You can't be part of it?' Cord looked concerned.

'Under normal circumstances I'd be pleased to work on it, but I'm tied up with something else right now. Will be for awhile.'

'We need you on this,' Cord said. 'Mac's a journalist with a great reputation, but this is television and we're particularly anxious to have you involved. Having your name associated with this project is most important to us.'

'What made you think I'd be available?' Ransome said.

Cord shrugged. 'When I heard you were here, I talked to the network people who are going to be scheduling our programs. They were excited at the prospect of having you involved—the man who filmed the 'Cong arriving in Saigon. Shit, you're money in the bank.' He was smiling, but there was something in his eyes—anxiety, or a threat.

'If you had been able to put if off for a few weeks . . .' Ransome said, testing him out, trying to see what was happening.

'We're talking about big bucks, Jack. It's carte blanche as far as you . . . both are concerned,' remembering to include McGregor, but concentrating on Ransome.

Ransome shrugged.

Cord looked at McGregor directly. 'How does fifty thousand per episode for each of four episodes sound? For each of you.'

McGregor was impressed. He looked at Ransome. 'Could you take some time off?'

Ransome shook his head. 'Sorry, Mac. But you'll get someone else. That shouldn't be a problem. I can think of a dozen guys who'd jump at it.'

'We might be able to go higher,' Cord said. 'Maybe a share of the points on all overseas sales. Could be worth a lot of money to you guys.'

Ransome wondered how far the man would go. 'If you need it now, I can't do it. That's it, I'm afraid.'

'Try and persuade him, Mac.' Cord was vexed. 'This whole thing could stand or fall on the two of you being involved.'

Putting pressure on him through Mac was a bit too crude. It was beginning to sound distinctly tailor-made. Ransome decided to push him a little.

'Come on,' he said, 'there must be half-a-dozen television guys who could do this assignment on their ear.'

'But we want you,' Cord said. 'And Mac here, of course, with his inside knowledge and his grip on the language.' He sat back and downed the last half of his beer. 'Mac, could you excuse us for awhile. There's something I need to talk to Jack about.'

McGregor looked surprised and offended. He stood up. 'Sure, I need to take a leak anyway.' He went off through the crowded dining room.

Cord leaned over the table like a salesman about to make his pitch. 'How much do you want, personally—

paid in any way you want, in any country you want—to do this project?'

Ransome laughed and shook his head. The mask was peeling off rapidly. 'I've said I can't do it. I don't know how else to tell you that I'm presently not available. You don't have enough money to get me to change my mind.'

Anger was beginning to show behind Cord's eyes. 'It might be smart to switch over to something less dangerous than your present assignment.'

'What assignment is that?' Ransome said, sparring.

Cord shook his head impatiently, like a bull irritated by a barb. 'I get to hear things. I hear that you're getting yourself into shit a mile deep. Get smart. This is a good project I'm offering you.'

Ransome had had enough. 'Who do you really work for, Dr Cord?' He wondered if the man would come right out and say it.

Cord said nothing. He sat back staring at Ransome. There was a touch of high colour on his cheeks.

'Why are you trying to buy me off?' Ransome said.

Cord said, 'You're making a mistake, Ransome, believe me. You're into something that could turn really ugly.'

'I thought it already had,' Ransome said.

The big man shook his head disdainfully. 'You haven't seen anything yet, my friend. You may think you're a hard-head, but if you get into trouble here in Japan—as a foreigner—you haven't a prayer, pal.'

Cord stood up. His face was sour. 'You should recognise who your friends are. You've got my number. If you get smart and change your mind, you call me.'

Chapter 19

Two days after her husband failed to return home, Mrs Kokesei Minao went to her local police station in Funabashi and reported him missing. The police were polite and attentive. They took down her husband's details: name (Junko), age (thirty-four), appearance (they asked for a photograph, which she delivered later that day) and occupation (laboratory assistant with a food processing company). She was asked if he had any distinguishing marks. At first she remembered none, but later, when delivering the photograph, she told them her husband had an appendicitis scar, and that he had once broken his ankle skiing; he had a steel pin in it. He also had a small blue butterfly tattooed on his left buttock.

They then asked her a series of embarrassing and awkward questions about her personal life and that of her husband: the state of their marriage, whether he was a heavy drinker, whether he had previously stayed away from home, and so on. Routine, they explained. She was obliged to admit that their marriage was neither happy nor unhappy, that he drank neither more nor less than his fellow Japanese, and that from time to time he did not come home at nights.

She told them that at such times (she admitted it was quite often) he invariably used the excuse that he had important work to do that went late into the night. He would sleep at the office. Mrs Kokesei was adamant that she had no reason to disbelieve her husband.

The police promised to do what they could to locate

him. She was asked to inform them the moment he turned up. Subsequently, a copy of Mrs Kokesei's signed statement went forward to the Missing Persons Department for processing.

Chapter 20

Kaizei had set up two interviews in Yokohama. On the way there, Ransome told him about Cord's warning.

Kaizei was puzzled. 'I can understand why my fellow countrymen are getting ugly about this, but where do you guys fit in?'

Neither of them could imagine why Cord was involved. This new factor ended Kaizei's optimistic mood. When he had picked Ransome up in a taxi from the front of his hotel he'd had the look of eager anticipation, the pent-up excitement, of the reporter with exclusive inside news of a good story.

Aoyama had given him another batch of names. 'One of them lives in Yokohama, so we can do him at the same time as we do Yonoi.'

'What's so special about this Yonoi character?'

'He was one of those in Sakurai's group photograph, in fact, the third highest ranking officer of Section 731.'

Ransome was impressed. Maybe now they were getting to the meat of the matter.

Kaizei said, 'Yonoi Eiji, once a medical doctor, now a very successful corporate lawyer. Specialises in medical legal cases and copyright ownership of chemical formulae. Very impressive guy. Lives in the penthouse above his own law office building. I've talked to him once before. Mr Aoyama gave me his name awhile ago. When I asked him to do an interview on Section 731, he was horrified. He didn't want to know. At first he denied everything, then he got hostile.' Kaizei grimaced. 'Offered to have me—"silenced".'

'To have you killed?' Ransome said.

'Not in as many words, but his meaning was clear. I'm certain he's behind the various attacks on me.'

'Would he be connected with the people who abducted me?'

'God knows.'

'If he wouldn't talk before, why is he willing now?'

'Good question,' Kaizei said, grinning. 'He suddenly leaves a message at my answering service—would I contact him to make a convenient time. I'm pretty sure it's a trap.'

'And we're going to see him?' Ransome made a sceptical face.

'Yeah, but he doesn't know when. It's going to be a big surprise.'

The train slowed down. Kaizei looked out the window. 'Lovely Yokohama,' he said. 'The Emperor had the city built on a disease-ridden swamp as a suitable place for you foreigners.'

The Emperor, thought Ransome, sounds a bit like Reiko's father.

An icy rain was falling over the bleak cityscape. It seemed to him that all the way from Tokyo they had been travelling through one endless marshalling yard flanked by an unrelieved jumble of concrete buildings: factories cheek-by-jowl with ugly apartment blocks festooned with damp washing. He felt vaguely apprehensive.

'By the look of it,' he said, 'nothing has changed.'

Kaizei laughed. 'Welcome to the swamp,' he said.

* * *

They decided to interview the hospital cleaner first. They changed trains at Yokohama and travelled the one stop to Kannai. There, outside the station, Kaizei hired a car, a new Honda. He had an address with him but, driving through the Yamashita district, stopped at the first police box and went inside to ask the way. A moment later he reappeared in the company of a young policeman, who came with him to the car and pointed the way on Kaizei's roadmap.

The policeman noted Ransome's presence in the car. Ransome nodded to him with a smile. He had the feeling that, if ever he were asked, the man would remember him.

For about twenty minutes they drove north, away from the harbour and through gloomy industrial suburbs. On the way, Kaizei stopped once more to check his map. At last they arrived outside a run-down redbrick building. Kaizei identified it as the hospital they were seeking. He parked the car and went inside. After ten minutes he reappeared.

'He's off duty at lunchtime.'

'You talk to him?'

Kaizei shook his head. 'Don't want to frighten him off. I told one of the staff that I was his cousin from Hiroshima. She's going to point him out to me. Meanwhile, let's get some shots of the hospital and grounds.'

Ransome checked the power on his camera. They spent the next half-hour taking shots to establish backgrounds for the interview. Even if the man refused an interview outright, they planned to try to take some pictures of him.

Their timing was good. No sooner had they finished taking the shots than a sleety rain began driving diagonally into their faces. Kaizei went inside the hospital once more. Ransome waited in the car.

Fifteen minutes later, Kaizei appeared, framed in the staff entrance doorway of the hospital. Ransome started the camera rolling. He caught the man perfectly in his lens as he came through the door after Kaizei.

Masaka Amoi was a skinny little weed of a man who barely came up to Kaizei's shoulder. He was wearing a blue baseball cap and a transparent plastic raincoat over a white hospital cleaner's uniform. As he came out, he opened an umbrella. Kaizei moved close to him and took his arm. They crossed the street and turned the corner. Kaizei stayed close to Masaka, talking intently as they walked. The little man looked frightened and hostile.

Ransome put down the camera, wound up the window and started the Datsun. He swung around the corner after them, driving very slowly along what appeared to be a high street, busy with shoppers scurrying to dodge the rain. Halfway along the next block, he saw them go into the doorway of a bar. Above the door there was a crude yellow plastic sign showing a topless girl.

Fifty metres past the bar, Ransome found a parking space. He parked, locked the car and walked back to the bar, carrying the camera in his shoulder bag.

The Rolling Stones were extolling the virtues of Long Tall Sally. It took awhile for his eyes to get used to the gloom. The place was painted black. Under some muted orange lights he could see maybe a dozen men in the place. None of them appeared to have noticed him. They were intent upon the gyrations of a skinny girl who was dancing on the bar. She appeared to be naked. What was certain was that she had absolutely no sense of rhythm.

He spotted Kaizei and Masaka in a booth opposite the bar. They were sitting facing each other, talking intensely. Ransome went to the bar, said 'beer' to the barman and sat on a stool where he knew Kaizei would see him. The barman poured beer from a bottle into a tall glass. Ransome offered him some change. The barman took what he needed and went back to join the customers, who were crowded at one end of the bar within touching distance of the naked girl.

Ransome waited, sipping the beer. It was going to be

difficult to take pictures in the available light.

At length, Kaizei rose and crossed to him. Masaka stayed where he was, sitting forward and staring down at the table as though he had seen a ghost.

Kaizei said, 'This is not a happy man.'

'Will he be interviewed?' Ransome said.

'He asked for money.'

'We going to give it to him?'

Kaizei shook his head. 'I found it cheaper to offer not to tell the hospital authorities about his past.' He flashed a predator's grin at Ransome. 'So he said yes, but he won't appear on camera.'

'I doubt that I could get an image in this light.'

Kaizei raised his eyebrows. 'That's a thought. Back in a minute.'

He crossed back to Masaka and slid in beside him. For several minutes he talked at him with great force, leaning over him, intimidating and dominating. Suddenly, both men stood up and headed towards the entrance. As he passed Ransome, Kaizei beckoned him to follow with a movement of his head.

The two sat down in the booth nearest the door and furthest from the music. Ransome picked up his beer and his camera bag and joined them. He sat opposite Masaka. The man looked at him with an expression of considerable dislike and resentment. Kaizei made no move to introduce him.

At close quarters, Masaka was an unlovely creature. His bitter face was cadaverous; the eyes seemed too big for his head. Ransome would have bet on cancer. Masaka said something to Kaizei. When he spoke he showed a lot of bottom teeth. They were broken and uneven.

'He wants assurance that no-one will be able to recognise him if he agrees to appear on film.'

Ransome made a meal of his reply, talking earnestly, shaking his head and pointing towards the orange lights.

He took his camera from his bag, pointed it at Kaizei, looked through the lens and opened it up to its fullest. Even then Kaizei's face was no more than a shadow. He handed the camera to Masaka. The man took it and looked through the lens at Ransome. He stood up and said something to Kaizei.

'Smart fellow. He doesn't trust you,' Kaizei said. 'Wants to change places.' Kaizei stood up and went to the bar.

Ransome stood up and sat on the opposite side looking towards the orange light. The girl had moved from the bar onto the lap of one of the customers. The music was now muzak, at half the volume.

Masaka looked through the lens at him. Ransome stared back. The man was evidently satisfied. He put the camera on the table and, once more, changed places with Ransome.

Kaizei returned with a bottle of whisky and three glasses. He poured Masaka a drink and a smaller one for himself and Ransome.

'Start the camera when I put down my glass,' Kaizei said. He sipped at his drink and began to talk earnestly with Masaka.

Ransome picked up the camera, adjusted focus and aperture and practised zooming in and out on the faces of both men. Kaizei put down his glass. Ransome began filming.

They winged the interview. At first Kaizei did not translate for Ransome's benefit all the questions he asked of Masaka, nor all the replies he received. Later, he explained to Ransome that he had been worried throughout that the man was going to break off the interview and, literally, run for it.

Certainly Masaka was nervous. He licked his lips constantly and his eyes moved nervously from Kaizei to Ransome. From time to time he would look around as though afraid of being overheard. But, watching him through the lens, the overwhelming impression Ransome gained was that of his resentment. It exuded from Masaka like a magnetic field. Every question brought bitterness and anger to his face.

Gradually, he loosened up. He drank thirstily and the liquor worked on his tongue. At first, Masaka was intent on establishing that although he had known what was going on at Harbin, he had had nothing to do with the work there. He claimed to have begun as a camp guard. He claimed to have seen nothing of the prisoners after they had been inducted into the camp. He even claimed to have disapproved of the work of the Section.

But then, halfway through the second tape, Masaka began to get interesting.

Kaizei admitted afterwards that he had almost given up on the man. He had learned nothing that he had not heard before from one or other of the men he had interviewed. Casting around blindly, he asked the question, 'What else did you do? Were you just a guard?'

Masaka said, 'No, I was always good with cars. I did some driving. Drove the officers around in their fancy cars.' A curl of the lip.

Kaizei began translating the questions and answers into English for Ransome's benefit.

Kaizei: 'Which officers?'

Masaka: 'The brass. I finished up the general's personal driver.'

'Which general?'

'The top man. Ishii. General Ishii,' Masaka said.

For a moment Ransome watched the man draw himself up in pride.

'Took him everywhere. His mistresses, the brothels. What an appetite for women he had,' awe in his voice. 'He trusted me absolutely. Not that it did me any good. They cast me off like dirty underwear after it was all over.' The skeletal face twisted with rage.

Kaizei: 'Who cast you off?'

'The brass, who else?' Masaka laughed bitterly. 'The rest of us have lived like dogs ever since, but they did alright out of it: big jobs, lots of money, guarantees they wouldn't be touched.'

'What guarantees?'

Masaka shook his head, showing teeth. 'They knew they were going to be looked after.'

'But you said guarantees.'

At this point, Masaka looked behind him and dropped his voice. 'I was *there*. I know they did some kind of deal.'

'You were where?'

Masaka seemed surprised by the stupidity of the question.

'Tokyo,' he said. 'After the surrender, I came back with him on his personal staff. The general insisted. He relied on me—always on time, the car always shining. He was scared of driving and he knew I was steady. A sober type,' the vestiges of a long-buried pride in something showing in the angry eyes.

When Kaizei finished the close-to-simultaneous translation he remained silent, creating a vacuum into which words might be drawn.

Masaka went on, 'It was the big staff car, that day. A brute to drive. It had to be the big car. There were five of them went to the meeting, the general and the other four senior officers. Afterwards, they were very pleased with themselves. All jokes and smiles. All of them talking at once, about some deal they'd done.' Masaka shook his head in angry disbelief. 'They would talk in front of you as though you were a dumb beast. The things I could tell you about their sex lives!' he said. 'But I was no dumb beast. I knew something was on.'

'What sort of deal?'

Masaka twisted up his face in thought. 'I don't know

the details. But I do know they were very happy about the future.'

Kaizei asked, 'Why do you say that?'

Masaka looked annoyed. 'On the way there, they were as nervous as hell. They were saying things to the general like, "Do you think they'll agree? What if they say no?"— that kind of thing. They were frightened they'd all be hanged. Afterwards it was a different story.'

Masaka downed another drink. 'It must have been a great arrangement. Not one of them was ever touched afterwards. I've kept track of those bastards, seen their names in the paper from time to time. Whatever it was, it set them up for life. They all got on with becoming rich and successful while the rest of us poor bastards waited for the axe to fall.'

Kaizei said, 'Where was this meeting?'

Masaka looked surprised again. 'At the headquarters.'

'What headquarters?'

Masaka replied as if surprised to be asked.

Kaizei looked at Ransome. He said, 'You're not going to believe this.' Then he gave it to Ransome in English. 'The occupation army headquarters. The Americans. Their meeting was with MacArthur's staff.'

Ransome heard himself say, 'Jesus Christ!' He kept right on filming.

Kaizei, staying matter-of-fact for Masaka's benefit: 'And what happened afterwards?'

'The next day I drove the general over to a store in Ikebukuro someplace. It was one of the few buildings still standing.'

'A store?'

'A big warehouse.'

'And?'

'Well, that was it. There were a couple of American brass there. They had three big trucks and a dozen soldiers. They loaded up the filing cabinets.'

'How many filing cabinets?'

Masaka shrugged. 'Forty, fifty maybe.'

'Then what?'

'Then, nothing. The general got them to sign a paper. They all saluted each other and shook hands and I drove him back to his house.' Masaka looked triumphant, like someone who had just solved a puzzle. 'So, that's how I know it must have been a deal. How else could the Section have been kept a secret all these years if the Americans hadn't agreed to say and do nothing?'

* * *

'We *knew*?' Ransome said, 'and we kept it a secret?'

Kaizei drove in silence for a time. Then he said, 'In all the interviews I've done, no-one has ever mentioned a deal with the Americans.'

'Not even Aoyama?'

Kaizei shook his head.

Ransome said, 'That could explain the approach by Cord. Someone has a vested interest in keeping us away from a story about a secret deal.'

He felt real excitement. Everything had suddenly changed into a higher gear. 'You think Masaka can be believed?'

Kaizei shrugged. 'Who knows? Normally, I'd doubt I could believe anything a bitter bastard like him might say—and yet, somehow, I believe this.'

'Maybe he's just making a big fellow of himself.'

'But why would he make up an extraordinary story like that?'

Ransome agreed. 'You say this Yonoi character was a heavy in the Section. If there was an American deal on, maybe he would have known about it.'

Kaizei said, 'You bet your life he would.'

Chapter 21

Kaizei knew the way. They went first to the law office on the fifth floor, but did not enter the foyer. Instead, he led Ransome to the left, around a carpeted corridor. They came to the discreet polished steel door of a private lift. It had padded leather walls and thick carpet. To the soft strains of a Mozart clarinet concerto, they were borne aloft to the penthouse.

Yonoi was a cool customer. If, when he opened the door, he was surprised to discover Kaizei and Ransome, he did not show it; his face remained neutral. Kaizei said something to him. Without a word, the man turned on his heel. He led them along a short hallway with black-tiled floors then into a vast, glass-walled room with an impressive view past a rooftop garden out over Tokyo Bay. Below, there were ships passing, seemingly close enough to touch. Beyond, there was a logjam of shipping in Yokohama's busy harbour. Ships of all sizes—ore carriers, cargo ships, tramp steamers, container ships, a few sleek navy vessels, tug boats and yachts—were coming or going or straining at their anchors with their bows facing into a stiff southerly gale. White-tops iced the waters of the bay. Away to the east the Boso Peninsula rose up, a dark mass against darker clouds.

White. Everything white. At one end of the room there was a single futuristic-looking steel and leather chair, a glass coffee table and a reading lamp. There was nothing else in the space that was personal; neither books, ornaments, nor pictures on the walls.

At the other end of the room, which appeared to serve as office and conference area, Yonoi motioned them to be seated. He sat opposite them on one of a facing pair of white leather divans. Between them there was a white marble coffee table. On it was a pile of files, one of which was opened. He closed the file, tidied the bundle neatly and slid it sideways so that it aligned with one edge of the table.

Ransome studied his subject. Yonoi was of medium height, slim and fit-looking in a black pinstripe suit. He wore a conservative striped tie, held in place by a gold bar. The hair was spiky, receding slightly at the forehead and jet-black enough to suggest regular dyeing. He must have been in his late sixties, but looked nearer fifty. Yonoi's face was a curious mixture of wear and preservation. The cheeks were smooth, as though they were covered in the flesh of a younger man, but the eyes were old, caught in a web of worry lines. There were shadows under them that told of sickness past, present or to come.

Yonoi looked up at Ransome. The eyes betrayed contempt and dislike. He said something to Kaizei. Ransome caught his own name.

Without taking his eyes off the lawyer, Kaizei said, 'He knows who you are.'

Doesn't everyone, thought Ransome.

Kaizei and Yonoi spoke for a time. Yonoi gave the impression of someone who was reining in anger under a veneer of obligatory politeness. Kaizei looked relaxed and confident. Ransome fought against the frustration he felt at not being able to understand what was being said.

After a time Kaizei said, 'He's agreed to be interviewed.'

'Here and now?'

Kaizei nodded. 'He's even keen on the idea. Wants to set the record straight. Our line of inquiry is all a misunderstanding, apparently,' this without changing expression, or tone of voice.

'And the cheque's in the mail,' Ransome said, wondering how much English Yonoi might understand and not really caring. He found it easy to dislike Mr Yonoi.

As Ransome unzipped his camera bag, Yonoi rose and crossed the room to a desk that stood against the wall. He picked up the handpiece of a cordless telephone and walked through a door further into the flat.

Kaizei was on his feet immediately. He crossed the room fast and disappeared through the door. Ransome heard a sharp exchange between them; raised voices. After a long moment, the two men came back into the room.

Ransome raised his eyebrows questioningly.

Kaizei said, 'I told him if he made any call he wouldn't get his chance to set the record straight.'

'Best we provide the surprises,' Ransome said. He felt nervous. They might have ambushed Yonoi, but this glacial apartment was an elegant cage from which it might be hard to escape.

Yonoi was expressionless. He put the handpiece in front of him on the marble coffee table and sat down. He took a cigarette case from his inside pocket, lit up and sat back, watching them with a calm expression.

Ransome checked the camera and rigged the tripod. A quick view through the lens and he nodded to Kaizei to indicate he was ready. Kaizei switched on his tape recorder. The interview began. Yonoi spoke with fluency. Kaizei translated Yonoi's answers.

Yonoi: 'You ask me why I've agreed to do this interview. There are several reasons. First of all, it is known in certain quarters that I had the honour to serve the Emperor in the medical corps and held a high rank. I am therefore most anxious to see that the reputation of the corps, and my role in it, is not harmed. I have my own integrity to protect. I am proud of my record of impeccable dealing in all matters.

'Secondly, having thought carefully about this television investigation you are conducting, I think it proper to try to set the record straight. I understand that you have been talking to various ex-servicemen from my old section who may not be in possession of the full facts of the matter. These low-ranking men may not have been aware of the outstanding humanitarian work that was done by a special, elite section.

'Yes, I am aware of certain rumours that have surfaced recently concerning the Section. You have my word for it that all such allegations are completely untrue. I should know. I was a senior ranking officer, well aware of the policy decisions that were taken concerning the medical program we undertook. I therefore can speak with full authority.

'Yes, it was a scientific unit that dealt with medical matters. Top medical people were involved in what was vital war work. Yes, it was called "Section 731".

'Yes, it was commanded by General Ishii. If I may say so, one of the great men of our time. A medical visionary.

'No, I have never heard the Section referred to as "The Devil's Brigade". Never.

'The mid-thirties? I can't answer your question about the exact date. But I believe it was after we liberated Manchuria. Our forces suffered a great deal of sickness and death in unfamiliar country. Primitive levels of hygiene and endemic disease among local populations put our servicemen at risk. The need for greater medical knowledge was recognised at that time. The Section was established then.

'Yes, there was military significance to our work. Of course there was. Our brave fighting men were serving the Emperor on fronts from the arctic regions to the jungles. They were faced with all kinds of diseases and problems that could cripple them to the extent that they could not carry out their tasks. Our job was to develop antidotes for malaria, beri-beri, tropical ulcers, frostbite. Anything we could do to alleviate the suffering of our serving men was scientific knowledge worth having. So we conducted various programs to find cures. The work was undertaken entirely from a humanitarian point of view. I was then, and am now, proud of the work we did.

'Offensive military significance? What do you mean?

'Germ warfare? No. Nothing like that. Our work was purely humanitarian. It was about the prevention and curing of disease, not about propagating it.

'Look, I don't know who could have made such a gross accusation, but certainly, to my knowledge, such experiments were never undertaken, nor even contemplated.

'No, I personally was never involved in any programs involving the development of offensive medical weapons.

'Human guineapigs? Ah, now we're getting to the bias you demonstrate in your approach to this whole subject. You must be familiar enough with the scientific method to know that at some advanced stage, new compounds, drugs and methods of treatment have to be tried out on the humans that they are designed to help. The literature is full of examples of scientists who have been the first to experiment on themselves with their new discovery.

'Come now! You use the term "experiments on humans" as though this were something imposed upon unwilling victims. Nothing could be further from the truth.

'Yes, there were certain carefully monitored experiments involving prisoners of war, but these were always on a voluntary basis.

'On what basis did they volunteer? The prisoners did so on the basis of receiving special privileges.

'Deaths? Yes, there were a few unfortunate accidents when experiments went wrong. But accidents do happen.

Science is not, contrary to the popular view, an exact thing. There were a few deaths.

'Two or three. Half-a-dozen at most.

'I can't be specific about numbers of prisoners. The nearby prisoner of war compound was outside my jurisdiction. At the height of the war it contained, perhaps, as many as a thousand.

'Staff? Once again, at this distance in time . . .

'More than a hundred? Possibly.

'More than a thousand? No, I doubt it.

'*Maruta*? Logs of wood? No, the term is not familiar to me. I can honestly say I have never heard that term applied to captured enemy personnel. And certainly not by me.

'The camp was closed at the beginning of 1945. The Russians were advancing and we came home to help defend our beloved country.'

At this point, Kaizei asked him about the American deal.

Yonoi paused for a long time before answering. He was not a successful lawyer for nothing. He had enough control to keep his composure.

'Documents? Medical records? Handed over? I know of no documents given to the occupation forces.'

Kaizei pressing now.

Yonoi: 'You say you *know* about them? Then ask the Americans.' He gestured contemptuously towards Ransome.

'You say it was a Japanese who told you this? I don't know who your source is, but the allegation is a complete fabrication. There *were* no documents to hand over. As far as I am aware, all our records were lost between Harbin and Japan.

'What deal? There was no deal involving a pardon of the men who served in Section 731. Why would the Americans want to prosecute us? What had they to pardon us for, anyway? We had done nothing wrong.

'Your information can come from as high a source as you like, but I can promise you it is nonsense. I was, after all, the general's third in command. I was present, along with at least two other staff officers, at any discussions he had with the Americans. He did not do a private deal with them.

'Normal discussions to do with the handing over of our surrender, that's all. There were, as I remember, some complications about our section, because of the secrecy under which we worked. The Americans had not known of the Section. We gave them as little cooperation as we could, as it happens. At that time they were engaged in some vengeance hangings of high-ranking Japanese Imperial Military personnel who had only been carrying out orders and were made the scapegoats.

'I think I have answered your questions fairly and fully. If you stick to the facts and avoid the kind of sensationalising implicit in this line of questioning, frankly I doubt if you have a story worth telling. Now, if you'll excuse me, I have work to do.'

Yonoi's expression changed. Watching his face through the lens, Ransome suddenly saw his teeth show. The man was smiling a triumphant, barracuda smile. He was looking beyond the camera lens.

'We've got company,' Kaizei said.

Ransome jumped to his feet.

Three young men had come into the room. Thickset, crop-headed and blank-faced. Two of them carried baseball bats.

Kaizei was already on his feet. He walked around the glass table and stood alongside Yonoi.

Yonoi said something to the men. The third one produced a knife. They started to cross the room, coming fast. Ransome gripped the camera tightly; it was the only weapon he had.

Suddenly, they stopped. They were staring towards Yonoi.

'Come behind the desk,' Kaizei said.

Ransome turned. At full arm's length, Kaizei was holding a small pistol to Yonoi's head. The foresight was jammed under the man's left ear. Yonoi was rigid. There was a look of implacable hatred on his face.

Ransome was surprised. He had never thought of Kaizei being armed. 'Good thinking,' he said, relief flooding.

Kaizei barked an order at the three men. They looked at Yonoi. From the expressions on their faces it was obvious they wanted to keep on coming. There was a long silence. Yonoi spoke. The foresight did not waver.

The three put down their weapons, carefully. They raised their arms.

Kaizei spoke again.

Very slowly, the three men lay face down with their hands behind their heads.

Ransome went round the table. Facing the three men, he picked up the knife and the baseball bats. He went to the glass doors leading out onto the roof terrace. He slid open the door. An icy blast rushed in. He was about to pitch the bats onto the far side of the terrace when the thought occurred to him. 'Why don't we park them out here?' Ransome said.

Kaizei caught his eye. He gave a brief grin. 'Good idea. Check it out.'

Ransome went out onto the terrace. Quickly he went around the perimeter. The wind roaring in off the bay clawed at him, freezing the skin of his face. There was one door only. It seemed to be that of the building's fire-stairs. It was locked.

'It'll do,' he said.

Yonoi stood up, ignoring the pistol aimed at his face. He began shouting at Kaizei, who stood listening with a cynical expression on his face. Finally, Yonoi turned to Ransome. He spat out a comment like a poison bait.

Kaizei said, 'It's not every day you get called a mercenary jackal.'

Ransome managed a smile, but he felt vulnerable. He wanted out of this.

Within a minute Yonoi and his three men were standing on the exposed terrace beyond the plate glass.

'Come on Katie,' he said, 'let's get out of here.'

They grabbed their gear and left.

In the lift, Mozart had been replaced by Vivaldi's *Four Seasons*—the movement called 'winter'.

Chapter 22

'That's a bad bastard,' Ransome said as they left the building.

'You're not wrong,' Kaizei said. 'Let's just assume he'll take some action. I'd feel a bit vulnerable in a train.'

And so, rather than risk going back to Tokyo by rail, they kept the hire-car.

Kaizei drove hard, his eyes glittering with excitement. 'An American connection! Wow!' He threw back his head in triumph.

'Yonoi was fairly convincing in denying a deal was done,' Ransome said, straight-faced.

Kaizei shook his head in admiration. 'Yeah, he's very good, that guy. I didn't believe a single word he said.' They burst out laughing.

'Jesus, Jack, I thought this thing was big, but I had no idea how big. If we can crack this story a lot of people are going to be very embarrassed.'

'How far is it likely to go?'

Kaizei said, 'All the way to the top, my friend,' he said with relish. 'All the way.'

Ransome said, 'I've a contact in Washington who might be able to help me dig out something on the US connection. I'll call him as soon as we get into the city.'

Near Tokyo, Kaizei said, 'In that little outburst at the end, Yonoi said some interesting things: that the true patriots had not lost the war and that they had never stopped working for the final victory of the Japanese people. And that when the time came,' Kaizei made a sceptical face, 'traitors like me would be the first to pay.'

'What do you think he means?'

'I don't know. Right-wing lunatics like him worry me.' Kaizei looked sober. 'There's always the chance they'll get to be in charge of the asylum. And right now they are in full cry. All these student riots, the challenges to the Prime Minister from inside his own party—it's getting to be serious.'

They returned the hire-car and took a cab to Yuraku-cho. The station concourse was thronged with commuters retreating from a day in Tokyo's commercial trenches.

They agreed that this central city location would be their assembly point for all future journeys. Ransome deposited his camera in a luggage locker; the less he had to carry, the less conspicuous he would be. He took the videotapes in his carrybag. He would post them from his hotel.

'That, Jack, was one hell of a day,' Kaizei said, confident and jaunty, pulling down the brim of his black fedora. 'You right for tomorrow? If I can sort out the address, we might have another interview.'

Ransome said, 'Only if you promise to wear the Raymond Chandler hat.'

Kaizei smiled back from behind his mirror sunglasses. 'I'll call you.'

Ransome watched him limp off up the stairs to the train platforms. In a moment he was just another anonymous figure swallowed by the surging river of people.

* * *

He was in luck. When he called the Foreign Correspondents' Club from the station, McGregor was there filing copy. 'Sure you can make a Washington call from the club,' he said. 'You're at Yurakucho?' It was only a minute's walk. He would wait in the twentieth floor foyer.

They had a quick drink together while Ransome waited

for his call to be placed. McGregor was due at a British
Embassy party. Within five minutes Ransome heard his
name being paged. He farewelled McGregor, downed his
drink and hurried to the telephone. After a succession of
strange peeps and electronic signals, the operator said,
'Your call to Washington.'

Lloyd Brucchi's mellifluous voice came on the line.
'Brucchi. How can I help you?'

'È Lloyd Brutta Faccia?' Ransome said.

Brucchi paused for a moment then he laughed.
'Ransome, you bastard! What are you doing in Japan?
Selling that lousy film of yours?'

'No, actually I'm getting deep into the shit, Lloyd.'

'So what's new?' Brucchi said.

'I need your help,' Ransome said.

'Well, that's new, for a start. What can I do for you?'

'First of all, let me tell you that what I'm going to ask
you is confidential.'

Brucchi paused for no more than a second. 'Uh huh,'
he said. 'You want me to call you back?' One thing you
knew about Lloyd Brucchi was that he was smart.

'I'd like that.'

'Where are you ringing from?'

'The Foreign Correspondents' Club.'

'Number one, Shimbun Alley? No shit, how come they
let a reprobate like you into that hallowed place?'

'Robbie McGregor signed me in.'

'That Scotch prick never did have any taste. Give him
my regards. It's going to take me maybe five minutes.
What's the number there?' Ransome read it to him.
Brucchi hung up.

Ransome thanked the telephonist for organising the
connection and told him he was expecting a return call.
'We can bring the phone to your table, Sir,' the man
said.

'Thanks, but I'll take it here.'

He walked around the foyer wondering what Lloyd Brucchi would think of the amazing story they had uncovered in Yokohama.

He had last seen Brucchi in Washington when he had been there promoting *No Man's Land*. Brucchi had interviewed him for his network television newsmagazine and, with great enthusiasm, had shown clips from the film. It had led directly to a network sale worth a great deal of money to Ransome.

They had celebrated Ransome's success together. Brucchi proved to have an inexhaustible supply of attractive women—Washington politics and journalism groupies—to draw upon.

He had met Brucchi first in Kampuchea, when the man had been working for NBC. Since then, Brucchi had given television news away and had turned author. He had begun his literary career by writing a Pulitzer-prize-winning book on the Kampuchean and Vietnamese conflicts. If anyone could dig out the material he needed, Brucchi could. He had a brilliant sense of history and, most useful of all, a nose for revealing research. Much of the material he had published in his book came from classified sources. It had caused untold embarrassment to the United States Government. Almost certainly Brucchi's phone would be tapped.

Five minutes stretched to ten. Ransome watched the comings and goings of the club members and read the various noticeboards. On one wall there was a brass plaque, dedicated to a long list of journalists 'missing believed killed' in the South-East Asian wars. He read through it with interest. About half of them Ransome had known. A familiar name jumped out at him: Kaizei's. Katie ought to get his name off that thing, Ransome thought. Somehow it was unlucky.

The call came through.

'Getting paranoid in your old age?' Brucchi said, as

though the conversation had been running on uninterrupted.

'No, but I thought it might be smart to be discreet.'

'Well, to tell you the truth,' said Brucchi, 'things at my end are distinctly un-secure. I'm sure the bastards listen in to every call I make or receive. But I'm using a public phone now, so what's the problem?'

Ransome said, 'I need someone to help me with some delicate research; someone who's a specialist in the Mac-Arthur occupation era, from '45 onwards a couple of years. Probably classified stuff. You know anyone?'

There was a long silence while Brucchi gave thought to the question. 'Post-war Japan's outside my own competence,' he said, 'but let me see who I can dig up for you. How long you going to be at that number?'

'How long do you need?' Ransome said.

'An hour, maybe less.'

'I'll be here.'

Brucchi hung up. Ransome grinned to himself. Typical of Brucchi, to be too discreet to ask him what the story was about. In Vietnam, no-one had ever been given a tip about a story by Lloyd Brucchi. The first anyone ever heard of his many journalistic scoops had been when watching the news.

* * *

'S-u-m-n-e-r,' Brucchi said. 'Julia Sumner. A very good doctorate at Harvard on the subject of post-World War II Japanese history. You might remember her. She was at one of the bashes we went to together, when you were here in bullshit city—at the British Embassy as I recall. Tall, angular, model-girl type who wears those "clever" glasses to promote the fact she's got a genius IQ. She remembers you. She had quite fancied getting into your pants.'

'Now you tell me,' Ransome said.

'As I recall, she was doing a special assignment for the

Democrats then, digging out even more dirt on Nixon, if that were possible. She was with Senator Gerry Cambridge that night.'

Ransome had no memory of Julia Sumner. The week there with Brucchi was now a blur of faces seen through a champagne mist.

'She's ex-directory, so write this down.' He read off the telephone number. Brucchi said, 'I've told her a few lies about you so she won't hang up when you call. She's good, Jack. I've used her myself a couple of times. Entirely trustworthy, you can depend on that. And she's the perfect researcher—the instincts of a bloodhound. She'll go down to the end of any burrow you point her at. Her other animal instincts are that she charges like a wounded rhino and, although I don't have the good fortune to be able to speak from personal experience, she's said to be hornier than a jackrabbit, which probably accounts for the fact that she enjoys remarkable insider's connections in government and the bureaucracy.'

They talked on for a time. Ransome told him about Kaizei.

'I heard he'd bought it,' Brucchi said. 'Good to hear he survived. Only met him a couple of times. Put me in mind of someone who'd strayed from a kung-fu movie. Anyway, let me know how this all pans out and, if you need any more help, you know my number. Julia's out of town a couple of days, but then she'll expect your call. Take care.'

Ransome thanked him for his help and rang off.

                              * * *

He was back in his new hotel, the Otani, by six o'clock. The foyer was crowded with tourists and fashionable-looking people having after-work drinks or meeting before dinner. He picked up his key at the desk. Reiko had returned his call of the previous day. She had called at four o'clock and wanted him to ring her. The prospect gave him considerable pleasure. It could not be long now before they were alone together.

He inquired about postal arrangements. Yes, he could post packages from within the hotel, but he was too late to do so tonight. The post office opened at eight in the morning. He asked could he use the hotel safe? Yes, but could he wait for a few minutes, please? The desk superintendent had been called away on an urgent matter. Ransome was exhausted. He said he would come back down later.

By the elevator, he stood aside to allow an elderly lady dressed in an exquisite kimono to enter ahead of him. A young American couple smiled at him—the smile of mutual strangers in a strange land. He smiled back. Just before the lift doors shut, two well-dressed Japanese men ducked in. The other passengers buttoned their various destinations. Ransome pressed the twenty-fourth floor button. One of the Japanese men pressed for the twenty-fifth floor.

The lift shot upwards. The old lady got out at the fourth floor, the American couple at the nineteenth. 'Have a nice day,' they chorused as they left.

He suddenly became aware of the two men in the lift with him. There was something about them that made him uncomfortable. They stood with their backs to him. They were not as tall as he, but thickset, filling their well-cut suits the way weightlifters do. The thick necks and the cut of the hair spoke of the street rather than the boardroom. They had not spoken to each other since the upward journey had begun. Ransome felt his heart race. He took a tight grip of the handle of his carrybag. He knew he was in trouble.

The lift began decelerating with a stomach-stopping motion. He glanced up at the indicator lights: twenty ... twenty-one ... twenty-two ... twenty-three ... The lift stopped with a discreet whoosh. The doors slid open. He stepped out. There was no-one else in sight in the passageway. The two Japanese stepped out with him. He turned and faced the one on his left. The man grinned. Ransome tried to go past him. The grinning man blocked him. Ransome instinctively ducked away from him. At that instant, he was felled by a blow on the back of his neck.

Ransome had been in enough football fights to know how to handle himself. He came to his feet quickly enough. He tried to headbutt one of them, but failed to connect. A sideways cleaver-like chop to his ribs delivered some bad news: they were professionals.

Neither of them spoke throughout. They inflicted damage and pain on him with controlled savagery and economy. This was no hit and run attack; he was being deliberately beaten. It lasted perhaps no more than a minute, maybe two; it seemed like forever.

He felt as though he would retch to death; the blood in his mouth was choking him. When at last they had stopped holding him and hitting him and had finally smashed him to the ground, he wedged himself against the wall, assumed the foetal position and protected his head and guts with a carapace of shoulders, forearms and knees.

After a final kick which caught him agonisingly on the thigh, one of them tore his carrybag from his shoulder, half turning him from the wall. He could see them waiting for the lift, the two adjusting their suits, buttoning and tugging them back into a perfect fit, all the while staring at him with expressionless faces. The lift came. They stepped into it and were gone.

Ransome sat up, leaning against the wall of the passageway. Another lift stopped at his floor. The doors opened. Some passengers came out and saw him. Their faces told him that he was a mess. He blacked out.

Chapter 23

The soft touch of fingers on his cheekbone. He found himself looking up into the concerned face of a young man. There was a stethoscope around his neck. A hank of black hair hung down over his face, making him look absurdly youthful to be a doctor. The room seemed full of people. An anxious-looking older man in dark suit, bow tie and striped trousers watched him from the foot of his bed. A young housemaid was carrying a basin of water towards the bathroom. The bellhop was standing by the door.

'Mr Ransome?' the doctor said. Ransome nodded, thinking, they got the videos. 'Do you know where you are?' His voice was soft, the curious British accent suggesting study in someplace provincial, like Liverpool.

'Yes,' Ransome said, 'in my room.'

'Where?'

'In the Otani,' thinking, as soon as they see those videotapes, that poor little bastard in Yokohama is liable to end up dead.

The doctor nodded, satisfied that Ransome wasn't disoriented. 'How do you feel?'

'Sore.' He felt as though he had been over a cliff.

The doctor sat on the edge of the bed and looked into Ransome's eyes with an ophthalmoscope. 'Look up . . . left . . . right . . .' He sat back, without expression.

'Anything broken?'

The doctor shook his head.

Ransome explored his face with his fingertips. There

was a dressing on his forehead, and another on his cheek-bone. The whole side of his face felt tender. He tried the bridge of his nose. It felt no more bent than usual, ridged with six breaks from football. He ran his tongue around the inside of his mouth: the taste of blood and the feel of broken skin where his teeth had gashed open the inside of his cheeks.

He tried to raise himself. A pain shot through his solar plexus. The doctor shook his head, but Ransome gingerly sat upright then, carefully, stood. The dizziness passed quickly. He took a deep breath.

The worried man in the suit spoke. 'Mr Ransome, please. What happened?'

'Two men beat me up.'

The man looked so anguished with worry that Ransome felt sorry for him. 'In the hotel?'

'Right outside my room door.' Ransome walked through to the bathroom. The housemaid was wiping blood from the washbasin. The whites of her eyes showed as though she had suddenly found herself locked in a small cage with a madman. She fled. When he looked in the mirror, he understood her reaction. He looked fear-some: dressings, bruising, smudges of yellow antiseptic.

A pair of frantic eyes met his in the mirror. The manager was standing looking at him from the doorway. 'Did you know the men who attacked you, Sir?'

Ransome shook his head.

'Have you ever seen them before?'

'No.'

'Did they steal anything?'

Ransome thought for a moment and decided to say nothing about the stolen videotapes. Should the police be called in, the fewer awkward questions the better. 'No,' he said, 'they snatched my bag, that's all. Nothing in it of any importance.'

The man was puzzled. 'Not your wallet, or money?' It

was clear he was wondering what kind of criminal company his hotel guest kept.

'No.'

'We must apologise for this, Sir,' the manager said. 'Such things have never happened before. Our security is most first class. Will you be making insurance claim on us?' he asked, getting to the nub of the matter.

Ransome managed a reassuring smile. 'No,' he said. He walked back into the bedroom. The little man hurried after him.

'You do not hold us responsible?' on his face, a glimmer of hope showing.

'It's not your problem. It can only be a case of mistaken identity. I'll be alright now, thank you.' He offered his hand to the manager, then to the doctor, who looked at him with obvious scepticism. He obviously thought very little of the 'mistaken identity' explanation. 'Thanks for patching me up.'

'I am on the staff here,' the doctor said, 'should you need me again.'

Ransome was not sure if the irony was intentional.

They left.

Suddenly, pain overcame him. He began to shake. The whole front of his body was sore to the touch. His kidneys ached. The hinge on his jaw seemed a poor fit. He lowered himself carefully onto his bed.

Ransome wondered how long it would be before someone viewed the stolen videotapes. He kept thinking about the bitter little man in the topless bar. The shots of Masaka leaving the hospital clearly identified him; the tapes would incriminate him. From that moment he could be in deadly danger. There was no way he could reach Kaizei so that the man could be warned, and to recruit Reiko to the task was unthinkable.

* * *

Masaka and Yonoi fused and melted together like

Bill Warnock

corrupting flesh. Sometimes they became the two stone-faced thugs, wearing suits made of tattoos. They had him trapped in an elevator, the doors of which kept opening on empty corridors. There was a dancing girl in a bar with orange lights, then a sterile room without any colours at all. The walls of the room became the steel sides of ships passing through narrow, ugly streets crowded with box-like apartments, all festooned with damp washing. A great crowd of Japanese commuters with blank faces was endlessly pursuing him.

He woke, sweating. He looked at his watch: seven o'clock. Outside it was pitch black.

The phone beside his bed began to ring. As he reached for the handpiece he let out a groan of pain. His beaten stomach muscles had locked into one agonising bruise.

'Jack?'

He came fully awake, his head clearing as though he had breathed smelling salts.

'I called earlier,' Reiko said, a touch of anxiety in her voice.

'I know. I'm sorry,' he said. 'I was in Yokohama all day and, on the way back, I had a slight accident.'

'Oh, no!' she said. 'A crash?'

'No,' Ransome said. 'Actually, I was beaten up by two jokers in the hotel.'

'Beaten up? Are you alright? Have you seen a doctor?'

'I'm okay. Nothing broken, just bruises, that's all.'

'Were you robbed?'

'No.'

'Then why?'

'It's a long story. I'll tell you about it when I see you.'

'Where did this happen?'

'In the passageway, outside my room. I should stay in a better class of accommodation.'

'You don't sound too good,' Reiko said.

'I'm a bit sore.'

She paused. 'Too sore to see me now?'

'Tonight?' The prospect was tempered by doubt that he would be much good as company.

'Here, now,' Reiko said. 'I'm downstairs in the foyer.'

Ransome laughed painfully. She never failed to surprise him. 'Come on up,' he said. 'Room 2411.'

'I know,' she said.

He hobbled to the bathroom and brushed his teeth, gingerly, tasting dried blood. There was nothing he could do about the dressings. He probably looked better with them on than off.

An urgent, gentle knocking. He made it to the door and opened it.

Her smile of greeting instantly became a look of shock. '*Sheisse!*' Reiko said. She swore in German better than in English. She came into his arms, holding him carefully as though he might break, looking anxiously at his face to try to gauge how badly he was hurt. 'You look terrible,' she said, gently touching the dressing on his brow.

'And you look good enough to eat,' Ransome said. Her exotic beauty always slightly shocked him. She was bareheaded, the asymmetric cap of raven hair with its dramatic zed-slash fringe shining like patent leather.

She raised her eyebrows lewdly and grinned. 'Normally, that would be a delicious idea,' she said. Her lips touched the dressing on his cheek then played gently on the edge of his mouth. 'It's been so long,' she whispered, her voice catching as though she was close to tears. 'Can you be kissed?'

'I'll taste of blood,' Ransome warned.

'You will taste wonderful,' Reiko said, her voice hoarse. 'It's been too long, Jack. Don't ever let it be so long again.'

Her mouth slackened under his. They kissed with the beginnings of that familiar, tense ardour he had remembered so often of late. Their tongues engaged. Her arms went around his neck. Involuntarily, he flinched.

She drew back hurriedly. 'I'm sorry. I'm hurting you.'

'It's okay.'

She shook her head. 'No.' She led him to the bed, helping him lie back. The pain flooded to the surface as he moved. She was right. He was in no shape for anything.

'A bath,' she said. She slipped off her ankle-length leather coat.

He watched her as she went into the bathroom. He liked the way she moved. He closed his eyes, listened to the water running.

When he opened them again, she was kneeling on the floor beside him looking into his eyes, her hands busy with buttons and zips. She eased him out of his clothes, grimacing as she saw the weals and bruises already dark on his flesh. Then her lips were against his bare chest, pressing against his aching body like some magical healing sponge. The pain receded.

At length, she helped him into the shoulder-deep tub. She bathed him, tenderly. The intense heat steeped more of the pain away.

'What happened?'

He told her about the two men, leaving out the reasons for their attack.

She said, 'You weren't robbed, so it's something to do with the assignment you're doing here with your Japanese friend, right?'

A certain diplomacy was called for. This was dangerous territory: the less she knew the better, as well, and how would she react to the details of the grisly tale he was helping uncover? Had she so thrown off her cultural roots that she could deal with his involvement in something this touchy?

Kaizei seemed to have no problem with it. For him, it was more than just a journalist's investigative scoop. It went further. It was personal. He was approaching the project with the zeal of someone who wanted to expunge a stain on the honour of his nation.

But Reiko was different. Because of her European sophistication he never really thought of her as Japanese. But she *was* Japanese and now she was living back among her own people, her own culture. He had no way of knowing how she felt about Japan's recent past. 'It may be,' he said, well aware of how unconvincing he sounded.

'You *must* give it up, whatever it is. You must!' She spoke with fervour. In the dim light of the room her eyes gleamed with concern. 'I don't want you killed.'

'Who said anything about being killed?' he replied, seeing again the image of the distorted face of the old man in the block of ice.

She looked at him steadily. 'Jack, I never have understood why you do the kind of work you do.'

She helped him dry himself and get into bed. She poured him a brandy.

He dozed briefly after that, awakening to find her undressing—her belt coming loose, the silk shirt slipping over her head, her skirt falling. As always she was wearing nothing under her clothes, her fluid, long-hipped body caught in the light from the bedside lamp. Her skin had the smooth patina of antique ivory.

She lay in his arms. They did not make love.

A strange time passed, charged with unresolved passion: Ransome half-drowsy from the brandy and the painkiller; Reiko lying beside him, sometimes up on one elbow looking at him with a tender gaze.

They talked. She said, 'If my mother hadn't died, I would never have left you. The timing was so awful. I was just about over all that nastiness with Willy, feeling good about us. But I had to go, you know that.'

'I should have come with you.'

She gave a little shrug. 'Yes, maybe.'

'I was a bit bewildered when you didn't reply to my letters. It occurred to me that maybe you'd run out on me,' looking at her, trying to read her reaction.

She said, 'I thought it was over. My mother dying. Coming back to Japan. It seemed that fate was working against me—against us.'

'I even wondered whether or not I should contact you when I arrived in Japan.'

She shook her head, laughing in disbelief. 'I'm so glad you did,' kissing his eyes, his throat. The pain had receded to a safe distance. His mind was sharp, if oddly detached; remembering.

For her, their liaison had occurred at an unhappy time. The time they had spent together had been shadowed by the problems of her separation: the ugly behaviour of Willy, his threats to go back to Germany with the children.

Her discovery of her own ardent sexuality which, until Ransome, had lain dormant, complicated things for her. Their lovemaking had triggered off something in her. She had consumed him, avidly, as someone dying of thirst gulps down water. At the time, he had felt as if she were, at least in part, using him to assuage years of lost opportunities. 'I wish you weren't such a generous lover,' she had said to him once.

Here, now, in this room, she seemed a free spirit, as though all her previous complexities had been mended by time. The moment felt good—relaxed and complete.

Reiko said, 'You cannot believe how strange Japan seems to me now. When I got your call the other day I had already decided you were out of my life and that I was doomed to be here forever. Your timing was uncanny.'

Ransome said, 'I've been thinking about you ever since you left.'

She came up on her knees, looking down at him. 'Pity

about this,' gesturing towards his bruised body. 'Today was the day *I* was going to make love to *you*.'

'I should time my beatings better.'

'That day at the zoo and, later, at my father's house—I spent the whole day wanting you desperately.'

She leaned forward and kissed him with slow tenderness. 'If I didn't know before, I know now. I love you, Jack.'

She swung her legs off the bed and stood looking down at him. He reached for her. She pressed his hand against her belly. 'When you are feeling better, I promise you it will be worth the wait,' she said, smiling.

He began to sit up.

'No.' She shook her head. 'I don't want to go, but I must. My father will already be thinking dark thoughts.' She grinned. 'What a pity he's not right.'

He lay watching her slipping on her skirt, her blouse. 'You can't stay the night?' only half-serious, knowing that it was impossible.

Reiko shook her head. 'I really wish I could, but the kids . . .' putting on the ankle-length leather coat and cinching the belt tight around her narrow waist. She sat on the edge of the bed and took his hand. 'By the way, do you happen to have a copy of your film with you?'

'*No Man's Land*? Yes, a video copy. Why?'

With a wry look, Reiko said, 'My father said he would like to see it.'

Ransome stared at her.

She laughed. 'I'm as surprised as you look. It came out of the blue. What's more, you're invited to dine.'

'Good God,' Ransome was astonished. 'He practically said I wasn't welcome. Didn't he tell you we had a quarrel?'

She shrugged, 'He suddenly seems to find you "interesting".'

'Better leave it until these cuts and bruises have healed. You don't want him to think you're going out with a thug.'

She laughed and kissed him, briefly and finally. 'I don't think you're a thug. Just mad. I really must go.'

Ransome said, 'It's going to be alright—you and me.'

She smiled. 'Yes, maybe it is. But won't you please promise to give up this investigation of yours before something even worse happens to you? I couldn't bear to lose you, Jack. I've never felt so good about us as I do right now.'

Ransome said nothing.

She looked unhappy. 'At least think about it, will you?'

'If I were a gentleman,' Ransome said, 'I'd call you a cab.'

She laughed, rueful. 'I have a car downstairs.' She picked up the phone, called reception, all the while gazing into his eyes. Her soft voice seemed to move a register higher as she issued instructions in her own tongue.

She hung up and came and knelt beside the bed, slipping her arms around his neck and kissing his ear. 'And I'll be waiting to make love whenever you're able,' she whispered.

For an instant she was a silhouette framed in the door. 'Next time,' she said, 'try to be in one piece.' Then she was gone.

Chapter 24

Kaizei rang at six. 'The usual place in one hour?'
    'Yes.'
Before Ransome could tell him of the loss of the tapes he had hung up.

He took four videotapes and bought a canvas and leather carrybag in one of the outrageously expensive hotel shops. He walked from the hotel, glancing quickly around to see if he was being followed.

The air was like dry ice. There was a north wind. Pale clouds raced above the city, presaging snow.

He hailed a cab in Akasaka. The cab driver looked with curiosity at his bruised face and the spectacular dressings but said nothing. He left the cab at Hibiya and walked through a department store, checking his back.

At Yurakucho Station he collected his camera from the luggage locker, stowed it in the bag and walked up to platform eight against a tide of commuters cut from the one pattern, business-suited and rigid with early-morning ambition.

Kaizei was sitting on the bench reading *Time* magazine. Ransome sat down beside him.

'Sweet Jesus,' Kaizei said, staring at Ransome. 'What happened?'

Ransome told him about the attack in the hotel.

'They were telling you something—not trying to kill you?'

'Seems like it. If they'd wanted to kill me I couldn't have done anything to stop them. Now the bad news.

The hotel post office was shut. They got the tapes from yesterday.'

The implications of that silenced Kaizei for a time.

'Our friend from the hospital is deeply in it,' Ransome said.

Kaizei jumped to his feet. 'I might be able to reach him. Let's go!'

He limped off through the concourse at speed. Near the entrance there was a bank of telephones. Kaizei rang the intercity exchange for the number then the hospital in Yokohama.

Ransome watched him as he spoke to someone at the other end.

Kaizei put his hand over the mouthpiece. 'They've gone to look for him.' He gnawed his lip as he waited. Ransome felt the same anxiety. They had inadvertently put the bitter Masaka in terrible danger. After a time Kaizei nodded to Ransome to indicate that Masaka was on the line. He spoke intensely to his listener for some time then, with a grimace, hung up.

'What did he say?' Ransome asked.

'He said, in as many words, fuck us both. He's going to lie low for awhile. Says he's got some leave owing.'

'Nothing else we can do.'

'This is going to get nastier,' Kaizei said. He examined Ransome's face. 'They really worked you over, didn't they?'

'It wasn't much fun,' Ransome said.

'You want to go on with it?' Seeing Ransome's expression, he laughed. 'Sorry,' he said.

* * *

Genba shuffled forward trailing the great silken yellow sweep of his elaborate costume. He offered the dowry gift of the sword and bowed low before the Shogun's messenger. Danjo, his eyes wild with anger, placed his hands on the sword and made a loud speech of thanks. Genba bowed ever deeper. Suddenly Danjo plucked the gleaming blade from its scabbard. With a single stroke, he beheaded Genba. The sorcerer fell dead. The assembled courtiers expressed their amazement with startled gestures and loud shouts. A court attendant lifted the bloody head by its hair and held it up for all to see.

An old man in the audience near Ransome and Kaizei shouted out with glee. Patrons leaned forward, peering through their hired opera glasses to see the corpse. A family in front of them, eating busily from boxes, paused for a moment, then went on feeding.

Danjo rose and began to explain the plot to the courtiers in a stylised, singsong voice.

Kaizei whispered, 'He's telling us that he had come to rid the house of the evil spirits that had haunted it.' He flashed a cynical smile. 'Just like us.' Suddenly he pointed, 'There! Did you spot Nikaido?'

As he spoke Ransome saw, behind Danjo, his first glimpse of the man they had come to see, the shadow dresser Nikaido Nobusuke—not the man himself, but rather the edge of a plain dark-brown costume revealed for a moment. Nikaido was one of a troop of unseen stagehands who, from behind, discreetly arranged the players' costumes whenever they moved about the stage. Had Kaizei not pointed out their presence, Ransome might not have noticed they were there.

The star, Danjo, made his ceremonial farewells and exited grandly, rolling his eyes and making exaggerated ritual arm gestures. The shadow dresser, Nikaido, was unseen now, moving behind the hero as he moved. A final roll of drums. Danjo vanished. The courtiers sat still in one final tableau, then the striped brown and blue curtains were pulled across.

The packed house cheered and clapped. The audience rose and, in a cheerful mood, made their way under the vaulting beams and the red lanterns of the Kabukiza Theatre.

Once in the foyer Kaizei said, 'Be back in a minute.' Heading for backstage, he vanished into the teeth of the crowd still streaming from the auditorium.

For possibly the first time in his life, Kaizei looked inconspicuous. He was wearing a sober business suit and tie, his shoulder-length hair shorn. With the *yakuza* and the police in Tokyo looking for him he was always at risk, but at least his profile was considerably lower.

Ransome walked about the packed foyer taking in the sights: the elegantly suited men, the women dressed in their beautiful dark evening kimonos. On the red walls there were vivid posters of the season's star actors. Looking at them made him think of Nikaido. Was there ever a more self-effacing job than that of a shadow dresser, whose success was measured by his skill in not being noticed, by his anonymity?

Five minutes later Kaizei returned, elated. Previously, the man had refused all requests to interview him. 'I told him about the trade-off—the Harbin data in return for a secret amnesty. He got very angry about that. No-one had ever told him. He didn't believe it at first, but now he's agreed to talk to us. We meet him at his place in an hour's time. He's given me a mud map. It's somewhere near the Tsukiji fish market.'

Snow flurries over the city showed silver in the streetlights. They leaned into the wind whipping up from the harbour and made their way along the Harumi-dori towards the markets. They killed time in a warm *kissaten*, drinking coffee and, at Kaizei's suggestion, sake.

Kaizei was optimistic. 'It'll be a hell of a lot easier to persuade people to talk now that I can tell them about the American deal.'

'Would be inclined to make you slightly pissed off,' Ransome said, 'if you'd been hiding for the best part of fifty years not knowing you were in the clear. Presumably none of them knew except the commanding officers?'

'Seems that way,' Kaizei said. He downed the last of his sake.

'Ishii and his henchmen just kept the secret to themselves and went on getting rich, knowing they wouldn't ever be touched?'

'Right.'

Ransome shook his head. 'With friends like Lieutenant General Ishii and his pals,' he said, 'you don't need enemies.'

The market area was deserted; the stalls boarded up, the streets empty. Following Nikaido's directions, Kaizei quickly found the little temple that sat at the heart of the market. It stood beside the canal that had once been part of the spider's web of moats protecting the Imperial Palace.

They went past the bridge and over the canal into a narrow street that ran parallel to it. There they found the house, an old broken-down, two-storey place wedged between a warehouse on one side and a fishmonger's on the other. There was an ornate upstairs verandah overlooking the street. They went along a narrow passageway half-blocked by empty rubbish bins and up an unlit flight of stairs to the first floor.

Nikaido opened his door before they could knock. He stared at Ransome then looked at Kaizei as though seeking assurance that the *gaijin* was to be trusted. As he opened the door wider, he peered beyond them down the stairs into the dim passageway below.

They entered.

The first thing that hit was the smell, a curious mixture of dampness from the canal, fish from the surrounding markets, the decay that came from the old building itself, and the contents of Nikaido's astonishing flat. The place was like a second-hand bookstall, floor-to-ceiling with

stacked books and mouldering magazines. The tiny
hallway was crammed with them as was the room overlooking the canal into which Nikaido led them. It was a
blackbird's midden of treasures.

He went to a tiny kitchen in the corner and poured
three cups of green tea. To make room for the cups, he
pushed aside the piles of newspapers and theatre programs that covered the table to a depth of several inches.
He ushered them to sit down around the table.

Nikaido was a fragile, wizened little man. He held
himself with his extremities tucked in, as though he
were still hiding behind the costume of one of the play
actors, trying not to allow the edges of his being to spill
outside the frame. His face was hollowed and his skin
sallow from too little daylight, but from behind the
dried-out face the eyes glittered with a bright intelligence. He wore a thickly padded green jacket with
tracksuit trousers.

Kaizei switched on his tape-recorder. He said, 'I'll translate as we go.'

There being too little floor space to allow for the use
of a tripod, Ransome hand-held the camera, panning
back and forth to cover the conversation.

Nikaido asked a question.

Kaizei, aside to Ransome: 'He still can't believe there
was a deal.' He turned back to Nikaido and spoke at
length. Ransome recognised the words 'Yokohama' and
'Yonoi'. As he listened to Kaizei speak, the old man
seemed to shrink ever smaller.

Nikaido asked, 'How could our officers have so
betrayed us? We were loyal to them. We were all sworn
to a vow of silence. We kept our vow. No-one ever spoke
of what happened there in Harbin, although it must have
been eating us from the inside like a cancer.' His face
showed sorrow.

It occurred to Ransome that he was watching an old

man who had just found out that he had wasted the last half of his life.

Nikaido told them his story.

'After I came back to Tokyo and the war finally ended, surviving was all that mattered then. I can remember the surrender, with everyone stunned and weeping with the shame of it. And the Emperor's voice on the radio! No-one had ever heard him speak before. It sounded so strange: thin and weak like a woman's voice.

'At that time I lived near Ueno Station. It was about the only area that had survived the fire-bombing. There were big concrete buildings where everyone crowded in for shelter. It was a hell-hole—angry soldiers who wanted to go on with the war, prostitutes trying to make money from the Americans, thieves and madmen.

'But you could survive there. There was money to be made. Everything was scarce. I traded things with the Americans—black market things. I met a lot of them and Australian soldiers at that time. They seemed to me to be good men. No different from good Japanese. Maybe better, in some ways. They fed us. We were the conquered people, yet they kept us alive. Nobody starved. Would we have done that? Thinking about that changed me. It was the first inkling I had about Western liberalism. Until then I had understood and respected only the bushido tradition.

'Things got better remarkably quickly. In a couple of years, for most people, the war was like a recent dream. But not for the likes of me. There were things I could not forget. I found that I could not go on in medicine. I kept seeing the faces of the poor devils we had so tormented—in the interests of science! I could not bear to be with people. I needed to be alone. Not to talk.

'I began to educate myself. When I was a young medical student I was so busy passing examinations that I never read anything outside the textbooks. I began to

read books about art, literature and philosophy. I had
always liked the kabuki tradition and one night when I
was there—it was the New Year season and they were
doing *Kotobuki Soga No Taimen*, always one of my favourites—I met an old family friend who took me backstage.
From that moment on, I knew that this was what I
wanted to do. I hung around the theatre and I finally
persuaded them to give me a menial job. I just wanted
to be part of it—not an actor out there in front of the
public, but someone behind the scenes. In the years that
followed I did everything: painted sets, cleaned, learned
everything I could about kabuki. Years passed, then there
came the chance to be a shadow dresser. I jumped at it.
I knew I had found the perfect place to hide.'

Kaizei asked: 'What were you hiding from?'

Here, Nikaido looked frightened. 'The past,' he said.
'The faces of those men.'

Kaizei: 'Can you talk about the camp at Harbin?'

A long silence.

Kaizei (gently persuading): 'What unit were you in?'

Nikaido (distant): 'I became involved in the freezing
experiments. I was expert in low-temperature technology. I had done my thesis on the effects of extreme cold
on human tissue. We were studying the effects of frostbite, mainly. Many of our troops would be fighting in
conditions of extreme cold.'

His flow of words had slowed to a trickle. As he went
on remembering, there were long pauses between each
sentence as if he were dredging up each image from the
muddied depths of his subconscious. 'It's very cold in
Harbin in the winter, bitter cold. We would take the prisoners outside in the evening at sunset. Their arms were
bared and, if it was not cold enough, we would accelerate
the freezing process with jets of air.' There was an odd,
detached quality to his voice as though he could not
believe what he was saying. 'This was done until their

frozen arms, when struck with a short stick, would make the sound a board gives out when it is struck.'

Here Nikaido began to weep. In the several minutes that followed he sobbed piteously. Ransome kept the camera running. Finally, the man composed himself. He looked up at them both. He seemed to fill more space. Whatever guilt had wracked him for all these years had lifted, if only momentarily.

Kaizei began to question Nikaido once more: 'The freezing experiments? Were you in charge of them?'

'No! There were six doctors in our team. I was just one.'

Kaizei's next question stopped Nikaido in his tracks. He shook his head vigorously, indicating that he wanted the camera and the tape-recorder turned off. Kaizei stopped the tape-recorder and nodded to Ransome, who laid his camera on the table.

Kaizei said, 'I asked him who was in charge. He won't say.'

He repeated the question.

Nikaido replied, rolling his eyes upwards and gesturing around the decaying room, saying something in a mysterious voice. Kaizei asked him another question, but he looked nervous and shook his head.

Ransome was fascinated by the theatrical alarm of the old man. The acting was pure kabuki, but the fear was real.

'He says this man is everywhere—all around us, even here—but he won't explain what he means by this.'

Nikaido whispered urgently to Kaizei.

'He wants us to go. He says it is too dangerous to speak about such things and that he has told us enough.'

'Why does he say it's dangerous? Is he being watched?'

Kaizei asked the question. Nikaido was silent for a time, then he began to speak to Kaizei in a low, frightened voice. Kaizei listened intently, his face immobile.

When he was done, Kaizei appeared astonished. He

pressed with another question, but Nikaido shook his head and remained silent, pursing his thin lips as though to demonstrate they would have to be forced open.

Kaizei looked strangely at Ransome. 'You're not going to believe what he's just told me.'

'What?'

Kaizei shook his head. 'Not now. We've got to go. The man is angry. He feels betrayed. He wants us out—now,' picking up his tape-recorder. 'I'll tell you what he said later.'

They packed up quickly. Before letting them go, Nikaido checked the stairs outside his door. He did not speak, did not shake hands. As they left, he covered his face with his hands.

In the dark passageway below, a rat scuttled from a pile of rubbish. Their footsteps sounded too loud on the wooden stairs.

The bright neon of the Harumi-dori beckoned. Ransome and Kaizei, clutching their coats about them, set off towards the light. Overhead signs rattled in the gale. Papers and plastic bags blew against the gutters. Somewhere, a steel rubbish bin was rolling with the sound of kettledrums. Along the narrow pavement on the opposite side of the street two men scurried in the direction of the temple by the bridge, walking fast.

Ransome asked, 'What am I not going to believe?'

Kaizei said, 'He warned us off. He said, "You don't know what you're getting into. You cannot realise what has been going on." He said "they" wanted his special knowledge of low-temperature technology.'

'Who's "they"?'

'When I asked him that, he said, "I dare not tell you." He said, "they" had been following up some successful experimental work he did in Harbin all those years ago.

He said that there had been some kind of chemical break-through and they wanted him back. He said he "resisted their blackmail" when they wanted him to work for them.'

'When did this happen?'

Kaizei looked at Ransome oddly. 'That's the ugly part. Less than a year ago.'

'Jesus.' Ransome stopped in his tracks, feeling the ground opening up. In the yellow streetlight, Kaizei's gaunt face looked like a skull. 'After the war they must have kept right on going.'

Kaizei said, 'It looks that way.'

Chapter 25

At the Foreign Correspondents' Club reception desk Ransome was told there had been a message from a Ms Sumner in Washington. He booked a return call and went to the lounge, looking for McGregor. There was no sign of him. He ordered a drink. A few moments later he was paged. He identified himself to the waiter who came to the table carrying a telephone handpiece. He plugged it in to the jack in the wall.

Julia Sumner's voice was intriguingly throaty and low. 'Lloyd told me your hotel calls were being bugged, so I'm already interested,' she said. 'That stuff is where I'm at, my friend. Brucchi says you're okay. Actually, I think I remember you— red hair, right? We were introduced at a press club bash.

'I made a point of catching up with *No Man's Land* last night. I wished I'd seen it before we met, I might have made a fool of myself.'

Ransome laughed, intrigued by her directness. 'Maybe I should arrange prior screenings when I visit next time.'

'Do that,' she said. 'Me, I think you must be quite mad, Ransome. How you didn't get your pretty ass shot off filming that stuff I cannot comprehend. It's somewhat impressive.'

'Thanks.'

Julia Sumner said, 'So, shoot,' all business now.

'Lloyd suggested you might be interested in helping me run down an interesting lead.' He backgrounded her on the story so far: about the mysterious General Ishii and Section 731 and the possibility of a deal done in 1945 between MacArthur and the Japanese High Command concerning some medical research.

'A secret deal in 1945? Oh, Momma!' she said. 'I know that period pretty well. I did my thesis on the occupation, but that one's news to me. How fascinating!' her voice revealing her excitement. 'What else can you give me?'

Ransome said, 'I'm guessing now, but one of the people we talked to mentioned germ warfare. To me that makes more military sense than the other stuff we've been hearing. We haven't yet caught up with anyone who actually worked on such a program, but we may. We've a few more people to see.'

'Germ warfare?' Julia said. 'Yeah, I think I've got a line on a couple of guys who work in that business. Okay, I'll start digging this end.'

Ransome suggested that she leave a message at the club whenever she wanted to talk.

'Before I go,' she said, 'run that story past me again—about the filing cabinets.'

Ransome told her as much as he could remember from Kaizei's translation of his conversation with Masaka.

She asked, 'Can you remember the exact location of where the meeting between this General Ishii and our occupation forces was supposed to have taken place?'

'Ikebukuro, as I recall, but I'll have to check. Kaizei, my partner would remember. He has audio tapes of the interview. Unfortunately, the video I did of the interview was knocked off.'

'Stolen?'

'Right out of my tiny white hand,' Ransome said.

'Could you go back to your source?' she said. 'It could be important.'

'That could be harder today than yesterday,' Ransome said. 'I have an idea the fellow who told us the story is in hiding.'

Julia was silent for a time. 'If there's any truth in this, Jack Ransome, you're onto some very heavy stuff. Any story that has been kept under wraps since the end of the war is liable to blow up in your face. Do keep in mind that our security guys can play very rough pool in defence of state secrets. You be careful, my friend,' she said quietly.

'I will,' he said. 'One last thing. Will you see what you can dig up about a guy called Dr Harold V. Cord. He claims to work for an outfit called Worldtrade Inc. He read out the address from Cord's business card and told her about the Cord approach.

Julia said, 'You think he's involved?'

Ransome said, 'He didn't even try to hide it.'

* * *

There was still no sign of McGregor in the main lounge, the library, nor the press room. He found him at last sitting alone in the side bar. In the corner, a television set was playing without sound: one of the interminable game shows. A toothy host was urging pretty young housewives to greater heights in a floor-scrubbing contest.

McGregor turned and saw Ransome's face. 'Jesus,' he said, 'you look like you've been through a windscreen.'

'It wasn't a windscreen,' Ransome said. He was going to be asking McGregor a favour, so he thought it only fair to fill him in on what was happening. He told McGregor about the beating and about the fresh accounts of war crimes they had uncovered. McGregor sat open-mouthed. At the end, he said, 'Jesus, this is fissionable material. No wonder people are getting knocked off. And you getting bashed suggests you're getting too close to the truth of it.' His excitement showed on his face.

Ransome said, 'I think that the lawyer in Yokohama probably tipped off someone in Tokyo. Whoever it was thought they'd get a look at the tapes and warn me off while they were at it.'

'You don't sound too warned off to me,' McGregor said.

Ransome gave him a wry look. 'Don't let this calm look fool you, pal. I'm scared shitless. These guys play rough.'

'Where is Kaizei?'

'Good question,' Ransome said. 'Maintaining a low profile out there someplace, digging out the next piece of the mosaic.' He had developed an underlying sense of dread as he waited for his friend to call. 'I too am trying to keep a low profile, and since I don't particularly enjoy having my face rearranged, I was wondering if you could help me change hotels, more or less on a daily basis.'

McGregor laughed. 'Sure.'

'The trouble is,' Ransome said, 'if I book under my own name, about two minutes after I change hotels, the police are going to know where I am. My name's associated with their murder inquiry. And after that business with the *yakuza* in my cell, I suspect that if the police know, other people are going to know.'

'So what do you need?'

'Will you make the hotel bookings for me, using your name and your passport? I'll use the rooms and pay you. I'll be harder to track that way.'

'Tell me when.'

Ransome said, 'Starting today.'

'Right,' McGregor said. 'Drink?'

'A beer'll do.'

When the drinks came Ransome said, 'I'm planning on doing some research. You said this library's pretty good. I want to see if there's anything official—news stories, official accounts of the war—anything where the senior people involved crop up. I'd like to read anything they've got on a General Ishii and another officer of high rank called Yonoi—the lawyer who I think had me bashed.

The army medical unit is called Section 731.'

McGregor wrote the names down. When they finished their drinks, he led Ransome to the library. At the desk he spoke to the one of the librarians in fluent Japanese. 'Give them half an hour and they'll dig out anything they've got. It's a very comprehensive library. If those names are on record they'll have it, or they'll find it for you.'

They went back to the lounge and ordered another drink.

Ransome looked out at the view. The rain drove at the twentieth floor windows. Far below, the vast Imperial Gardens looked sodden. Leafless trees shrunk from a driving wind. A passenger jet, its lights flashing damply, was swallowed by a cloud.

'Remember the tropics?' Ransome said, shaking his head ruefully. The cold weather and constant rain had begun to depress him.

'Getting to you, is it?' McGregor grinned. He had been notorious for complaining about the heat all the time he had been in Vietnam. 'It's good Edinburgh weather— bracing and healthy. The trouble with you, Ransome, is you don't know a climate fit for humans when you see one.' He said, 'I find it difficult to believe this business about your mob doing a deal with war criminals. Surely that can't be right?'

'If it's true that the Japanese *were* researching biological warfare, maybe MacArthur's people thought the material was worth doing a deal about. Post-war was paranoia time. Why else would your friend Dr Cord have tried to buy me off?'

'You sure he was?' McGregor was sceptical.

Ransome said, 'You heard from him again?'

McGregor shook his head. 'Haven't seen him in here since.'

The librarians had found nothing. They assured McGregor that they had searched their files and tapped their outside information sources. There was no mention of a general called Ishii, nor of a high-ranking officer called Yonoi, nor of an army medical Section 731 in any index they could find.

'Curiouser and curiouser,' McGregor said, intrigued. 'Sounds to me as if something nasty's been deep-sixed. Would you like me to dig around, see what I can find out?'

Ransome thought about it for a moment. 'Mac, I'm not trying to protect the story. You're welcome to share it. For me, it's simple. If things become too difficult, I can always simply leave. But you and Suroko have to live and work in Japan.'

McGregor said, 'This is one hell of a story, Jack, and I'd love to help. There are a few sources from whom I might be able to dig out some useful information that might not be available to you.' Seeing Ransome's expression, he said, 'Don't worry! Being a devout coward, I'll be discreet, promise you that.'

'I'd be glad of your help,' Ransome said, 'but watch yourself, for Christ's sake.'

McGregor went off to the bathroom. Ransome idly flicked through the pages of the *Japan Times*. It was the first time he had seen the local English-language newspaper. The front page was filled with a new factional split forming in the government. Californian Senator Calvert Hudson was complaining about Japan's unfair imbalance of trade.

Near the bottom of page seven, his eye was caught by a local news item. A man had been found frozen to death in the refrigerator of a morgue of a private hospital in Yokohama. The authorities had not yet released the victim's name.

In the pit of his stomach he felt a sickening lurch. Ransome knew who it was. In his mind's eye he could see the bitter little man in that sleazy bar staring at the naked dancer.

Chapter 26

No word from Kaizei. Ransome wondered if he had seen the news item about the death in Yokohama. He fought off the depression that had claimed him all day. If only he had deposited the tapes in the hotel's safe.

Reiko's chauffeur stopped the car, opened the rear door for him and held an umbrella over him all the way to the front porch of the house. He knocked at the door, flashed a smile, bowed and went back to the car. Ransome grinned to himself. He could get used to this chauffeur-driven life.

The front door was opened by a motherly-looking middle-aged woman dressed in a kimono.

'Mr Ransome?' She bowed and invited him inside.

Ransome had worn a suit for the occasion and an elegant woollen overcoat. The overcoat was the first he had ever owned. He had bought it in one of the hotel's shops, having succumbed, finally, to the continuous freezing weather.

The woman took his coat then led him through the hallway. He dallied for a moment admiring the Portuguese screen. Subtly lit by ceiling spots, it looked even more beautiful at night.

Reiko's father was standing waiting to greet him by the door of the main room. He bowed, then offered his hand. 'Good evening, Mr Ransome.' He did not smile. He eyed Ransome's face, looking concerned. 'My daughter told me of your unfortunate incident.'

Ransome had forgotten the wreck of his face. The cuts

and bruises were less painful. That morning, the doctor had removed the stitches from his cheekbone, now covered by a small dressing. He said nothing. There was no point in explaining.

'I was sorry to learn of it,' Takanichi said. 'It looks painful. It was good of you to come.' The man seemed awkward. There was no warmth in his expression.

'Thank you for asking me,' Ransome said, thinking, it looks like a fun night. 'Reiko told me you would like to see my film.' He handed him the videotape. 'I'll leave the tape with you and you can return it when you've seen it.'

'Tonight,' said Takanichi. 'Surely my daughter said? We should like to see it tonight, after dinner.' He turned back towards the room as though to include someone else in the conversation.

The beautiful room was lit as carefully as a film set. In a soft pool of light by the windows overlooking the garden, stood another man.

'Mr Ransome, this is my nephew, Mr Takanichi Shoji.'

Shoji Takanichi was impressive. He was in his forties, powerfully built, a thick crop of healthy-looking hair side-parted and carefully smoothed down with pomade. A prominent, well-shaped mouth gave the impression of massive self-satisfaction. The eyebrows reared up at the tips like grey wings.

He bowed slightly. Ransome found himself looking into a pair of shrewd eyes; he was aware of being weighed up.

Shoji offered his hand. He smiled warmly. 'Welcome to Japan, Mr Ransome,' he said. He spoke English with a strong accent and some hesitation, as though he seldom used the skill. 'My uncle has told me a great deal about your work. I invited myself here this evening so that I could see your documentary.'

At that moment Reiko came into the room. He had

never before seen her dressed in a traditional kimono. She had transformed herself into a beautiful lady of some ancient Shogun's court, her lacquer-black hair caught behind with combs, her slim figure accentuated by the fall of cyclamen-coloured silk.

She came to him, bowed and then smiled in a roguish way, as if to let him know that she was acting a part, a young woman playing dressing-up games. He badly wanted to touch her. He offered his hand.

'Welcome, Mr Ransome,' she said. 'I am sorry I was not here to greet you,' very formal. Except that she held her grip a trifle longer than was necessary, it was as if they had never met formally. He thought of her naked in his arms in his hotel room.

'You look lovely,' he said. 'That kimono is exquisite.'

'Thank you,' she said. 'It was my mother's.' She was looking at her father. Ransome caught the look of half-pride, half-sorrow that flickered across his face.

Reiko turned back to him. 'How are your bruises?'

'Better,' Ransome said.

'I told my father and my cousin about your beating.'

'I am sorry to hear that you were attacked,' Shoji Takanichi said. He looked concerned. 'We are dishonoured by such incidents.'

Ransome shrugged. 'I was unlucky, that's all.'

'Were you robbed?'

'Not of anything valuable,' Ransome said.

Reiko's father spoke. 'My daughter tells me it may have been because of the work you are doing here.' He sounded disapproving, as if serious bad manners were involved.

'Perhaps,' Ransome said, not backing off. 'It might just have been a coincidence.'

'Japan can be a dangerous place,' Shoji said, 'for a foreigner.'

Ransome said, 'Tokyo seems a lot safer than other cities I've visited.'

'Surely, Mr Ransome, you are not beaten up in every city you visit?' Shoji smiled at his own joke.

'It is time for dinner,' Takanichi said. His face was bleak.

Reiko led the way through a sliding screen into a dining room. It was spare and restrained in style. The walls were in muted natural colours. Tatami mats covered the floor. On three sides of the room there were painted black screens adorned with pale pink camellias. There were no other decorations. On the fourth side, an intricately worked black iron stove warmed the room.

'I hope you like traditional Japanese food, Mr Ransome,' Reiko said, game-playing still. He smiled at her and assured her that he did.

The meal was superb: course after course of delicate, beautifully presented foods. Reiko picked out tidbits for Ransome and explained the various dishes. They enjoyed their private game of hostess and honoured guest, well aware of the sexual tension that underlay their actions in sharing food under the gaze of her father and cousin.

Throughout dinner, Reiko's father hardly spoke. He looked like a man who wished he were someplace else. Shoji did most of the talking. He quizzed Ransome about his work as a television news correspondent. He sounded out his impressions of Japan. He wanted to know how Japan was regarded in Asia and America. The more he spoke, the more easily his English flowed. Ransome judged him to be very bright, very insightful. With the journalist's habit, Ransome countered with questions of his own.

First he questioned his host. 'I understand you are a tunnelling engineer, Mr Takanichi,' he said.

Reiko's father spoke of his work with understatement, as though he were merely a functionary, but from his oblique answers to the questions, Ransome was able to deduce that Takanichi was, in fact, the owner of a

company with major Japan Rail contracts. His present
project was tunnelling through a mountain in Kyushu,
the southern island. Ransome turned to the nephew.
'And you, are you an engineer also?'

Shoji shook his head and said, 'No. I have business
interests of various kinds, but not in engineering.'

Reiko looked directly at Ransome and said, 'My cousin
is too modest to tell you that he is a politician—a cabinet
minister in the ruling party, the Liberal Democrats.'

A politician—of course! He might have guessed, he had
met enough of them. The arrogance, the shrewd manner,
the impression he gave of being a well-informed
insider—it all added up.

Shoji shrugged, as though all this were irrelevant.
'Tonight, all politics are behind me,' smiling broadly at
Ransome. 'I am a man dining with his family and their
welcome guest.' He raised his glass to Ransome.

Ransome caught the look of venom that Reiko's father
gave his nephew. What the hell's going on? he thought.

'Now that dinner is over,' Takanichi said. 'I think we
shall have some music. Reiko?'

Reiko rose at once. She gave Ransome a strained smile.
'Duty calls,' she said, and left the room.

Ransome was pleased. In the time they had spent
together he had often asked her to play for him, but she
had always refused. At that time, her unhappiness with
her marriage and her life had led her to give up music
completely. She had just promised him she would go
back to it when the news of her mother's death had
come.

'You have heard my daughter play?' The question was
pitched like a probe for information.

'Only on tape. She is very good.'

They were seated in the lounge once more having
coffee and cognac when Reiko reappeared. She was
dressed in Western clothes: a lovely full-length blue silk

dress with a modest neckline and short sleeves. 'Cellos and kimonos don't mix,' she explained to Ransome with a smile.

She sat on a low chair by the grand piano at the far end of the room, facing the three men. She settled to her instrument without fuss. The cello glowed in the soft light, caught within the frame of her spread skirt. Ransome watched fascinated by this fresh manifestation of Reiko: the serious musician. Her face changed, taking on an expression that he had not seen before—intense and inwardly focussed. There was a moment of stillness, then the sonorous music of her cello began to pour out.

Afterwards, Ransome could not remember how many pieces she played. Not much of the music was familiar to him, but he knew that she was good; there were no false notes, no hesitations. As she played, her slim hands moved on the strings with a steely suppleness, her dark hair fell over her face. Her body seemed to fuse with her instrument and the thrilling sound of the cello filled the room.

Between pieces she would look directly at him. He realised she was playing for him alone.

In her last piece, the instrument changed in character, speaking in the plucked Japanese sounds of koto and samisen. When the lovely, haunting melody was over, Reiko flashed a relieved and happy smile, stood and bowed.

Ransome applauded and was joined by Takanichi and his nephew.

She crossed the room and kissed her father's cheek. Takanichi's face was glowing with pleasure and pride. She came and sat close to Ransome.

'That last piece was especially beautiful,' he said. 'What was it?'

She gave a dismissive shrug. 'It's something I wrote.'

'*You* wrote it?'

She nodded, modestly. 'It's based on a famous haiku by Moritake.' She thought for a moment. 'In English it goes,' closing her eyes as she searched for the right words, '"Fallen petals rise back to the branch. I watch. Oh! . . . butterflies!"'

'It was lovely, and you play wonderfully.'

'Thank you,' she said. 'It wasn't bad. I'm back in practice, or at least I should be! I have to give a charity recital next month in Hiroshima—a fundraising event for victims of the bomb.'

'The cello is surely very old?'

Reiko made an odd little gesture that might have been annoyance. 'Very old and very rare and very expensive,' looking embarrassed. Takanichi was smiling indulgently at her. 'My father spoils me. He gave it to me as a present when I returned. But now it's your turn, Jack.'

'Yes,' Takanichi said, 'will you show us your documentary now, Mr Ransome?'

'If you'd like that,' Ransome said.

They sat in the lounge room watching *No Man's Land*. Ransome had seen it a score of times and, as had become his habit, concentrated instead on watching the reactions of his audience.

Neither Takanichi nor his nephew changed expression during the forty-five minutes, but Reiko's face mirrored her feelings. Ransome watched the subtle changes play as she took in the most striking images from those awful wars: the napalmed children, Van Trong's death in the fire-fight in that first Kampuchean push (the terrible despair on Kaizei's face as he dragged their fellow journalist backwards through the waterlogged paddy field), the exhausted faces of the soldiers, and the panic on the faces of the civilians fleeing before the victors sweeping into Saigon. She seemed particularly affected by the images of a school hit by a random bomb attack—the teachers running from the blazing building carrying the wounded and dead children, a young teacher shouting at him '*Voyeur! Voyeur! Voyeur!*' with hate in her face for the stranger who recorded the horror but did nothing—images that haunted his dreams.

After the last still images of death and destruction that accompanied the credits, the video cassette ran out.

There was silence. The men exchanged glances. It was impossible to read what they were thinking.

Reiko's father rose and put the video recorder on rewind. It whirred back quietly.

Shoji said, 'I must congratulate you, Mr Ransome. A remarkable film. I have never seen a war in such close-up.'

Reiko looked at Ransome with an astonished expression. 'You filmed all that?'

'Yes,' Ransome said.

'You were there . . . in all those scenes? Every one?' She looked shaken.

He nodded.

'I had no idea,' she said. She rose and began refilling their glasses.

Shoji said, 'Reiko has told us that you are making a documentary about Japan. What is the subject of it?'

Ransome concentrated on choosing the right words. He didn't want to insult his host's nephew. 'I apologise if this seems rude, but I don't usually talk about my projects. I think it tempts fate to speak about something you haven't yet done; so, if you don't mind, I'll say only that it's a contemporary documentary with a historical theme related to the Second World War.'

'Well whatever it is Mr Ransome, after what we have just seen I'm sure it will be done well.' Shoji smiled at him warmly. 'If there's any way I can assist you, please don't hesitate to let me know.'

Ransome judged this offer to be one of those polite things powerful people say, not expecting to be taken up on it. 'Thank you,' he said.

'I mean it,' Shoji said. 'You tell my cousin you need my help, and she'll see that I am informed.' He smiled at Reiko, who bowed her head briefly.

Again Ransome picked up some undercurrent of uneasiness in the relationship between the three of them.

Reiko rose. 'Jack, will you excuse me please.'

'Are you alright?' She seemed disturbed and unhappy.

'I just found it . . . the work you do . . . a bit . . . violent, that's all.' She turned to her father. She spoke in Japanese to him, asking something.

He replied in English, for Ransome's benefit, 'I will see that Mr Ransome gets safely home.'

Reiko said, 'Thank you for showing your film, Jack.' She shook hands. 'I hope to see you soon.' She bowed to all three men. After she had gone, her perfume lingered.

Takanichi topped up Ransome's glass. 'How long were you there?'

'In Vietnam? Eight years. In Kampuchea, two.'

'Were you ever wounded?' Shoji asked. He had an odd sceptical way of asking a question as though the answers he was hearing were somehow amusing.

'A few times. Minor things only. Only three times seriously. The last one put me out of action for a time,' Ransome said.

'Only three times in ten years?' Shoji said.

Ransome said, 'I was lucky.'

'Yes, you were.' Shoji leaned forward and filled up his own brandy glass. He held the bottle up to Ransome and Takanichi. Both shook their heads. 'Your film is evidence that you are a brave man, but why do you do this thing— attend wars? Are you fascinated by violence, danger and death?'

It was a question that had been put to Ransome a hundred times as he had gone around the various film festivals promoting his film. He still did not know the answer. 'I'm not fascinated by death,' he said. 'Curious about it, perhaps. But I'm more interested, I think, in watching people being resilient.'

'Resilient?' Shoji seemed not to know the meaning of the word. He asked a question of his uncle. Takanichi said a word first in Japanese then in English. 'Enduring.' Shoji understood the alternative translation. He nodded.

'Were you ever a soldier?' Takanichi asked.

Ransome shook his head. 'No, I was too old for conscription to Vietnam.'

Four years too old. It had worried him at the time, missing the chance to know if he were made of the right stuff, if he could be resilient, if he could remain graceful under pressure—if he could be the man his father was.

Shoji looked at him. 'Your bruises: my uncle has already suggested that you may have been attacked because of the assignment you are doing. Is this possible?'

Ransome decided upon vagueness. 'Possible, but unlikely. We're dealing with history.'

'I thought,' Shoji said, 'you mentioned that it was contemporary.'

Oh, you're quick, Ransome thought. 'It's both,' he said, smiling.

Shoji looked at his uncle. 'There are those in our society who would hide the past at any cost. A pity. Today we are trying to run a different, more open kind of Japan.'

Takanichi said nothing. Changing the subject, Ransome addressed him. 'Where did you serve, Mr Takanichi?'

'All over,' said the man. The guarded expression of a member of a defeated army was on his face. How much do you admit to the victor? How much of your old pride is allowed? 'Singapore, the Philippines, New Guinea.'

'Engineers?'

Takanichi nodded. 'Yes. I was mainly concerned with

engineering problems: roads, airstrips, railways.'

I wonder, thought Ransome, if he helped plan the railway my father sweated blood to build? But he had no quarrel with this man. That was a long time ago and this was Reiko's father.

Shoji flashed a smile at Ransome. 'My uncle is too modest. He was on the General Staff, planning the Malaysian invasion and later in New Guinea and Burma. He finished the war as a Major General.'

Takanichi looked at him with protest on his face. He made a self-deprecating movement with his hands and shoulders. 'Why embarrass our guest?' he said curtly.

'In military terms, a great personal success,' Ransome said.

Takanichi acknowledged the compliment with a slight inclination of his head, relieved a little by the neutrality of the statement.

'My father fought against you,' Ransome said. 'He served in the Philippines. He was a war correspondent— a cameraman but—unlike me, he was not a civilian.'

Takanichi and Shoji looked uncomfortable. There was a question to be asked. Neither of them wanted to ask it. Takanichi, the host, broke first. 'Did your father survive?'

Ransome shook his head. 'No.'

There was an awkward silence.

'War is a terrible thing,' Shoji said.

Ransome allowed them some relief. 'It was all a long time ago,' he said quietly.

Shoji said, 'Yes, it is good that we can now put that unhappy past behind us.' He drained his glass and rose to his feet. 'Why don't I offer our American friend a lift back to his hotel?'

They went together to the front door. Reiko's father handed Ransome his cassette. Shaking hands, he said, 'Thank you for allowing me to see your film. Most impressive.' His eyes were bleak.

As soon as they appeared at the front door, a black Cadillac stretched limousine drew up to the entrance. There were two men in the front seat: the chauffeur and a powerfully-built young man in a dark suit who jumped out the passenger side and opened the door for them. A bodyguard, Ransome noted with interest. But then, Shoji was a cabinet minister.

Ransome thanked his host and slid into the interior of the limousine. Shoji came in after him. The car crunched smoothly around the circular drive. For a moment the white face of Reiko's father was caught by the headlights, then the car shot through the open wrought-iron gates into the street.

'Which hotel?' Shoji asked.

Ransome said, 'Yurakucho Station will be fine, thanks.'

'We can take you to your hotel, it's no trouble.'

'Thanks, but I have things to do at the press club.'

Shoji wound down the glass and instructed the driver. On the short drive back to the city, he was friendly and animated, pointing out various places of interest, concerned about Ransome's comfort. At one point Ransome said, 'Did your father serve in the war, Mr Takanichi?'

'Unlike my illustrious uncle,' Shoji said, smiling, 'my father did only an inconsequential desk job.'

'What branch of the services was he in?'

'Planning—that kind of thing,' Shoji said. 'He has often regretted not being a fighting soldier, but in wartime we do not always get to choose the role we would prefer. We can only serve. We can only obey orders without question. He never left Japan.' The shrewd eyes held Ransome. 'Maybe all men share this regret: not being able to prove oneself. It often occurs to me. I've never been required to risk my life. Perhaps that's why you do the job you do, Mr Ransome: to prove yourself.'

'Perhaps,' Ransome said.

They swung past the blackness of the Imperial Gardens into the neon-bright Ginza.

Before Ransome got out, Shoji handed him his card. 'I meant what I said about being of assistance. Do not hesitate if you need my help.' They shook hands. 'I may be able to open doors for you that might otherwise be closed to a visitor. Being in government,' smiling, 'I'm not without some influence.'

Chapter 27

'Been mixed up in any other murders lately?' Mc-Gregor had said on the phone.

'Why do you ask?'

'Your policeman wants to talk to you. He asked me to set up a meeting.'

Uto.

Ransome had suggested the neutral ground of the Tokyo Hilton. He regretted the choice now; he felt vulnerable in the wide-open spaces of the foyer. Twice he had changed taxis on the way there, but the nervousness persisted.

From the atrium dining room on the lower level, the tinkling sound of 'A Foggy Day in London Town' carried up from the white grand piano to the main foyer. Ransome watched the police inspector crossing the foyer through the crowd of guests and businessmen attending various conventions. Uto's face was neutral, but not unfriendly. They shook hands.

'I'm sorry to hear you were attacked,' Uto said, studying Ransome's face.

'Drink?' Ransome asked.

'Coffee, please.' Ransome ordered from the pretty waitress. Uto turned to watch her walk away. He smiled when he saw that Ransome had observed him.

'How are your wounds? Are you in pain?' Uto said.

'Who told you?' Ransome asked, wondering if he would be given the truth.

'The hotel reported it.'

'I didn't ask them to,' Ransome said.

Uto shrugged. 'I had asked them to keep me informed about you.'

Ransome was not surprised, but it annoyed him, nonetheless. 'When I come, when I go, who I see—that kind of thing?'

'Yes Mr Ransome, that kind of thing. I'm sorry.'

The waitress arrived with coffee and a plate of pink sugared almonds. Uto said something to her. She looked embarrassed, but then smiled at him and said '*Hai!*'

He took a pen from his inside pocket. As she poured their coffees she said something to him rapidly: a number. He wrote it down on his serviette. The girl laughed and covered her mouth, amused by this. She walked away, conscious of being watched, swaying her hips with subtle exaggeration.

'Presumably, 'Ransome said, 'she's going to help you with your inquiries.'

Uto smiled. 'I hope so,' he said. He took a sugared almond delicately. He had long spatulate fingers and prominent veins. Ransome wondered if the policeman had ever worked with his hands.

'Is it usual for visitors to Japan to have their movements reported to the police?' Ransome kept it amiable. He was sure the beating was not the reason Uto had telephoned him.

'No, it's not.' Uto bit through the almond. 'We have enough troubles of our own without concerning ourselves with the actions of our foreign visitors. But you are a concern of mine, Mr Ransome.' He popped the rest of the almond into his mouth delicately and immediately reached for another. 'That beating you had is the kind of thing that worries me about you. This is the second time you've been involved in violence since you arrived.'

'How do you know it's only the second?'

The policeman's eyes widened slightly. 'You've been attacked again?'

'Wouldn't you have known about it if I had?'

Uto considered him for a time, then shook his head. 'I don't command enough resources to have you followed. I might be able to protect you better if I did.'

The reply interested Ransome. The man was wanting to protect him?

Uto sipped his coffee, watching Ransome closely over the rim of his cup. 'Did the attack persuade you to give up your investigation?'

'Is your department anxious that it should have succeeded?'

Uto looked ruffled, but did not reply.

'Inspector Uto, is this an official visit?' Ransome said. He suddenly felt that it was not. When Uto had called wanting to see him, he had assumed it was something to do with the death of the frozen man in the hotel room. Since that night there had been no follow-up from the police.

Uto met his eye for a time, then smiled slightly. He twisted around in his armchair to gaze around the sumptuous foyer. 'Look about you, Mr Ransome,' he said. 'Marble, deep carpets, expensive furniture, musicians playing for your pleasure, caviar, champagne, servants to fetch and carry for you. Anyone who can afford it, can enjoy such things. Today's rich live better than our most powerful emperors ever did.' He swung back and took another almond. 'You're not staying here at the moment.'

'No.'

'Where are you staying?'

'I'm between hotels,' Ransome said.

Uto noted the evasion. 'You must be well off, Mr Ransome, to stay in such hotels as this. What does it cost? Five hundred dollars a day?'

'Something like that,' Ransome said.

'How does a journalist afford this?'

Ransome laughed. 'I spent about ten years of my life not drawing much of my pay.'

'When you were in Vietnam and Kampuchea?'

'There wasn't that much to spend it on save for booze and women. And I don't go for booze that much.'

'Are you married?' Uto asked.

Ransome shook his head. 'No wife and no kids, no mortgage payments. So I can stay in decent hotels.'

Uto said, 'The rich and powerful in my country can buy anything they like. They can buy people, they can buy silence. Some think they can even buy history. Did you know that?'

The anger inside the man was being allowed out on a tight leash. Ransome wondered what was coming.

'From what I have learned, you did not report a biased view of Vietnam and Kampuchea. I have been reading about you. You were in trouble with your own authorities for reporting things they would have preferred people not to know about. Is this not so?'

Ransome shrugged a 'maybe'.

'You asked me if this was an official visit,' he said. 'Yes, Mr Ransome, it is. Officially, I'm trying to find your friend Kaizei in connection with a murder inquiry.' He smiled, making a rueful face.

Ransome said, 'I can't tell you where Mr Kaizei is. I don't know. But even if I did, I wouldn't tell you.'

Uto looked at him keenly, as though genuinely puzzled. 'Why would a Westerner risk injury by becoming involved in something that is occurring in Japan, a country which has nothing to do with him?'

'Kaizei asked me to help.'

Uto looked sceptical.

Ransome felt the need to explain more. 'I care about him a great deal. He wanted me involved.'

Uto remained unimpressed, his silence expectant.

Ransome didn't like talking about it, but the man wanted to know, so he was going to tell him. 'Ever heard of a place called Khe San?' he said. 'Look it up. The north-west highlands of Vietnam. I was there once, briefly, doing a piece about a siege that was going on. I didn't spend a lot of time with our own forces in Vietnam; mostly I found the best stories with the Vietnamese. But that was one story we both covered, Kaizei and I. The reason I got out of there in one piece was my friend Kaizei. The details don't matter, but the upshot is, as we say, I owe him one. So when he asks me to come to Japan, I come. Then, when he tells me what the story is, I stay because I want to, because I'm a journalist.'

The reply seemed to irritate Uto. 'Come now, Mr Ransome, I'm sure you have many stories you can cover in your own country. What's so important about this story you and he seem to be so obsessed by?'

'You really don't know what the story is?'

Uto shook his head. 'No, I don't. My problem is I do not know what it is you are doing here.'

Ransome was puzzled. 'Then how come you're warning me off?'

'Am I warning you off?' another sugared almond, 'or am I just warning you? You see, my orders come down from high places. Let's just say that someone important must think what you are doing is of interest.'

'What is this?'

The inspector said, 'Mr Ransome, I am sometimes called upon to handle certain "delicate" matters. Apparently I have a reputation for being able to close files that otherwise might later prove embarrassing to certain highly placed people. Sometimes I am made aware of the details: an indiscretion by a minister with a woman, or a financial scandal that would be best swept out of sight.

Sometimes, as in this case, I am simply instructed to find out what is happening.'

The policeman looked uncomfortable; embarrassed or frustrated, it was hard for Ransome to tell. 'I have been led to believe that whatever it is you're working on may involve political, security and diplomatic matters. I have an inkling that it may be something to do with the Second World War, but I haven't been given the details. My job is to find out discreetly.'

'And, presumably, frustrate my investigation?' Ransome said.

Uto looked away.

Now there is a man who should be in another line of work, Ransome thought. He sensed a sympathy from Uto. His neutral face was betrayed by eyes filled with a great unhappiness. Ransome took a decision.

'War crimes,' he said. 'That's what our story is about, Inspector—the ghosts of old war crimes rattling around Japan.'

'War crimes?' Uto's eyes showed revulsion. 'What kind of war crimes?'

Ransome said nothing.

'You have proof?'

'We're getting proof.'

'Are you going to tell me more?'

'I'm sorry, I can't—not right now.'

Uto sat in silence for a time. 'Ah,' he said at length, smiling slightly as though something had meshed in his mind, explaining many things. 'Mr Ransome, thank you for telling me that. It has helped me understand my instructions more clearly.'

He sipped his coffee and ate the last almond.

'Do you know we Japanese are currently rewriting the history of the last war so that our children will not know what actually happened? We did not invade China, nor Manchuria; we "liberated" them. We did not attack Pearl

Harbour; we leave that out of the history books altogether. There were no railways built with slave labour; prisoners were paid and worked willingly for the greater good of the Great South East Asia Prosperity Sphere.' Uto shook his head in disgust. 'Do you know this version of history?'

Ransome said nothing.

'You're right, Mr Ransome,' Uto said. 'There are old ghosts rattling about in this country. The noise they make distracts us, worries us, reminds us of things we do not wish to be reminded of. We Japanese have a choice. We can live with our ghosts. We can learn from the mistakes of our past. We can try to change ourselves and become part of the world. But not everyone thinks this is a good idea. There are those who believe we did nothing wrong in our past, that we can do no wrong. Such people will, if they can, write the ghosts out of our collective memory, or they will have us put such a lid on the coffins that our ghosts cannot rise to the surface and embarrass us with the sometimes hidden crimes of our past.'

Uto looked at Ransome blankly for a moment, as though he had become entranced with his own words.

'There's one other thing the rich and powerful can buy, Mr Ransome. I almost forgot it. They can even buy history.'

Ransome said, 'Why are you telling me this, Inspector?'

Uto gave a small shrug. 'I had not realised before just how much danger you are in. And I'm afraid that I cannot be of any help to you. All I can say is, be very careful.'

He stood up and offered his hand. Ransome stood. 'Goodbye, Mr Ransome, and next time you see Mr Kaizei, please ask him to contact me. It is now especially urgent that he do so.'

As Uto passed the cashier's desk, Ransome watched

him stop for a moment to speak to the pretty waitress. She laughed at something he said, covering her mouth with her hand. She bowed and smiled. The inspector walked on through the foyer. The doors slid open for him. A police car glided up to the entrance. Uto got into it. The car drove off.

Ransome sat thinking about the conversation. Why did Uto appear to be sympathetic? From what the man had said, he seemed to hold strong political and philosophical views. Were there political forces within the police force itself, with Uto ranged on one side? Ransome wondered if it might have been smarter to tell the strange inspector more.

* * *

The departure of the policeman left him feeling nervous. From the foyer of the Hilton he rang the Foreign Correspondents' Club desk. They told him there had been a call from Washington. McGregor had booked a room for him at the Hyatt. He walked there, keeping an eye open for anyone who might be following him.

The foyer was crowded. Once more he checked to see if anyone was paying him special attention. In the hurly-burly it was impossible to tell. At reception he was guided to the guests' international telephone service in the first floor lobby.

In the phone booth, waiting for the connection, he checked his back, feeling edgy.

Julia Sumner answered, sounding irritable, her voice thick with sleep. 'Jesus, do you know what time it is?'

'Sorry,' Ransome said. 'But the message did say "call when you get in". Frankly, I forgot to check Washington time.'

'A working girl is supposed to get her beauty sleep and, for your information, it's two o'clock in the morning.'

'Shall I call you in the morning?'

'It's too late, I've turned into a haggard crone already.

Hang on a minute while I dig out my notes.'

Ransome hung on, giving a quick look around to see if he was being watched. Julia was back on the line within a few seconds, her voice no longer sounding tired.

'Goodness,' she said, 'you *have* tipped over a nasty little rubbish heap, haven't you? First the bad news. There is no such Japanese Army medical unit as Section 731, at least not according to any war records available to the great unwashed public in the USA. And neither is there any record of your General Ishii. There ain't no such general. If General Ishii and Section 731 did exist they are two of the best-kept secrets of World War II. How's that for starters?'

Ransome said, 'For starters, that's very interesting indeed.'

Julia laughed. 'Thought you'd like that. A contact of mine tells me that certain documents pertaining to occupied Japan that were supposed to come loose under the thirty-year freedom of information rule have disappeared, or have been given a later date.'

'Can they do that?'

'Not legally they can't, but of course in the interests of that useful catchall "national security" they can do anything. But now for the good news. That lead you gave me about some kind of medical deal has really paid off. I think you might just have uncovered something very, very nasty buried in the cellar.' She sounded impressed. 'This phone okay?'

'Yes. Public phone in a hotel.'

'This'll take awhile. You taking notes?'

'Yes.'

Julia began, 'I had to dig very deep indeed. You talked about a deal to do with medical research. I didn't get anywhere with that. My normal research sources and contacts didn't help. There was no public record anywhere of a deal done between the United States and

Japan to do with the passing on of medical research information. No-one in government seemed to know what I was talking about.

'I began again. I figured that if your information was correct, then there should be some record of such a transaction. And, if there was no record, I assumed that anything buried so carefully for all that time must be potentially explosive. You mentioned germ warfare experiments.'

'Yes,' Ransome said.

'Well, when I began asking about the development of BW . . . bullseye!'

Ransome felt a quickening excitement.

'My friend at the Pentagon, who owes me a favour, was intrigued enough by my questions to ask some questions of his own.'

'He must owe you some favour,' Ransome said. The lobby was suddenly filling with people: well-dressed couples who looked like guests on their way to a wedding reception.

She laughed, mock-mysterious. 'You cannot believe how big a favour this guy owes me, Jack. Anyway, my friend spent time with some of the Old Hands from the World War II germ warfare projects. We, of course, were into that grubby business with our ears back. I suspect the atomic bomb saved us from even greater excesses. From them, he picks up some vague talk about—and I quote—"a vast amount of information about new methods of biological warfare" being shipped out of Japan late 1946, early 1947. According to him, the Old Hands talked in terms of "the great leap forward" in knowledge around that time.'

Ransome pressed back deep under the perspex canopy of the callbox, feeling the pressure of the crowd.

Julia went on, 'So, my friend comes to me with this and I say yeah, but what about the deal? He says, what deal? So I ask him to get me some more. So, back he goes to his boffins. Sure, they say, there was a deal. They're not sure of the details, but one of them uses the phrase "immunity from war crimes prosecutions" and my Pentagon friend becomes really interested. He's shaken by the thought that the United States might have done a deal to shield war criminals. He asks the Old Hands how they feel about that. They say, "So what? the information was great and cost us nothing. We couldn't have duplicated such research." One of them says, with real regret, "No-one would allow us." What do you think of that?'

The crowd had grown. No-one seemed to be paying him any attention, but his nerves were beginning to jump. 'I think that's fantastic.' Ransome could feel his blood racing. Kaizei's story was beginning to grow rapidly, like an alien creature in a test tube. 'Is there more?' he said.

'There will be,' Julia said. 'My guy is still digging for any details of the deal in writing. And I'm chasing up a few other leads.' She paused. 'This is a dynamite story, Jack. Does what I've told you confirm your findings in Japan?'

'It exactly confirms it.' The crush around him had grown. Someone in the crowd caught his eye.

'I was going to ask you . . .' sounding hesitant.

'Shoot,' he said, affecting calm, thinking: end this call, get out of here, his eyes searching the moving column of guests for the man who had been looking at him.

'We talked fees last time, but I'll do this research for free if, when you are going to break the story internationally, you'll let me be first in with the newspapers in the States.'

Was the face familiar, or was he just being paranoid?

'If my mate Kaizei has no objections, you're on,' Ransome said. 'But just keep digging for me, will you? We're bound to get nothing but official denials this end.

Your confirmations in the States are absolutely vital. Copies of documents would be useful.'

'I'll call you as soon as I have anything,' Julia said.

'Anything on Cord?' There, not ten metres away, a young Japanese who seemed familiar. The man glanced at him, then looked away. Wasn't he one of the three *yakuza* who had abducted him? The driver?

'Nothing I can nail down,' she said. 'On the surface he appears to be a cleanskin, but my nose tells me he's not. He's been in too many hotspots like Vietnam, Laos and Nicaragua to be just a businessman. But if Worldtrade is a front for some outfit, my information is that it isn't CIA. Your Dr Cord intrigues me, so I'll keep asking.'

The man was five metres away, looking at him directly now. Ransome said, 'Julia, I've got to hang up right now. You've been great. I'll thank you personally first time I'm in Washington.'

Julia said, 'You want to put that in writing?' She blew him a kiss and hung up.

He struggled frantically against the noisy tide of wedding guests. He found a door marked 'exit'. A flight of emergency stairs. He ran down them, hearing his shoes panicking in the concrete stairwell. Through another door. He found himself in a shopping arcade lined with boutiques bearing names like Givenchy, Yves St Laurent, Hanae Mori.

He came out into the street, his heart pounding, knowing that his nerve had begun to go.

Chapter 28

There was work to be done, but Masaka's grisly death in Yokohama had shaken them both. Kaizei hadn't known about it until Ransome told him about seeing the newspaper report.

'It was my fault,' Ransome said. 'If I'd posted the tapes of the interview . . .'

Kaizei said, 'No, my fault. He died for no other reason than us wanting to know things.' He looked like a man at the end of his resources.

'This is a horrible story we're covering, Katie. People are getting killed. Why are we doing this?'

After a long pause, Kaizei shrugged unhappily. 'I don't have a choice. Not now.'

'I know,' Ransome said, feeling trapped. 'It's weird. In the past couple of years I've been bored absolutely shit-less. I've found myself reading about places like Somalia with something approaching longing. I must be mad. *We* must be mad.'

* * *

Kaizei had organised more interviews in Tokyo. They proved mainly abortive. Three of the first four failed to show. Kaizei was vexed. 'The heat must be on,' he said.

The fourth interview was with a man who had also been threatened but chose to ignore the threats, Dr Kabagawa Naito.

For some reason, Kabagawa would see them nowhere else but in the floating gardens, a lovely city park called Hama Rikyu that lies on the bank of the Sumida. It is overlooked by a booming expressway, but high stone walls muffle most of the other sounds of the city. A narrow canal, crowded with yachts and motor launches, separates the park from the city's market.

They had the place to themselves. It was bitterly cold. Their breath steamed in the freezing air. The bare trees stood with their feet in patches of yellowish mist.

The old doctor was hard work to film. In spite of the hour, he was half-drunk and maudlin. As he talked, he kept walking round and round the garden—past the lovely tea-house which was one of the Emperor's favourites, past the duck ponds where hardy teal were fishing industriously in spite of the ice forming on the edges. But he remembered his part in Section 731—'The Devil's Brigade' was his term for it—with remarkable clarity. It was an appropriately chill morning to hear what he had to say.

Kabagawa: 'The prisoners were put out in temperatures of minus forty degrees celsius, or they were chained into ice baths or to the row of freezing cabinets so that a single limb could be frozen. Afterwards we would try various ways to resuscitate the flesh. But when the frozen limbs were soaked in hot water, the tissues crumbled. There was no way of saving the log's life other than chopping off the limbs.'

Again: 'We learned a great deal about measuring skin temperature, how long it took to produce gangrene, how to treat frostbite.'

Again: 'Two naked men were put in an area forty to fifty degrees below zero and our researchers filmed the whole process until they died. They suffered such agony they were digging their nails into each other's flesh.'

Again: 'The candidates for freezing were often hand-me-downs from the different germ teams, and from there they were either vivisected (if they survived freezing), or killed in the poison gas, grenade, or flame-thrower tests.'

More than any others, these ghastly images were to stick in Ransome's mind and, in the nights that followed, invade his dreams.

Later, at Kabagawa's suggestion, they caught the river ferry from the little pier on the canal and went up the Sumida River under the warp of lovely bridges that stitch Tokyo together. He talked all the way upriver as far as Asakusa where, without warning, he disembarked, asking them not to follow him.

* * *

Ransome stood by the window looking down at the new cityscape—the view from another hotel, the third in as many days.

Somewhere out there in that impossible maze of streets Reiko was in a car moving towards him. Not half an hour ago her soft voice, filled with infinite promise, had fluttered like a butterfly on the telephone.

Tokyo sparkled icily below. It was the first sunny day since his trip to the zoo with Reiko and the children. The weak winter sunlight had dissolved the city's haze, giving clean hard edges to buildings and vivifying the colours. Below, to his right, on the roof of a building, tiny figures in red tracksuits were playing tennis on eight emerald-green courts. Far to the left, where the dark copse of trees marked the gardens of the Meiji shrine, a dramatic stadium hung suspended as though from skyhooks.

How did this intricate and random machine keep working? he wondered. Who could even conceive of its mechanism? He had a vision of a tidal wave of timber and concrete and steel rolling out over the countryside, obliterating fields, trees, rice paddies, villages and towns. The scale of it made him feel inadequate; his present quest, futile. And there was the new dimension of fear. Tokyo was no longer simply alien, it was hostile.

* * *

Trailing kisses downward: mouth, nether lip, the hollow

of neck, outside curve of breast, the spiral of navel, the warmth of belly, the moistness of inner thighs against his cheeks. Down, down to the honeyed epicentre of her, the wet locus of her, his tongue a lever artful enough to move the world.

She gave a little gasp. Her knees relaxed outward. Her back arched. He tasted the sweet essence of her. Looking past her flat belly, past the flattened swell of breasts, seeing her head fallen sideways on the pillow. For a moment her eyes opened and she smiled at him from someplace far away. Mouth and flesh fused. A seamless, timeless darkness.

She cried out, rearing half up, catching the back of his head in her hands, fingers entwined in his hair, pressing him against her until she was spent.

Her dark exhausted eyes were wide, staring at him as though seeing him for the first time. 'Damn you,' she said, smiling. 'Just when I thought I'd got you out of my system—you show up.'

At first Reiko had seemed restrained (he was to learn why later), but their first kiss undammed something in them both. They rushed headlong into a private place of blood-racing, well-emptying passion. Ransome was taken to his limit by her joyous abandon.

At one point she whispered, 'I cannot get enough of you,' something akin to desperation in her eyes. She loomed above him in the half-light of drawn curtains. He looked up at her, the light catching the subtle curves of ribs and sweetly engineered breasts, her black visor of hair shadowing her lovely face. A seamless amalgam of flesh, a silken weightlessness, a release.

'Was that alright for you?' the eyes feline and questioning and amused—knowing the answer.

Ransome laughed with pleasure. 'You cannot know how good it is for me.'

'Ever since I came back here, I kept thinking about

making love with you that first time,' Reiko said. 'The beach. Remember?'

Yes. He remembered that night: Imperia Beach with the lights of San Diego Harbour away in the distance, the flash of the lighthouse turning in the blackness, the feel of her skin warm against the cool sand. That night had been the beginning of it all. Something wild had happened to her. To them both.

'Do you know that in those few times we had together you taught me all I've ever really known about sex. And now, since you arrived, I can't stop thinking about you, wanting to be with you.'

'Maybe we're making up for lost time,' Ransome said.

Before Reiko, he had always managed to compartmentalise his life. It was either work or, away from the action, play. The women he had been involved with were always the objects of all-stops-out, there's-no-tomorrow affairs. A week in Saigon, weekends in Bangkok or Hong Kong—white-hot intense passions that burned out like comets. Compartments. A beginning, a middle and an end. Afterwards, it was back to work. Not like this. Reiko kept intruding into his thoughts. He found himself torn between her and the reason he was in Japan. Now the two parts of his life were imploding into one point in time. He sensed that, in the end, he could be blown apart by it all.

Later, she lay beside him on the pillow tracing the contours of his face, from time to time kissing him gently.

'Poor scars,' she said, running her fingers lightly over the fresh cicatrix on his cheekbone. A warm, satiated smile, 'For a man supposed to be in pain, you don't do badly.'

He caught her hand in his and kissed the soft palm. Miraculously, after the point of satiation, he wanted her again. But now she was looking at him with a seriousness that stopped him in his tracks.

She ran a slow finger down his profile. 'How bad is this trouble you are in?' she asked.

'You mean about being attacked?' sensing that she meant more than the beating and wondering how much he should tell her.

She paused. 'My father told me to warn you that you are in more danger than you know. He said: "Tell your friend that there are powerful groups in Japan who believe that contemporary history is not the business of foreigners."'

Ransome stared at her. 'He said that? But he can't know what subject I'm working on.'

'He knows you were beaten up. You did tell me it was connected with your investigation. He knows you're a journalist here on an assignment. He's actually concerned for you.' She smiled ruefully. 'You cannot know how amazing that is. He thinks that you are on very dangerous ground, and that you ought to leave Japan.'

I'll bet he does, Ransome thought. One way to get rid of the *gaijin* suitor.

Reiko said, 'Will you tell me what it's about?'

He decided on frankness. He told her about being abducted and warned off, that it was something to do with an old World War II crime; no more than that, not the hideous details.

'World War II? It must be a terrible crime if people are still being beaten up because of it. How much have you found out?'

'We don't have any real proof yet, just hearsay. People we talk to give us a few details here, a few details there.' He could hear himself holding back now, not wanting to confront her with something that could stink like a corpse between them. 'When I've got more concrete proof I'll tell you about it.' It was an evasion. He knew it. She knew it.

'The men who attacked you, they could have killed you if they had wanted to, couldn't they?' Her face had closed. 'And the men who abducted you—I might never have seen you again.' She was frightened for him. And angry.

There was no answer to that. He remained silent, but gently touched her shoulder.

'You're crazy!' she said, not looking at him.

'The assignment won't take too much longer.' A softening lie. So far, only one rotting limb, a beckoning hand, had been exposed. The truth was that now they were going to have to dig all the way to the bottom of the grave.

She came up on one elbow, looking down into his face. A city neon shone in the pupil of her eye, a small square of orange set in the lustrous brown.

'Jack, will you give up this investigation,' her arm slipping around his neck, 'for my sake?'

Ransome shook his head. 'I can't.'

'For our sake.' She kissed him deeply. 'You must know I'm in love with you and that you're very dear to me.'

'That works both ways,' Ransome said, 'but I still can't let Kaizei down.'

She rose from the bed and crossed to the window, staring out at the city, distancing herself, wanting to show him her annoyance at his unwillingness to comply with her wishes. After a long silence she said in a low voice, 'Then will you do something for me?' Looking intently at him now, 'For us?'

'Depends,' Ransome said, feeling churlish that he would not commit sight unseen.

'Take up my cousin's offer of help.'

'He was only being polite.'

'He could be useful to you. He's very well connected, very influential. He might be able to arrange some kind of protection.'

'He can't waste his time offering help to every foreigner who gets into trouble. Why should he?'

'He's family.'

'But I'm not.'

Reiko was irritated by the remark. 'Look, even if he only helps you find out the information you are after, it will mean you can leave Japan all the sooner and be safe.'

'You want me gone then?' kidding her.

Reiko smiled. 'No, I want you alive, so that I can leave with you.'

Ransome considered for a moment. Access to government influence might do no harm. 'Okay, if you'll arrange it I'll talk to cousin Shoji.'

* * *

An hour later, she left. When he returned from escorting her to her waiting car, he threw himself down on the bed. He felt depressed. The putrefaction of an old crime in which neither of them had been involved intruded upon their relationship.

Later, he slept a troubled sleep. He dreamed of Reiko's father and her cousin. They fused into one soldier who seemed to be carrying him out of a paddy field that was under fire. As he awakened feeling troubled, an important insight, remarkable in its detail, slipped away over the edge of his consciousness like a bright coloured leaf whirled down a slipway.

Chapter 29

The autopsy on the man discovered in the burning car in the factory was completed five days after the body was found. Only some of the results were circulated through the usual police channels: that the man had sustained burns to fifty per cent of his body, mainly the upper torso and head, which was beyond recognition; that the teeth had been knocked out and the tips of the fingers removed, presumably to prevent identification. What was not circulated was the fact that the body appeared to have been in a frozen condition at the time of burning.

The report had been received and noted by the Special Intelligence Unit. It was for this reason that the health authorities were instructed by the Prime Minister's Department to ensure that certain information would be deleted from the autopsy report.

What was not specified in the police circular was the actual cause of death. This was listed simply as 'cause unknown'.

The autopsy had revealed that the victim appeared to have died as the result of massive internal organ and brain damage. Exhaustive analysis confirmed that the cadaver showed symptoms of both pneumonic plague and a previously unknown anthrax strain. Several other symptoms not previously associated with the viruses were detected. The man had suffered a complete breakdown of his immune system.

The concern of the medical professionals bordered on

panic. Efforts to establish the identity of the man were redoubled, concentrating mainly on 'missing persons' reports.

After certain organs were removed for further analysis, the body was burned. This time, successfully.

Chapter 30

The trappings of Shoji's political power were impressive. The cabinet minister's suite of offices were in the Diet building complex in Kasumigaseki with a leafy view of the ziggurat tower of the main building across the courtyard. It boasted sleek modern furniture and state-of-the-art internal communications systems. The discreet and efficient staff had ushered Ransome and Reiko from the frantic activity of the outside office to the undisturbed quiet of this inner sanctum.

Shoji sat opposite Ransome on a black leather couch, impeccably dressed in a silvery grey suit. He looked supremely at ease, managing at once to convey serious concern, authority and benign calm.

The small talk over, the coffee served, Shoji said, 'My cousin tells me that before you were beaten up you were abducted.' A keen look. 'You do seem to be involved in something extremely dangerous. I promised to help, Mr Ransome, so, what can I do for you?'

'I don't know that you can do anything,' Ransome said. Being there made him feel awkward.

'Protection is what I think is needed,' Reiko said. She was edgy and looked drawn.

Shoji grimaced, as though slightly put out that she had joined in the conversation. 'Reiko, as we politicians know, it's practically impossible to protect someone round the clock. Mr Ransome's only certain way of staying safe is to leave Japan, but,' here he smiled at Ransome, 'from what I have learned of you from your film, you may actually enjoy danger. Would you like to tell me what happened?'

Reiko withdrew behind her coffee, ruffled by her cousin's patronising tone, watching them both.

Ransome kept it brief. Shoji listened intently, then asked, 'The two men in the cell warned you off?'

'Yes.'

'But the police denied they existed?'

'Yes.'

'You say that the men who abducted you threatened you with death if you remained in Japan?'

'Yes.'

'Do you take the threat seriously?'

'Very.'

'Were your abductors and the men in the cell and the ones who beat you up the same ones in each case?'

'No. The men from the cell were not the ones who beat me up. The men who abducted me were different again.'

'You have no idea who they were?'

'No.'

'Do you believe the various warnings you were given to leave Japan were specifically to do with your investigation?'

'I believe so.'

'When you were beaten up in your hotel, was anything stolen?'

'Some taped interviews I'd shot.'

'Concerning your investigation?'

'Yes.'

Shoji took his time. 'This is very serious,' he said. 'I am deeply concerned. It would help me to know something about your investigation. It might give me some idea how to assist you.' He grimaced. 'When we met, and I asked you why you were in Japan, you were very discreet. Is it possible you can tell me more? Reiko has told me that it is something to do with World War II.' Shoji raised his eyebrows cynically. 'If I may say so, it seems very strange to be putting yourself at risk for a story so old.'

How much to tell him? Maybe, with his political clout, he might be able to gain access to material about Section 731: information, documents, proof unavailable to Kaizei. Then again, as a Japanese national, Shoji might not want to know. Ransome decided to risk it.

'My Japanese colleague and I are trying to track down a war crime that has been concealed.'

'Committed by which side?' Shoji asked.

Ransome gave him a brief description of the main thrust of their investigation. As he spoke, Shoji made notes on a small yellow legal pad.

Ransome said finally, 'The thing we are trying to establish is the existence of such a camp in Harbin. Do you happen to know? Or could you help us find out?'

The politician swung round in his chair to stare out of the window towards the grey tower. He remained perfectly still for several minutes.

Reiko met Ransome's eye. She said nothing.

When he turned back, Shoji's face was grave. 'This is not an easy thing to hear, Mr Ransome. You are a guest in our country and I believe you are entitled to the fullest protection, regardless of whatever journalistic assignment you have undertaken. It would sit very badly on us were you, a journalist of repute, to be harmed, or in any way impeded in your work. However, I do not believe this story can be true. I hope it is not. Do you have proof?'

'We are beginning to build up some detailed evidence which suggests that it may be true.'

Shoji reached under his desk. A moment later a slim young man entered. Shoji spoke to him for some time. The young man took notes.

Reiko smiled uncertainly at Ransome.

The young man bowed to Shoji, to Ransome and Reiko and left the room.

'Mr Ocha, my personal assistant, will undertake some immediate research to see if we can track down this Section 731 of yours, and the general, Ishii.'

'Thank you,' Ransome said, 'that could be very helpful.'

Shoji said, 'I must say I hope that Mr Ocha will be able to help disprove your theory, which I find,' his face showed distaste, 'repugnant.'

Ransome said nothing.

'About protection. My cousin is right. I do believe you may be in great danger, Mr Ransome. You really would be best to leave the country on the next plane. However, I cannot insist so, short of that, a word in the right places may be able to provide some measure of police protection for you. But I think you understand that this is not possible on any twenty-four hour basis.'

'Please, no,' Ransome said, 'it's not your responsibility to protect me. I would prefer that you did not do that.'

Shoji nodded as though approving Ransome's decision. 'As you wish.'

Reiko shook her head, exasperated, but said nothing.

Ransome felt embarrassed now. He hadn't wanted to be there in the first place. For her benefit he said, 'I'll be extremely careful. You've been very kind to give me your time.'

Shoji stood. 'If my assistant finds anything, I will be in touch with you through Reiko.'

He bowed to Reiko and shook hands with Ransome. His face was grave. 'I would feel happier, Mr Ransome, if I were helping you with a more positive story, something that might bring our two cultures closer together rather than risk driving a wedge between them. I can't help thinking that it is a long time after the war to be digging up such a terrible story.'

Chapter 31

The town of Kamakura lies in a green valley surrounded by a perfect circle of heavily-wooded, steep-sided hills. To the south, the one break in the ramparts opens out onto the sea. In the year 1142 a great tidal wave drove in over the grey volcanic sands of Yuigahama Beach, funnelled through the narrow break and dragged everything back out to sea.

Later Kamakura became the political centre of Japan. The first imperial court of Minamoto Yorimoto was established there. Buddhism was a powerful force then. The warrior class of that twelfth-century shogunate took up the Buddhist teachings of loyalty and fealty. From this intricate mixture there developed the dark beginnings of the bushido philosophy and the samurai code.

Now Kamakura is a bustling, leafy little seaside town, a haven for day trippers: in summer coming in their thousands to swim in Sagami Bay, in April to enjoy the cherry blossom festival and, all the year round, to visit sixty-five Buddhist temples that grew up around the court.

The temples range from grand to touchingly domestic in scale. They nestle discreetly on the tree-clad slopes among the walled houses of the rich who make their home in the ancient and charming town, a convenient hour from Tokyo. There was just such a modest temple on the steep hillside above the home of Sanko Yuichi, the man they had come to see.

They arrived in Kamakura at ten o'clock in the

morning. While Kaizei was trying Sanko's number from a payphone on the promenade, Ransome crossed the road overlooking the bay.

At either end of the great curve of beach he could see a cluster of huge resort hotels clinging to the headlands, and away to the south a chimney-like lighthouse stood on a headland.

By the concrete steps that led down onto the beach a sign in English and Japanese read: 'In case of earthquake be cautious of tsunami. Even without a tsunami alarm pay attention to the surface of the sea. Evacuate immediately from the beach in case of unusual appearance.'

On the way from Tokyo Kaizei had told him the ancient myth of how Japan lay on the back of a turtle. 'What does the turtle stand on?' Ransome asked. Kaizei said, 'It's turtles all the way down,' laughing outright for the first time since they had been together.

Ransome looked out to sea and thought of tidal waves. The surface did not look unusual, save for whitecaps that churned all the way to the horizon. Under the frowning winter sky, the water was almost black. He wondered what he might do if the sea suddenly reared up and rushed at him. Run? He had an image of himself and the town behind him, and all the people in it swirling out helplessly into the dark waters of the bay. And what then would be the point of this search for truth that he and Kaizei ventured upon with such determination?

Ransome walked down the wide beach to the water's edge. The dingy grey sand was littered with sea wrack and plastic bags anchored by rotting kelp, remnants of the long-dead summer. The icy wind that had swept the beach clear of people and boats insinuated itself through his clothes. He thought of clean golden beaches and of suntanned girls and the flat heat of the Californian sun on his skin, and felt dispirited.

A few minutes later, Kaizei joined him by the ocean's

edge. He, too, was depressed. 'No answer,' he said grimly. 'My information is he never leaves the place. I hope we haven't come on a wild goose chase.'

They drove through the empty streets of Kamakura— the gift shops, ice-cream parlours and coffee shops boarded up for the winter—and from the railway station in the main square followed Kaizei's map to Sanko's address.

The house seemed deserted. Kaizei's knocking went unanswered. Ransome waited in the car while Kaizei questioned Sanko's neighbours. One of them told Kaizei that he had been there earlier that morning. They decided to keep a lookout from the temple above the house.

The temple gatehouse above the road was empty. Perhaps the cold had driven the attendant away. They left coins in the tray on the counter and walked up the slippery wooden steps set into the slope between the bamboo poles with their wildly fluttering prayer flags. The hillside was thickly covered in larches and oaks, and on the crest of the hill above there grew a dark frieze of pines.

At the top of the stairway they reached the ledge upon which the little wooden temple was built. The ground was sodden underfoot. From a spring somewhere higher up on the cliff-face water dripped down.

They passed though a tiny graveyard carved out of the side of the stony cliff; tiered, black and grey marble memorial plinths; bamboo jars of faded flowers; wooden prayer sticks; stone incense lamps and bowls. Along the temple wall, a line of ancient stone Buddhas, their faces half-obliterated by time. On one grave, there was a full Kirin beer bottle as though a thoughtful mourner had sent a message of good cheer to the departed. The wind sang in the treetops, and high overhead, a kestrel hawk wheeled, looking for prey.

From the narrow terrace in front of the temple they had a clear view of Sanko's huge house set in its walled and sculptured garden. The house was built of honey-coloured timber, the architecture half Danish functional, half Swiss cuckoo clock. From their perspective the complicated steel roof glistened in the chill rain.

During the hour they waited, perhaps a dozen cars drove along the road. At twelve-forty, just when they were about to give it away, a dark Nissan sedan swung into the driveway.

*　*　*

Much later, driving back to Tokyo, Ransome remembered the odd feeling he had had when Sanko first opened the door. As Kaizei was explaining why they were there, the man's expression had been that of someone greeting an expected and welcome guest. He had bowed and smiled at them and then, without a word, led them into the house.

Their feet rang on the polished wooden floors. Everything was timber: the walls, the ceilings. The rooms seemed empty, as if Sanko were a new tenant waiting for the furniture to arrive, but when they came to Sanko's study at the rear of the house it was different.

The room was tall-ceilinged, warm and comfortable. It ran the full width of the house. On a small table a percolator bubbled away, filling the space with the aroma of fresh coffee. The walls were lined with bookcases. There were bright-coloured curtains and easychairs facing out into the garden through big double-glazed windows. A word processor and a printer were on a desk facing the view. Beyond the high stone walls, the rounded hills of Kamakura rose up.

Their host invited them to sit. He poured coffee for them, then sat down expectantly.

Kaizei spoke to him in Japanese for some time. Ransome observed the man. Sanko Yuichi had run to fat.

His face hung with loose wattles and multiple chins. Behind spectacles with lenses as thick as the bottom of milk bottles, his eyes were diminished to black specks. His hair was a wild but thinning grey mop. His clothes were comfortable: a roll-neck blue sweater and black trousers worn with soft ankle-length boots.

Something Kaizei said to him made Sanko laugh and shake his head.

'He doesn't mind being filmed,' Kaizei said. 'He has some English but he won't speak it. "Make me famous," he said.'

Ransome took the camera from his bag and set it up on its tripod. Maybe I will, he thought.

Kaizei started his tape-recorder. His first few questions set Sanko off in a flow of words that sounded so fluent it might have been rehearsed.

Kaizei: 'You were a member of Section 731?'

Sanko: 'Yes, from 1937. November of that year.'

Kaizei: 'You don't seem surprised to see us.'

Sanko: 'I knew you would come some day. Somebody was bound to.'

Kaizei: 'Did any other members of the Section tell you we were conducting an investigation?'

Sanko: 'I have heard nothing about you from anyone. Since the war ended I've had no social contact with fellow members of the Section, not to my knowledge. Nor have I sought any of them out.'

Kaizei: 'Ever attend the Section's reunions?'

Sanko: 'Do they have them? I cannot think of anything worse.'

Kaizei: 'No-one has tried to prevent you speaking to us?'

Sanko: 'No.'

Kaizei: 'No threats?'

Sanko: 'Even if I had been pressured, I would not have been deterred. How can anyone threaten an old man like

me? What do I have to fear from anyone about death? I
am glad you are here. I can unburden myself.'

Kaizei: 'What was your role?'

Sanko: 'I originally trained as a biochemist. I volunteered to serve in the water purification unit.'

Kaizei: 'The water purification unit?'

Sanko: 'Its full name was the Epidemic Prevention and
Water Supply Unit. That was the cover name given to
the biological warfare project.'

Kaizei: 'What do you mean by the term "biological
warfare"?'

Sanko: 'Exactly that. We were developing various
strains of diseases to use as weapons.'

Kaizei: 'What sort of diseases?'

Sanko: 'The deadliest ones you can think of: bubonic
plague, pneumonic plague, anthrax, typhus, cholera. It
was the key project. Chemical warfare was the reason for
the Section's existence. Ishii—'

Kaizei: 'Lieutenant General Ishii?'

Sanko: 'Yes. Ishii persuaded his superiors that microbes
could become an inexpensive weapon capable of inflict-
ing great casualties.'

Kaizei: 'Was the concept a success?'

Sanko: 'We had some successes. By 1941 we were man-
ufacturing big amounts of bacteria. Eight tons a month
was our maximum capacity.'

Kaizei: 'Eight tons?'

Sanko: 'Eight tons a month. We would skim the bacteria off the surface of the culture medium like cream.'

Kaizei: 'You personally, what was your work?'

Sanko: 'The unit's work was very wide ranging, but the
principal task of my own section was to develop new
strains of plague.'

Kaizei: 'Did you succeed?'

Sanko: 'Yes.'

Kaizei: 'Was it ever used in warfare?'

Sanko: 'Yes, in China. There were several successful trials. One experiment I monitored was in Shangde in Hunan province. That was in November 1941. We fed fleas on plague-infected rats and dropped them over the target area in loose envelopes of cotton and paper. Some wheat was mixed in. The idea was that rats would be attracted to the wheat, giving fresh hosts for the fleas to feed on.'

Kaizei: 'Did it work?'

Sanko: 'Yes, there were subsequently some plague-attributed deaths. I don't think there is any doubt it worked as a weapon. Ishii was a brilliant organiser. It was his concept. He was in charge. The whole place was self-contained: sophisticated germ- and insect-breeding facilities, testing grounds, an arsenal for making germ bombs, an airfield, special planes, and a crematorium.'

Kaizei: 'A crematorium?'

Sanko: 'For the prisoners of war.'

Kaizei: 'Who were experimented on?'

Sanko: 'Yes.'

Kaizei: 'What kind of prisoners?'

Sanko: 'Mainly Chinese, Russians, Mongolians. Some special prisoners: spies, security risks, saboteurs and the like.'

Kaizei: 'How were the prisoners used?'

Sanko: 'To try out the various theories.'

Kaizei: 'In what way "try out"?'

Sanko: 'Lethal dosages, for instance. But in the pursuit of exact scientific information about the progress of a disease in various time frames, sometimes individuals would be selected out of the group and sacrificed.'

Kaizei: '"Sacrificed"?'

Sanko: 'Killed. We usually used morphine. Depending on the experiment, we would pass on any spare organs to people in the other programs. There was always a waiting list.'

Here there was a long pause. Sanko said nothing for such a long time that Ransome almost stopped filming.

Sanko: 'I've thought a lot about the work I did. Europeans—like your cameraman there—had scruples about using the bubonic plague as a weapon of war. But we Japanese were not burdened by the legacy of the Black Death. Nor did we have scruples about using human guineapigs. After all, the *maruta* were not Japanese, so the killing was made easier.

'You can tell your friend that, had atomic bombs not been dropped on Japan, we were technically ready to use germ warfare on the United States and we would have done so. But this does not excuse Hiroshima, or Nagasaki.'

At this point Sanko looked directly into the lens, directing his remarks to Ransome. It was only later, after reading the translations, that Ransome realised why.

'I do not consider the crimes I was implicated in any worse than that inflicted upon those tortured cities by the dropping of the bomb. But crimes they certainly were. Halfway through the war, I grew up suddenly when I realised I was involved with something shameful.'

Another long silence.

'One image sticks in my mind. The prisoners in the special section were obliged to have injections every morning.' Sanko closed his eyes. 'I can see a line of bare arms thrusting out of the judas holes in the cell doors.'

He opened his eyes and looked out into the lovely winter garden. 'I came to be filled with pity for the prisoners, who suffered vilely through the privations we inflicted upon them. They were treated with complete callousness, as though they were objects that had ceased to exist from the earth. I came to see this clearly. The rest of my time in Harbin was a nightmare.'

'And afterwards?'

'Afterwards?' Sanko laughed shortly. 'There was no

"afterwards", only time to be filled in until the grave. After the war I was sickened by what I'd been involved in. I gave up science. I wanted nothing more to do with it. I became a writer. I've been doing it ever since—with some success,' he gestured to the house around him.

'What kind of things do you write?'

'I write for daytime television. Romances. No-one was ever hurt by someone writing a romance.'

'Do you have any records of the Section: photographs, regimental memorabilia?'

'No. At the end of the war I burned every single record I had. I even burned my uniform. Not that such gestures make any difference. The terrible thing is that nothing has changed.'

Kaizei pressed. 'Any names you can pass on, so we can widen our investigation?'

'Names? Ah, yes,' here a tired and cynical smile. 'I know all the names, all the top men. You'd be surprised if you knew who they were and how well they have survived. But I won't reveal them.'

Sanko was staring out the window in silence. Abruptly, he stood up. With an odd, distracted smile he said something at length to Kaizei.

Kaizei translated. 'He says everyone has to live with their own conscience, and that he has waited thirty-seven years for us to help him unburden his. He asks us to see ourselves out.'

'He waits thirty-seven years to confess?' Ransome said. 'What if we hadn't turned up?'

Sanko spread his hands to show that he had nothing more to say. He went to the door, then hesitated. Speaking in a low voice, he said something urgently to Kaizei.

Kaizei seemed astonished by whatever it was he was hearing. He pressed the man with questions, but Sanko shook his head firmly. He bowed briefly and left the room. They heard the sound of his footsteps fading.

Kaizei's face seem to have seized. 'You know our golden rule about confirming a story with two separate sources?'

Ransome suddenly knew what was coming.

'He's just confirmed what we heard from the shadow dresser. He says that less than two years ago he declined a highly paid offer to work for an organisation research-ing the transmission of disease as a weapon of war—the same work and some of the same team he worked with in Section 731.'

'Sweet Christ,' Ransome said. 'Did he name the organisation?'

Kaizei shook his head.

At that moment, from somewhere upstairs, there came the unmistakable sound of a gunshot.

They stared at each other. Kaizei closed his eyes. 'Oh no,' he said. Ransome suddenly understood about the thirty-seven year wait.

They found Sanko Yuichi lying half off the narrow cot that was the only piece of furniture in the room. In his hand was a rusting gun Kaizei identified as standard officer issue, Imperial Japanese Army, World War II. Sanko's brains were spread over the bamboo headboard and the wooden wall behind.

Chapter 32

They left Kamakura like fugitives, Kaizei driving too fast in the rented Toyoto. Both of them were feeling sick about what had just happened. They saw none of Sanko's neighbours on their way out and had no idea whether the sound of the shot had been heard. Kaizei said that as soon as their journey was over he would advise the Tokyo police of the suicide.

Halfway back, Ransome broke the silence. 'Remember that old dilemma we used to talk about—is truth changed by the presence of a camera?'

Kaizei nodded. 'Yeah. How much are they reacting to the event, and how much are they acting for the audience?'

'How badly did we change truth back there? We produce a camera—a man kills himself. The ultimate effect.'

'We're changing a lot of truth right now,' Kaizei sounded unnerved. 'Three people have died already, two because we talked to them, one because we planned to.'

Ransome said, 'If what Sanko said is true—if something secret is still going on—maybe *that's* the reason people are being killed.'

Kaizei looked sick. 'Maybe that's what Aoyama meant when he said "keep on digging".'

'Maybe we've been asking the wrong questions.'

'Or even worse,' Kaizei said, turning his eyes from the road to look into Ransome's face, 'maybe we're after the wrong story.'

* * *

In the next five days they crisscrossed Japan by car and train, taking action always to throw off anyone who might try to be follow them. They interviewed seven ex-members of the Section in Kagoshima, Kyoto and Osaka. They heard variations of the same grim story: other experiments, other horrors, other inhumanities. They listened to selective memories at work: rationalisations, excuses and—occasionally—remorse. The interviews were excellent and would make startling television.

But through all this both Ransome and Kaizei felt badly distracted. They shared an uneasiness, a common journalistic instinct that their present assignment had become redundant, that there was another even more terrible story somewhere below the surface.

With each interview Kaizei probed for further evidence of this. He questioned each man closely, bullying at times, in an effort to establish the truth of what they had heard from Sanko that bloody afternoon in Kamakura. Did they know of ongoing experiments? Not one of their interviewees knew what he was talking about and none of them gave the slightest sign of evasion. They had to be believed.

'Maybe I misunderstood Sanko,' Kaizei said.

'We've got two sources, Katie. The theatre man said much the same thing. And didn't your father's friend, Aoyama, say there was more? "Keep asking questions," he said, "and you'll come to know."'

Kaizei stared at him, something like fear on his face. 'Maybe we should go north again before too long,' he said, 'and try to persuade Mr Aoyama to tell us whatever else he knows.'

The next day, travelling on a half-empty Japan Airlines commuter flight to Kobe to interview another of the men in the rose grower's photographs, he handed Ransome an envelope. 'Present for you,' he said.

Inside were the photographs of the group heads of

Section 731. Ransome had seen them last at the farm-house of the rose grower, Sakurai.

On the back of each, Kaizei had pencilled in the names Sakurai had given them: Kanaka, Osatko, Hamada, Obe, Watanabe, Yonoi. In the middle, General Ishii. There was a question mark behind two of the figures in the group, the men whose names the old man had not been able to remember.

Ransome looked at Kaizei, questioning him.

Kaizei shrugged. 'I went back to see if he would lend them to me.'

'He agreed?'

Kaizei made an amused face. 'He wasn't home. I borrowed them.'

'He's not going to be too happy about that.'

Kaizei shrugged. 'Something so unique and powerful deserves the widest possible audience.' He seemed very pleased with his theft. 'Those are the originals. When I have time, I'll return them to him.'

Once more Ransome examined this yellowing record of the men who had run the secret activities in Harbin. They stared out boldly and confidently from their hidden past.

Seeing these arrogant faces once more made him remember the strange dream he had had the night before: groups of soldiers posing endlessly for photographs, each group dissolving and becoming another; officers, soldiers watching sumo wrestlers—sometimes in close-up, sometimes in long shot—all fused together with wedding shots of Reiko's parents and her children.

Kaizei said, 'Since they're the only photographs we've got of these guys, it would be a shame if they got lost . . . or were stolen. Can you have them put in your hotel safe?'

'Sure,' Ransome said, 'I'll organise it when we get back.'

'For some extra security, I've had them copied. How

about you post off a set to your friend in San Diego?' He
handed Ransome two other copies of each photograph.
'A set for him and a set for you.'

Kaizei pointed to one of the officers in the original
photograph. 'Osatko ... dead—a stroke last year. This
one—Watanabe—I'm told was killed in a road accident
ten years ago. But him, he pointed to another in the
group, 'he's our next interview ... if we can get near
him.'

Ransome read the name pencilled on the back of the
man's image. 'Captain Obe Kukuei.'

'From what I've managed to find out about him,' Kaizei
said, 'Obe was in charge of the experimental vivisection
team in Harbin. He's said to be an active member of
several extreme right-wing organisations and from all
accounts is a card-carrying fascist. He's unlikely to be
cooperative.'

'He's agreed to talk to us?' Ransome said.

'No way. We're going in cold turkey.'

'Where?'

'Kobe University. He teaches at the medical school
there. Guess his subject.'

'Surgery,' Ransome said.

* * *

Kaizei had said they were going in cold but, in fact, as a
cover designed to get close to their man, he had organised with the university to do some filming in the medical
school, ostensibly for a documentary for American television on the life of Japanese medical students.

The university's public affairs officer, a bright young
woman called Naka Somo was effusive and helpful. They
spent two hours filming on the campus. Somo pointed
out Obe to them and they even managed to get some
footage of him coming and going to lectures. Kaizei asked
her if she could organise an interview with him. She
made a phone call on their behalf.

After a long discussion she put down the phone. 'Dr Obe is willing to be interviewed. He can spare you an hour after lunch.'

Somo agreed to have lunch with them. Kaizei showed some of his old form by flirting with her outrageously. She had formal English and a driving ambition to break into television. She questioned them like an interrogator, seeking the magic formula with which to change her career.

At two o'clock she ushered them into Obe's study and, with much deference to the old man, introduced them. After listening to a brief reiteration of the nature of the documentary from Kaizei, Somo bowed and withdrew, smiling. Obe invited them to begin.

Through the eyepiece Ransome studied the man as he answered Kaizei's questions. Obe was a lean man in his mid-sixties whose military bearing spoke of cold showers and little forgiveness. His bony face was characterised by an under-slung jaw. It gave him the look of a river pike: voracious and determined. Perhaps to compensate for the unfortunate jawline, Obe had cultivated a small but thick moustache. His hair was thick and crew cut. His skin shone as though it had been first flayed, then polished with pumice.

As they had planned, Kaizei began by questioning the man in a low-key way about the training of students and his methods of teaching surgical techniques. Obe answered confidently at first, but seven or eight minutes into the interview, when Kaizei asked him 'After your graduation you served in the army?', a look of concern appeared on his face. The interview had obviously taken a direction he had not expected.

Obe replied, 'Yes, I did.'

'What work did you do in the army?'

Obe paused for a moment, uncertain how to go on. 'I served in the medical corps in Malaysia during the Great

Pacific War. Then later, in 1944, I ran a surgical team dealing with burns victims after the fire-bombing of Tokyo by the Americans.' At this point he glanced towards Ransome, looking right into the lens.

Kaizei then asked: 'Were you able to refine your surgical techniques in the war situation?'

'Yes. It was an excellent opportunity to be able to deal with more extreme cases that one would not see in peacetime circumstances.' With this remark Obe drew his shoulders back and straightened slightly, the pose of the tough-minded medical pragmatist willing to face the harsh realities of war.

Kaizei's hand came into shot here as he slid a photograph, face down, across the desk to Obe. Ransome followed the man's hand as he picked up the photograph, then captured his face in close shot as he stared at the image. There was a look of shock on his face. The underslung jaw dropped, the mouth opened.

Kaizei said: 'Did you not, in fact, develop your surgical techniques in Harbin?'

Obe did not reply. He continued to stare at the image.

Kaizei: 'Is it not so that you were the leader of the surgical group in Section 731?'

Obe's voice was no louder than a whisper. 'Where did you get this photograph?'

Kaizei: 'Is it not so that you experimented on prisoners of war there?'

Obe's face worked briefly as he took a grip of himself. 'What has this photograph to do with me?' His eyes were blazing with anger.

'That's you in the second row.'

Obe stared at the picture once more. He shook his head; whether to deny Kaizei's accusation or out of sheer disbelief that the photograph existed was not evident. 'No,' Obe said emphatically. 'Not so. I do not know any of these officers.' The voice had risen a notch.

Kaizei said, 'Kanaka, Osatko, Hamada, Yonoi, Watanabe. In the middle, your commanding officer, Lieutenant General Ishii. And third on the left—Obe. Captain Obe Kukuei.'

Obe shook his head emphatically, his eyes wide with alarm.

Kaizei said, 'We have spoken to Yonoi. He has identified you.'

'No!' Obe had lost his confidence. He seemed profoundly shaken. 'Yonoi would never betray a comrade!'

Suddenly Obe stood up. He shouted something at Ransome.

Kaizei said, 'He insists you turn the camera off. No harm done. We've got enough.'

Ransome switched off and sat back.

Obe began to tear the photograph up into tiny pieces. He shouted something at Kaizei.

'He says it's a fake.' Kaizei was close to laughing. There was a glitter of excitement in his eye.

Ransome smiled. 'That's why he's taking it all so calmly.'

Kaizei said something to Obe, then translated for Ransome's benefit. 'I've told him we know it's not a fake and that we have copies.'

Obe began to shout once more.

Kaizei translated. 'He insists on having the tape in your camera.'

Obe rushed round from behind his desk. He tried to take hold of the camera. Ransome put a hand on the man's chest and shook his head. Obe seemed for a moment poised to strike him, but then he swung on his heel and went back to the other side of his desk. He began to punch a number.

Kaizei said something to him. Obe stared at him, then slowly put down the handpiece.

'What's going on?' Ransome said.

'He was going to phone the police. I suggested we would phone the media and offer to sell the interview. He doesn't seem too terrifically keen on that idea.'

Obe began to harangue Kaizei in a low voice. Kaizei translated as he talked. 'He's heard through the grapevine that some journalist is spreading lies about the work of the Section. He denies that he was in it. He denies that anything we have accused him of is true. Now he wants to know how much we are willing to accept to leave him out of it. He says that this could be bad for his name.'

Kaizei replied to him. Obe looked anguished. 'I told him our purpose is not blackmail but exposing war crimes.'

Obe began to speak again.

'He says he will tell us nothing. He hopes the Devil takes us. He says I'm a communist and a traitor to my country. He tells me that he has connections in the right places to see that I am dealt with. He says that when the present government is defeated it won't be long before people like me face the treason judges.'

Ransome said, 'Has he done any experimental work lately with his old colleagues from Section 731?'

Kaizei asked the question.

Obe stared at him. He answered contemptuously, looking like a man accused of an absurd offence.

Kaizei said, 'He says he knows nothing about any experimental work still going on.'

Obe strode across the room to the door and held it open, inviting them to leave.

Kaizei said something to Obe. It sounded like an insult.

A muscle was jumping under Obe's right eye. His glare was that of a madman. They went out through the door.

'What did you say?' Ransome asked.

Kaizei gave a wry smile. 'I told him he was a disgrace to the medical profession.'

Chapter 33

The Takanichi Rolls Royce arrived, slowly picking its way through the ambulances and police cars. The entrance of the collapsed rail tunnel was lit by floodlights. Sleet angled down on the stark scene of emergency workers entering and leaving the tunnel mouth.

Reiko left the car accompanied by her chauffeur, who held an umbrella over her head. She was saluted past various policemen. Detouring nearer the tunnel mouth, she watched as a stretcher was carried out. The victim was in a body bag. A woman in the crowd shrugged off a policeman and ran weeping towards the stretcher. She was restrained by two emergency workers.

Reiko climbed the outside flight of stairs and entered the demountable site office. The chauffeur remained outside under the streaming umbrella.

'You spend all your life building up a reputation,' her father said, 'then something like this happens.' He was alone by the window, looking out at the scene of the disaster. 'They keep finding more bodies! There's no doubt about it now. The police have established sabotage. Who could have done such a thing?' The old man sounded bitter.

Reiko said, 'Tell me about your brother's past.'

Takanichi turned to face her. His face was half-collapsed by grief. 'Your American is causing worse trouble than you know.'

Reiko was savage. 'Are you afraid of the truth?'

'No, but our family honour is involved.'

Reiko shook her head impatiently. 'What hold does Shoji have over you?'

Takanichi shook his head, denying, but there was no conviction in the gesture. He said in the voice of a defeated man, 'Just persuade him to get out of Japan.'

'You just want him out of my life,' she said, angry now.

Takanichi showed his frustration. 'Go with him if you must. It no longer matters. You are no longer a Japanese woman, you are something I do not understand. Don't you realise how much danger he is in? There are people who will kill your . . . lover, or whatever he is to you, if he gets in their way.'

Reiko said, 'Who would kill him? Shoji? You?'

Her father was silent for a moment. He collected himself with an effort and said, 'I don't want to see him come to harm. If I wanted to harm him, I would have said nothing.'

Reiko shouted at him, 'Why? Just explain why!'

Takanichi slumped down in a chair behind a desk. 'Daughter, we all have a past. Or all families do. Ambitious politicians often want to bury theirs. Let me tell you about my brother.'

Chapter 34

'Don't want to be melodramatic,' Ransome wrote from the Foreign Correspondents' Club, 'but the situation is somewhat hairy. Just in case I don't get back, here's what I want you to do about releasing the material.' He detailed his instructions and mailed the letter, together with all the latest video footage, to Martin Garrett. Writing the letter felt rather like writing his will.

* * *

As soon as Ransome's voice came on his line, Brucchi said, 'You bastard.' He sounded amused. 'Whatever corpse you've exhumed has begun to smell. If you're not careful, you're going to get my favourite lady arrested.'

'She's not in trouble, is she?'

Brucchi laughed. 'Nothing that she can't handle. You don't know the Lady Julia. All the same, she's going to have to be careful. A couple of days ago she was told by a senior Agency official to lay off asking questions about Japanese medical research circa 1945.'

Ransome felt exhilarated. The old rule called for two confirmations of every fact. Here was further evidence that there was an American connection.

Brucchi went on, 'The said gentleman warned her sternly that the matter has been accorded a high-priority national classification and that she was in danger of breaching the National Security Act, which is why *I'm* calling you. She felt that might be more judicious. She doesn't fancy looking out through the bars.'

'Tell her to leave it alone,' Ransome said. 'I don't want her getting into bother.'

'There's more,' Brucchi said, his voice fruity with conspiratorial pleasure. 'You're going to love this. Yesterday she was grilled for three hours by two Company men about her interest in the matter—fairly straight-up stuff, but finally she was asked if she knew a busybody called Ransome.'

Better and better, Ransome thought. There *must* have been a deal back in 1945. Who else was worried about Kaizei and him digging up old corpses? And what were these allegations about something presently going on? And why were people dying? And where did Cord fit in?

'When Julia rang her contacts, they were suddenly all keeping very quiet. Her man at the Pentagon was on the carpet, being asked why he was suddenly taking an interest in germ warfare. By the look of it, they've all been warned off.' Brucchi laughed. 'Whatever this is all about, my friend, it must be semi-serious.'

Ransome said, 'Semi-serious it is, and I'm really grateful to both of you. But please tell Julia she's done enough. I'll keep her informed of progress through you, Lloyd, if that's okay with you.'

'Sure,' Brucchi said. 'Sounds like you're onto a hell of a story, Jack.'

'It might even be bigger than we thought,' Ransome said.

* * *

He caught the underground at Hibiya, clinging to the strap in a crowded carriage. The teaming underground below the city somehow paralleled the dark secrets he was helping to uncover. He didn't know this place, nor these people. He was more aware of being an outsider than ever before.

He watched the faces of the jammed-together passengers, each impinging on the space of half-a-dozen others, each occupied with their own private thoughts. Few of them spoke. Most were salarymen and women office workers, neatly dressed, carrying their briefcases and handbags. As the train came to each station, groups of them would rush the doors in a frantic scrum. Another group would crowd aboard to fill the spaces left behind.

Everything was clean and well-lit. Even the paper advertising posters that hung from the roof of the train were in mint condition. Not one of them was torn or marked with graffiti. Discipline.

Automatically now—for he had adopted the habits of a hunted man—Ransome searched faces for that too-long-held gaze, seeking out the dangerous profiles of strangers glimpsed once too often. He was shocked when he found himself staring into a pair of eyes that blazed with hostility. They belonged to a tough-looking man of about fifty, unkempt and wearing ragged and dirty overalls. On the seat beside him he had laid out the tools of his trade, a shoemaker's awl and some sharp knives. He was making a pair of traditional Japanese wooden-soled sandals, working with dexterous hands.

When his eyes left his work, the shoemaker regarded the people around him darkly, muttering under his breath. The passengers stayed well clear of him, avoiding his eye. No-one attempted to occupy the seat he used as a bench.

When he found Ransome looking at him, the man picked up his knife and pointed it balefully. He said something in a loud contemptuous voice to his fellows. It sounded like an obscenity. Diplomatically, Ransome turned away and took to studying the advertising posters. The man laughed wildly. An office girl giggled, then smiled warmly at Ransome, offering politeness to the insulted stranger. He smiled back, unnerved, wondering how much anger lay under the orderly surface of this society.

* * *

'I need to see you,' Reiko said at the first sound of his voice.

'The feeling's mutual.'

'Can I come over?'

'How soon can you get here?'

'I'll leave now.'

He told her his new address: the Ginza Tokyu. With McGregor's help he had moved there the day before.

He showered and dressed in front of the television. On the screen, the results of the earthquake. There had been a tunnelling disaster somewhere; there were rescue teams in masks, stretchers with bodies coming into the glare of the arc lights, anguished women waiting for news of their men, ambulances driving off, lights flashing. Scenes from the student riots, thousands of motorbike-helmeted kids armed with staves, battling with riot police. The truth in ten second grabs—the edited overkill of television news.

He went down to the foyer to meet her.

* * *

Outside, to the north and east, they could see lightning flickering silently against the black backdrop of sky. Rain streamed down the windows. Tokyo's neon skyscape painted her ivory body with soft, ever-changing colours: reds, greens, gold and turquoise. She was a warm, languid chameleon by his side.

Reiko said, 'I always loved the actual physical feeling of making the notes, feeling the texture of the polished wood and the strings that combined to make such a lovely sound.' Taking his hand, she said, 'Because being a successful musician was so important to my father, I was always by myself, practising. Because I had such a very lonely childhood, everything went into that instrument. I used to talk to it as though it were alive. I loved the thought that I could be very private with my cello and whisper to it and convey to it my most secret feelings,' smiling at the memory, her face taking on the soft contours of a young girl. 'It began to assume human qualities. It became a person to me, but more than a person . . . my first love.' She kissed his hand and looked at him fondly. 'It doesn't seem so important now.'

She slept.

Ransome stood by the bed looking down at her. Her round breasts rose and fell evenly. Her mouth had parted. The full nether lip betrayed a hint of sweet bruising.

It occurred to him that he had never heard her tell of her childhood. He knew little about her. She knew equally little about him. There had been no other dimension to their affair, words only about passion, about love. There had been only a shared present. Now it was different. It made him desire her all the more.

Half an hour ago, she had seemed in pain as she reared over him, her head flung back, the pulse on her neck beating fiercely. Then the familiar half-amused, half-amazed smile. 'You do that to me every time,' she had said.

When she awoke her face was shadowed, her mood sombre. Ransome studied the sweep of her profile.

She rose and went to the window. He realised that she was trembling. He crossed to her quickly and put his arms around her.

'I don't know who I am,' she said. She sounded desperate. 'My father went south first thing this morning. There's been an accident on his project.'

'Serious?'

'Very. A cave-in on his tunnel. Twenty dead so far.'

Ransome said, 'I think I caught something about it on television when you were on your way over.'

'The news gets worse by the minute. He was shattered when he left this morning believing that there might be three dead. I can't imagine how he'll survive this.'

'How did it happen?'

'I don't know. The police think it's sabotage. I just

hope it's not negligence. That would be the end of him. He's obsessed with his business integrity.'

She lay back on the bed, staring up at the ceiling. In a low voice she said, 'If you're a woman and you make your escape from Japan, you should never come back. I used to find myself an alien in the West, now I find myself an alien here. I have no country now.' She rolled free from his arms and lay silent for a time.

'Where we are together is our country,' he said.

She made a rueful face. 'You can't believe how crushing it's been to live in that house,' turning towards him. 'My father treats me like a wayward child. I can't imagine what I've done, but even before you came he was barely civil. He thinks because he spent a fortune on that damn cello that he owns me.' She lapsed into a troubled silence, then: 'Maybe it's because of my mother's death. He's so alone.'

'He must be concerned for your welfare,' Ransome said, smiling at her. 'For starters he doesn't want you to have anything to do with me.'

'It's me he doesn't approve of, or what I have become.'

'Why?'

'Living abroad for so long, I suppose,' Reiko said. 'Marrying a *gaijin*, divorcing. I think he sees me as a disgrace to the family honour.' She laughed, drily. 'I'm out of touch with ideas like family honour. It's a terrible thing to admit, but I could very easily dislike my father.' She threw her arms around him. 'Hold me!' she said.

They lay together in silence, but he sensed that she had something more to say.

'Jack,' she said, 'I want to leave Japan, but sometimes I think I'll never get away again.'

'Of course you will.'

'But where to go?' close to tears.

He said, 'When you want to leave, you can just leave.' He smiled at her. 'When I go, why don't you come too?'

She sat up, 'Do you mean that?'

'Yes I do,' Ransome said, certain about his feelings for her now as never before.

'How serious about me . . . about us . . . are you?' She gazed at him with an unwavering look.

'Very serious indeed,' Ransome said.

'I'd like to leave now. Just get out. Tomorrow. I just want to book tickets for me and the kids and go. Will you come with me?'

Ransome was hearing the subtext: I need you. You've got to get out of here. You're in danger. That's what this is all about. He kissed her gently. 'Sure, let's go together. We can go in a few days time.'

She closed her eyes, shaking her head in frustration. 'No, it has to be now.'

Ransome said, 'Look, I'm nearly done on this assignment. A few more days won't make any difference, surely? And you'll need time to pack and sort out your affairs.'

'Jack, there aren't any days left.' Ransome saw fear in her eyes.

'You're thinking about me, aren't you?' he said. 'That I might come to harm.'

'It's not just that,' she said, tears springing to her eyes again. 'Of course I think you're in danger, but this whole thing could wreck things between us. That's what's really important. We've got to get away from here. Both of us.'

Ransome wondering, What's this all about?

'You know something,' he said.

'No!'

He could tell by her face she was evading.

'Yes! I do know something. Something my father told me.' She looked at him angrily. 'I can't tell you what it is, but I just know you must not stay here in Japan!'

She got out of bed and began to dress.

'I only need a few more days and I'll have done what

I came to do,' he said, trying to flush out whatever it was she had in her mind. 'Can't you tell me?'

She shook her head, blindly. 'Jack, *please!* If we don't leave, we won't survive what's going to happen.'

She left a few minutes later with the distracted air of a messenger who had delivered bad tidings and was in a hurry to leave before she could be killed for it.

Chapter 35

Uto walked straight into the room followed by a stone-faced young assistant in plain clothes.

Ransome was impressed. It hadn't taken the police inspector long to find out where he was staying.

Uto did not introduce his colleague.

'When did you last see Kaizei?'

'Day before yesterday.'

'Where?'

'Here, in Tokyo.'

'What were you doing together?'

'We had been interviewing a man.'

Uto did not ask who, or where.

'What time was it when you saw him last?'

'Ten o'clock in the evening.'

'Was that the very last time you saw him?'

'Yes.'

'You haven't seen him this morning?'

'No.'

'Heard from him since then?'

'No.'

'Any idea where he is staying?'

Ransome wished he did know. With Kaizei under threat of death his long silences were unnerving. He shook his head.

Uto gauged the response, his eyes hard.

'Will you please get dressed,' he said. 'I should like you to accompany me.'

'Where?'

'Just to help us with our inquiries.'

Seven-fifteen a.m. The streets were already heavy with traffic.

'How did you know where I was?' Ransome was unnerved by the speed with which he had been tracked down.

Uto was silent for a time, considering whether to explain. 'Hotel registrations,' he said. 'Your name didn't come up on the central computer and McGregor is not a common name. I guessed that it must be your friend who booked you into your hotel.'

The police inspector did not speak on the rest of their journey, his face still as though it were carved in old whalebone.

* * *

The central wholesale market at Tsukiji stretches over several blocks of downtown Tokyo, bounded on one side by the Harumi-dori, on the other by the docks where the fishing fleet anchors. It is the major food market of the city, selling fresh fruit and vegetables, meat and just about everything else that can be eaten. But fish is king at Tsukiji. Even in the freezing cold air of an early winter's morning, the smell of fish was strong.

The streets and narrow alleys between the shops and market stalls were jammed with people: cooks, chefs and housewives, salesmen, shopkeepers and tourists, stall owners, businessmen, butchers in bloody aprons. It sounded like a riot in progress. The air was filled with the cries of the stallholders and hawkers, music throbbed from a hundred tapes.

Uto's driver put a flashing light on the roof but, even then, the car had to force its way through the packed streets. Workers gobbled hot noodles at narrow stalls, or crowded around burning braziers trying to unfreeze their chapped hands. Ancient porters manoeuvred impossible loads on long-handled trolleys through head-high stacks of frozen fish. Boys holding trays of hot food aloft swerved through the crowds on bicycles, miraculously keeping their balance.

It was only when the driver ran the car up onto the pavement, hard against the wooden walls surrounding an old Buddhist temple that Ransome knew he had been there before. Last time he had been there, Tsukiji market had been a deserted, windswept place. A chill like a block of ice formed in his gut.

Uto led off through the crowd, heading for the canal bridge. It was practically impassable. Tough-looking men manned temporary stalls selling army surplus equipment, cheap crockery, handicrafts and souvenirs, stacks of radios, cassettes, cheap watches and the kinds of things that fell off the backs of trucks. Hundreds of their customers and market workers crowded the parapet, looking down into the canal.

With some shouting and brute force, the young policeman cleared a space by the edge of the bridge.

Below, on the canal, Ransome could see a small rowing boat. Around it, four heads of masked divers bobbed in the green waters. Ransome was filled with a sense of dread; he knew who they were looking for.

Among the jumble of nondescript warehouses and sheds that crowded the bank of the canal he could see the building they had visited, with its ornate roofline and the upper verandah that made it look like a goldrush hotel.

On the canal side, the building fell one further storey down to the water's edge. Just above water level there was a small verandah that doubled as a landing. There was a rail around it and a few steps leading down into the water. On the landing were a group of uniformed police and several more divers in their yellow wetsuits, canary bright against the sombre greys of morning.

On the opposite side of the canal there was a greasy

black wall of ancient, sweetly interlocked granite boulders, evidence that the waterway once had been an outer moat of the Imperial Palace. All round the banks there was an encrusted scum of plastic bags, rubbish and things unspeakable. A street block away, the canal ran under another bridge already choked with early-morning traffic.

Two police divers swam to the landing and were lifted out. Another two lowered themselves into the murk, their yellow suits disappearing into water thick and green as the spill from a chemical factory. After a moment, they sank out of sight.

Uto turned to Ransome. 'You've been here before?' He knew the answer.

Ransome nodded. 'A few nights ago.'

It was impossible to read Uto's expression. He turned away and asked a question of some onlookers. There was a volley of replies. He did not seem to pay attention, but immediately pushed through the crowd and led off in the direction of the street entrance to Nikaido's house.

Instead of going up to the old man's apartment from the passageway, Uto went past a uniformed policeman and down a rickety flight of wooden stairs. It brought them onto the landing stage. 'Wait here, please,' he said.

Ransome stood watching. Uto went to an older, uniformed officer, whose impressive insignia suggested he was in charge. They spoke for several minutes. The officer glanced over at Ransome briefly then ignored him. The police and divers on the landing were intent on the work of the divers who appeared and disappeared, time and again, into the depths of the canal. They paid him little attention. One of the uniformed men held a radio receiver to his ear.

A yellow arm suddenly speared upwards through the oily surface. A diver reared half out of the water as though he had been frightened by something below. Excitedly, he pointed directly beneath him, ten metres out from the landing. There was a flurry of activity. The other divers converged on the spot like seabirds diving for fish.

There was a long stillness. At length, the waters stirred, thickly. A yellow head appeared, then three more. The divers were dragging something that showed pale as it came to the surface.

Slowly, they swam nearer to the landing. Several policemen crowding the landing steps briefly obscured Ransome's view. They reached down, took a grip of the drowned corpse and lifted it onto dry ground like a landed fish.

Uto stooped over the naked figure for a moment then turned and beckoned Ransome with a slight movement of his head. Ransome crossed the landing, dreading the sight.

Nikaido looked like a stick man made of chalk. His body was all skin and bone. He looked no bigger than a child. His penis was shrivelled and had practically disappeared into the thick bush of grey hair. His face was screwed up in a death agony. It was the same expression Ransome had seen on the face of the old man in the Shinjuku hotel room. Tortured? he wondered.

'This was the man you were interviewing?'

Ransome nodded, dumbly.

Uto said, 'You know his name?'

'Nikaido.'

The policeman nodded. 'You know what he does?'

Ransome said, 'He works—worked—in the Kabuki theatre.'

At that moment, a uniformed man clattered down the stairs and went directly to the officer in charge. He saluted smartly and spoke for some time. The officer came and spoke to Uto.

'Let's go,' Uto said, and followed the policeman back up the stairs.

They passed through Nikaido's building out into the busy street and turned left. The next-door building was a two-storeyed brick warehouse. By the entrance, two uniformed men were keeping onlookers back. One of them saluted Uto. They entered the building, a coldstore. They went through an insulated door into a gloomy cavern of chill.

An extraordinary sight greeted Ransome. Row upon row of enormous yellow fish stretched as far as he could see. There must have been a thousand of them, each the size of a man all identical as if stamped out of a mould, each one gutted, each with a gaping mouth: tuna. Everything was yellow. The low mist of freezing air that hung over the carpet of fish, blurring the edges of the dead creatures, had caught the yellow colour of their flesh. The dozen men who stooped over the fish, slicing the choice cuts, wore yellow shirts and headbands. Their long flensing knives hung from yellow sashes.

A lone policeman stood on the far side of the freezing room. Uto walked to him. The man handed Uto some clothing: tracksuit trousers, some underwear, a pair of high-sided boots, a thickly padded green jacket. He pointed to where the clothes had been found wedged between two of the huge fish.

Uto showed the clothes to Ransome. 'Do you remember what Nikaido was wearing when you saw him?'

Ransome had recognised the green jacket. He nodded. He touched the material then jerked his hand away. It was frozen.

'Hasn't it occurred to you, Mr Ransome, that the next body we find could be your friend Kaizei's, or your own?'

Uto handed the clothes back to the policeman and walked out of the freezer room. Ransome took one last look around the killing ground and followed him.

The driver had brought the police car to the front of the building. Ransome got in, Uto slid in from the other side. The car moved slowly forward, bulling its way through the crowd.

Uto said, 'You learn anything from that, Mr Ransome?'

'I've been learning a lot of things since I saw you last, Inspector.' Ransome leaned his head back against the seat and closed his eyes. This thing was growing like a cancer. 'I think it's time we talked.'

Chapter 36

The policeman took him to a breakfast place in Shin-juku on the first floor of a beaten up building.

Uto ordered Sapporo beer for them both. They picked at a bowl of seaweed snacks.

Ransome looked around the dim bar at the faces of the patrons. Most of the tables were taken by groups involved in intense conversations. They were a motley mixture of young and old, hippie-looking types and a few impressive-looking older women. The light inside the bar was an odd yellowish colour. It gave the faces a line and shadow effect.

The beers arrived. 'A favourite bar for university staff,' Uto said. 'Some people think it's a hangout for subversives and left-wing revolutionaries—people like your friend Kaizei. I like it,' he gave a small smile, 'because I don't meet policemen here.' He swallowed the first inch of his beer and put the glass down.

'The police have been ordered to redeploy all available resources into a major man-hunt for your friend. He has no chance of evading us.'

'He hasn't done anything,' Ransome said.

'So?' affecting cynicism. 'We're going to hang the killing of Nikaido on him. Somebody, or some pressure group with influence, intends to get him out of the way to block your inquiry. One way or another they'll succeed. When we catch him, he'll be out of the way—even if, later, he can prove he's innocent.'

Ransome stared at Uto. He wondered whether he gave a damn about guilt or innocence.

Uto said, 'You had something to tell me?'

Ransome wondered how much to give. He was tempted for a moment to say nothing. 'There have been more than two killings,' he ventured. 'Another man we interviewed died locked in a refrigerator.'

'What other man?'

Ransome told him about Masaka's death in Yokohama.

'You had also interviewed him before he died?'

'Yes.'

'Is that it?' He looked as if he did not want to hear the answer.

Ransome hesitated. Should he tell him about Sanko Yuichi? 'You may have seen a phone-in report of a suicide in Kamakura,' he said.

Uto looked puzzled. 'No, suicide reports don't come over my desk unless they involve something we are engaged upon. I don't know about that. Who?'

'A man called Sanko—a television writer. He shot himself.'

'How do you know?'

'We were there when he did it,' Ransome said.

Uto's eyes widened.

'Just after we interviewed him he went into another room and shot himself. When we got back to Tokyo, Kaizei anonymously reported it to the police.'

Uto stared off into space, thinking hard, trying to fit pieces together. A bitter smile formed on his face. 'You two conduct very dangerous interviews,' he said. The smile vanished. 'Mr Ransome, you admit that four men connected with you are dead. You must tell me what is going on here.' Uto spoke with deadly force. It was time.

Ransome said, 'Have you heard about Section 731, Inspector?'

'Section 731?' Uto's face told him that the words meant nothing to him.

In the next half-hour Ransome watched the man's face slowly glaze over with horror as he told him about the secret medical installation that had been operated on the faraway plains of Manchuria long before the inspector had been born.

When Ransome finished, the policeman said, 'I could use another drink, how about you?'

When the drinks came he filled both their glasses. 'Why is your friend doing this?' he said.

Ransome took his time answering, thinking about the question. The way Kaizei was driving himself was almost obsessive. The more he learned, the more he seemed determined to root out this ancient canker regardless of the personal cost. 'Out of a sense of shame is probably the best explanation I can give you,' he replied.

Uto looked away. 'Yes,' he said, 'that must be it.' Turning his gaze back, he said, 'I happen to think it's time we Japanese buried our past, or at least faced up to it.'

'Do you think you can?'

'Those in power can't,' Uto said. 'They've been running things to suit themselves for so long that they cannot contemplate any other version of history and events.' There was a look of sadness in his eyes. He glanced around the bar. 'Not all of us think that way,' he said. 'Frankly, as far as your exposé is concerned, I hope you succeed.'

Ransome was intrigued. Had the man switched sides? 'Why are you saying that?'

Uto shrugged. 'You two are not criminals, you are journalists. A policeman's business is with crooks.'

'Whatever happens, we will succeed,' Ransome said. 'We've already sent all the evidence we need out of the country.'

Uto laughed as though he had heard the punchline of a good joke. 'If you are as smart as I think you are, Mr Ransome, you will follow it at once.'

'Soon. In a few days, maybe a week.'

'I doubt,' said Uto, cynical now, 'that you have that long. I know from my own people that you are being careful. We've found it impossible to keep track of you all the time, but, given the will and the manpower, you would be relatively easy to tail. Whoever finds you may also find Mr Kaizei, so be sure you don't lead anyone to your friend. It could cost him his life.'

Ransome nodded, sobered by the advice.

For a moment, Uto seemed distracted. 'Japan needs brave men willing to speak out,' he said, 'but it appears that they die for it.' It was as though he were talking to himself. 'Your friend Kaizei interests me a great deal. We have a very thick file on him going back before his time as a journalist in Vietnam. He's always been something of a thorn in the side of authority, even when he was quite young. A prince of lost, left-wing causes,' he laughed.

'You said "we" have a file on Kaizei. Who's "we"?'

Uto thought for a while, considering whether to answer, but he said nothing.

Ransome was annoyed by this. 'Now that you know the story we're uncovering, are you going to go on tracking down Kaizei?'

'It's out of my hands,' Uto said. 'But at least now I am beginning to understand. I need to meet him. Do you think you could arrange it?'

'I'm not sure he'd take the chance.'

Uto said, 'I promise that our meeting would not lead to his arrest.'

'I'll ask him.'

Uto gave a twitch of a smile and stood up. 'I'll take you back to your hotel.'

As Ransome rose, a group of patrons at the table directly facing him also rose to leave. They crowded around one of their number, a man who remained seated, looking over his shoulder at something on the table in front of him. For a frozen moment under the yellow lights of the bar, they were a tableau, like a group in an old photograph posing for the camera.

In that instant Ransome made a startling connection. The meaning of his dream about Takanichi and Reiko's cousin was suddenly known to him. Reiko's strange, agitated behaviour would be explained by this, were it true. He was overcome by a sense of excitement. He could not wait to test out his insight.

He jerked his attention back to the policeman. Uto raised his eyebrows, quizzically, sensing that something had affected him, but Ransome did not explain.

Chapter 37

'I'd prefer not to meet at the Foreign Correspondents' Club,' Ransome said. He'd been into the Yurakucho building that housed the club several times too often of late. It was the obvious place for anyone to tag him, and there was no point in giving free kicks to the opposition.

'The scene getting somewhat heavy?'

'I'm in paranoia country, Robbie, and it isn't Time's wingèd chariot I hear at my back.'

'I know a place,' McGregor said.

McGregor took him to a watering hole in Akasaka. It was called The Glasgow. Inside, the ceiling and walls were covered in dark oak panelling. Glass cases all around contained a collection of rare Scotch whiskies. A barman polished glasses industriously behind a gleaming oak bar. There was an impressive array of bottles and racks of magazines and daily newspapers. The studied effect was that of a discreet private club. Muzak played quietly.

On one wall there was a map of Scotland surrounded by the tartans of the various clans. A poster showing a steam train bore the legend, *As the train leaves for Glasgow, I drink a toast to myself.*

'You can see why I come here,' McGregor said with a grin. 'Glasgow was never like this.'

'They missed a chance,' Ransome said. 'The muzak isn't bagpipes.'

'Another reason I like coming here.' McGregor laughed loudly.

They sat at a table for two in the corner of the bar, well

away from the other patrons. Small groups of young businessmen dressed in identical suits sat in over-stuffed leather chairs and divans, chatting over drinks or leafing through magazines. They paid no attention to the foreigners. Ransome ordered a coffee from the waitress; McGregor, a whisky.

McGregor said, 'I did some digging in the archives for you. There ain't no such animals as Section 731 or General Ishii. Someone appears to have wiped the slate clean.'

Ransome said, 'It doesn't surprise me, but thanks anyway.'

'So what is it you want to ask me now?'

'A new line of inquiry. If it won't jeopardise Suroko in any way, I wondered if you'd help me dig out some biographical stuff?'

McGregor grinned. 'I've always thought you a tenacious bugger, Ransome, but are you getting any closer to pay dirt?'

'Maybe. But what about Suroko?'

McGregor's expression closed. 'I'll be very discreet.'

'It could be dangerous.'

McGregor looked at him. 'When I was in Nam, Ransome, I made a point of staying as far away from you as I could, which is how I survived. But I was smarter then. Tell me what you need to know.'

* * *

They had the ground floor of the lovely house to themselves. The children were asleep upstairs, the housekeeper with them. It was warm. Reiko's own recording of the Bruch cello concerto was playing in the background. They drank French champagne and lay back on the divan wrapped in each other's arms, enjoying the moment.

'How lovely,' she had said. 'Yes, he's still away. Come over. Have you eaten? Shall I send the car?' sounding as excited as a schoolgirl.

He had felt wretched. Tell her! Tell her why you are going to her house. He had said nothing.

He had caught a taxi. The front gate had been open, the light on the porch lit. Reiko had greeted him wearing a beautiful purple kimono with a rose pink *obe*. The colour matched the roses he had brought her. She had been thrilled by them. As they had embraced just inside the door, he had become aware she wore nothing under the kimono. The *obe* had fallen away. They had made love on the floor in front of the Portuguese screen.

They had eaten together, Reiko playfully parodying her perfect hostess role as though she were a geisha, serving him an elaborate Japanese meal boxed 'in the Kyoto style'. They had drunk sake and wine. He had been taken upstairs to see the sleeping children. They had shifted the photographs from the top of the grand piano and she had played for him. Ransome had never heard her play the piano before. He had stood by the end of the keyboard watching her as she concentrated on the piece. It was then that Ransome's feeling of duplicity had begun to reassert itself: he was here for another purpose.

'You seem troubled,' she said, her eyes soft with concern.

He shrugged it off. 'What's happening with your father?' changing the subject.

Her face darkened. 'I spoke to him this morning. They are still bringing the bodies out, and they haven't yet worked out what caused the explosion. The media are harrying him, saying terrible things about him. A journalist wrote an article two days ago blaming his company for "inadequate safety standards".' She sounded disgusted. 'One thing about my father, he has always prided himself on the standards of his company. He is very depressed.'

Ransome was impressed by her loyalty to her father with whom she seemed only to quarrel.

'The one thing I want to do right now is leave Japan. But I can't go now. My father needs me here. Not that I can do anything much for him. I offered to go down south to look after him, but he doesn't want that. So, in a couple of days, I'm going to take the kids skiing. I promised them I would and I have the chance to use a ski lodge up at Matsumoto. The kids love the idea, they've never skied. Do you mind? It's only for a few days.'

Ransome felt relieved. He needed to concentrate on finishing the project. 'No, I don't mind. If I wrap things up on the documentary, I might even join you.'

Later they went, very marriedly, to bed. She said, in answer to his question, 'The staff have the night off except for Akiko, who's deeply shocked but accepting. She was like a second mother to me when I was growing up. She doesn't approve, but she understands.' A wry look, 'All the same, perhaps you should be gone by the time the children wake up.' She had laid out a tooth-brush for him.

They climbed into her bed but lay in silence for a time.

Reiko said, 'Something's troubling you. It's Kaizei, isn't it?'

What had she heard? He questioned her with a look.

Hesitating, Reiko said, 'You were right the other day. I did know something. Before he left, my father told me that the police are after Kaizei.'

'Where did he learn that?'

'My uncle told him. He hears about such things.'

'Did he also tell your father why the police want Kaizei?'

'For two murders,' she said, looking unhappy, not having wanted to talk about this. 'That's what worried me.'

'And your father told you that I was implicated.'

She nodded unhappily.

'It's true, they are after him,' Ransome said, 'but he didn't kill anyone. There are people who want him out of the way. The trouble is he has no way of proving he's innocent.'

'And you?'

'I'm not a suspect.'

She sagged with relief. 'So what's going to happen?'

Ransome said, 'We'll sort it out,' trying to sound confident. 'The people who did the killings are looking for Kaizei.'

'Aren't they also after you?' she said, searching his face.

He shrugged. 'They're not so likely to touch me, a foreigner. There are political implications in knocking off *gaijin*,' smiling at her, 'I hope.'

Reiko caught both his hands in hers. 'Jack, please be careful. Please! Whatever it is you're involved in, I don't want anything to happen to you. I need you.'

He stared at her, kneeling beside him, naked. He tried to imprint her image on his mind, wanting to take from this night something perfect. Maybe that way they could survive the treachery he planned. The sight of her rounded, ripe body, matured by two births, pleased him as never before. How ironic. It had never been so good.

They slept.

As dawn broke, he kissed her finally and insisted that she stay in bed. Sleepily, she used the bedside phone to order a cab for him. It would pick him up at the front gate. She promised to call him from the Shiga Heights ski resort when she arrived. She watched him as he dressed, insisted on one final embrace.

He walked downstairs through the silent house. On the way through the lounge room, feeling wretched with guilt, he took the thing he had come to borrow.

* * *

Ransome left Tokyo like a man running from some terrible truth. The connection he had made filled him with excitement but also with apprehension. If his hunch proved to be true, the personal implications were appalling.

The *shinkansen* speared its way towards Nagoya through an eerily beautiful, snow-painted landscape. Factories and ugly suburbs were now transformed into something pristine, unspooling past the windows like a high-speed black-and-white film. The train sounds were hushed. The smooth speed gave the impression that the train was running always downhill.

He thought of Kaizei in the north someplace making contact with his source, Aoyama. It could be days before he would surface. For this reason Ransome had decided to act on his own, without waiting for his friend to show.

Around him commuters were packed. Opposite, a young salaryman studied a printout and made notes. From time to time girl attendants came through the carriage with trolleys of food and drinks. Using sign language he managed to buy a coffee and some potato chips. The barrier of language made him feel vulnerable and inadequate to the task he had set himself. Beside him, two little girls with dolls' faces watched Ransome and giggled behind their hands.

Little girls. He remembered those he had seen dying that day in the North Vietnam primary school. 'Voyeur!' the teacher had screamed at him as he had filmed the carnage. 'What a terrific sequence,' people said now. *Voyeur*. Maybe she was right. Maybe that's all he was.

Now the train was slicing through open country. There were market gardens studded with tomato stakes like beds of nails; lumber yards; tired little villages with sagging rush fences and orchards of leafless trees; an anonymous little town with a Zero fighter on a pedestal in the square, a little graveyard at the edge of the town and, beside it, a ten-high stack of car bodies.

For a time, the track ran parallel to the sea, following

the contours of the hills running down to the white-topped waters of Ise Bay.

Ransome felt as though he and Kaizei were struggling in a rising tide of corruption. Why am I doing this? he asked himself. Am I addicted to violence, a junkie unable to operate without my daily fix? Is there something wrong with me that I must always be close to the bloodshed?

The train turned inland once more, through miles of frozen rice paddies packed together like computer chips. Over and over to the rhythm of the train, Ransome thought, I should have told her . . . I should have told her . . .

The *shinkansen* rushed past a crossing. Blinking red warning lights and lowered boom gates held back a couple of farm lorries and some people on bicycles. What do they do with their lives, he wondered, the drivers of these trucks? In their collective unconscious did they know about the camp at Harbin? And if they did, would they care?

The train ducked under a series of tunnels—one, two, three—then burst out of the darkness into the light once more. A city; factories—grey, prison-block-like buildings. The train slowed. Nagoya.

Ransome got out, hurriedly, nervous now at the difficulties that lay ahead. The bright red lights on the smooth snout of the *shinkansen* slid obliquely away around the curve.

Ransome had brought his international driving licence and English language handbook with him. He knew only that the man he was after lived close to a village near a town called Kasugai about fifteen kilometres inland from Nagoya. At Nipon Rent-a-Car he hired a Toyota with chains on the tyres. With the help of the clerk, who spoke rudimentary English, he worked out the route. It still took him an hour and several frustrating stops at service stations to get out of Nagoya on the right road. He drove on through the white countryside feeling like a blind man. The falls of snow had been light. The granite bones of the mountains showed through their white skin of snow.

He found Kasugai, an ugly little town full of rubbish-filled waste grounds and liquor shops, no more than a faceless stop on the way to somewhere more important. He stopped there to ask directions. The red and gold flashing neon sign above the Star Hall *pachino* parlour dominated the main street. The sound of the *pachino* balls, endlessly rolling ball-bearings, sounded like static in the chill air. There was a coffee shop called, charmingly, The Maison Dank. The girl was friendly, but had no English. The name Sakurai meant nothing to her.

Two hours later he had not found his destination. He had driven back and forth along all the roads leading out of the town looking for familiar landmarks, but had failed to find Sakurai's farm. He had almost decided to give up when, on a road to the west of the town, he came to the perfume factory he remembered seeing. Around a curve and there, above him, was the giant ferroconcrete statue of the Buddha. This was the valley!

Ten minutes later he spotted Sakurai's house caught in a fold of mist, the same pile of sawn timber covered by the same red canvas sheet, the same pink rug hanging from an upstairs window of the neighbour's house across the valley.

As he drove up to the house, he passed an old woman on a bicycle bearing aloft an open umbrella that acted like a sail. She smiled a toothless smile and passed on, heading for the road. A cleaning lady, perhaps? A visiting lover for an old man?

But Sakurai was not home. Ransome decided to wait it out. He sat in the heated car with the engine running against the biting north wind. Twenty minutes passed.

A tractor appeared driving along the road from the direction of the town. It turned into the driveway. Ransome got out of the car. The tractor was dragging a trailer piled high with bales of hay. Sakurai was driving. He drove straight into the garage. Ransome followed him in.

'*Konnichi-wa,*' Ransome said.

The old man was already out of the enclosed cabin unloading some groceries. He looked at Ransome gravely. '*Konnichi-wa,*' he said. He peeled off his thick gloves, but did not offer to shake hands. He reached into the tractor cabin and took another box of supplies. Ransome offered to carry it. The old man met his eye for a moment then allowed him to take the package. Without a word he set off towards the house. Ransome followed.

As soon as he had put his box down in the kitchen, Ransome reached into his inside pocket for the two photographs Kaizei had taken. He handed them to the old man. He had learned the right word: '*Sumimasen,*' he said.

Sakurai glanced at them and put them, face down, on the kitchen table. '*Domo arrigato,*' he said, with a small smile, acknowledging the apology. He filled a kettle, laid out two teacups and went upstairs.

Ransome looked around the house. Every top surface was crammed with pots of seedlings. After a few minutes he heard a toilet flush upstairs.

Sakurai reappeared, having exchanged his coat for a thick woollen sweater. He made tea for them both and indicated that Ransome should sit by the kitchen table. They drank their tea in silence.

Ransome picked up the photographs and laid them before Sakurai. He pointed to the faces in turn, first the Lieutenant General. 'Ishii,' he said.

Sakurai nodded.

Ransome pointed to Yonoi and spoke the name.

'Yonoi,' Sakurai confirmed, without hesitation.

Ransome pointed to each of the officers in the group in turn.

Sakurai identified each one. 'Kanaka, Osatko, Hamada, Obe, Watanabe.' He paused for a long time as Ransome's finger pointed to the two unidentified officers. He tapped impatiently at the photograph, shaking his head and screwing up his face as he tried to force the names into the front of his mind.

Ransome remained silent. He was determined to give Sakurai every chance to say the names unprompted.

Suddenly Sakurai grinned like a lottery winner. 'Ah!' Excitedly he pointed to the image of one of the officers. 'Kitano! Kitano Masaji!' he said.

Ransome took out his notebook and wrote the name down. It would be interesting to see whatever had become of this man. McGregor might be able to find out. He repeated the name to Sakurai. The old man nodded.

Running his fingertip across the faces, Ransome said, 'Ishii ... Yonoi ... Obe ... Kanaka ... Osatko ... Hamada ... Watanabe ... Kitano ...' He stabbed a finger at the dark-haired man to Ishii's left.

Sakurai stared at the face for a long time, tapping his forehead with his knuckles as though trying to knock the name loose. At length he shook his head in frustration. The name simply would not come into the old man's mind.

He sat back and sipped his tea, staring out of the window towards the looming mountains. As Ransome watched, Sakurai's arms crept around his chest as though they had a will of their own. He began to hug himself close as though he were freezing cold, his eyes wide, his whole body shaking and shivering. He stopped and looked at Ransome. Once more he clutched his chest and mimed a shivering man.

For a moment, the mime puzzled Ransome. Was the man saying the weather was cold?

Sakurai pointed to the man in the photograph, then repeated the mime.

Ransome made the connection. The unidentified officer had been in charge of the freezing experiments. A surge of excitement took hold of him. If only Sakurai could remember the name.

He nodded to show that he understood. The old man stood up shaking his head wearily, closing his eyes, showing his disgust at the memory that had been evoked.

Ransome took another photograph from his pocket. He laid it down beside the group shots. The old man stared at it uncomprehendingly, then looked at Ransome. Ransome gestured towards the photographs, moving his hand between the two, inviting Sakurai to reconsider them once more. For a long time, Sakurai stared. Suddenly, he made the connection. He turned and nodded emphatically to Ransome. He pointed to one man in each of the two group shots. It was the same man: a thickset body; a bony face topped by a distinctive crop of hair, side parted; eyebrows that flared up towards the hairline.

Ransome pointed to the commanding officer. 'Ishii,' he said, then pointed to the unidentified man hoping now to jog the name from the recesses of Sakurai's memory. But Sakurai shrugged half-irritably. It was clear he was not going to remember the name.

Ransome rose, hiding his frustration, bowed slightly and said, '*Domo arrigato gozaimasu.*'

Sakurai stood in the sleety rain watching him go. Ransome turned the ignition then reached out of the window and shook the old man's hand. Sakurai's grip was firm. Ransome sensed in the old man an approval of his quest. He engaged the clutch and drove slowly down the drive.

Behind him, there came a loud shout. In the rear-vision mirror he could see the old man running after him waving his arms. Ransome slammed on the brakes and reversed back up the drive. He wound down the window when he came opposite Sakurai.

'*Hai! Hai,*' Sakurai said, very excited now. He held up his hand to hold Ransome in place and ran back to his house.

Ransome watched him go, puzzled. Had he left something behind? A minute later, the old man trotted back to the door of the car. '*Hai,*' he said, his chest heaving. He collected himself, then once more did his grotesque mime of the shivering man. He pushed the group photograph inside the car and pointed at the unidentified officer. Sakurai spoke a name, very clearly, then repeated it.

Ransome's feelings were mixed as he contemplated the implications of the terrible connection he had just established. It was the name Ransome had guessed he might hear.

* * *

The train rushed through the twilight towards Tokyo. The man sitting next to him on the *shinkansen* was reading a comic filled with exaggerated images of ecstatic blonde *gaijin* women being brutally possessed by Japanese men. None of the characters seemed to have genitals. A fat young man across the aisle gobbled fish and rice from a wooden box.

Outside, the landscape looked ghastly. The snow had been turned to slush by a drizzling rain. Yellow industrial lights marked the perimeters of late-working factories. Shining bitumen reflected the vivid, candy-coloured neon signs of garages and factories and department stores still at work. It was as though the whole country was a tireless beast that never slept.

The train stopped briefly at an industrial city somewhere on the Kanto Plain. On the opposite platform

Ransome could see another train, bright as day in the winter's gloom. Faces of city workers stared out into the night. The image made Ransome think of a cattle truck. The *shinkansen* surged out of the station leaving them caught in a time warp.

Chapter 38

Worried that he hadn't heard from Kaizei, he took the risk of going into the Foreign Correspondents' Club in case there was something there. The desk advised him that the only message was from a Mr Ocha.

Ocha? Who the hell was Ocha? He dialled the number.

'*Mushi mushi.*'

'Mr Ocha?'

'Yes.'

'Ransome.'

'*Hai!* Moment, please. Mr Takanichi is calling.' Ah yes, Ocha—Shoji's smooth personal assistant.

Shoji came on the line. 'Mr Ransome,' the voice was cool. 'Do you progress with your investigation?'

What tone to strike: pending success? Failure? Ransome said, 'It's hard to ever prove anything, Mr Takanichi. Verification is always the tricky part.'

'My Mr Ocha has been working very hard on this serious question you raised. I cannot say that I am unhappy with what he has found. From a most thorough search of military archives he has been able to establish that these stories you have heard are not what they seem.'

Fascinating. Ransome wondered how the news would be couched.

Shoji said, 'For your benefit I am arranging to have translated some copies of documents which show that there *was* a military hospital in Harbin, and that the commanding officer *was* a General Ishii. His major work was in water purification and disease prevention, vital work to do with the health of troops. That part is true. But you will be disappointed I suspect, Mr Ransome, that there is no evidence we have been able to find of any medical experimentation on prisoners of war. None.'

'Is it possible there was a cover-up?' Ransome said.

Shoji laughed. 'The sceptical journalist! Yes of course that is always possible. But I have strong reason to believe that is not the case here. With my influence, I am sometimes able to open doors that lead to even the most heavily classified archival material. I'm sure that if anything illegal had taken place at Harbin, Mr Ocha would have found traces of it. He had free access to much material not usually available and is extremely diligent. I should say, Mr Ransome, without fear of contradiction, that nothing went on at Harbin that was not normal military practice.'

Ransome said nothing.

Shoji said, 'I suspect the stories you have been hearing are based on rumour and exaggerations. However, you can judge for yourself. I will arrange for you to receive copies of this material for your own examination. I am convinced that when you see this documentation it will put an end to the matter.'

Seeing how an official cover-up was handled would make interesting reading. Ransome said, 'Thank you for going to all the trouble, Mr Takanichi. I'm extremely grateful for your help.'

'I hope you will find better things to write about us, Mr Ransome.' The tone was chilly.

'There is much about your country,' Ransome said, 'that I greatly admire.'

'I am pleased to hear that, Mr Ransome. If I can be of any further help, please let me know.' Shoji hung up.

Ransome stared at the handpiece. 'Wow,' he said.

On the off chance that McGregor might be someplace in the club, he had him paged, but he wasn't in. Ransome went to the library to catch up with the news.

On the front page of the English-language *Asahi Evening News*, a familiar face caught his eye. Under a heading 'Gangland Slaying' there was a photograph of a funeral procession. In the centre of the front rank of sober-suited mourners was an angry-looking little man with a great crop of white hair and a primal slash of eyebrow—unmistakably Frogface.

Flanking him were the two big men who had been present when Ransome had been given his bloody demonstration of the penalties for small errors. The gaunt-faced Mirrorglasses was wearing a white raincoat, Frogface the Younger a dark suit and tie like all the other mourners. The caption did not identify the mourners.

Ransome read the text quickly. It would be interesting to know who Frogface really was.

More than 1000 gangland identities attended the funeral of Yamamoto Masahisa, second-in-command of the Ihari-gumi syndicate, gunned down three days ago in a luxury apartment building in Suita, Osaka Prefecture.

Four hundred police patrolled the area surrounding the mansion of the syndicate leader, Ihari Kinichi, where the funeral was held. No incidents were reported.

The murder—one of several that have occurred in the past week—is the culmination of a gang power struggle which has been going on for several months. It has now flared into open warfare. 'We fear the Ihari-gumi will not leave the killing unavenged,' said Chief Kamoda Osamu. 'The coming clashes will probably be extremely vicious.'
(more on page 8)

Ransome turned to the background article and read it carefully. It told him only that the Ihari-gumi was a breakaway group that had split from the bigger Yamaguchi-gumi *yakuza* syndicate and was seeking greater control of the unions involved in the meat trades.

He took the newspaper to the library desk and was shown the copying facility in an anteroom. He made a copy of the photograph and the article. Kaizei might have some idea how it all fitted together.

On the way out, he checked at the reception desk, but there was still no sign of McGregor. The friendly man on the desk, who had begun to recognise him, said, 'There's some mail for you Mr Ransome.'

A manilla envelope with a Washington postmark. He went into the press room and, in the privacy of one of the booths, opened the envelope. There were a few pages of photocopied documents and a covering letter. The date was January 24th.

Dear Jack Ransome,

Classified, of course, and I'd be obliged if you would protect this source.

See you stateside sometime.

Best of luck,

J.

There were four documents.

The first showed a simple technical sketch design of a ceramic bomb. At the bottom left-hand corner of the document there was a box of specifications headed 'Ha bomb experimental fragmentation bomb for anthrax'. The sketch was dated 5th January 1946. It was marked 'Drawn from sketch submitted by Lt Genl Shiro Ishii'. The heading on the single sheet of paper was that of 'E' Division, Fort Detrick, Frederick, Maryland. The bomb itself was detailed with fuses and casing sizes. A cross-hatched section was marked 'Bacterial fluid'.

The second of the documents was a letter. The stationery was that of the 'Supreme Commander of the Allied Powers, Military Intelligence Section, General Staff'. It was a recommendation that a Japanese biological warfare expert held by the Americans and interrogated for information classified as 'Top Secret' information now held by the US Chemical Corps—was not under any circumstances to be given over to the Russians, who were claiming the man was a war criminal. It was signed with the initials CAW and dated March 1947. The words 'Top Secret' were stamped on the top of the letter. A stamp on the bottom left-hand corner read, 'Restricted, confidential, secret and classified'.

A third document was headed 'War Department, Classified Message Centre, Incoming Classified Message'. It carried a May 6th, 1947 date. Ransome ran his eye over the document. He picked up the words '. . . reluctant statements by Ishii indicate he has superiors (possibly General Staff) who authorised the program . . . Ishii states that if he is guaranteed immunity from war crimes in documentary form for himself, superiors and subordinates, he can describe the program in detail . . . Ishii claims to have extensive theoretical high-level knowledge including strategic and tactical use of biological warfare on defense and offense . . . Ishii confirms authenticity (a) Human experiments (b) Field trials BW against Chinese.'

There was a note appended to the letter: 'Possible that Japanese General Staff, even Emperor, knew and authorised the program.'

The Emperor? Ransome gave a little whistle, remembering Kaizei's prediction: 'It will go all the way to the top.'

Lloyd Brucchi hadn't been wrong about Julia Sumner. This material was dynamite. Here was proof that the story they had been uncovering was true. Ransome felt a profound sense of satisfaction and not a little relief.

The last document was a report from a Dr Edwin M. McColl, Chief, Basic Sciences, Fort Detrick, Maryland. It was dated December 13th, 1947. It was several pages long. Ransome flicked through it. Towards the end, some phrases caught his eye: '. . . the material obtained is a financial bargain . . . evidence gathered has greatly supplemented and amplified previous aspects of this field. It represents data which has been obtained by Japanese scientists at the expenditure of many millions of dollars and years of work. Information has accrued with respect to human susceptibility to those diseases as indicated by specific infectious doses of bacteria. Such information could not be obtained in our own laboratories because of scruples attached to human experimentation . . .'

Ransome read the sentence again. '. . . because of scruples attached to human experimentation . . .'

'Jesus Christ,' he said out loud.

A journalist busy typing in the next work booth swivelled on his chair and looked at him curiously. 'You okay?' he asked. The voice was English.

'Yeah, thanks,' Ransome said, 'I'm fine.' He smiled at the man. 'Just finding it difficult to deal with something I'm reading, that's all.'

Chapter 39

Uto looked at his watch. 'Do you think he'll come?'

It was already ten minutes after the agreed time.

Ransome nodded. 'Yes,' he said. Had he been wise to trust the policeman? He scanned the crowd for people who might be plain-clothes police, looking for the too-casual lounger, the lingering glance. Uto stood with his hands comfortably in the pockets of his tweed overcoat. 'How do we know we can trust him?' Kaizei had said.

The echoing passageways of Shinjuku underground railway station were chill as a freezing chamber. A few yards from where they stood, half-a-dozen tunnels met at a brightly lit junction lined by ranks of ticket-selling windows, brilliantly designed advertising posters and ticket-vending machines. There were busy kiosks selling newspapers and magazines, drinks and sweets.

Commuters in their thousands poured in and out of the tunnels, sweeping past in a ceaseless stream. They moved like automatons, following the arrows and the signs, making their connections, catching their trains, riding the moving staircases—eyes staring straight ahead.

Somewhere Ransome had read that three million people used Shinjuku Station every day. He could believe that. He stared at the faces, looking for Kaizei, but his eyes were drawn constantly to the derelicts camped in the passageway a few yards away.

A dozen gaunt men with unkempt hair flowing from under filthy headbands sat with their backs to the wall, staring straight ahead as though frozen in a trance. Many of them were young; a few very old, as fragile looking as stick insects. Jammed hard alongside the pale yellow tiled walls was a jumble of cardboard packing cases, the kind used to protect refrigerators and stoves. From them protruded feet and legs and heads swathed in aluminium foil against the cold. Forty or fifty of them lay there within plain sight, under the very feet of the passengers. These were the shelters of the dispossessed.

A whole family, husband, wife and several ragged children wrapped in filthy blankets sat around a portable gas burner, cooking. The commuters swerved around them, looking away, perhaps seeing themselves reflected in the ravaged and hopeless faces.

Uto had been watching them. 'Our hidden poor,' he said.

'Bit of a surprise.' Ransome was shocked. He had seen no sign of such poverty in the city before. He wondered how much more of it was hidden under the glossy surface of Tokyo's success.

'We don't talk about them. We don't write about them. We don't even think about them, or we try not to.' Uto's voice was cynical now. 'A lot of ordinary Japanese pay a high price for our economic miracle. For them, Japan is a miserable, third world country.' The policeman's tone betrayed anger.

At that moment, Ransome spotted Kaizei. He was fifty metres away, walking in the faceless ruck of commuters. Ransome could see his head turning constantly as he checked his rear. He was dressed in a dark blue salaryman's business suit, carrying a briefcase, hair neatly combed.

Twenty metres away he looked directly at Ransome and raised his eyebrows quizzically. Ransome glanced quickly at Uto. He was looking the other way. Ransome nodded 'all clear'.

Kaizei kept on going, limping past them, looking straight ahead. When he was twenty metres further on,

Ransome touched Uto's arm. 'Let's go.' For a second Uto was puzzled, but then he walked beside Ransome with a neutral expression on his face.

Keeping Kaizei in view, Ransome stayed at the exact pace of the crowd. It began to thin out as commuters swung off into other passageways and boarded the escalators that took them down into the rumbling earth. A stream of commuters turned left, and left again, Kaizei with them. Ransome and Uto followed.

They came out into a busy, glass-covered, lower-ground-level plaza that surrounded the foot of a gigantic modern building. They crossed the landscaped space. A pair of external elevators—one of red glass, one of green—scuttled up and down the walls of the building like jewelled insects. Kaizei kept on walking. He disappeared through the crowded main entrance.

The atrium was dominated by a water-operated clockwork timepiece, rising thirty metres in the air, like something out of the set of *Metropolis*. Shops and restaurants were doing brisk lunchtime business.

There was no sign of Kaizei. He would be checking to see that this wasn't a trap.

They walked across the atrium under the steel beams of the great timepiece. Suddenly the mechanism whirred; huge pendulums swung and counter-balanced under a weight of spilling water; cogs meshed, then the quarter hour sounded a single peal like a cathedral bell. Tourists gawped.

Ransome spotted Kaizei watching them from the balcony that looked over the atrium at first-floor level.

They went up the escalator. As they rose, Ransome watched Kaizei anxiously searching the ground floor behind them.

The strain was showing on Kaizei's face. Ransome hugged him and said quietly, 'I'm certain he's come alone.'

'Sure,' said Kaizei, looking at the policeman with a watchful expression.

Ransome said, 'Inspector Uto, Mr Kaizei.'

They bowed briefly to each other, but did not shake hands, nor smile. They looked like boxers meeting at a weigh-in.

Uto said, 'Mr Ransome has been telling me something about your investigation.'

Kaizei nodded. 'What did you want to see me about?'

'I wanted to ask you some questions, but in the last few days something else has come up.' Uto took from his pocket a photograph. 'I thought you ought to know that we have this.'

He handed the photograph to Kaizei, who studied it with a blank expression on his face. He passed it to Ransome.

It was a detail blow-up of Kaizei from a telephoto shot that must have been taken somewhere in South-East Asia. It was several years old. Kaizei's hair had been shoulder length then. The bandanna round the head made him look different, but it was otherwise an excellent likeness. He was looking straight into the lens. Jesus, who had taken this shot all those years ago? So much for Katie's superstitious fetish about never having his picture taken. So much for his comforting theory that no-one in Japan knew what he looked like. He said, 'A nasty surprise.'

Kaizei made an odd unhappy grimace.

Ransome addressed Uto. 'Where did this come from?'

The policeman shook his head. 'No idea. Maybe a press agency library in Europe, or the States. It came to us through Interpol. There is no limit to our resources when something is wanted badly enough,' looking at Kaizei, 'and your picture was wanted very badly indeed.'

'How long have you had this?'

'Two days,' Uto said. 'Long enough for it to be on the

wall of every station house in Tokyo Prefecture.'

'Let's eat,' Kaizei said flatly.

Restaurants were cheek by jowl around the first floor. They chose a corner booth facing the door. They ordered sashimi and drank green tea. For a time they ate in silence, Kaizei bolting his food as if he were starving. Suddenly he said, 'What do you want to know?'

'Anything you can tell me, Mr Kaizei,' Uto said. 'I have too many unsolved deaths.'

'Do you mind if I speak in Japanese, Jack? It'll speed things along.'

Ransome shook his head.

For twenty minutes Kaizei spoke without interruption, sometimes in English but mostly in Japanese. Uto listened without expression.

Ransome, watching these two men, thought how different they were: Kaizei, the radical, the rebel, a man with a world view; Uto, the disciplined product of the conservative Japanese system, and yet, curiously for someone with his job, a nail that maybe had not been hammered all the way in. They seemed comfortable with each other, these two.

When Kaizei finished talking, Uto asked several questions in Japanese. Then, in English for Ransome's benefit, he said, 'You must realise that the whole thing is now out of my hands. Even if it's the police who catch you, I can't guarantee you'll be safe.'

Kaizei looked at him coolly. He picked up the photograph, studied it for a moment, then held it up to the policeman. 'You said this photograph is only in Tokyo Prefecture?'

Uto shook his head. 'Until this morning, yes, but right now thousands of prints are being distributed. By tomorrow your face will be known in every police station, port and terminal. Going out of Tokyo is not going to help. No place will be safe.' Uto dabbed at his mouth with a napkin. 'Don't just leave Tokyo, Mr Kaizei, leave Japan. Now. Today.'

Kaizei stared at the policeman for a time, then bowed his head. '*Domo arrigato.*'

Uto gave the briefest of nods.

'I've promised Inspector Uto that we'll tell him anything else "interesting" that we uncover,' Kaizei said, with a conspiratorial smile.

So he hasn't told him our worst fears, thought Ransome. Shouldn't we tell this policeman everything we suspect, now that we have him here? He said nothing.

Kaizei swallowed the last of his green tea and stood up. 'I'll be in touch, Jack.' He embraced Ransome, bowed to Uto, slung his coat over his arm and walked quickly out of the restaurant.

He was swallowed at once in the crowd of office workers and shoppers. For a moment, Ransome saw him at the top of the escalator as he was borne downwards out of sight.

'Can't you persuade him to get out while he can?'

Ransome shook his head.

Uto picked his teeth with an orange toothpick. 'If he doesn't, he hasn't a chance, you know that?'

Ransome said, 'Thanks for telling him about the photograph. That'll help.'

'Don't count on it making any difference, Mr Ransome,' Uto said. He sounded tired. 'Whoever it is who wants him will find him in the end.'

Chapter 40

'You asked me to do some research.' From his inside pocket McGregor took a single sheet of paper and some newspaper cuttings. He laid them on the table in front of him. He looked at Ransome. 'First tell me how you came to meet Shoji Takanichi.'

'I'm practically related to the guy,' Ransome said. 'He's Reiko's cousin.'

McGregor looked puzzled.

Ransome had never told him her surname. 'Reiko Takanichi. At least she was, until she married her German music professor. Reiko Takanichi Hauser. Her father is Eiji Takanichi. He's an engineer.'

'My God, you are mixing in powerful company,' McGregor said.

'You disapprove?' Ransome said.

McGregor shrugged. 'Shoji Takanichi is very heavy in politics,' a cynical smile. 'He scares the bejesus out of me and a lot of other people besides. Is he in some way connected with your investigation? Is that why you're interested?'

Ransome kept his tone neutral, not wanting to tell McGregor any more than he had to. 'He offered to help. Said he might open some doors for us. I wondered how much clout he had.'

'He's got clout to burn.'

'What did you manage to dig out?'

McGregor tapped his papers with a finger. 'The life and times of Shoji Takanichi,' he said. He glanced at his notes. 'Takanichi Shoji. His father, Junichiro, was a medical doctor, his mother a one-time minor film star, Akiko Hamatsu. He was born 1950, graduated from Tokyo University 1972 as an economist. Studied in the States two years at Stanford. Has been married twice; the first marriage was into a notable family, his present marriage is to an ex-showgirl. There are no children from either marriage. According to my translator's reading of the material, there was a nasty inference one could draw from the reports of his first wife's death by suicide.'

'What inference?'

'That he treated her badly.'

The waitress came and took their order. McGregor waited until she was gone before continuing.

'You'd be surprised how hard it was to find out anything about this character,' McGregor said. 'There was very little on record about him. Presently, as you know, he's a member of the Liberal Democratic Party, a cabinet minister with special responsibilities for economic development of the export food industry.

'Business interests?'

'Never had to work. He took over his father's business when the old man died two years ago. His father made a huge fortune by being heavily into the fish and meat business, as well as foodstuffs of other kinds. The company has coldstores everywhere. Shoji Takanichi seems to be moving more into the entertainment industries. He already has controlling interests in quite a few ski resorts. They say he's a millionaire many times over. However you cut it, he's very very rich.'

'What sort of reputation does he have?' Ransome said.

'Ah, now comes the interesting bit. In all this digging I've been doing, there's been one common response, like a Greek chorus: be it the father or the son, you don't cross a Takanichi with impunity. A guy I know on the

Asahi Evening News who writes financial stuff told me that business rivals who have taken him on have suffered in various ways: strikes, harassment, personal violence, accidents. This guy says that Shoji's connections with criminal elements in the meat industry—although never properly established—are spoken of freely.'

'The *yakuza*?'

McGregor shrugged. 'It's hearsay. It's all very oblique, but it's spoken of in that casual way that suggests Shoji Takanichi's shadier connections are accepted as matter of fact by those who know how the system works. But certainly your girlfriend's cousin is a very powerful man, and it's power he's not frightened to use.'

Ransome said, 'I told you about the guys who abducted me.' He put the copy of the newspaper photograph in front of McGregor. 'There they are.'

McGregor stared at the photograph. 'The Ihari-gumi. The *yakuza* who control the meat industry. Saying goodbye to murdered friends. Jesus, Ransome, you're dangerous to know. These boys are in the heavy team.'

Ransome said, 'You said there's speculation that a special relationship exists between Shoji Takanichi and the syndicates who control the meat business. You didn't hear this gang mentioned, did you?'

McGregor shook his head.

'Thanks for digging up this stuff. You've been busy, Mac.'

'I was lucky to find anything at all. Talk about a low family profile! The father was totally anonymous: never permitted interviews, had no public profile. Son Shoji, of course, is a different matter, being a cabinet minister. And right now he's in the middle of a huge political brawl.' He handed the newspaper cuttings to Ransome.

They were from the *Asahi Evening News* and the *Japan*

Times. One was headed 'Second Takanichi Faction Meeting', the other 'Takanichi Accused of Disloyalty'.

McGregor said, 'Shoji Takanichi has a so-called policy study group. In fact, it's a faction on the extreme right of the Liberal Democratic Party. They had a secret meeting several weeks ago, but it was leaked. A couple of other scheduled meetings were postponed. Maybe the numbers weren't propitious. Anyhow, this second meeting was quite significant. The numbers of Dietmen attending went up by nine. Your girlfriend's cousin is making progress—which is putting the fear of God into the Prime Minister's supporters. Now that his numbers game looks like getting serious, the shit's beginning to hit the fan.'

McGregor finished his whisky. 'Remember that procession we saw, the day you were arrested? Shoji's supporters. And the number of right-wing demonstrations and riots has increased sharply in the last few weeks.'

'Putting pressure on the government in the streets?'

'Looks that way. It's a pretty serious moment right now.'

'What's he after?'

'Shoji Takanichi?' McGregor grinned. 'The big one. Failing that, he wants to usurp the Deputy Prime Minister so that he becomes the logical successor when the Prime Minister goes, which, what with bad health and the bribery scandal, may be sooner than later. So, my friend, you may soon be related by marriage to the most powerful man in Japan. How do you feel about being related to Son of Ice Man?'

Ransome stared at him. 'Why do you call him that?'

McGregor said, 'Some journalist tagged Shoji's father, "The Ice Man"—something to do with old Junichiro being cold-blooded and ruthless in business.'

Ransome considered McGregor soberly. 'There's

another, rather grimmer reason why he was called that,'
he said.

McGregor's eyes brightened, 'You going to tell me
what the fuck this is all about?'

Ransome gave it to him, all of it, chapter and verse.

* * *

He rang from the Okura, his latest hotel. Reiko picked up
on the first tone. 'There's something I have to tell you,'
he said.

'Tell me what it is.' She sounded tense.

'No, I must see you,' he said.

He waited for her in the crowded foyer, rehearsing the
words with which he might tell her what he had
discovered.

She came in through the sliding doors, stylish in a
camel-coloured coat, her hair tied in a bright scarf.

Guilt spoiled his pleasure at seeing her. The act of
taking the photograph from her father's house the last
time they were together suddenly seemed doubly under-
hand. He should have told her of his suspicions and
asked her permission.

Her eyes were anxious, and she clung to his arm,
urgently. In the lift they kissed passionately all the way
to his floor.

They made love with something akin to desperation.
Afterwards, she talked about her father with the nervous
air of someone trying to distract. He stalled too, wanting
to avoid the issue. He knew he should have interrupted
her flow, thinking: tell her now, but the effects of his
revelation were likely to be terrible. He let her talk on.
What had happened between them was so good, and
now it was in terrible jeopardy.

She told him that her father was still in the south-west,
wrestling with his tunnelling problem. The accident at
his project had developed into a full-scale disaster. The
death toll was rising by the day. Several of the injured

had since succumbed. 'It's awful for him. He's terribly depressed. He has never had a fatal accident at any of his projects.'

'How's he handling the inquiry?'

'Badly,' Reiko said. 'Have you seen the newspaper reports?'

'Yes,' he said. He had seen the coverage on the front page of the *Asahi Shimbun* he had bought in the hotel foyer while he waited for her. More dead workers had been brought to the surface. The official inquiry into the disaster had begun. Takanichi was attending daily. So far, the evidence was going very badly for him and his company. The phrase 'criminal negligence of safety standards' had featured in the article; not sabotage.

'When is he coming back?'

'I don't know. Not before it's all over. Some of the trapped men are still alive. He's there supervising the rescue operation.'

She became silent, her eyes searching his face. She seemed about to say something more.

He could put it off no longer.

He kissed her gently and said, 'You know I care for you, don't you?'

'Yes,' Reiko said, 'I know that.'

'Whatever happens, keep that in your mind, won't you? I need you to believe that.'

Reiko was looking at him, trying to read him. 'Something is wrong, isn't it?'

He nodded.

She paused for a time, then asked, 'Is it bad?'

'I'm afraid it is,' he said, wondering if they could survive it. 'It's something that may embarrass your father—and you.'

'In what way "embarrass"?'

'The story I'm covering with Kaizei. I've suddenly discovered that your uncle was involved in it.'

She edged away from him, her eyes darkening. 'How was he involved?'

Tell her.

He told her what he had discovered about her uncle's past.

She listened in silence. When he was through her eyes played over his face.

'Have you known about it long?' Her face was blank, her voice edging towards cold. Implications of 'Is this the reason you've been interested in me?' were beginning to form, he could sense it.

'I've just found out, believe me,' Ransome said. 'It's all very awkward, a horrible coincidence. There were over two thousand doctors involved. He happened to be one of them. Before the past few days, I didn't know about your family's connection with it.'

'How did you find out?'

He reached into the drawer of the cabinet beside the bed and took out the framed photograph. He handed it to her. 'I recognised him in a group photograph I was shown by an ex-member.'

She stared at the photograph.

'I borrowed this to double-check.'

'From my father's house?'

He nodded, feeling numb.

'You shouldn't have taken it without telling me,' she said.

'I know. I'm sorry.'

She got out of bed as though being there in his room was an awkward case of mistaken identity. She stood by the window looking out.

Ransome said, 'I had hoped it would prove to be untrue.' He watched her standing there, feeling her slipping out of his life. But he couldn't blame her. It was family. Blood is thicker and all that.

She turned to look at him. Her eyes were filled with

disgust. 'But it is true,' she said, speaking in a whisper. 'My uncle *was* involved.'

Ransome was shaken. She knew! Was that why she had been so keen that he should quit? He said, 'How long have you known?'

'I began to think there was something going on the night you came to show your film. Shoji set up that meeting. He asked my father—who didn't want anything to do with you—to arrange it so that he could meet you. They hinted at some family problem, something in the past. They didn't go into details. But the other day I confronted my father about it.'

Ransome said nothing.

'Look, my father and my uncle never got on. Never. And he has no time for Shoji. But Shoji's still family.' She shook her head, dazed by it all. 'The night you came— that was the first time my cousin has been in our house for as long as I can remember. They asked me to do what I could to stop you going on with your investigation. Shoji said that it would be bad for him politically if it were known his father had been involved in some past scandal. My father has known about it for a long time. For him it's about family honour,' she said, the contempt spilling out.

How much does she know? Ransome wondered.

'I didn't want you to be in danger. Shoji said there were people involved—other people, not him—prepared to do anything to stop the secret coming out. He thought it best if you left Japan. I took you to him that day because I wanted him to guarantee your safety.'

She was silent for awhile, looking away from him, alienated by what they had told each other.

'I don't care about my cousin or the reputation of my uncle, who was a hateful man, but when this comes out my father is bound to be particularly badly affected. He has enough problems on his hands at the moment. Is it absolutely necessary that you go on with your investigation, right now?'

'Even if I gave up, Kaizei would go ahead.' At that moment Ransome would have walked away from it all if he could.

She said, 'Jack, it's history. It all happened a long time ago. What gain is there in revealing it all these years later?'

'Reiko, did Shoji tell you that people are being killed *now* because of it,' he said.

She stared at him, aghast. 'Killed? Now?'

He believed her: she did not know. So he told her the things he had been holding back, about the killings. He stopped short there, not speaking about the new developments he and Kaizei had uncovered.

When he was done she sat stunned and silent, then, in a low voice, she said, 'Why haven't you told me this before?'

'It was nothing to do with us—or so I thought.'

She laughed ruefully. 'It is now. Shoji—is he involved?'

Ransome shrugged. 'I don't know,' he said, wanting to drive as few wedges as possible.

She seemed to make up her mind suddenly. 'They didn't tell me about this. I need to talk to my father.'

As she finished dressing he said, 'Reiko, keep in mind what I said about the way I feel.'

She gave a little nod, then began to weep. 'Why did this have to happen?'

He crossed the room and held her in his arms.

'It was all going so well for us,' she said.

Chapter 41

He didn't want to meet Cord, but when McGregor had passed on the American's request for a meeting on the neutral ground of the Foreign Correspondents' Club, curiosity had won.

Cord was in the side bar watching a baseball game. The sound was at threshold level. He was the only customer. 'You wanted to see me,' Ransome said.

'Watch this guy,' Cord said, not looking round.

A black man was at bat. The pitcher wound up and let fly. The batter uncoiled sweetly. The ball flew high up into the packed stand.

'The bastard's got an eye like DiMaggio,' he said, shaking his head in wonder. 'Couldn't get a game in the States.' He turned around. 'Drink?'

Ransome shook his head. 'No, thanks.' He wasn't planning on letting his guard down.

Cord gave a little grimace. 'How goes your little project?' He raised his whisky glass in a sarcastic toast.

Ransome had a feeling that Cord had stopped playing games. 'Why? Are you thinking of making me a bigger offer this time?'

'Let's not beat around the bush, Ransome,' Cord said. 'There won't be another offer.' The eyes were suddenly cold. 'Me—I'd buy a plane ticket.'

'How so?'

'If you read my lips you'll see that I'm reciting a little signal,' exaggerating his lip movements. 'You are heading into serious danger.'

'You're threatening me?'

Cord grinned, a bored expression on his face. 'Call it what you like. Warning you, threatening you, I really don't give a flying fuck what label you hang on it. If you want my best advice—just leave it alone. As you already know, they play rough in this country. And with you standing on too many toes, believe me, they'll play rougher yet.'

'Is that what you came to tell me?' Ransome said, feeling the anger rise. He swung off the bar stool and stood facing Cord. 'You're a bit late, pal. All the interviews—tapes, transcripts, the lot—are already out of Japan in safe hands. Our story's going to run, regardless.'

'That's a real shame,' Cord said, with something like regret. 'But it doesn't make any difference to you. Let me be specific. You'd be advised to get your ass out of Japan with all deliberate speed, and here's for why: there's a contract out on you and your Japanese journalist friend.'

Ransome wondered if Cord held the contract. 'Doctor Cord,' allowing his disdain for the title to show, 'your kind make me puke. We're talking about what might be the greatest scientific obscenity in history and you think you can keep the lid on it by threatening me?'

'Oh, come on!' there was a contemptuous expression on Cord's face, 'don't give me that bleeding hearts crap. So these guys make the Nazi experimental program look like a mercy mission, so what? It was fucking wartime. Who sticks to boy scout rules then? The scientific fallout is what counts. It was vital defence knowledge. We'd never have gotten such information without spending millions—even then it would have taken years. What do you expect us to do, throw it back like a fish too small to keep? Don't be goddamn naive!'

Ransome looked at Cord. He thought, There really are two kinds of people. 'What a crapulous argument! Our government lets three thousand war criminals go scot free in return for some putrid scientific research. You think there's a justification for that?'

Cord shrugged. 'It's history. So what, our chosen boys get into power here? That's just politics. Geopolitics if you like.'

'Screw your geopolitics,' Ransome said. 'I'm talking about what's going on now.'

Cord said, 'Smart Japanese don't like left-wing politics any more than we do.' He grinned. 'We don't want sensible politicians with ideologically sound views being embarrassed by ancient family mistakes.'

Disgust welled over. 'Christ!' Ransome said, 'is there no depravity you people won't be part of? How much money are you pouring into the present research?'

Cord stared at him, a shadow of puzzlement flickering on his face. 'What the hell are you talking about? Present research? What present research?'

He doesn't know, Ransome thought. He doesn't bloody know! Cord and he had been talking at cross purposes. The people behind Cord had been protecting the Japanese to keep hidden their secret wartime deal and to save some right-wing Japanese politicians from embarrassment. Was it possible the people involved in the new research had told Cord nothing?

Cord caught him by the lapels. 'What fucking research?' His voice had risen an octave. There was alarm on his face. Here was a man who had been left out of it.

Ransome slapped off Cord's grip and backed away a yard, looking into the man's astonished eyes.

'Sounds like you guys've been screwed,' Ransome laughed. 'You really don't know that some of the people you've been protecting for the past forty-odd years have been going on with the same ugly work? They didn't tell you?'

'What kind of research?' Cord sagged as though someone had kicked away his props.

Ransome found himself almost sorry for the man. 'You'd better ask them—just in case their targets aren't your targets.'

Chapter 42

In spite of the rigid barrier nursing techniques that had been applied, two doctors and four nursing sisters at the quarantine hospital Funabashi had died, all within the past week. A third doctor was in intensive care. His prognosis was grim. In rapid succession his various immune processes were breaking down. His suffering was terrible.

All the victims had been directly concerned with nursing the man in the blue Datsun.

A series of emergency meetings of the National Medical Council Epidemiology Committee was called. Drastic action was decided upon. In close liaison with the Prime Minister's Department, the Minister of Health approved their emergency plan. Total secrecy was insisted upon. This was based on the advice of the Prime Minister's Special Intelligence Unit, as always, principally concerned with divining the possible political fallout. In this time of crisis the public's possible reaction to news of a biological epidemic could not be accurately gauged.

Within twenty-four hours, in a massive secret operation, all known contacts of the afflicted Funabashi staff—over two hundred people—were rounded up and taken to the island. There they were placed under strict quarantine and round-the-clock observation.

Chapter 43

The disembodied voice on the telephone had become flesh.

Julia Sumner said, 'Did you get the documents I sent?' She was enjoying surprising him.

Svelte was a word Ransome had never been able to use during his brief and disastrous stint as an advertising copywriter. He would have used it to describe Julia. She was tall: six feet, plus heels. She was wearing a stylishly cut dark blue-grey woollen suit with a cream silk shirt. She wore a necklace and pendant earrings of a complementary blue. There were two gold rings on her right hand, one set with a prominent emerald. There was an expensive-looking gold watch at her wrist. Svelte was exactly right. She gave the impression of someone seeing the world with a sense of ironic amusement.

Her confident eyes were very blue, something he hadn't seen much of lately in this country of brown eyes; even features, a narrow face, a straight nose, short ash-blonde hair that shone the way hair shines in the shampoo ads. The lean, athletic body said mid-twenties, but he judged her to be in her late thirties. Pale shadows under her eyes suggested she might be a touch over-stressed.

Her phone message, left at the desk of the Foreign Correspondents' Club, had brought him here to the United States Embassy at Kasumigaseki. Her name at the front entrance had gained him immediate entry. She had been waiting for him when he arrived, escorted by a Marine guard; a firm handshake, the flesh of her hand smooth as a child's. Now they sat opposite each other across a low steel and glass table in a small sitting room on the second floor.

'Yes, they were very helpful indeed,' Ransome said, thinking, What is she doing here? 'They confirmed all the facts we are uncovering here in Japan. I was planning to call you to say so.'

Brucchi had said they had met in Washington and that Julia remembered him. Odd—he had no recollection of her at all. Admittedly, Washington had been a boozy, good-times blur, but you could hardly forget Julia Sumner. Maybe she had had her powerful personality focussed on someone else at the time. Right now he was aware of its searchlight force as she considered him frankly. He said, 'So by turning up in the flesh, so to speak, you've saved me a call.'

'And I've saved myself getting woken up in the middle of the night.' She smiled, showing a row of expensive, very white teeth.

'Sorry about that,' Ransome said. 'What brings you to Japan?'

'You,' she said. 'Or, more accurately, your investigation. I wondered if you'd be willing to expand on what you have told me already.'

'In what capacity are you here? As a researcher? Journalist? What?'

'Presently, let's call it research,' she said.

'Do researchers normally have the run of the American Embassy?'

Julia Sumner laughed. 'I'm no ordinary researcher.'

'Indeed you are not,' Ransome said.

She acknowledged the compliment with a small inclination of her head.

'Lloyd Brucchi told me you had run into some flak by asking too many awkward questions on my behalf. I hope that won't have serious repercussions for you.'

She shook her head. 'That's not going to be a problem, long term. If things start getting too rough I have a certain "immunity",' smiling with the word. 'You see from time to time I do some confidential work for a senator friend of mine—let's leave his name out of it for the moment—who's running a small senate sub-committee examining . . .' she paused here, looking for the right word, 'loose cannons in the basement of the White House. There are, presently, a couple of them crashing about. "Patriots" they'd call themselves, but their brand of patriotism is causing certain people concern.'

Ransome said, 'It never occurred to me that the basement of the White House would be the last refuge of scoundrels.'

She made a cynical face. 'You must be joking,' she said. 'Recently you mentioned a name that tripped a flare.' Julia paused for effect. 'Cord. My senator was very interested to know about that.'

Ransome stared at her, thinking, what game is this? 'I rather thought you and I were talking in confidence. Have you been talking to your senator since the beginning?'

She shook her head, looking concerned. 'No. Please don't get me wrong. I treated your assignment with total discretion—still do—but when you asked me about Cord I was worried on your account. I heard some things about him in relation to another matter I was working on for the senator. I thought it wise to tell him about Cord being involved here in Japan. I promise you I gave away no specific details about what you are investigating.'

Ransome weighed her up. 'Go on,' he said, nodding to show that he accepted her explanation.

Julia said, 'You see, the senator's committee has been interested in Cord for some time. I'm on the committee payroll doing research—not that too many people know that—so I know what's happening. He hoped you might be willing to share any specific information you have about Cord—what he's doing in Japan, what he's told you about himself, anything you've got that might be useful to us.'

'I thought he must work for one of your agencies,' Ransome said.

Julia shook her head emphatically. 'No way.'

Cord: a patriotic loose cannon and a freelance. That made him nervous. 'So who's running him?'

She raised her eyebrows. 'Who indeed? The senator asked me to come to talk to you personally.' She cocked her head on one side, looking at him with a shrewd grin. 'He's impressed by my powers of persuasion. The question is: are you?'

Ransome laughed. She was disarming in the extreme. 'What do you want to know?'

'Thanks,' she said. She stood up. 'You mind if I tape record this?'

He shook his head.

She went to an elegant oak bureau against the wall and returned with a small Sony recorder. She set the microphone between them, switched on, then, checking that the tape was running, spoke the date and said, 'Interview with freelance journalist Jack Ransome.' Her eyes met his. 'Mr Ransome, have you met a man called Dr Harold Cord while you have been here in Japan?'

The interview took half an hour. He told her everything he remembered about Cord from their meetings, and about Cord's warning during the confrontation he'd had with him the day before. He told her as much about the deal that had been struck by General Ishii and the occupation forces as he deemed wise, but chose to tell nothing of the fears he and Kaizei entertained about the new obscenity they had uncovered.

When it was over, she switched off the tape and put

the recorder back on top of the bureau. She said, 'Why are you doing this?'

'We're off the record?'

She nodded.

'My friend asked me to. And I was bored. And I was glad to be able to come to Japan. And it's more fun than a poke in the eye with a burnt stick.'

The smile did not reach her eyes. 'I wouldn't count on that remaining the case,' Julia said. 'There's another reason why I was asked to come personally.' Her face darkened. 'My senator wants you to know that Cord is very dangerous. Very, very dangerous.'

'In what way? Physically?'

'Exactly,' Julia said. 'I've seen his file. It doesn't make reassuring reading. Cord keeps bobbing up in the middle of the grubbiest situations. He was in the thick of the uglier things that went on in Vietnam and Kampuchea. He was one of the most enthusiastic proponents of the now somewhat discredited Phoenix program.'

'Winning hearts and minds with a bullet, right.'

'And methods of persuasion it's best not to ponder. More recently he's been busy in Central America and in the Middle East. Where Cord is, pain usually follows hard by. I am to warn you to stay clear of Cord at all costs.' She reached across the table and put her hand on his forearm. 'I agree. You'd be a waste, Ransome, if you got yourself totalled.' She smiled a bright, provocative smile and allowed a silence to hang.

Chapter 44

The flight north to Sapporo was horrendous. An hour was lost at Haneda Airport before take-off, waiting for a weather clearance. As it was, the Japan Airlines Boeing was tossed about by fierce headwinds. Ransome wondered when the local airlines considered it too dangerous to fly. The turbulence did not seem to worry the planeload of Japanese. Most of them were dressed in ski clothes. They chattered like excited parrots and ate and drank non-stop.

On the trip he never saw the earth below them, save for a few seconds on take-off and again when through a single break in the clouds he looked down on Tsugaru Straits between Hokkaido and the mainland, the icy grey waters enclosed by snowcapped mountains. But as they circled over Sapporo the cloud cover cleared. It was a lovely sight. The mountains and the city had been buried in a vast white blanket. He watched with trepidation through the screen of the cockpit camera which gave the passengers a pilot's eye view of the approach and landing at Chitose Airport.

Kaizei looked dashing in a ski cap, dark glasses and an orange parka. He seemed hardly able to contain his excitement. When he grinned at Ransome, his gaunt face cracking in half, Ransome thought how frail he seemed, how over-stressed. Chasing this particular ambulance was costing his friend dearly.

'You're green,' Kaizei said, amused. They had shared

enough helicopter trips together for him to know how badly Ransome reacted.

'Never have subscribed to the theory of flight,' Ransome said, his stomach settling at last.

There was an enormous crush at the airport. The crowd made Ransome nervous; he was mindful of Uto's warning about leading someone to Kaizei. But though he had had a sense of being watched from the time he had left his hotel that morning, it was impossible to tell.

He thought he caught someone observing them too closely: one of a group of foreign tourists. But they were so rugged-up in winter clothing—hats, scarves and dark glasses against the snow glare—that he couldn't see the man's face. Without a further glance in Ransome's direction, the man, carrying skis and a huge rucksack, moved away with his fellows and disappeared out into the white world beyond.

Outside the terminal, snow was falling steadily. Kaizei had a hire car. As Ransome slid into his seat, Kaizei said, 'The American involvement. All true.' He pushed a manilla folder into his hand. 'All in there.' He stared at Ransome. 'And our worst fears—also true. At least I think so. Have a look while I warm up the car.' He started the engine.

Ransome opened the file. It contained a typed transcript of an interview, several single-spaced pages in English. There was a black-and-white photograph on top of the transcript.

'I couldn't persuade the lady to be filmed. She said she was no longer beautiful.'

The faded print showed a pretty young woman, her hair piled high upon her head, smiling at the camera, holding a bouquet of flowers. She was flanked by two American army officers. They looked pleased to be there.

'1946,' Kaizei said. 'General Ishii's beloved only daughter Harumi with her father's house guests, the two

US Army interrogators. The one on the left,' pointing to a handsome young man with an Errol Flynn moustache, 'is Major Alvin Thomas. The other is Harvey Walker, a captain. She told me they spent most of 1946 debriefing General Ishii.'

'Christ,' Ransome was impressed. 'How did you find her?'

'Mr Aoyama. When I told him what we'd heard about the Japanese brass buying immunity from the Americans, he was distinctly pissed off. It was the one key piece of information he didn't have. "Why don't you ask the general's daughter," he said. "Maybe she knows if that's true or not."'

'You didn't know there was a daughter?'

Kaizei shook his head. 'No. He'd never mentioned her before. She lives here, in Sapporo. He told me yesterday morning. He knew where she lived, even gave me her phone number, which is ex-directory. I phoned her straight away, told her that her father was a hero of mine,' making a mortified face, 'and that I was writing a book on the "forgotten patriots of the war".'

'She agreed to see you? Just like that?'

'Just like that. I went straight over there. A tough, bright old lady, is Harumi. She's obviously got money— a chic apartment in a building above the swank part of town. She talked for three hours. She made no bones about it. The occupation forces did do a deal: the research data from Harbin in return for complete freedom from prosecution. She reckons the idea of the trade-off came from the US officers, not from her father. She says he only agreed to the idea to save the lives of his men. She reckons this guy,' pointing to the photograph of Major Thomas, 'literally pleaded with her father for top secret data on germ weapons.'

Ransome shook his head in disbelief. 'What an obscenity. They must have known how that data was obtained.'

'She knows everything. They used to come every day. Ishii was sick, so she sat in on most of the interviews. She could type, so they used her as a stenographer. She'd type out daily transcripts of the interrogations. She even delivered them to the American GHQ at Ichigawa garrison. Read it later at the hotel. It's all in there,' Kaizei said. 'Fascinating stuff.'

He drove out of the car park and headed into Sapporo. He avoided the centre of the city and made for the eastern suburbs.

The mountains seemed no more than an arm's length away when he stopped the car in a narrow backstreet. Save for a couple of older houses, the architecture of which might have belonged in Siberia or Alaska, it could have been a suburb anywhere: modern bungalows with steep roofs piled high with snow, high wooden fences, cars and family vans parked nose-to-tail down one side of the street.

Kaizei sat for a time in the car, watching through the rear window. The street was empty. After awhile he was satisfied that no-one had followed them.

'Do you think he'll talk?' Ransome asked.

Kaizei grimaced, unsure. 'I hope so. I think so. I told him we had dug out something new he might be able to help us with. He said he would, if he could.'

They got out. He locked the car. They walked to a house fifty metres back along the street. It was different from the others. It was a three-storey building made of white-painted brick. A flight of stairs led from the street to the first-floor level.

'Doctor's surgery,' Kaizei explained. 'That's what Aoyama does,' smiling oddly, 'he specialises in treating old people.'

They entered. An old woman sat behind a narrow steel desk. She recognised Kaizei and smiled with pleasure, showing a set of steel teeth. 'Mrs Aoyama,' Kaizei said. Ransome smiled at her. She bowed.

Aoyama appeared at a door. '*Konnichi wa!*' he said. He shook hands with Kaizei and Ransome.

He looked different from the nervous but robust man Ransome had first met in a Tokyo hotel room. His white doctor's coat gave him a certain authority, but his face had caved in with anxiety. He looked shrivelled with age.

'Come.' Aoyama led them upstairs to a small study on the top floor lined on three sides with shelves crammed with books and box files. The fourth wall was glass; beyond it, no more than a kilometre away, a wall of white mountains. Although it was only late afternoon darkness was already claiming the sky.

For several minutes Kaizei and Aoyama talked rapidly together. The old man seemed angry.

Kaizei said, 'He's had two telephoned threats in the past few days. I've assured him that we've protected him as a source.'

Ransome said, 'Maybe one of the contacts he has given you has betrayed him.'

'He's badly rattled. They were both direct threats of death.'

'Yet he's still willing to talk?' Ransome knew that Kaizei had told Aoyama about the killings. No wonder the old man looked so gaunt. 'He's a bit game.'

'He's more than a bit angry that he was never told about the amnesty,' Kaizei made a rueful face. 'Had he known that, he says, he would never have wasted the last thirty years of his life hiding here on Hokkaido. I'm beginning to know how he feels,' this ruefully.

Aoyama said something, pointing at the camera.

'He won't be filmed this time.'

Ransome shrugged. No-one could blame Aoyama. They had him on tape already revealing the ancient crimes he had catalogued in the days of Section 731. This time their reason for seeing him was far different.

From his inside pocket Kaizei took the two Harbin photographs. He handed them to Aoyama, who studied them with a growing look of excitement. He said something to Kaizei. 'He wants to know where we got them. He's never unearthed a single picture of the top men before.'

Ransome said, 'Can I lead him through the names?' Kaizei looked surprised. 'I'll tell you why afterwards.'

One by one Ransome read out the names of the officers in the group. Aoyama said '*Hai*', after each name. Ransome pointed to one of the two unidentified men. 'Who is this?'

Aoyama looked at him then back at the image. His face screwed up as he tried to remember.

'Kitano Masaji?' Ransome said.

'*Hai*,' Aoyama said.

'How do you know that?' Kaizei asked, his face registering surprise.

'I went back to see the rose gardener, Mr Sakurai.'

Kaizei stared at him.

Ransome pointed to the last unidentified man. 'Who?' he asked Aoyama. The old man paused, then shook his head vigorously. He looked scared.

'Ask him if he knows the man's name,' Ransome said.

Aoyama said something.

Kaizei translated. 'He says he can't remember.' Sharply, he asked Aoyama another question. Aoyama remained silent.

Without showing it to Kaizei, Ransome handed Aoyama another photograph. 'Does he recognise anyone in this photograph?'

Kaizei was puzzled. 'Where did this one come from? Sakurai?'

Ransome said, 'I'll tell you in a minute.'

Kaizei asked the question.

Aoyama's face was betraying alarm. He seemed extremely agitated.

Ransome guessed that he knew but was unwilling to speak. 'Maybe he's wise not to recognise the connection.' He showed the photograph to Kaizei. 'Recognise him?'

Kaizei saw the common factor at once. He pointed to the unidentified officer in the Harbin group. 'Same guy. Who is he?'

Watching Aoyama's face as he said it, Ransome said, 'Takanichi Junichiro.'

Kaizei said nothing. He, too, was watching Aoyama.

'The rose gardener made the connection,' Ransome said. 'He was at Harbin. He knew them all. So was Mr Aoyama. He must be able to confirm that the two men are the same.' He looked at the old man. 'Is it Takanichi?'

Aoyama nodded without waiting for Kaizei's translation. 'Takanichi Junichiro,' he said, the words coated in bitterness.

Kaizei said, 'Jesus H. Christ, no wonder people are being killed! His son is the biggest fish of all, Jack. In a few weeks time, Shoji Takanichi could be in power.'

He said something more to Aoyama. The old man looked embarrassed. He spoke for several minutes in a rush of words, his head bowed.

Kaizei said, 'He admits he recognised Takanichi, but says he was too frightened to say so. He has known Takanichi's connection to Section 731 from the start. But he also knows how ruthless the father was—and Shoji Takanichi has the same reputation. It was all very well confessing and even naming the others involved, but naming a Takanichi scared him. Shoji is too powerful and too dangerous.'

'Ask him which section Takanichi headed up.'

Aoyama replied, distaste on his face.

Kaizei translated. 'The freezing experiments.'

Ransome addressed the old man directly. '*Domo*

arrigato gozaimasu. Tell him we think he's a brave man.'

Kaizei translated and Aoyama bowed, gravely.

'Now let's ask him the other question.'

Ransome watched Aoyama's face as Kaizei's question registered. The old man turned away from them and sat in silence looking out towards where the mountains crowded close to the edge of the city. He seemed profoundly sad. When he spoke it was in heavily accented English.

He said, 'Yes, what you ask is true. I have known for long time now that some ex-Section members went on with an experimental program. I do not know what area they work in. I do not know who they are. I do not know where they work, but in the past years, as I have been researching, I have been hearing hints of this.'

Kaizei said, 'Have you any evidence?'

A long silence, then, 'Some papers. I have some papers you can have. About four years ago two of the most brilliant Section members told me at different times that they had worked on such a program. I kept notes of our conversations.'

'Can we see them?' Kaizei said.

'I keep them in another place.' He gave a small apologetic smile. 'I did not want such things in my house. My ex-colleagues were ashamed of what they were doing.'

'What kind of program was it?'

Aoyama's expression set. He said nothing.

'Biological warfare?'

Aoyama stared at them both, his eyes panic-stricken. Then, as though his resolve had collapsed, he gave a slight nod.

'Do you know if they still are working on the program?'

Aoyama shook his head. 'I believe they were planning to leave the project, but I do not know what happened.

I have not heard from them since.' He stood up. 'Tomorrow morning I will have the papers here.' The interview was over.

Walking to the car, Kaizei said, 'Where in God's name did you get that photograph?'

'It's a copy of one I saw on top of a grand piano at a house in Akasaka.'

'Who is the other man in the picture—the high-ranking one?'

Ransome said, 'A man who had nothing to do with Section 731. Reiko's father.'

Kaizei stopped dead in his tracks. 'You're kidding me.'

Ransome said, 'I wish I was.'

Chapter 45

No-one could remember ever seeing a woman in the Akizawa sumo wrestling gymnasium at Ueno before. As they worked out, straining to lift the enormous barbells or practising the forty-eight ritual falls, lifts, throws and twists, the big men stared at her insolently through the glass wall of the gymnasium office. From time to time, the cabinet minister's three guards, playing cards just beyond the door, looked up from their hands, made coarse remarks, then went on with their game guffawing at their own jokes.

Inside the office Shoji said, 'So, my father was at Harbin. So were hundreds of doctors.' He shrugged. 'So, I didn't choose to reveal that to your *gaijin*. But in fact I told your nosy friend all he deserves to know about things Japanese—which is precisely nothing!' He laughed. His secretary Ocha, standing behind him, smiled discreetly.

Reiko said, 'What sort of Japan do you want? How do you imagine we can continue to bury the past?'

Shoji's eyes were on the activities of the wrestlers outside. Their loud shouts filtered through the glass. 'There is nothing in our past we need be ashamed of,' he said.

'Then who is trying to cover it up? Who ordered that people prepared to speak out about that obscenity were to be killed?'

Shoji said nothing.

'It suits your political ambitions that your father's past should not be known.'

'Are you accusing me?'

Reiko did not reply.

He gestured to Ocha. 'Give her the files.'

At that moment, the big Hawaiian entered the gym through the street door. He waved to Shoji. The cabinet minister rose, gave his champion a huge smile and a two-handed victor's salute.

On the desk, directly in front of Reiko, Ocha stacked up a dozen dusty files.

Shoji sat down once more. He said, 'Japanese Army Medical Corps records. You want to know the truth about Harbin? Read these!'

Reiko picked up one of the files and glanced through it.

'Experimental, yes it was, but my father was only involved in work that was scientifically pure—and morally impeccable. Take them! Read them!'

Reiko said, 'Do you expect me to believe this is the whole story?'

Shoji stood up. Contempt now: 'Personally I don't care what you believe. If you prefer to hear the lies of your *gaijin* lover, or this friend of his, Kaizei—who happens to be a renegade journalist who would stop at nothing to harm me politically—so be it. If you prefer to malign your own family on the hearsay of troublemakers,' slamming his fist down on the files, 'then do so!'

Despite herself, Reiko jumped with fright.

Shoji rose abruptly and crossed to the door. 'Some advice—and best you take it!' stabbing a finger at her. 'If you value his life—get him out of Japan!'

'Don't you dare harm him!' She could not control the fear in her voice.

Shoji stopped and stared at her, disdain on his face. 'No wonder your father is disappointed in his ... corrupted ... daughter.'

He left the office.

Shaken to her core by the level of his intimidation, Reiko watched her cousin for a time as he made his way slowly through the gymnasium, stopping and shaking hands with various of the wrestlers. His guards ended their game and followed him, chatting and laughing and horsing around. At length she collected herself. She swung on the secretary and gestured angrily at the pile of files. 'Bring them!'

She left the office and, ignoring Shoji who was now in conversation with the Hawaiian and his handlers, went out into the street where the car was waiting.

In the office, Mr Ocha slowly began to collect the files.

Chapter 46

The icy white sails of the half-sized Sydney Opera House soared up against a black, star-studded winter sky. Across Keoi Square the frozen turrets of an ancient Japanese castle glinted in the bright-as-day floodlight. A three-metre high samurai warrior galloped on a semi-transparent crystal horse. The bare trees wore jewelled necklaces of fairy lights and icicles.

The square was packed with people, mostly families with round-eyed children, muffled with coats and scarves and woolly hats against the freezing wind. Bands played and searchlights bounced off the ice sculptures of intricately carved animals, Disney characters, emperors, warriors and geishas, space ships, sailing junks and steam trains.

Kaizei said, 'Most things you remember from your childhood seem disappointingly small when you see them as an adult, but this gets bigger and better. My father used to bring my sister and me up from Hakodate every year to see it.' His face was aglow, remembering.

He looks about eighteen, Ransome thought. Kaizei's elation about their successful interview that evening was still with him, sustained by all the excitement around them.

Previously, Kaizei had been troubled by the moral implications of his countrymen being guilty of terrible crimes. Now he appeared to have regained his journalist's front-page enthusiasm for the project. Ransome was aware of the irony—his own enthusiasm had withered in

the light of the involvement of Reiko's family. And there
was the disturbing involvement of his own people. He
wondered how his father might have viewed the amnesty
had he survived.

The distracting smells of vegetables and noodles drew
them towards the open stalls. They bought coffee and
went on walking around the square.

A line of high-sided trucks was emptying loads of snow
beside an unfinished Greek temple. A group of sculptors
standing on scaffolding platforms were fluting the
marble columns with their ice axes. To one side of the
vast square, a fountain had frozen solid, its water fixed
in a single moment into the shape of a surreal flower.
The clock on the tall communications mast showed ten
o'clock.

'What about Reiko? How's she going to take it?' Kaizei
said, reading his silence.

Ransome shrugged unhappily.

'Is it going to screw things up for you?'

'It's going to be awkward, let's put it that way.' It was
going to be much worse than awkward. He dreaded the
prospect of hearing her verdict, the prospect of losing
her.

'You want to drop it?'

Ransome shook his head.

'I suppose we could leave Shoji out of it,' not managing
to sound convincing.

'No,' Ransome said. Kaizei was making a remarkable
offer, but it wasn't on. 'We'll take this one all the way
down the line. I think we should confront Shoji.'

'He'd never talk to us,' Kaizei said.

'Maybe he will, maybe he won't,' Ransome said, 'but
first I need to hear where Reiko stands. I owe it to her.'

Kaizei studied him for a time then said, 'Thanks, Jack. This
is the big one. We had a great story before, but Shoji's
involvement makes it sensational. And tomorrow we might

have some real evidence about something even bigger.'

They arrived at their *ryokan* and sat around in the blue and green kimonos that came with their room, eating dinner.

Kaizei gave him his copies of the Ishii transcript, the tapes and photograph. 'Let's get this stuff out of Japan as soon as we can, shall we? You'll find it interesting, especially the bit at the end.'

'What does the general's daughter think of her old man now?'

'I asked her that.' Kaizei reached over and took the transcript. He flipped through it. 'From the beginning, she lived in Harbin just outside the camp. In a mansion. She said it was like something out of *Gone with the Wind*. Knew what was going on in the camp. Said she thought it was terrible, that she felt sorry for the victims. She has a curious view about her father. She said, "What he did, or was alleged to have done, in the line of duty as a medical officer and soldier in the Imperial Japanese Army should be denounced by any moral standard."' Kaizei emphasised the words. 'Then she goes on: "Even so, one must not forget that it all happened under extremely unusual circumstances. It was war."' Kaizei made a cynical face. 'Heard that excuse before?'

Ransome laughed sourly. 'Yeah, it sounds vaguely familiar.'

Kaizei handed the transcript back to Ransome. 'But it's the bit at the end I want you to read. I've marked the passage.'

Ransome quickly flipped over the pages to the end. He read:

H. I.: They treated him as though he were a piece of fruit to be squeezed out to the last drop. So, to secure the lives of his devoted men, he told them some secrets. But no more than he needed.

The last sentence had been marked with a yellow transparent marker, as was the next section:

K: Does that mean there was information he did not tell them?
H. I.: Of course. Do you take him for a fool? Why should my father pass over to the enemy the most vital pieces of knowledge?
K: Do you mean he held back some of the research secrets?

Here, Kaizei had typed in 'no answer'.

K: Who has this information now that your father is dead?
  (No answer)
K: Do you have it?
H. I.: It is in good hands.

Ransome read through the section again carefully, to make sure he fully understood it. 'Are these her exact words?' he asked: "Why should my father pass over the most vital pieces of knowledge?"'

Kaizei looked troubled. 'I've run the tape over and over again. That's exactly what she said. There *was* information Ishii didn't pass on. As she was saying it, I remember feeling certain that it was something significant. When she clammed up . . . it was the way she looked—somehow—triumphant. Like she held a vital secret no-one else knew.'

Ransome said, 'If they got off to a flying start with "the most vital pieces of knowledge", I wonder how far along the biological warfare track scientists could go in all these years?'

Kaizei said, 'Doesn't bear thinking about, does it?'

* * *

They were having breakfast when Aoyama's message came. The *ryokan* dining room was packed with middle-aged skiing enthusiasts. Ransome had passed on the

Japanese breakfast of rice, steamed vegetables and boiled fish soup with an egg in it. He stuck to black coffee.

The young woman from the front desk came to their table. She handed a slip of paper to Kaizei. He read the message and jumped to his feet, his face white. He asked her a question. She replied.

'Trouble?' Ransome could see that it was.

'A phone message. Aoyama is waiting for us now in the square. Why?' Kaizei looked agitated. 'There's something bad happening, Jack. I can feel it.'

* * *

Sapporo was laid out like an American Midwest city: all straight lines and wide boulevards. The design was guaranteed to catch and funnel every nuance of the northern gales.

Keoi Square was like a deserted film set. The crowds of the night before were gone. In the distance, at the far end of the square, Ransome could see workmen shovelling snow from a pavement. A snowplough was clearing drifts that half-covered a line of food stalls. From a loudspeaker someplace there came the sound of music. The high-pitched electronic tune was oddly familiar to Ransome, but the wind snatched it away before he could recognise it. They waited, looking round anxiously for Aoyama, but there was no sign of him.

From the telecommunications tower they walked slowly through the square to the far end, searching for the old man; past the sculptures and the empty food stalls; past the leafless trees gilded with snow, hung with skeins of black cables and coloured lights. No Aoyama.

Snow flurried around the bases of the ice palaces and castles and blurred the carefully sculptured garments of the statues. Save for the workmen, there was no-one in the square.

They went around the outer edge of the square, moving slowly through the garden of white statues, leaning into the fierce wind. Mythological creatures grinned coldly, samurai swordsmen lunged, Donald Duck capered. High above, windblown snow trailed like smoke from the girdered heights of the telecommunications tower.

They went around a second time. Not a sign of Aoyama. They were in a quandary. To keep searching? To leave? To phone his home? They had been there half an hour. Still no sign. A car drove slowly past, but kept on, to disappear around the corner.

Perhaps he was sitting in a car? There were a few parked around the perimeter streets half-buried in snow. They peered in the windows of each one, scraping the snow from the windscreens. All were empty. By the Grand Hotel corner the music was louder. As the traffic lights at the deserted street crossing changed—red, yellow, green—the tunes changed with them. Now a marching song, then that maddeningly familiar tune.

'For the blind,' Kaizei explained. 'So they know when to walk and when to stay.'

What was that tune? Kaizei was on edge. Finally, he shook his head at Ransome. It was useless. 'He's not going to turn up,' he said, shouting into Ransome's ear against the shriek of the wind. 'Something bad has happened to him.'

'Maybe someone wanted us out of the way,' Ransome said.

Kaizei looked at him blankly. 'Let's go to his place.' They began to walk, hurrying now.

There was some traffic on the street now: ghostly, slowly moving cars half-dissolved by snow.

Ransome stopped at the corner and looked back. For one last time he swept his eyes slowly across the full width of the square. His gaze had gone past the ice garden when he sensed that something did not quite fit. Beside a gigantic statue of Goofy, there was a life-sized tableau of Snow White and the Seven Dwarfs. Something was wrong with it. There was an eighth dwarf.

Ransome began to run. He shouted to Kaizei, but his shout was plucked away by the wind.

Aoyama's face was covered in a two-inch thick layer of ice. Through the glassy prism his face was strangely distorted, as though his features had melted like candle grease.

They stood staring in horror at the ice-encased body of the old man. He was upright, but sagged within the frozen armour. It appeared that whoever had killed the old man had taken the trouble to prop him upright and hose him down with water through the arctic winter's night.

Kaizei began to scream out a wild gibberish, clawing at the ice covering Aoyama's dead face. His hands made no impression on the icy coffin.

Ransome grabbed him by the shoulder. 'There's nothing we can do,' he shouted into his ear.

Kaizei flung off Ransome's grip. He kept on tearing at the ice, now beating at it wildly with his fists. At last he stopped, his shoulders bowed. When he looked around, tears were streaming down his face.

'I should never have begun this!' he shouted. There was a crazed look about him.

Ransome said, 'Let's get out of here.' He gripped Kaizei by the arm and half-dragged him away from the grisly statue. Kaizei seemed broken by it all. He walked like an automaton.

There was a sudden lull in the wind. Their feet crunched on the snow. The roar of the snowplough could be heard for the first time. The electronic music from the street crossing sounded loud in the chill air.

Two things occurred to Ransome at the same time. He remembered the name of the elusive tune, the words suddenly springing into his head: *Guin' a body, meets a body, coming through the rye.*

And he knew that the half-familiar figure he had seen at the airport when he had arrived in Sapporo had been Cord.

At the corner, the lights changed from green to red; with them, the music. 'Coming through the Rye' became a rousing Japanese marching song.

Chapter 47

Snow flurries above Tokyo. The temperature: close to zero.

Aware that whoever was responsible for the killing was right on their heels, they had not stopped to ask questions. Changing plans, they had travelled back by train.

Kaizei had hardly spoken a word on the six-hour train ride to Hakodate. His face was drawn with sorrow. Aoyama had been his father's friend and a man who was genuinely remorseful about his past.

It would not have surprised Ransome if he had decided to give up. He thought again of Aoyama's burning house. He had filmed it as Kaizei had driven past the end of the street: red fire engines against the blinding white of the snow, black smoke rising above the fire-blackened building. He wondered again what had happened to Mrs Aoyama. Had she died in the blaze?

Looking out the window at the lights twinkling on the black hill that rose behind the port city where he had been born, Kaizei said, 'I had no idea the opposition would be this big. We really are going to have to get out of Japan—both of us—and fast.'

'How about we try to talk to Shoji first?'

Kaizei's eyes widened, then he laughed outright. 'You haven't changed, you mad bastard, have you?' He shrugged. 'Yeah, why the hell not? How do you propose to arrange it?'

'Reiko might be able to help. It's family,' he said, the irony masking his gnawing fear that this would probably never be the case. 'Anyhow, there's no harm in asking.'

'Ah,' said Kaizei, serious once more. 'Now I know you're kidding me.'

* * *

They had bucketed in a force two gale in the big ferry across the black straits to Aomori, drinking beer and trying not to be sick.

The clockwork Japan Rail schedule was not affected by the weather. The sleeper train had left the rail siding wharf for the south exactly on time.

Southwards. A restless, broken night on their narrow bunks behind the green curtains listening to the rhythmic clack of the rails. The smell of unwashed flesh. A few stops where Ransome peered out to see the patterned earthworks of frozen paddy fields raised like the veins of leaves. Twice they were shunted for twenty minutes, the only sound the click of steel hammers on the wheels, then through the giant marshalling yard that doubled as Tokyo's outer suburbs to the early morning bustle of Ueno Station.

Ueno had been packed with early-starting workers. Making their way through the throng, Ransome had said, 'I keep getting the feeling there's an army of people following me. Do you think I'm turning paranoid?'

Kaizei had looked around. There could have been half a hundred people on their tail and they would not have known. 'You'd be a fool if you weren't,' he had said.

Now Kaizei had gone to ground once more. He had not said where, but he had left Ransome a number where he could be contacted in case Shoji Takanichi agreed to an interview. He would be in touch in the next twenty-four hours. From the station, Ransome called McGregor who readily agreed to put him up. He sounded slightly drunk.

On the train he had scribbled an explanatory letter to Martin Garrett in San Diego covering all the story so far, telling him everything he knew and guessed. He found a post office on the station concourse. Two copies of the photograph he had purloined from Reiko's father's house went with the letter, together with the Ishii file and the Sapporo footage.

* * *

'She's been fired,' McGregor said bitterly, 'and of course she blames me.' His apartment was a wreck and it smelled bad: stacked unwashed dishes and discarded clothes, bottles everywhere.

'She's gone back to her mother's.' McGregor's face was ravaged by grief.

'Should be me she blames.' Ransome felt mortified by McGregor's state. If he had not come to Japan, the man might still have his lover.

'No reason given,' McGregor said, gulping a whisky. 'The pressure came from someone high up in government. She was helping me get together that dossier on the Takanichis—father and son— for you.' Seeing Ransome's expression, he held up his hand. 'I know you said don't involve her. Our decision. She did it with her eyes open.'

'Did she?' Ransome said.

'Maybe you're right,' McGregor said, 'maybe it would've been better if I'd never set eyes on you again.'

'You want me to go?' Ransome said.

McGregor smiled foolishly and poured a long whisky into his own glass. 'No?' holding the bottle vaguely in Ransome's direction.

Ransome shook his head. As a distraction from the painful subject, he gave McGregor the present he had bought him on the way. 'Call it a "thank you" present or call it an apology—whatever,' he said, feeling like a pariah.

McGregor opened the package and set the bowl on the table. It had cost a great deal of money at the antique shop he had found on a street off the Ginza.

'Jesus Christ,' McGregor said, looking suddenly sober. 'Kobe ware. You've got good taste Ransome.'

'The man at the antique shop has good taste.'

McGregor took the bowl and held it under a side lamp, allowing the light to play on the subtle ceramic surface. 'This is a beautiful piece. I don't know how much you paid for it and I won't ask, but thanks anyway.' He put the bowl down alongside three others. He rose. 'One good present deserves another,' he said. He went into his study.

A moment later he was back. 'In pursuing my research on Takanichi Junichiro I've discovered something interesting.' He laid a piece of paper in front of Ransome. There were several neatly typed paragraphs on the page. 'Let me tell you about the father of your future family member Takanichi Shoji. Wow, you're going to love this!' shaking his head in wonder. 'The Japanese Physiological Society published a learned paper his old man gave at a big conference on food technology two years ago, just before he died. He was described as the world's leading authority on—quote—the science of human adaptability—unquote. In that year he gave talks on the subject to conferences all round the Pacific rim. How do you like that?'

Ransome was no longer capable of being surprised. He did not respond.

McGregor said, 'I had it translated by a pal of mine. The paper was a review of his life's work on "the comparative resistance of different races and age groups to extreme cold". He proudly claimed scientific veracity for his work since he boasted—admitted ... confessed ... what's the right word?—to have used living bodies, for Christ's sake.' McGregor looked sick. 'Of course they were all volunteers. He doesn't mention coercion. He doesn't mention Harbin. Apparently it all took place in some mythical place best left unidentified. And every scientist listening to or reading this shit doesn't really want to know how he came about the knowledge. And, if people in high places in Japan do know, I'll tell you how much they care: Takanichi was a long-serving consultant to the Japan National Frozen Foods Council and to the Japanese polar expeditions.' McGregor gave a short, disbelieving laugh. 'You like it, Jack? Me, I can't handle it.'

Ransome felt compassion for McGregor. Everything had gone bad for him in the brief period he had been helping with the story.

He said, 'You've been a terrific help, Robbie. I owe you one. When I get back to the States I'll send you copies of the photographs and all the transcripts in case you want to do a press story from this end.'

McGregor managed a smile. 'It's a nice offer,' shaking his head, 'but no, don't waste your time sending anything. I'm out of all that crap.' He was calmer now, but his voice was full of pain. 'Been doing some serious thinking. I've decided to give up journalism for good, Jack. I've done it without thought for twenty years now and it's time to do something more worthwhile.' He lay back on the divan and took a deep breath. 'You know those primitive tribes who believe that when you take a photograph you capture a man's soul? They're right. That's what we journalists do every day of our lives. We tell someone's story, we steal their soul. Sometimes we even wreck their lives.'

Maybe McGregor was right to give up journalism— maybe none of them should lift the stones to find out what was underneath. What right had they, Ransome wondered. By the very act of observing events and not taking part, they changed them.

'Don't fret, Jack, Su will be back,' McGregor said unconvincingly. He picked up the bowl. 'I thought, when Suroko left me, I would leave here. But then I realised that there's one immutable, unchanging thing about this country that I love: their art.' He held the bowl up in front of his eyes. 'Look at this thing. Bloody lovely. Art's one thing these people really know about. They've taken it about as close to perfection as anything I know. So to hell with everything else. Screw politics and screw all the corrupt bastards who are in it. I'm going to stay here and I'm going to concentrate on writing about art. I sometimes think I hate this place, but the truth is, Jack, I love Japan.'

Chapter 48

He had to know what she was thinking. He needed to tell her what he had found out.

When he called Reiko's number, her father answered. Ransome identified himself. 'May I speak to Reiko please,' feeling awkward.

'I'm sorry, she is not here.' Takanichi sounded cool.

'Can I leave a message for her?'

There was a pause. 'Mr Ransome, I would like to talk to you.'

Why would the man want to talk to him? To try to buy him off?

'When?' he asked.

'The matter is urgent and vital,' Takanichi said. He sounded grave. 'Can you see me tonight? I can come to your hotel this evening if you are free.'

It must be important. Takanichi was the man you came to see, not the other way around. But there was no way they could meet in McGregor's flat. 'Alright. How about eight o'clock at the Imperial? I will leave my name at the desk.'

'Thank you, Mr Ransome. I will be there.'

* * *

Reiko's father had aged ten years since Ransome had last seen him. He was grey-faced, his lines deeper-etched with exhaustion and care.

His chauffeur was standing in the foyer with him, but when Ransome appeared he was dismissed.

Takanichi bowed slightly. They shook hands. Ransome

ushered him over to a small lounge on one side of the great foyer. They slid into a high-backed banquette which gave them privacy. Ransome invited him to have a drink. Takanichi declined.

'I am sorry to hear about your tunnelling problems,' Ransome said. 'Is it true what the newspapers say—that the tunnel collapse was sabotage?'

Takanichi shook his head as though trying not to hear the words. 'Please, do not talk about this, Mr Ransome, I am here for another reason.'

'But if evidence were coming to light that your tunnel was deliberately mined, wouldn't that end the speculation about negligence?'

'Of course there was no negligence!' Takanichi was ruffled.

'Who would have done such a thing to you?'

The old man paused. 'Perhaps I will have a drink.'

Ransome ordered whisky for them both. While they waited for their order, Takanichi said nothing. He appeared to be composing himself as though for an ordeal. The drinks came.

Takanichi sipped his whisky. 'I would like to know if this investigation of yours is the reason for your interest in my daughter.'

It took Ransome by surprise. 'No!' he said, shaking his head emphatically. He was shocked that Takanichi might think he had simply used Reiko as a stalking horse to get close to some story connected with her family. 'Not at all. I had no idea she could possibly be connected. I knew your daughter and cared for her long before I ever knew about this story. You must believe that.'

Takanichi considered him for a time. He nodded slowly. 'Yes, I think I believe you, Mr Ransome. You do not strike me as a liar.'

Speaking carefully, he said, 'I do not know in detail what your investigation is about, Mr Ransome. You said it was a matter of history. But it touches my family. I realise that my late brother is implicated.'

Ransome said nothing, trying to gauge what might be coming.

'I am well aware that there are aspects of my brother's past which, if they became public, could bring dishonour to our family.' Takanichi's voice was apologetic but detached, as if to show that he was not tainted by it.

'I realise that you are a professional journalist doing your work, but I beg you to reconsider. What is the point of dragging this up? It's a 45-year-old crime. My brother was a young man when he volunteered for that work. Where will the gain be for such matters to come out now?'

Ransome said nothing.

'You cannot understand the disgrace this will cause. It is not only for the sake of my family honour that I ask this, but for your sake and my daughter's. Reiko thinks very highly of you.'

Poor bastard, thought Ransome. He looks to be at the end of his tether.

He said, 'I'm sorry that you and Reiko have been dragged into it, but my colleague would go on with it whether I were involved or not. The story has its own volition. We can't pretend it's not there. We will go on with it.'

Takanichi was silenced by this.

'Crimes have come out,' Ransome said. 'Confessions have been made. Have you any idea how bad this is?'

Takanichi had the look of a debater whose only argument had been nullified. 'You told my daughter that there had been killings.'

With genuine regret, Ransome gave him the details.

As he listened, Takanichi remained perfectly still.

'Three of them were murdered,' Ransome said. 'Another committed suicide. All the deaths have been directly connected with our investigation.'

The old man's expression was set into a waxen mask.

'It's an obscenity,' Ransome said, thinking, you're not getting off the hook, pal. 'Do you really think we should end our investigation?'

Takanichi stared at him. A flicker of emotion moved over the grey face like a shock wave on the surface of a still pond. After a time he shook his head.

'I wondered if your nephew, who is a powerful, well-connected man, might know something of this. That's why we're anxious to speak with him.'

After a moment, Takanichi gathered himself and sat back. He said, 'I have never admitted it before, but I have always known about my brother's wartime involvement with that despicable business. However, although I knew you were beaten,' his voice was almost a whisper, 'until you told my daughter I had no idea there had been murders. I cannot believe that my nephew is involved in that.'

'I have no way of knowing that he is,' Ransome said. 'We have met other men— old comrades of your brother from Harbin—who, in my view, would be capable of murder. Maybe they organised the killings. If your nephew would agree to speak about his father's involvement with Section 731 at least he could clear his own name of implication in these murders. Would you help arrange an interview with him? That way we may get to the truth of the matter.'

Takanichi gave a short, incredulous laugh. 'Take my advice. Don't even think about it. I know from seeing your film, Mr Ransome, that you are not without your share of nerve, but I did not think you a fool. Leave Japan at once.'

'I can't do that. Things have gone too far along the track for us to pull out now.'

Takanichi looked hostile. 'You cannot understand

what danger you are in if you continue with this.' There was urgency in his voice. 'It must be obvious to you that whoever is behind these attacks is totally ruthless. And you have my nephew to contend with. He is a very powerful man, Mr Ransome. Politically, at this time especially, he cannot afford under any circumstances to have his father's unfortunate past revealed. He is determined to stop your investigation. I'm not suggesting for a moment that he would resort to violence, but he has a reputation for using his power.'

'I'd still like to talk to him. There's something else your nephew may know about.' He told Takanichi about the terrible new truths they were uncovering.

When it was over, sorrow showed on the old man's face, stark as an obscenity daubed on a white wall. He sat in silence, his eyes focussed elsewhere. Suddenly he stood up, looking agitated. He lurched away from the table a few metres. For an instant he appeared to have lost his balance.

Ransome jumped to his feet, but the man had composed himself. 'Thank you for agreeing to see me,' he said. 'I must go.'

'Will you tell Reiko that we have spoken?'

Takanichi said, 'I will tell her. No doubt if she wants to talk with you she will be in touch.' He stared at Ransome as if seeing him for the first time. 'You have destroyed my family, Mr Ransome.'

Ransome shook his head. 'No, Mr Takanichi. I am no more responsible for your brother's past than you are.'

The old man took this in. He gave an odd smile, then bowed and walked away.

Chapter 49

The police car slowed. Ransome recognised the street and the old converted warehouse building.

Three other police cars were parked half-up on the pavement. There was a small crowd of people standing staring. Two uniformed men standing guard at the entrance hall saluted Uto as he led the way inside. Another policeman was manning the apartment manager's office. Walking up the stairs, Uto said, 'You've been here before?'

'Yes.' Ransome felt sick to his stomach. 'Kaizei stayed here at one time with a friend of his.'

There was blood on the walls and floor of the foyer outside the loft.

Uto said, 'The manager heard screaming. She called the police then came upstairs as far as here. Now she's in hospital. She has a slashed face and a hand so badly cut she may lose it.'

'She see who did it?'

Uto shook his head. 'She's too shocked to remember anything.' He paused then said, 'She thinks there were two men, but there may have been three, she can't remember.'

Christ, had they taken Kaizei? Ransome forced away the thought.

There was another uniformed man at the door of the apartment. He saluted Uto and unlocked the door.

In the flat there was blood everywhere. The place was wrecked: furniture broken, pictures ripped from the walls; there were bloody slashes in the upholstery of the divans and chairs. Two white-coated men were taking fingerprints.

Uto led Ransome into the bedroom. Under a sheet spread over the bed there was a body. Dark blood was seeping through the sheet from below.

Uto paused by the body and looked at Ransome. 'You must have seen a few dead bodies.'

'Yeah, one or two,' Ransome said. He steeled himself.

Uto uncovered the face. 'You know her?'

Ransome stood staring at the hideously disfigured face that had once been beautiful. He felt his gorge rise. 'What in God's name did they use?'

'Samurai sword. Our gangsters, if that's who did it, favour it as a weapon of revenge.' Uto spoke with distaste.

Ransome was drowning in blood. He took a grip of himself. He had liked the lively Eiko. Another innocent bystander; he had spent years of his life seeing them caught in the crossfire of conflicts not their own. Poor Eiko, she had drunk her last Krug champagne.

He looked at Uto and nodded. 'Nakasone Eiko,' Ransome said. 'A good friend of Kaizei's. He stayed here with her for a time until it got too hot for him to stay in the same place.'

'What do you know about her?'

Ransome shook his head. He was not going to tell Uto what he knew about her life as the mistress of some film tycoon and the girlfriend of a diplomat. 'I only met her once. Great girl. Full of life.' He had a mental picture of her tottering up the hallway in her ridiculous heels. '*Was* full of life,' he said, thinking, Before we entered it, Kaizei and me.

'Could Kaizei have done this?'

Ransome shook his head wearily. 'No, never. He really cared for Eiko. He couldn't have done that,' gesturing towards the bloody sheet.

'They were lovers, Kaizei and this girl?'

'I'd be surprised if they were not—at some stage. But certainly old friends.'

Uto covered over the face with a certain tenderness. 'We don't know if she was tortured or just slashed to death. It might be a random killing, or revenge—someone jealous—but most likely someone trying to find Kaizei.'

'Did Kaizei get away, or was he taken?'

Uto looked at him. 'We don't know the answer to that.'

Ransome said, 'Did anyone else see people leaving?'

'If they did they haven't come forward. Most people mind their own business, look the other way. If he did escape, any idea where he might have run?'

'No,' Ransome said. 'There's a lot of people out there who want him stopped.'

Uto gave a wintry smile. 'And you, Mr Ransome,' he said, 'and you.'

Outside again, Uto commandeered the police car. He was silent for several minutes, driving carefully through the heavy traffic at the Rappongi Crossing. 'I doubt if your friend Kaizei can run for long,' Uto said. 'Whoever is after him has obviously decided he has to go. And if they have employed the crime syndicates . . . they will keep after him until he is dead.' His face showed his disgust.

Ransome said nothing. Out in the Kampuchean paddy fields the troops used to say that The Lady was near when they sensed someone was going to die. It was not necessarily you, but someone nearby. He could feel her near now.

Hailstones began to angle against the windscreen. They looked lethal, driving in like tiny hand grenades. They rattled on the roof of the car. The windscreen wipers could not keep up; Uto slowed.

Ransome liked Uto. He felt he could trust him. This police inspector who could sound official one minute and personally involved the next had spoken as though he cared about what might happen to Kaizei. Telling him more of what this was about might help keep Kaizei alive.

'There's something I didn't tell you before, Inspector.' He took from his wallet the cutting of the newspaper photograph of the *yakuza* funeral and gave it to Uto. As the policeman examined it, Ransome told him how he had been warned off. He said, finally, 'I wonder if these people might be behind it all?'

'We need to talk,' Uto said.

'Do you mind if I have something to eat while we do?' It had occurred to Ransome that he had not eaten anything all day.

* * *

Uto parked the car and led him through several streets to a brightly lit cutting under the *shinkansen*'s elevated track at the frayed edge of the Ginza: porno movie-houses, cheek-by-cheek massage parlours, the smell of noodles from open sidewalk stalls no bigger than packing cases. They sat in a noisy bar eating *yakitori* and grilled mushrooms and drinking beer. Ransome was the only foreigner in the place.

Uto laid the cutting on the counter.

Ransome pointed to the little man. 'He seemed to be the boss. Those two,' indicating the henchmen, 'were with him when he turned on his little demonstration about mistakes,' seeing in his head the boy slice off his finger; feeling, once more, the tightening of stomach muscles.

Uto studied the group of mourners. 'When did this happen?'

'Not long after you questioned me about the first death.'

'Any idea where they took you?'

'No. They blindfolded me on the way there and back.'

Uto said, 'The docks around Shinagawa, I would think. That's his territory.'

'Yeah, I saw cranes and ships. You know him?'

Uto said, 'Kinichi Ihari. *Kumi-cho*—the godfather—of the Ihari-gumi. You were lucky. A very bad man.'

'What could be his interest in warning me off?'

The policeman frowned. 'It seems out of his line. His syndicate controls the meat workers.' He held his hand downwards, the thumb tucked in and waggled his finger like the four legs of a beast. 'All his people are *buraku-min*—the untouchables; people who handle dead flesh. They are considered to be the lowest of the low, our national private disgrace. You'll find them in the tanneries or the sewers and hidden behind walls in our cities and in separate sections of our cemeteries. We treat them even worse than we treat our Koreans, or our returned war orphans.' Distaste was written on Uto's face. 'There are things in our society that don't bear thinking about. But although they are outcasts, under Ihari they are very well organised and one of the most effective *yakuza* syndicates. But why?' Uto wrinkling his brow, puzzling it out. 'Why would he be involved in warning you off? Did they give you any idea?'

Ransome shook his head. 'Maybe he was part of Section 731? Maybe he's got that to hide?'

Uto looked doubtful. 'It's possible.'

'Or would he do a paid job for someone else?'

'Could be.' Uto was thinking. 'The present gang war that's on between the various *yakuza* syndicates has some political undercurrents, but I don't know enough. And I can't see how you are connected.' He scowled in frustration. 'You should have told me before.'

'I'm sorry now that I didn't,' Ransome said.

'I need to talk to Ihari's son. He's smart. Maybe even smart enough to tell me what this is all about.'

Ransome pointed to the bigger of the two henchmen in the photograph. 'This him?'

Uto nodded.

'Frogface II.'

Uto laughed. 'We call them *buotoko* — ugly. Ugly I and Ugly II—father and son. I'll have a talk with him.'

'There's something more, Inspector,' Ransome said, 'but it's so appalling I don't even know if I can believe it myself.'

'How bad?' Uto said.

'Very.'

He told Uto about the information they had been given hinting at ongoing work of the Section 731 biological warfare team.

When Ransome was done, Uto said, 'You have proof of this?'

Ransome shook his head. 'Only hearsay. But if it is true, it explains why people are being murdered. Three of the dead men were directly involved in biological warfare research. Two of them told us they had declined invitations to work on the program. Aoyama died because he had the facts. Unfortunately we never got to see the files he claimed to have.'

'Did any of them name names?'

'No.'

Uto gave a disappointed grimace.

Suddenly, his manner changed. 'Perhaps it would help you to know something about me.'

Ransome felt as though the man had taken a decision about him.

'I work,' Uto said, 'in a special Police Intelligence Unit which is seconded to the Prime Minister's Department. When you were arrested in that hotel, Kaizei's name came up on our computer—the arrest report mentioned his name which had been written on that threatening note. We found this very interesting. We had been aware for some time that Kaizei was involved with some kind of investigative journalism. There had been hints and rumours about possible political fallout. This had caused concern. The unit keeps watch on people like your friend, along with hundreds of other people who, for various political reasons,' smiling cynically, 'interest us.'

He filled both their glasses.

'I came into it personally because for some time I have been investigating the level of politicisation of the police force. When you were threatened in a cell by men who subsequently vanished from the police records we thought the connection between you and Kaizei must be worth watching.'

'So you believed my story.'

Uto shrugged, 'Why not? Why would you make it up? Kaizei had been very discreet. There seemed to be a wall of secrecy around everything. We had not been able to track down what it was about. We decided to target you. For a start, you were easier to keep in sight than he was. Now, from all you have told me, we were right. It is very political indeed. The implications are frightening.'

'Your unit is attached to the Prime Minister's Department,' Ransome said. 'Is your Prime Minister going to be embarrassed by what Kaizei is investigating?'

'That's a typical journalist's question, Mr Ransome,' Uto smiled. 'The answer is "no". The Prime Minister has proved willing to bring out into the open some embarrassing episodes from World War II.' The smile turned into a wolfish grin. 'But some of his conservative opponents might be very embarrassed indeed.'

'And that would be useful, politically.'

'In the present state of crisis,' Uto said, his eyes darkening, 'it might be crucial.'

For a moment Ransome considered telling him of the Takanichi family involvement with Section 731, but he decided to say nothing for the time being. He had no way of knowing how the fallout might affect Reiko.

'How serious is the politicisation of the police?'

'Alarming. There is a significant section of the force whose loyalty can no longer be depended upon in the event of a right-wing coup. You're caught up in something bigger than you can imagine, Mr Ransome.'

He took a card from his wallet. 'In case you're foolish enough to stay in Japan, and you get into trouble,' writing a telephone number on the back of the card and handing it to Ransome, 'call that number—anytime, day or night.'

Chapter 50

The Takanichi Rolls glided silently through the security gates. The two guards closed the gates behind it and watched as the car rolled quietly on the white gravel of the driveway to stop in front of the house.

The chauffeur, Akira, opened the car door for Takanichi. The man got out of the car slowly. The chauffeur watched him walk past the two young men guarding the steel and glass front door of the house and into the white marble hallway beyond. Takanichi's normally vigorous gait had become that of an old man.

In Shoji's study Takanichi sat opposite his nephew across a bare teak desk. Making no attempt to hide his disgust, he said, 'What are you doing, continuing to involve our family in this filth? Your father lied to me about his research—worse, he betrayed Japan by keeping on going with his disgraceful experiments—and you follow in his footsteps!'

Shoji's contempt was equally naked. 'Betrayed Japan! My father often said that your kind didn't have the stomach for the real fight. In 1945, content to think that losing the war was the end of it, you all sat back, defeated to your soul, content to make money.'

'At least it ended the disgraceful things your father and his criminal friends were responsible for in that camp. Or it should have.'

'That defeat was only temporary! My father understood that—as I do.' Shoji took a grip on himself. His tone became conciliatory. 'What I have done is to build on the basis of my father's work. This is superb technology. It makes useless all other weaponry. There's a huge market for it.'

Takanichi looked aghast. 'You would sell such weapons?'

'Of course. What are we supposed to do with our new science? Sit on it? Go broke while other countries catch up with us? In fact, we've just completed our first sales contract to the Middle East. Alone it's worth hundreds of millions.'

Takanichi rose. 'I came to tell you I intend to stop you in any way I can.'

Shoji stared at the older man. He said, 'Uncle, you know I can't allow that. Believe me, you don't want to finish up on the wrong side in this. The collapse of your tunnel should have reminded you that you are in a very vulnerable business.'

Takanichi paused for a long moment, astonished. 'Are you telling me that you were responsible for the explosion in my tunnel?'

'Let's just say that the leaders of strategic businesses—especially organisations that depend greatly on government contracts—need to fully understand their responsibilities in the new Japan. Get on with being an engineer, Uncle. You're out of your depth in politics.'

Chapter 51

C row Castle loomed up, its towering granite *donjon* night-black against the white-clad mountains. The train slowed.

The bright young student who had been practising her English with him all the way from Nagano pointed out the window. 'Matsumoto,' she said. She smiled widely and shook hands. 'Thank you for Engrish lesson. Goodbye, American.'

Ransome smiled at her distractedly. All the way his mind had been crowded with images of poor, dead Eiko and thoughts of Kaizei. Was he safe? Had he been taken? Was he alive? He had no memories of this trip. Some mechanical part of his brain had brought him here to see Reiko.

The skiers rose eagerly, donning parkas and backpacks, adjusting woollen hats and gloves, anxious to be at the virgin slopes.

He phoned the number from the callbox in the little station. There was no answer. Call from the station when you arrive, her message had said.

What the hell is going on? Ransome thought. The man on the desk of the Foreign Correspondents' Club had read it out to him over the phone. 'I must see you urgently. Will you come tomorrow? Reiko.' There had been detailed instructions on how to get to the resort and the telephone number to ring when he got there. Before he had caught the train he had tried. There had been no answer.

The station quickly emptied of skiers. Ransome stayed in the phone box trying the number over and over, anxious now. He was cold. Either there had been some kind of misunderstanding or Reiko had been delayed. Perhaps she was out skiing with the children? The stationmaster eyed him curiously, but soon went inside to the warmth of his glass-fronted office.

Perhaps she had driven in to collect him?

He walked out of the station onto the street. Matsumoto looked like any other mountain resort town at the height of the snow season. There was a cluster of steep-roofed hotels and boarding houses, ski shops, restaurants and coffee shops. The streets were narrow, thronged with skiers, and noisy with snowcats. The wheels of every car were fitted with chains.

No sign of Reiko.

He went back to the stationmaster, but the man had no English. Ransome thanked him and walked back out into the main street.

He found a tourist information office near the station. The pretty young woman behind the counter spoke passable English. He explained his problem.

'Kozenkei-Ski? *Hai.*' She looked apologetic. 'Far to go. You have missed last bus. Not another bus today.'

'Can I get a taxi?' he asked.

'Taxi? *Hai,* I will order for you. Now?' He nodded. She called the taxi then walked out to the kerb with him. A few minutes later a green taxi pulled up outside the office. She leaned in and asked the driver a question. 'The fare will be five thousand yen,' she said. He nodded to show he could afford that much, shook her hand and climbed in beside the driver.

The taxi driver spoke no English. Ransome concentrated on the scenery. The road to Kozenkei-Ski was spectacular, snaking upwards through narrow, vertical valleys, heavy with freshly fallen snow.

Pine trees like black matchsticks clung to the walls of the valleys and bearded the tops of the mountains. The road was busy. Judging by the skis strapped to every car-rack, they were mostly cars coming down the mountains from the various ski resorts above.

Near the top of the range a whole wall of the mountain had slid away, revealing a mile-long scar of black soil. The root structures of ruined trees reached out of the moun-tainside like skeleton hands. Around the curving road, and before them was a ski resort spread over the shoulder of a ridge, a cluster of modern buildings at the centre of a web of ski-lifts.

The car park was crowded. There was a line of buses waiting to take daytrippers back to the town. The taxi pulled up outside the main building, a terracotta-coloured structure of brick, concrete and glass. Ransome paid off the driver and entered. Inside there was a central plaza full of ski-hire shops, coffee shops and dining rooms. Skiers in bright clothes clumped about. Some of them stared at him curiously: the only person present not dressed for action.

Near the entrance he found an office. The girl on reception had some English, but not enough for him to convey his meaning. She asked him to wait and went into a nearby locker room. A few moments later she returned with a deeply tanned young ski instructor. He listened intently while Ransome explained his problem. 'Her name is Mrs Reiko Hauser. She is here at one of the private lodges with her two children.'

The young man translated but the girl looked puzzled and shook her head. Ransome heard her repeat Reiko's name. It seemed to mean little to her. She checked a list then shrugged. The young man said, 'Sorry, there is no Mrs Hauser listed.'

Ransome felt slightly panicky. Had something serious happened to Reiko? He showed the ski instructor the phone number. 'Is there anyone else who might know?'

The ski instructor shrugged.

Ransome tried a different tack. 'Miss Takanichi,' he said.

Immediately, the girl behind the counter smiled. 'Miss Takanichi? *Hai!*' She seemed impressed. She spoke rapidly to the young man.

He bowed his head sharply at Ransome. 'Miss Takanichi, yes. Please come with me,' he said.

He led Ransome out onto the open terrace overlooking the huge, fan-shaped area where all the downhill runs ended. Dozens of fit-looking skiers were drinking coffee and watching their fellows swoop down from the mountains.

To one side of the valley, steep-roofed, red brick ski-lodges sprouted on the curving shoulder of the mountain, each of them with a clear view of the downhill runs. The ski instructor pointed to a lodge poised above all the rest. 'Takanichi Lodge,' he said. 'The top one.' He turned towards a big illustrated map to one side of the terrace. It showed the layout of the resort's seven ski-runs and of the private lodges. He identified the building.

Ransome looked in some dismay at the climb. It looked to be about a kilometre up the slope. 'How do I get up there?'

The young man smiled. 'Wait here please,' he said and went down a flight of stairs. Ransome watched him walk towards a large open hangar; inside it, a helicopter, a wide-tracked snowplough and a line of fire-engine-red snowcats.

A team of expert-looking skiers in identical blue and yellow clothes whooshed down the slope and pulled up gracefully outside the hangar, joining several other ski instructors who were lounging around.

The weather was changing rapidly. Previously it had been a cloudy day with moments of bright sunlight, but now, behind the mountains, a dramatic anvil of black cloud was forming. A sudden wind blew over some polystyrene coffee cups at a nearby table. A waiter hurried to pick them up.

At that moment, from somewhere high up on the slopes, a siren went off. The ski instructors were galvanised into action. Two red snowcats snarled into life. They raced up the nearest ski run, each with two men aboard. The helicopter was wheeled out of the shed. With a great roar, it lifted off with three men aboard. It heeled over and, no more than ten metres above the ground, raced up to the ridge to disappear down behind the screen of trees.

Skiers continued to career down the runs, pulling up in front of the terrace in a spectacular flurry of snow. The skiers on the nursery slopes paused for no more than a moment then went on with the serious business of staying upright while the weather lasted. Ransome tried to spot Reiko and the children, but the runs were hopelessly crowded.

The young man appeared on the terrace beside him. 'I'll take you up,' he said. He led Ransome down the steps onto the snow and across to one of the snowcats.

The young driver kept close to the edge of the cleared snow. Downhill skiers whizzed past them at electrifying speed. When they were three-quarters of the way up, the helicopter roared overhead, heading down the mountain, a red light flashing from above its cabin. Ransome turned to watch it swoop down. A group of instructors crowded around to unload the victim. Already from this high up, the main buildings looked no bigger than dolls' houses. About two hundred metres behind, two other snowcats were climbing the slope after them.

Opposite the topmost lodge, the young man swung the snowcat to the left and stopped, idling the motor as Ransome dismounted.

'Takanichi Lodge,' the young man said, nodding towards the building. He waved his hand and accelerated away. About a hundred metres down he passed the two other snowcats that were heading slowly up the steep slope.

Ransome looked at the lodge. It was bigger than its neighbours. It had an extra storey and a cantilevered, glassed-in observation deck looking out over the valley. Several pairs of skis stood upright in a ski-rack by the door. There was a reassuring column of smoke from the chimney. Reiko was here after all.

He crunched through the snow. There was a knocker on the polished wooden door. He knocked. The noise of the snowcats behind him grew louder. He knocked once more. The engines cut out. His knocking sounded loud in the silence. He looked around. The two riders had dismounted and stood watching him. They were not dressed in ski clothes but in heavy topcoats and balaclava helmets. They wore mirrored snow goggles and high-laced boots. Ransome suddenly knew what was happening. Behind him, the door opened.

'Welcome, Mr Ransome,' said Shoji Takanichi.

Chapter 52

'Where is Reiko?' Ransome said.

Shoji held the door open wider. He smiled and said, 'Come in out of the cold.'

Ransome walked into the lodge. The two snowcat riders followed him in, not quite crowding him, but close enough to intimidate.

Inside was a great vaulting space under an A-frame roof. There were cheerful, bright patterned rugs on the pine floor, comfortable-looking divans and red drapes by the huge windows that framed a view across the mountains. A fire burned in a black iron stove. A thin chimney ran up through the high ceiling. The place was stiflingly hot.

Had Reiko been a willing accomplice of her cousin?

Shoji said, 'Reiko is not here. She refused my invitation.'

'Did the message I received come from you? She has no part in this?'

The man looked at him with contempt. 'I sent the message,' he said.

Ransome believed him. He felt a profound sense of relief.

Shoji motioned the two men towards a divan near the door. They peeled off their balaclavas and goggles and sprawled back on the divan. The hard faces and blank expressions were familiar. The last time he had seen these two had been in a jail cell in Shinjuku. The one wearing red boots grinned at him like a wolf contemplating its next meal.

'This ski resort,' Ransome looked out at the white world beyond, feeling foolish and angered at having been duped, 'I suppose it's one of yours?'

'Of course.' Shoji was dressed in a dark business suit as though attending the office.

'You offered Reiko a holiday here?'

Another shrug.

Ransome thought: not bad—he knew I'd come when Reiko called. 'So what am I doing here?'

'Please sit down, Mr Ransome.'

Ransome sat.

'My uncle told me that you intended to try to interview me. So I decided to make myself available.' Shoji smiled, enjoying his moment.

The smile chilled Ransome. 'If you'd given me warning I would have brought my camera,' he said, thinking: what is the bastard going to do?

Shoji said something to his men. The *yakuza* wearing the red boots, the shorter, more powerfully built of the two, disappeared through a door.

Shoji went over to the huge window and looked out over the valley for a time in silence. He turned slowly and faced Ransome. 'I would not normally be interviewed,' contempt in his voice. 'I know about you journalists. Things would be edited and distorted. What would come out would be lies.'

Redboots came from the kitchen with a tray of tea. He laid it on the low table in front of Ransome.

Shoji came back and sat down opposite him. He waved his man away. He poured tea into two cups and slid a cup over the table.

'Thank you,' Ransome said.

'But since you have questions,' Shoji said, 'why not ask me now?' the barracuda smile challenging him.

His motives were obvious. The questions would tell him how much Ransome knew. But why not? he thought. The man would never agree to a formal inter-view. Why not ask him now?

The tea tasted good. 'Let's just confirm some facts,' Ransome said. He unbuttoned his jacket.

The tallest of the two men rose quickly. Shoji shook his head. The man sat down again.

Ransome handed Shoji the Harbin photograph.

He studied the print for a long time, his face expressionless.

Ransome said, 'Your father was in charge of the Section 731 hypothermia experiments in Harbin, was he not?'

'Where did you get this?'

'We have talked to many of his men from that time. We have statements, interviews. Some of them had photographs.'

'So, what is this?' derisive now, holding the print towards Ransome as though it were something without value. 'It's just a group of officers.'

Ransome said, 'But an interesting group, Mr Takanichi. Harbin Camp, 1942. That's your father, sitting on the left of the senior officer who is Lieutenant General Shiro Ishii, officer commanding Section 731. The names of all your father's fellow officers are written on the back of the print.'

Shoji turned it over and read the names. He shook his head. 'Someone who looks like him. A group of officers in some unknown place. It proves nothing.'

'He has been positively identified.' Ransome took the second print from his pocket. He handed it to Shoji.

The man stared at the picture. 'Did my uncle give you this? My cousin?' His voice had risen a register. 'Did they identify me?'

'No,' Ransome said. 'When I made the connection and realised your father was one of the group of officers, I borrowed it.'

'You borrowed it? With anyone's permission?'

Ransome shook his head.

Shoji's eyes showed a naked rage. 'You stole it!'

Ransome shrugged. 'Borrowed it. I have given the original back to Reiko and apologised for taking it. That is a copy.'

Shoji sipped his tea in silence. He gave a resigned smile as though making up his mind to stop evading. Speaking carefully, he said, 'You cannot possibly understand what my father's team was doing in Harbin. No matter how any journalist reports it, they will bring their own bias to it. Which is why those who worked in Section 731 never spoke about it.'

Ransome said nothing.

'Yes, my father did work in the scientific study of hypothermia. It was vital war work. Our men were fighting in conditions of extreme cold. There was little or no medical knowledge at that time of the effect of low temperatures on people: how they could be revived, how they could be saved, how they could be protected. He and his colleagues had a unique opportunity to derive important knowledge that could save countless lives. He was a scientist, a medical doctor. The work he was doing was as important as any being done at the time— and it wasn't even offensive, but rather, defensive. He wasn't involved in the development of bombs or plague bacilli; he was involved in the humane business of saving lives. The knowledge we gained has been invaluable scientifically. It was then, it is now.'

'Did he use prisoners of war for his experiments?'

'Yes.' This, curtly.

'Were they coerced?'

Shoji seemed puzzled.

Ransome tried an easier word. 'Were they forced?'

'Not at all,' Shoji said. 'My understanding is that they volunteered in respect of certain privileges they were offered.'

Ransome said, 'Many of the men we have interviewed say that the prisoners were forced.'

Shoji looked at him steadily for a long moment then gave the faintest of shrugs.

The bastard doesn't care.

'Your father had no moral strictures about using forced prisoners?'

Shoji looked puzzled. 'The fruits of his work were invaluable to our war effort.'

'I suggest,' Ransome said, 'that the fruits of his work were poisonous.'

'Words,' Shoji said, derision in his voice.

Ransome thought, there's something inhuman about him—a gene missing, perhaps. He said, 'Are you aware that the prisoners in Harbin were referred to as *maruta*?'

'They *were maruta*. It is a term we Japanese use for soldiers so lacking in personal honour that they surrender rather than die in action.' He smiled pityingly at Ransome. 'Your culture is different from ours, Mr Ransome. Your soldiers seemed to find no dishonour in surrendering. Neither did the Chinese, nor the Russians. So they were *maruta*: logs of wood.'

'I put it to you that the prisoners were often political people who had worked against the Japanese and were punished by being sent to the Harbin experimental camp.'

'I know nothing of that,' Shoji said firmly. 'You and your friend Kaizei have been doing all the research on this. You've turned up all kinds of information I have found very interesting. And some names of people who have broken their vows of silence. We'll be attending to them in due course. You probably know a great deal more about it all than I do. I must say you've been most determined in trying to create a scandal.'

'How many of the prisoners died during your father's experiments?'

'You tell me. I have no idea. In scientific experiments dealing with extremes there are accidents, miscalculations.' Shoji looked away. 'Presumably sometimes the experiments did not work. But I point out they were Russians and Chinese.'

'Are they less human for that?'

Shoji did not answer.

Ransome said, 'The Germans called their experimental victims *untermenschen*—subhumans. Apparently it helps not to be able to think of victims as human.' Ransome could feel the angry coal in his gut glow. 'Do you consider Americans, British and Australians subhuman?'

'Americans? British? Australians?' Shoji looked puzzled.

'We have been told that soldiers from those countries were used for the experiments.'

'I know nothing of this,' sharply.

'Is it not true that your father and Generals Ishii and Katano were party to a deal that was made with the US authorities after the war? That they agreed to swap their scientific knowledge for immunity from prosecution as war criminals?'

Shoji blinked. The names and the detail seemed to surprise him. 'You Americans approached my father and his colleagues,' defensive now, 'which goes to prove how important the work was, scientifically. They knew the value of it.'

'Did your father and his colleagues admit that the data had been obtained by experiments on humans who were given no choice?'

Shoji snorted with disbelief at the question. 'Do you think your authorities had any quibbles about how the knowledge was obtained? Some of the data that was supplied to them within areas like biological warfare was vital to their strategic Pacific interests.'

'Is it also true that the senior officers, including your

father, did not tell their men of the amnesty?'

Shoji looked offended. 'They did the deal to save the lives of their men. It was a pity they could not pass on the information generally, but it was a condition of the deal insisted upon by your side. But let me say emphatically, Mr Ransome, that what is important is that not a single man under their command was ever tried as a war criminal. The fact is, they were not criminals.'

'Your father must have gained great advantage in knowing he would not be prosecuted.'

'Yes, my father was one of the senior officers involved in the negotiations with the Americans, but he did not care what happened to himself. He and his comrades offered themselves as scapegoats to the enemy. They were willing to take full responsibility for everything done by the 731st Unit.'

Ransome said, 'Some of your father's men think they were double-crossed.'

Shoji laughed, arrogant now. 'Nobody understands. They think because they know part of the story they have the right to have an opinion.' He poured more tea into their cups. 'You Americans had great respect for our scientific achievements. Your interrogations of General Ishii lasted for two years. Your country derived immense value from our discoveries. Where do you think you got the technology to use germ warfare against the Chinese and the North Koreans in 1952, if not from Ishii?'

'But he didn't tell the American High Command all the secrets, did he?' Ransome was watching Shoji, assessing, wondering how much he might be prepared to admit. 'The key scientific breakthroughs were held back, weren't they?'

Silence.

The nearer you get to the front line, Ransome thought, the better the pictures. 'Tell me about present experimental work being done.'

'Present work?' Shoji affected puzzlement.

'We have come across evidence that certain experiments were continued by Section 731 scientists after the war.'

'Evidence?' Shoji stared at Ransome, amazed.

'And we understand this work is going on presently.'

'You say you have evidence?'

'Yes. Several ex-members of Section 731 have told us that they have worked on or have been asked to work on a biological warfare program. Each has, or had, a background of work either on Ishii's original plague program or on your father's hypothermia program. Three we have interviewed have been murdered. Others have died.'

Shoji screwed up his eyes. 'Are you accusing me?'

'I'm interested in what you can tell me about it.'

The man shook his head.

Ransome said, 'We have been told that on his death General Ishii handed over certain secret experimental data to one of his most distinguished and trusted officers.'

The statement caught Shoji by surprise. For a brief moment there was a change of expression, then his face was under rigid control again. Speaking in a whisper he said, 'Where did you learn that?'

Ransome said, 'The general's daughter.'

The man looked shocked.

The rub, Ransome thought, is that the nearer you get to the front line, the greater the risk you're not going to survive. He said, 'That officer was your father, wasn't it?'

Shoji picked up the Harbin photograph and studied the group of officers. 'Some great scientists there,' he said, his face softened with nostalgia. 'My father was one of them.' He put the photograph down. 'General Ishii was a genius. He knew more than any man alive about bacteriological warfare. He conceived the plans, he broke new ground in the culturing of bacilli, he invented the bombs that would carry them.'

He suddenly pounded the top of the table. 'Believe me, if he had been allowed to drop the plague bombs when we had them ready, the war might have ended differently. When the Emperor was betrayed by the cowards who ran the military, Mr Ransome, there were those, like my father, who did not consider the surrender anything more than a betrayal. Nothing was changed by that so-called defeat. He knew that the time for Japan would come again. And it has.'

Shoji rose and went to the stove. He stood warming his hands, looking back at Ransome. 'Yes, it's true. My father had the honour to be chosen by the general to carry on his work. And, as it happened, although biological warfare was not my father's area, his own work in low-temperature technology provided the key, the breakthrough.' He seemed to square his shoulders. 'He took Ishii's technology into a new dimension. You're very clever, Mr Ransome. Persistent. Perhaps you deserve to know the remarkable progress we have been making.'

He came and sat back down. 'I often wish that I had trained as a scientist and followed in my father's footsteps. As it is, I have only a layman's understanding of it. But I know this: science is a remarkable thing. With patience, time and money we can eventually find techniques to do almost anything you can think of. It took my father over forty years to perfect our present biological weapons, and we're only at the threshold of the knowledge. There are effective viruses we haven't even dreamed of yet.' His smile was terrible.

For the next twenty minutes, sitting comfortably on the divan opposite Ransome, he spoke about the work of his father's laboratory and of the terrible new weapon he had created.

To know is to die. After listening with growing disbelief to the horrors Shoji had outlined, Ransome knew he wasn't going to get out of there alive. He said, 'Where do you fit into all this?'

Shoji said, 'When my father died, I felt it important we kept his work going. For him, the development of this weapon was the key to Japan's destiny as a major power. His lifelong dedication to its development and the scientific breakthrough that he made has given us this power. It has obvious geopolitical implications for Japan, but for me it was just good business. There is a market for it.'

'You wouldn't seriously use this stuff?'

'Why not?'

'You use that weapon and what are you going to inherit? A diseased world.'

'No, not a diseased world. The weapon is subtle. Chemically, it is volatile. It has a finite life. It can be controlled with great accuracy. Its potency cuts out in two weeks, or three at most. But by then it will have achieved its aim and, with minimum decontamination, property and territory can be recovered safely.' He gave an arctic smile.

Ransome felt sick. 'What you're doing—it's obscene.'

'It is profitable,' Shoji said.

'Have you no scruples at all? You are responsible for those murders of your own people.'

Shoji shook his head tiredly. 'What is it you say? "You cannot make omelettes without breaking eggs"?' He stood up. 'Well, Mr Ransome, you have had your interview. I must leave you now.'

Both his bodyguards had stood up with him. Redboots came over carrying a topcoat. He helped Shoji on with it.

He went to the door, then turned and faced Ransome. 'For your information, Reiko's father died last night.'

At first the word failed to register with Ransome, then it hit. 'Died? How?' Not another victim of this trail of death he was running, surely? 'Did you kill him?'

Shoji flushed. He hesitated, as though the answer were none of Ransome's business, then said, 'No, he committed *seppuku.*'

Seppuku? Images from Japanese novels and films flashed through Ransome's mind: a kneeling man with a knife and a tight white sash strapped around his belly, a close friend standing by with a sword to administer the coup de grace halfway through the disembowelment. Christ, was this how Reiko's father had killed himself?

'Why?' feeling anguished, suspecting he knew the real answer: that he had given the old man sufficient reason to end his life by throwing up all the ugliness of his brother's past.

There was no mistaking the pain on Shoji's face. 'He misguidedly considered that certain of my activities compromised his honour.'

Ransome knew he had run out of time. He crossed to the window and looked out.

Far below, the lights of the ski resort had been turned on against the encircling gloom. The wind was rising. Somewhere in the house, where the wind had probed and found a weakness, the eerie moaning sound grew louder. Skiers on the downhill runs kept disappearing in flurries of driven snow.

He had to try something. 'You realise that there's nothing you can do to stop the story coming out? And that you're involved in it up to your neck?'

Shoji crossed back to the table. He picked up the two photographs and tore them in half. 'As for the past, there is no proof that my father was ever in Section 731. Harbin is history, but the present belongs to me.'

'We sent all our taped interviews out of the country. The people I sent them to will see that the story gets maximum exposure.'

Shoji nodded to his men. One of them dialled a number on a mobile phone.

'You are too late, Mr Ransome. In a few days there will be a sharp shift in power in this country. I will control a group of true patriots who will not shirk from leading Japan to its proper place in the world. With this weapon, and our willingness to use it, my followers and I will ensure that Japan will not be humiliated again, ever.'

Ransome said, 'My colleague Kaizei has the story too— all of it. When it comes out, what will happen to your political aspirations? You've double-crossed Dr Cord and his friends, whoever they are. They're not going to like that. They've been misguided enough to give you immunity and special protection as you've been making your grab for power. Do you really imagine they'll continue to back you? They'll drop you like you've got AIDS.'

'So? They'll be too late. And as for your traitorous friend Kaizei,' making a distasteful face, 'he is no longer a problem. We have him in safekeeping.'

A cold stone in the heart. Ransome tried to keep his feelings to himself, but the man knew he had hit home.

Shoji said, 'The police picked him up soon after he returned from Sapporo. Thanks to their cooperation, he is now safely in our hands. As soon as I return to Tokyo, where I am heading now, he will be dealt with as all traitors should be.'

Ransome wanted to smash him to the ground. 'So what happens now?'

'Now?' Shoji shrugged his coat more comfortably onto his shoulders. 'I go back to Tokyo. You have an unfortunate skiing accident.'

A skiing accident? So that was to be it. Jesus.

'You're sick,' Ransome said.

'Sick?' Shoji laughed cynically. 'I am a businessman developing a useful product, that's all.'

Ransome felt his disgust reach critical mass. Never argue with a drunk was the rule; nor a madman. He said, 'Have you tried out your new weapons on a few "willing volunteers" like the ones your father used in Harbin?'

Shoji flushed. 'You do not even begin to understand how politics and science work.'

Outside, the racket of rotor blades grew. Shoji turned away and said something to his men. Redboots came and stood behind Ransome. Blackboots produced a pistol.

Shoji said, 'I admire your determination. You are obviously not without your share of nerve, but you must realise there are political forces that cannot be threatened by the whims of journalists.'

He opened the door. 'Goodbye, Mr Ransome.'

Beyond, the resort helicopter hung poised just above the slopes. Shoji walked away without a backward glance. For a moment his silhouette was dark against the whirling snow.

The man with the gun said something to his companion. Ransome had half-turned towards him when the world exploded into white.

White . . .

Chapter 53

An engine roaring deafeningly in his ears. A tractor? For a second he was, once more, in the sun-blasted wheat field of his childhood on top of the big John Deere, watching the golden wheat crop being gobbled up. Then the world was white and upside down. And he was in pain.

Pain everywhere. His head ached fiercely. His ribs were being crushed as though by the jolting of a pile-driver. His arms and wrists were in agony; his hands seemed to be dragged behind him. He tried to move them and could not. He opened his eyes. A wall of ice was blurring past within inches of his face.

His face would be scraped off! Instinctively, he dragged his head away.

Inches away, a red laced ski boot. All the cues suddenly fitted together. He remembered what had happened to him. He knew where he was. He was face down and tied over the mid-section of a snowcat as it laboured up the mountain. And he knew where he was heading—towards a fatal accident.

The next bounce of the machine would cave in his entire ribcage. He tried to twist sideways. It was useless; he could not move a muscle.

Nausea, a rise of bile. He wanted to be sick. He was sick, vomiting wretchedly.

The snowcat slithered and bounced its way upwards. The engine roared on. Ransome blacked out.

Silence. Hands dragging him from the snowcat. His

arms seemed to be tearing loose. But suddenly his ribs
were free from pain. A wondrously comfortable cushion
of snow under his face.

Hands rolled him over, face up. He saw a dark sky,
scudding clouds close enough to touch. Black boots. Red
boots. Laced legs led up to two thick bodies and two
masked faces looking down at him. The angle distorted
everything. He turned his head away. The snowcat was
five metres from him. A pair of silvery skis rose up above
the body of the machine like the antennae of a red insect.

He felt strangely at peace. Maybe the Lady was present.
Maybe this was the moment. She had stayed out of his
life for a long time. But at that instant it occurred to him
that a ski accident meant one positive thing: they weren't
going to shoot him. His head began to work again. What
would it be? Tied to a tree and left to freeze through the
long winter's night; they come back and untie his body
in the morning? His head bashed in and left? Shit.

He struggled to sit up as best he could with his hands
bound behind him. The two men watched him impas-
sively. He let the nausea pass, tasting the bitter bile in
his mouth.

He was suddenly aware of the wind. It tore at his
clothes with icy hooks. He looked around. They had
stopped the snowcat in a shallow valley surrounded by a
grove of pines and some leafless trees that poked their
grey trunks out of the deep snow. Ransome judged that
they were up near the summit of the range. Past the
mouth of the valley he could see windswept and deserted
slopes of the mountain spreading out below. Thick white
clouds, pregnant with the next snowfall, were blanking
out the tops of the nearby ridges. The light was failing
fast. Snow was driving into his face and eyes. A flurry of
snow erased a stand of pines fifty metres away.

Redboots said something to his companion. The two
of them dragged Ransome to his feet. He had difficulty

standing; his legs seemed to have no strength. He sagged, but the men caught him again. They propelled him through the pristine knee-deep snow for twenty metres. They propped him up with his back to a tree.

Blackboots slipped off his gauntlet gloves and tucked them inside his jacket. He began to unbutton the front of Ransome's jacket. His nails were black and bitten to the quicks. On his right hand he was missing a little finger. The tough young face was impassive. It looked at Ransome with no more expression than that of a tradesman going about his work. The other man watched.

Blackboots spun Ransome roughly around to face the tree. There was ice caught in the rough bark pattern. He thought of Reiko and regretted wasting so much of his life.

He felt downward pressure on his wrists. The man was sawing at his bonds.

His hands came free. The blood rushed back along the veins. Ransome fell forward onto his knees, pressing his wrists against his chest and clenching his fists against the agony of it.

From behind, Blackboots tugged Ransome's jacket off. He handed it to his companion. Ransome felt his skin flinch and pucker under the knout of the wind. Suddenly he understood: they were going to leave him up here in the winter's night. The Lady wasn't simply present, she had come here for him.

Blackboots walked away. Ransome twisted his head to watch him.

For a moment the man was enveloped in a flurry of snow. He reappeared, a dark figure blurred at the edges. Ransome saw him lift the skis from the snowcat. He trudged back, gradually taking shape and substance as he neared, the skis over his shoulder. He stopped a metre away. Behind him, the snowcat disappeared, claimed by the snow curtain.

Blackboots speared one ski upright into a drift a metre

from Ransome's head. He came close, raising the ski like a baseball bat. Still on his hands and knees, Ransome flinched, anticipating the edge of it smashing into his face.

He ducked as the ski crashed against the trunk just above his head, once, twice, three times, the man swinging it against the trunk two-handed as though he were wielding an axe. The ski broke in half. One piece skidded behind the tree.

An unfortunate ski accident, Shoji had said.

Contemptuously, the man threw the other half of the ski at Ransome. The jagged, broken edge struck his arm and sliced into the snow.

Blackboots said something to his companion, jerking his head impatiently.

Redboots handed him Ransome's jacket.

Blackboots stared at Ransome for a moment. Snow was clinging to his face, turning it into a grotesque mask.

I'm not a fucking sheep to be slaughtered, pal. Ransome held his rage in check.

Wait.

Blackboots swung around and started towards the snowcat, twenty metres away. The snowflakes flurried. The man disappeared momentarily, then reappeared close to the machine.

For a moment, in a brief window in a white frame, Ransome saw Blackboots draping the jacket over the snowcat's saddle.

The snow whirled again and the window closed. Then the blizzard eased. The man reappeared. He was kick-starting the engine. The roar sounded feeble as it was plucked away by the wind. Blackboots sat on the driver's seat revving the motor and looking towards his companion. He edged the snowcat forward. The snow whited him out like an error on a blank page.

Ransome flexed his fingers, feeling the chill claiming

the flesh, the bones. The ski blade felt colder than cold. He twisted round to look at Redboots, half behind him to his right. Another white mask.

Wait.

The man reached inside his jacket pocket. He tugged at something. In his hand: a pistol.

'*Sayonara*,' Redboots said with a grin. He reversed the grip on the pistol, hefting it by the barrel like a club.

Ransome swung backhand as hard as he could. The jagged edge of the broken ski caught Redboots across the face. A spurt of red shocking against white. The man fell back with a cry, arms flailing. The snow claimed him like a trap.

Ransome forced himself to his feet. Agony. His legs seemed to be permanently bent.

An insubstantial snowcat was taking shape against the whiteness, the engine louder.

Redboots twisting around, grabbing for the pistol buried in the snow somewhere near his hand.

The ski was a axe. Ransome drove the blade down at the white snow mask. It caught the man across the throat.

The snowcat was near now, the motor howling in concert with the wind.

Ransome began running downhill, wilful snow pulling at his thousand-tonne legs. Momentum kept him going only for a few metres. He fell.

The snow cleared. The snowcat was ten metres away, coming fast. Blackboots was pointing at him. Aiming!

Ransome flung himself sideways.

A crack, two, three, four.

Snow against his face. He looked up. The white closed in. Visibility, nil.

He was on his feet, labouring like a drunk, his legs without feeling. Something black loomed up, a metre away. A tree. He fell beside it.

The high-pitched roar of a frantic engine. Ransome dragged himself upright.

Two metres away, on the far side of the pine, the snowcat roared past. The engine note faded quickly, losing a hopeless contest with the storm.

It was gone. There was only the banshee shrieking of the wind.

Keep right on going, you bastard, Ransome thought, heart pumping, fear draining away.

He waited, peering hopelessly into the whirly-whirly of snowflakes.

Downhill, he thought. Downhill.

Wrapping his arms tight around his body, he began to walk down through the white wall of a white room in a white, freezing world.

* * *

Black. Night. Something rough against his face, burning the skin.

He had no hands. No feet. No eyes. 'The arm when hit with a stick would give off the sound of a board being struck.' Where had he heard that?

Cold. That was it. He had never known cold like this. Would his arms give off the sound of a board? Something rough scraped his cheek painfully. He moved his head. If only he could get comfortable he could sleep and there would be no pain.

Suddenly Ransome knew that he was freezing to death. He willed himself to move. Nothing happened. The nerves and the synapses had all seized. This roughness? The bark of the tree. It had been the last thing he had seen, ice and snow lodged in its intricately patterned bark. He rubbed his face against it again, harder this time. He focussed on the pain and half-raised his shoulders off the freezing ground. He leaned his forehead against the rough blackness of the trunk, began to move his neck, his shoulders, trying to feel his arms and legs. With a huge effort he rolled himself over onto his side.

Move. Move, damn you!

He was on his hands and knees. He was clinging to the trunk of the tree. He was upright. The wind was shrieking. He thought of himself clinging to the tree, like a flag snapping from a pole, being torn to tatters.

He could see nothing, save one level of blackness darker than the other. Vertical black trees on a plane of black snow. He blew on his fingers. They seemed to have no feeling.

Downhill. As long as he kept going downhill maybe he might get lucky. He began to go forward. He took one step. His leg did not appear to be there. He fell forward on his hands and knees.

He struggled to his feet once more. He wrapped his arms around his chest and slowly began to stumble down the slope, falling every few steps and rising again, fuelled by a fierce rage. A fierce rage about Shoji Takanichi. Was he someplace nearby filming this for reasons of science? 'They dug their hands into each other's flesh.' 'Fuck him,' Ransome said, over and over again.

His eyes had begun to differentiate between trees and rocks, but then the snow began to fall. The blizzard closed around him like a wool press. He was a blind man stumbling and falling down the mountain unable to see his hand before him. Somewhere close, the Lady was stalking him. He tripped and rolled down a steep slope . . . down . . . down . . . to end against the bole of a tree.

The Lady was very near now. Her breath was chill on his neck. He could feel it. If he turned his head he knew he would see her.

All those years in the steaming, sweat-dripping paddy fields, she had lurked on the periphery of his vision like some patient, familiar ghost, wanting to take him in her arms, to soothe him.

Remember sweat, Ransome? Remember the steamy heat? He forced memories as though to wrap himself in them like a protective cloak. But he could not remember sweat, nor warmth. Not here, not now. Maybe warmth had never existed.

He stumbled on in the dark.

Come on Ransome, come on, come on.

How ironical that the Lady should have been here, high on this mountain, waiting for him. To look her in the face would end all this pain. He longed to look back, but knew not to.

He was one of them now; one of those poor wretches in Harbin chained into baths of ice, or with their limbs thrust into the row of steel freezing chambers. With his limbs chopped he would be fodder for the fragmentation tests, or the poison gas.

He came out of the trees. The snow was clearing. Through the flurries he saw the mountain rearing above him, black against the black sky.

He fell, screaming with rage. He rose and stumbled on.

*   *   *

The cold had seeped into the marrow of his bones. He sobbed with the pain of it.

Keep moving. Keep moving.

He fell. Rose. And fell again.

This time nothing would move for him. He got as far as his knees, but couldn't make it all the way up. His arms, his legs, all of him would sound like boards when they found him.

Ahead someplace, an explosion of yellow white. There was a familiar bucketing sound: thwack . . . thwack . . . thwack. For an instant, the face of the mountain was bright as day, then black once more. Lightning flashes, perhaps? Ransome closed his eyes.

*   *   *

Whiteness. A smooth white tent rises above him. Somewhere beyond the smooth fabric the Lady is out there,
waiting.

That bucketing sound? It eludes him, skittering around
the edge of his subconscious. He remembers the shriek
of wind.

Ransome sleeps. The tent closes around him. The Lady
moves nearer.

A flurry of snowflakes against the blinding light. A
powerful spotlight piercing the blackness. Backlit heads
appearing out of the blackness. Anonymous faces behind
ski-masks and goggles.

He can feel his toes. He wriggles them. The warmth.
The warmth. The sun on his bare skin, the wheat dust
like smoke in the lens. The golden light of the wheat.

A young, square-faced nurse with milk-bottle glasses is
looking down at him, taking his pulse. Her hair is black,
her eyes brown. It occurs to him to wonder if all Japanese
are black-haired and brown-eyed. Reiko flits through his
mind and is gone. The nurse smiles reassuringly. His
right hand hurts like hell.

The sound of rubber wheels, the clack of heels.

Voices.

A kindly-faced old man in a white coat reading some
charts by the foot of his bed.

He remembers whirling upwards through a blizzard.
Thwack . . . thwack . . . thwack. The roar of a tractor? A
snowcat?

Blackness.

Standing outside himself, Ransome watches the old
doctor watching a nurse unwrapping a bandage from
around his right hand. He feels nothing. His hand dis-
appears in a swathe of fresh white bandage.

Walls of ice rush past his face: closer, closer, stripping
away the skin, grinding the flesh away down to the skull.

A helicopter! Of course, that's it. The familiar thrashing

sound he had heard a thousand times in South-East Asia: helicopter blades whirling above the sweating green paddy fields.

* * *

When he awoke, the Lady had gone.

'You are lucky man, Mr Ransome,' the old doctor said. 'But, sorry about your hand.'

'My hand?'

'We had to take tip off your little finger. Frostbite. It should not too much affect you.'

Ransome stared stupidly at the bandaged hand. He thought about some men whose frostbitten flesh peeled off to show the bones beneath. They had had no anaesthetics, nor intensive care. He thought about losing a little piece of a finger and decided he didn't feel so bad about it. He was alive!

'*Yakuza*,' he said, managing a smile.

For a moment the old man did not understand, then he cackled. '*Hai*,' he said. '*Yakuza*. Lose one finger for each bad mistake. Good joke.'

'Anything else?' Ransome asked.

The old doctor shook his head. 'Concussion. You must have hit tree. You have hard head, Mr Ransome. And you suffer hypothermia. Lucky, we very skilled at dealing with problem here. Many cases: skiers, mountain climbers. Only five stitches in head and lost finger. Very sorry.'

He left, his leather-soled shoes clattering away rapidly into the distance.

Chapter 54

The battle for control of the largest power bloc in the Liberal Democratic Party stepped up. A group of right wingers associated with the study group set up by Takanichi Shoji moved a motion of no confidence in the Prime Minister.

The motion was triggered by Shoji's most virulent attack to date on American calls for relaxation of Japan's import policies. He called a press conference during which he demanded far greater defence spending, arguing that Japan was defenceless and entirely dependent on the United States.

Calls for factional unity were ignored. In an angry debate, during which several members came to blows, the motion was defeated only because a bloc of the Prime Minister's opponents abstained.

Later in the day, at Tokyo University, police were called in to remove students who had taken control of the administration building. Two thousand police battled the students for several hours before they cleared the area using tear gas. Three police and one student died.

Carefully orchestrated street marches in support of Takanichi's position took place in several parts of Tokyo: in Asakusa near the Meiji shrine and at the Rappongi crossing.

In front of the Diet building, five thousand students marching in lockstep refused to disperse when ordered. After a violent clash the march was eventually broken up by police using batons. Many students were pursued into the Imperial Gardens where a pitched battle lasting several hours took place.

Concurrently in Kobe, Nagoya, Sapporo and Yokohama there were marches and demonstrations by students and various right-wing organisations calling for the downfall of the government.

The Prime Minster issued an official statement in which he called for civil order, accusing 'certain reactionary elements' of deliberately organising unrest in a conspiracy to overthrow the government. He demanded the resignations of three members of his cabinet: Abe Takeo, Mayazama Susumu and Takanichi Shoji.

Chapter 55

'He asks why you were skiing in blizzard,' said the pretty girl. The uniformed policeman leaned forward to hear Ransome's answer.

'Got lost,' Ransome said.

The policeman said something to the interpreter. 'He said, did you not hear storm warnings?' Tell them nothing, he thought. 'What storm warnings?'

The policeman wrote a note, then prompted the girl with another question. 'He asks, why were you skiing in wrong clothes?'

So what does it matter if they think I'm a dumb *gaijin* tourist.

'How long have I been in hospital?'

'Three days,' the pretty girl said.

Jesus, three days. How long would it take Shoji to learn he had survived?

Ransome closed his eyes and went silent on them. After a time the policeman and the pretty girl went away.

Got to get out of here! He slipped out of bed. It was the first time he had stood up. His feet hurt like hell. He left his room.

In the passageway, opposite his door, a young policeman was sitting on a chair. A guard on his door? Was he in the bag already? The discovery shocked Ransome.

The policeman stood as soon as Ransome appeared, shaking his head. Ransome said 'bathroom', and kept on walking.

The word seemed to connect. The policeman walked

with Ransome along the passage past half-a-dozen closed
doors then round a corner. He opened the bathroom
door for Ransome then stood discreetly behind Ransome
while he took a leak.

Back in his room Ransome looked for his possessions.
His clothes were not in the room. He found his wallet,
minus money, in the drawer by his bed. His passport had
been taken. In the wallet, the plain white card with Uto's
number written on it.

When a nurse came into his room a few minutes later,
he asked about his passport. The young woman did not
speak English. He mimed making a phone call. She
smiled and shook her head.

His room was on the first floor. The white-clad mountains outside seemed to be within reach through the
double glazed windows. There were houses nearby, each
with a capping of thick snow. He pointed out the
window. 'Matsumoto?' pronouncing the name clearly.

The nurse smiled. '*Hai*, Matsumoto.'

At least he knew where he was. Got to get out of here.

When she had gone, he watched from the window.
There were a few people in the grounds of the hospital
bent forward against the wind.

It's freezing out there, Ransome thought. Have to find
some clothes and get away. Every minute he stayed here
put him in greater danger.

Half an hour later he went to the bathroom again. The
pattern was repeated, this time with a different
policeman.

The officer was vigilant, as if he knew Ransome had a
criminal intent. When Ransome asked him about making
a phone call, the portcullis of language was lowered.

He felt trapped. He began listening for the movements
of the policemen outside his door. They took turns,
changing on the hour.

Late in the morning he got lucky. He heard the sound

of the guard's boots diminishing into silence on the polished floor. He looked out. The passageway was empty. The policeman had gone off somewhere, maybe to the bathroom.

Ransome went out fast. He turned the opposite way. The first two doors he opened were those of private rooms, a patient sleeping in each. The third door was a kind of storeroom–office, filled with boxes of stationery, paper towels, toilet paper and sanitary napkins. On the wall behind the door there was a telephone extension. He picked up the handpiece. Almost immediately a voice came on the line. The receptionist. He hung up. How to get a direct outside line? He picked up and dialled zero. Again the receptionist's voice. He hung up once more. He tried dialling nine. This time, a continuous tone. He dialled Uto's number.

The dialling tone sounded over and over. Answer, damn you.

Finally, after a dozen tones, a guttural voice answered.

Ransome said, 'Inspector Uto?'

There was a long pause then the voice said, in English, 'Not here.'

Damn. Outside, the sound of running feet in the passageway.

'Who is calling please?'

The footsteps were nearer. He could hear doors being opened and shut. There was no lock on the door.

Ransome gripped the handle and braced his weight against it. There was no time to consider the implications. He had to chance it. Someone grabbed the door handle. Ransome resisted. 'Tell Inspector Uto, Ransome at Matsumoto Hospital.'

The handle rattled angrily. A body slammed against the door. Ransome leaned on it. 'Ransome. Matsumoto Hospital,' he said. He hung up and stepped aside. The door slammed open. The policeman half fell into the room.

'Not bathroom,' Ransome said, smiling at the frantic man.

*   *   *

Late afternoon.

Cord said, 'You must lead a charmed life, you son of a bitch.'

Ransome felt invaded. Cord filled the space with his bulk. He was wearing a black astrakhan fur hat and a heavy double-breasted tweed coat. It was like being in a small cage with a bear. How the hell did Cord know where he was? Who had told him? Shoji? But why would he send Cord? To finish off what he had begun?

How did they fit together, these two? Ransome was reminded of the snake ball he had seen once in the ruins of an old farmhouse: a globular cluster of reptiles all curled up together; venomous snakes entwined with lizards, toads and worms; natural enemies that, when awakened from their long hibernation, would prey on each other mercilessly.

'It's a fucking blizzard and they find you stumbling around in the snow. And you know what's funny?' The American was smiling, but the eyes were dead.

'Tell me what's funny,' Ransome said, thinking of Aoyama frozen to death in that northern square, fear burgeoning inside him.

'They weren't out looking for you. They didn't even know you existed. They were looking for some other poor bastards. Instead, they found you. I'm not sure whether I call that good luck or not.'

Ransome said, 'Did they find the ones they were looking for?'

'Yeah, they found them,' Cord said. 'Three of them. All experienced skiers. This morning. They were in a snowdrift. And a few more besides. Another guy with a snowcat.'

Shoji's hit man? He wondered if either of them had survived.

'What were you doing up there, Ransome?'

He said nothing. Outside, the light was beginning to fade.

'Coming down off that mountain at night in a blizzard?' Cord said. 'Not bad going, pal. They told me you were a hard nut. We'd been wondering where you'd got to.' He watched Ransome's face, then went on in a softer tone as though wanting his confidence. 'What the hell were you doing up there anyway? It's Takanichi's resort, you know that. Were you tracking him down?'

Ransome wondered whether to tell him what he now knew. 'How come you're here, Cord?'

'A little bird told me, so I rode to your rescue,' a sly, knowing smile.

Had his call to Uto backfired? Or had the Tokyo police picked it up when he was reported found? It had to be.

Cord carried an overnight bag. He placed it on the foot of the bed. He unzipped the top, and laid out a pair of trousers, a shirt, a woollen pullover and a topcoat. 'Your travelling clothes,' he said. From the bottom of the bag he dug out ankle-high boots with red argyle socks tucked inside. On top of the pile he dropped a plastic bag containing new underwear. 'We think of everything. So, let's get dressed, shall we?'

He lifted the chair from under the window and set it down beside the bed. 'Don't be shy. I won't peek,' settling down into the chair, unbuttoning his coat.

Ransome said, 'Why are you here, Cord?'

The American looked at him with a bland expression on his face. 'Thought I'd come and take you away from all this. Got a car outside. Can get you safely back to Tokyo before our mutual friend finds out where you are, 'cos if he does, you're in deep shit. In fact, you are dead. And we don't want that, pal, do we?' fabricating a smile.

Ransome twisted around and reached for the bellpush on the bedside table. Some company would make him feel safer.

Cord caught his wrist. 'No, let's not get complicated, shall we? We don't want problems getting you safely out of here.' He wasn't smiling now.

Ransome said, 'What do you want, Cord?'

'Unlike some people, Ransome, I don't want to kill you,' making a sweetly reasonable face, 'but I do want to ask you some important questions.'

'What sort of questions?' Ransome playing for time, thinking, how the hell am I going to get out of this?

'Questions about . . .' Cord looked up at the ceiling as though trying to pluck the right phrase out of the air, "the present obscenity". Wasn't that what you called it? You assumed we knew, didn't you. That we were party to it. Amazing, isn't it? It was you—a fucking journalist—who told us there was something going on. We never knew about Shoji's little project until you told us. We must be losing our grip.' Cord shook his head as though having difficulty believing. 'How's that for grateful? We help keep his old man's political ass out of the flames for years, but now Shoji, the big time politician, doesn't share the goodies with us.' There was an edge of indignation in his tone.

Ransome said nothing.

'Anyway, we've been following up and we've talked to someone and found out some things about what's been going down all these years.'

Talked to someone. Yes. Ransome saw again the old man encased in his icy coffin. Poor Aoyama. How much would he have told before he died?

Cord was still talking. 'It's heavy stuff. We figure you know a lot about it, a lot we need to know. So we want to protect you.'

Protect me? Ransome thinking, he gets me out of here and I'm history.

'Ask me your questions here.'

Cord shook his head. 'I'm talking about a lot of questions.'

Ransome said, 'I'm in no state to travel.' He held up his bandaged hand.

'Wrong,' Cord said. He gave a low whistle. The door opened. Two other men came into the room. One was Caucasian, the other Japanese. They stood by the door.

'Show him your shiny piece, Claude.'

From his pocket the man took a syringe.

'You can walk out of here,' Cord said, 'or we can carry you out.'

Ransome got up and slowly began to dress.

Three policemen entered the room. They looked smart in their dark blue uniforms and Sam Browne belts with the gleaming black holsters. It took a moment to register with Ransome. It was the first time he had seen the police inspector in uniform.

Chapter 56

He looked back out of the window, half expecting to see a pursuing car. Twin white columns of mountains reared up behind, propping up the ceiling of fat black clouds that loomed over Matsumoto. Orange streetlights gleamed cheerfully in the winter gloom.

Uto said, 'Did the local police allow you to make that call this morning?'

Ransome shook his head. 'They tried hard to make sure I didn't. I found an empty office with a phone in it. What'll happen to Cord and his pals?'

'My men will occupy their time for awhile,' a smile stalking his face. 'Who knows? There might be passport irregularities. Do they have licences for their firearms? that kind of thing.'

'We were just visiting a sick friend,' Cord had said with a sour, loser's grin at Ransome as Uto's men disarmed him.

He and his two men had stood by as Ransome had dressed in his own clothes. Uto had brought them with him when he arrived, carrying them in a plastic storage bag. They had been cleaned and pressed by the hospital. Ransome had taken the woollen pullover, topcoat and boots from Cord's pile. 'You don't mind, do you?' he had said, but not quite able to hide his relief.

As they left, Cord had winked and said, 'Here's looking at you, kid.' His eyes had promised retribution.

Ransome's feet were still swollen and tender. He had worn the socks but carried the boots as they went down the front steps of the hospital into Uto's waiting car.

Matsumoto's lights twinkled for a dying instant then were cut off by a bend in the road.

'Were they your men or locals?'

Uto said, 'I brought them with me. After details of your passport were sent to Tokyo Prefecture, apparently the locals came under instructions to hold you. I had to pull rank to take over.'

'Who gave them the instructions?' Ransome said.

Uto shrugged.

'Why were they holding me?'

'They may have just wanted to accompany you to the airport.' He raised his eyebrows sceptically.

Ransome heard the unspoken part. 'Or maybe not.'

Uto said, 'Your own embassy people and our passport office want you on a plane out.' He glanced up at the rear-vision mirror. 'So do I.'

'I won't go until I know Kaizei is safe,' Ransome said.

Uto pursed his lips and shook his head. 'Whether he's safe or not depends on who gets to him first.'

'Shoji has him,' Ransome said, watching Uto's profile. 'He told me the police had picked him up and handed him over.'

Uto looked startled. 'The police? Handed him over?' He shook his head as though wanting to deny the possibility. 'Not possible. I would have been told if he had been picked up.'

'You didn't know I'd been picked up,' Ransome said.

Uto was worried now. 'How long ago did you hear about Kaizei?'

'Three days. Takanichi told me just before he sent me up the mountain.'

Uto drove on in a stunned silence down the steep valley road, the chains on the wheels of the Mercedes biting into the icy curves. At length he said, 'If that did happen, if Kaizei was picked up by some of our people, then I wasn't told. And if it's true, and he was handed into some civilian's custody, then I'm afraid I don't like your friend's chances.' He sounded desolate. 'And it's not impossible. Takanichi Shoji carries enough political clout.'

They passed slowly through a small town where snow-ploughs were clearing the main street.

Uto took his hand off the wheel and reached into his topcoat pocket. He handed Ransome a manilla envelope with his passport and a plastic envelope containing the fifty thousand yen in notes that had been in the hip pocket of his trousers.

As Ransome held the wallet, he caught sight of his own hand. It looked unbalanced with the top joint of the little finger missing. He picked off the neat dressing. There was a neat line of stitches like small black splinters against swollen red flesh.

Uto saw him looking at the wound.

'Frostbite?'

Ransome nodded.

'Hurting?'

Ransome shrugged.

'What did your countryman, Cord, have in mind?'

'He was planning to ask me some questions.'

Uto turned and looked soberly at Ransome. 'Do you know something he doesn't?'

Ransome nodded. 'Yes.'

'Tell me,' Uto said. 'From the beginning.'

Driving fast along the near-deserted mountain roads, he listened in silence as Ransome related what Shoji had revealed. Uto was startled. He said, 'How long has this been going on?'

'Since 1937. Back in the 1940s, General Ishii planned to send a plague virus onto the American west coast by balloons. It was a crude concept, but it might have worked—if they'd had the time. Losing the war slowed things for a few years. But Shoji claims that his father started serious experimentation again just two years after the war. He began with the unique basis of the Ishii formulae he had inherited. He was working at it right up until he died.'

'How could he have kept it a secret for so long?'

Ransome said, 'The secrecy of the oath and the original deal with the occupation forces left him free of any historical connection with the crime. Shoji told me that when Ishii and the Section 731 heads advised the US military on the use of BW in Korea, his father stayed clear of it. He was a cleanskin in the biological warfare area.'

'He must have had a team around him?'

'All hand-picked men, not only rock solid scientifically but sharing his political views. As the technology became more sophisticated, Takanichi and his team started making significant breakthroughs. The DNA discovery enabled him to make a giant step forward. But Shoji claims that it was his father who personally made the significant conceptual leap—by harnessing his own freezing technology to biological engineering. Shoji claims the technology can produce off-the-shelf diseases: any foul disease you can think of and a lot you can't even imagine. It's all linked with the new recombinant chemistry.'

Uto let his breath out slowly.

Ransome said, 'It's a bit like those super glues. You know—each glue is ineffective on its own; bring them together and you need a surgeon to part your fingers. Shoji says that his father developed a technique whereby he could put bacilli in place, then, when he wanted to, he could add the triggering ingredient.'

'How is the weapon triggered?'

'Several ways,' Ransome said. 'It can be introduced physically—airdrop, missile, whatever—or another option is by electronic beam from a satellite. The pulse only has to pass over an already infected crop or a water supply, and immediately the chemistry begins to work. And people start dying.'

'Just like that?'

'Yes, if what Shoji claims is true. This makes the neutron bomb seem like a Christmas cracker. Doesn't harm property, only people. Apparently they can even control the length of time it remains lethal. They can quarantine off an area, walk in after everyone is dead. It's cheap to manufacture—a lot cheaper than the Bomb—easy to use and exact in its toll.

Uto said, 'A great contribution to the human condition.'

'So was napalm,' Ransome said. 'Why does anyone want to develop such shit? For Shoji's father it was about strategic power, nationalism—all that jazz. Apparently he wanted to ensure Japan's destiny as a major world player. With this weapon as a threat, he believed you Japanese could economically blackmail your rivals at will, or destroy your enemies.'

Uto said, 'And if his son gets into political power, who's to stop him?'

'I think Shoji subscribes to the same views but he's more into the economics of it all. He said, "Why not use it—there's a market for it."'

'He admitted all this?' Uto said, disbelief in his voice.

'He didn't intend that I should tell anyone.'

Uto drove in silence for a time. 'Takanichi Shoji's cover must be perfect,' he said. 'After what you told me, I tried to find out if there's any knowledge about any new biological experiments. I was given access to the highest levels of security. I found nothing. No-one knows what I am talking about. The opinion is that to sustain such a project in secret is totally out of the question. Did he give you any idea where these weapons were being made?'

Ransome shook his head.

Uto said, 'So the killings have all been to protect the new technology?'

'Yes. Harbin, act II,' Ransome said.

'What about the suicide in Kamakura?'

Ransome said, 'Sanko was another brilliant researcher from Harbin. He had also been approached to work on the program. Maybe that wasn't why he killed himself, but I think that knowing such work was going on again exacerbated an old guilt about the work he did in Harbin.'

'And the hospital orderly in Yokohama?'

Jesus, poor ugly little Masaka. 'That poor guy was just a pawn in the game,' he said. 'Masaka was no scientist, just the general's driver—a powerless functionary bitter enough to tell us something he knew, something that no-one was supposed to talk about.'

'And the girl?' Uto's face had hardened.

Ransome feeling sick, 'That was our fault. She should never have been involved.' The others had known what a dangerous game they were playing. Poor Eiko had known nothing. 'Maybe he ran out of places to hide, Inspector. He's been on the run for months now. He pushed his luck.'

'No, Mr Ransome,' Uto said, 'Mr Kaizei pushed her luck.'

Ransome nodded. There were no excuses.

Waiting to clear a *shinkansen* at a rail crossing, Uto said, 'You probably haven't heard, but two days ago Takanichi Shoji made his move on the government. His supporters are rioting all over the place. The political situation is very dangerous.'

'Is he going to succeed?'

'There are a great number of people who will fight to see that he does.' The train swept through the crossing. The gates swung up. Dusk was falling. Uto switched on his headlights. 'You haven't explained how you came to be in Takanichi Shoji's ski resort.'

Ransome told him about Reiko's family connection.

'You never told me your girlfriend was a Takanichi.' Uto sounded surprised and annoyed.

'I only established the connection between her uncle Takanichi Junichiro and Section 731 a couple of days before we last spoke,' Ransome said, wanting to explain. 'Until then, she wasn't involved.'

'I had reports of a woman visiting you in one or two of the hotels you stayed at.'

'Yeah,' Ransome said, wondering how much of his life was a closed book to the police. By the sound of it, not much. Uto must have been watching his every move.

Uto made another connection. 'I also had a report of you meeting an older man—a businessman with a chauffeur-driven car—in the Imperial Hotel on the evening before you came up here. Who was that?'

Ransome said, 'Reiko's father.'

'What was that about?'

'He asked me not to go on with our investigation.'

They crossed a steel bridge over a narrow river choked with ice.

Uto's face presaged bad news. 'Do you know he's dead?' He glanced at Ransome.

So it was true. 'Yes, Shoji told me. *Was* it suicide?' Ransome felt numb.

Uto nodded.

How would Reiko be feeling now? Thinking, I should never have become involved in this whole thing.

Uto said, 'The famous tunnelling engineer, uncle of top right-wing politician, has his biggest-ever tunnelling project sabotaged. He suicides. His death is big news. Especially now—just at the time his nephew is making his grab for power. Do you know if Takanichi was involved with his brother?'

'He knew about Junichiro's war record. Wasn't too keen on that coming out. Family honour and all that stuff.'

Uto nodded as though finding that motive acceptable. 'Did he know about the new biological weapon?'

'Not before I told him, I'd almost bet on it. He seemed genuinely shocked and angry about that, and about the killings.'

Uto looked sceptical. 'A motive for suicide?'

Ransome was made unhappy by the question. He said, 'I suspect so. Takanichi said it was something to do with family honour and I don't see a hell of a lot of honour in what his brother did, or in what Shoji is doing. To top it all, the sabotage of his tunnel and all those deaths affected him badly.'

'You said Shoji intends to sell it. To whom?'

Ransome shook his head.

'We've got to find out,' Uto said. 'He has to be stopped.'

They drove in silence for a time. Ransome thought about Kaizei, feeling a sense of despair building within him. He said, 'Kaizei wants to live. He isn't into family honour. Can you do anything about finding him?'

'I'll try,' Uto said. 'What you've told me might narrow down the number of people we can lean on.'

They made Nagoya in forty minutes, Tokyo in four hours.

* * *

Uto's safe house was a small apartment on the fourth floor of a block of flats in Kachi-doki. The unlovely concrete building smelled vaguely of blocked toilets.

'Two days,' Uto said, 'three at most, then you must leave Japan.'

'I need to make some calls.'

Uto thought for a moment. 'Alright, but don't give anyone this number.' He handed Ransome the key. 'Do not go out unless you have to, and be careful—you're hard to miss,' this with the ghost of a smile. 'Wear a hat, a scarf, sunglasses. Make sure nobody follows you back here.'

By the door, Uto slipped on his shoes and belted his trenchcoat. 'I'll see what I can do about finding your friend.' His expression didn't convey much hope.

Ransome made his calls. From the window he could look down along the Harumi-dori. It was choked with heavy transporters and huge, double-decker jinkers coming and going from the docks. Sleet was falling straight out of a sullen sky. That morning's fall of snow had been reduced to a black, glutinous slush.

He tried half a dozen times in the next two hours, but there was no answer from Reiko's number.

He rang the Foreign Correspondents' Club and asked the desk clerk to page McGregor. He hung on for five minutes but he was not in the club. He left a message: he would call back later and would McGregor advise the desk when he was going to be around?

His hand was painful and his feet still felt as though they had no circulation. Wearily, he lay down on the shabby sofa. He slept. He dreamed the Lady was near, stalking him silently through a palace of ice.

Chapter 57

They finally arrived at Higashi Shinagawa, a blighted cityscape of rail sidings, oil terminals, factories and docklands.

Uto's man swung off the expressway, switchbacked over a series of canal bridges and came to what looked like a factory behind a high, wire-mesh fence. 'My assistant will be there in ten minutes,' Uto had said on the phone. 'Don't open the door to anyone. I'll give him a key. He'll let himself in.'

It was a bleak and dismal place. By the gate, there were several police cars and an ambulance. Two uniformed policemen wearing oilskins came towards them, holding up their hands warningly. Uto's man did not wind down the window. He showed them an identification through the glass. They dragged the gates open. The car bumped across a series of rail lines deeply pitted with axle-deep holes filled with ice and black slush.

The driver stopped close under the eaves of the factory. He grunted and jerked his head at Ransome, indicating that he should get out.

They trudged over the slushy ground, sleet slashing at Ransome's face. A feeling of dread was overwhelming him like the nausea that precedes being violently ill. A small personnel gate was set into the steel roller door of the building. The driver went through it. Ransome followed.

Inside, it was harshly lit with neon lighting. The walls and floors were scrubbed clean concrete. This was no factory; it was a coldstore. Ransome had a depressing sense of deja vu.

At the end of a long corridor there was a group of several police, some in plain clothes. One of them detached himself from the group and came towards Ransome. Uto.

He shook hands, grimaced, then looked away, embarrassed: the gesture that told Ransome all that he cared to know.

'You've found him?' The question was redundant.

Uto said, 'I'm sorry. By the look of it, it would have been too late several days ago.'

Ransome said, 'Can I see him?'

'Are you sure you want to?'

'He was my friend.' But Uto was right, of course. Ransome did not really want to see Katie dead; he who had been so filled with life.

Without a word, Uto went to an insulated door. A uniformed man standing on guard depressed the lever and swung it open. Inside, the cold struck like a blow. Uto led him to the rear of the enormous chamber, past rack upon rack of frozen beef carcasses wrapped in white muslin.

Half-a-dozen police and medical orderlies were grouped around a stretcher. There was a body on it covered by a green sheet.

Uto was grim faced. He pulled back the sheet.

Kaizei. His face was almost unrecognisable, twisted as though by some unspeakable agony.

When Ransome stood up he noticed that there was a space between the carcasses directly above Kaizei's body. In the space, a meathook hung. There was blood on it.

Someone, perhaps Uto, pulled the sheet back over the dead face.

When Ransome looked up, he saw a ring of Japanese faces. They were looking at him with expressions of curiosity. They're thinking, how will I react? How will this civilian, this *gaijin*, take the sight of death? Christ, I've seen more death than all of them put together.

He walked away from them, pushing his way through a line of steel-hard, frozen carcasses that swung like pendulums after him as he passed. He wanted to be alone.

He walked beside the blank wall of the great freezing chamber thinking of his friend's crushing remorse about the deaths for which he had felt responsible. With each one, Kaizei had come close to calling the whole thing off. It was a pity he had not. Wouldn't it have been better if they had never begun? Had they brought back to life one single victim from faraway Harbin?

He thought of all the times they had spent together. He and Kaizei were survivors. They both went where the action was, but always they took care. They valued being alive. Never the unnecessary risk. That was what had bonded them as powerfully as any brothers. Ransome found some comfort in the thought that Kaizei hadn't died for the past, where he had begun this deadly journey, but for the terrifying present of Shoji Takanichi.

He half-tripped over something. For a long moment he did not recognise it. Something of plastic? Aluminium? Then he knew what it was. 'Latest state of the art,' Katie had called it. Thinking, Oh Christ, what did they do to my brother?

Ransome carried the limb back and handed it to Uto. 'Does Takanichi own this freezing works?' he asked.

Uto looked at him with pity. He did not bother to reply. He walked away.

It was then that Ransome wept.

* * *

That night, standing together on the Sumida River bridge, McGregor did some weeping of his own.

He had left Ransome a message at the club to call him at home. 'What the hell kind of trouble are you in?' he had said, sounding worried. 'A policeman called Uto just came by the apartment and picked up your camera.'

Yes, McGregor knew the Harumi-dori bridge over the Sumida River at Kachi-doki. 'I can be there in twenty minutes,' he had said. 'But it's bloody freezing, pal. Why do you want to meet there?'

'I need to get out of this place,' Ransome had said. He felt worse than he could ever remember.

It was a clear, frosty night. McGregor was dressed in an ankle-length fur coat. He looked like an overweight bear. They stood together on the arched steel span looking along the shimmering waters of the city's wide river. Reflections of the quartz lights from the fishing fleet dock were trailing on its black surface like yellow fire.

Ransome told him about Kaizei.

'I'm sorry,' McGregor said. 'Truly sorry. I know he was a great pal of yours.'

Ransome needed to talk about Kaizei, and for awhile, he did. McGregor was a good listener. That helped.

'When are you getting out of Japan?'

'First I have to see her,' Ransome said, ' find out what's going on in her head.'

A bus stopped fifty metres short of the bridge on the same side of the street. A lone passenger got off. He fell over and lay on the wet pavement, flat on his back. A falling down drunk.

The bus drove on over the bridge, past them. The drunk rose to his hands and knees. He pulled himself upright using the bus shelter for support. He walked a few metres away towards the docks, then spun around and began to walk onto the bridge. He was a little fellow dressed in a salaryman's suit. His legs seemed unable to keep him upright. He fell and rose again three times before he came opposite them.

Ransome said, 'Poor bastard.'

'Drunks,' McGregor said, disgusted. 'The whole country's full of them. Been on the subway late at night?'

The drunk's face was bloody, but he was singing a marching song. He seemed to be in no pain. He stopped opposite them and stared as though unable to believe the sight of foreigners. He said something that sounded like an obscenity and went staggering on to the city side of the bridge.

McGregor said, 'The carriages are full of men slobbering and puking over all the other passengers. Christ, underneath all this Japanese miracle—all this disciplined "success",' spitting out the word as if it were something rotten, 'is one weird fucking country.' Leaning on the parapet of the bridge, he stared out over the city. 'One of these days this place is going to go off like a bomb. I rather suspect it's happening right now. I've never seen the place this close to anarchy. The Prime Minister's bound to fall and, if he does, your friend Shoji will run the whole shooting match.'

Somewhere upriver a ship's siren gave a mournful hoot.

Ransome said, 'How's Suroko?'

McGregor turned. 'You know what's she's done?' There were tears in his eyes. 'She's gone to Hawaii with some American journalist from the *New York Times*. Not even a Japanese. Another *gaijin*. She's learned by her mistakes; she can repeat them all perfectly.' Suddenly McGregor turned and screamed out into the teeth of the wind, 'Screw you all!'

His shout carried out across the river. The words fragmented like spent fireworks over the great sweep of the Sumida. The big man wept like a child.

Ransome wanted to be home in the warm Californian sun. Out of this.

He hugged McGregor awkwardly around the shoulders, trying to give comfort. After a time the weeping ceased.

McGregor wiped his eyes with a handkerchief then leaned forward looking out to where the lights of the Tokyo Tower flashed high above the city. 'Sorry,' he said. 'Other directed anger.' He offered Ransome his hand. 'Kaizei was okay,' he said. 'A special kind of journalist. He had more courage than the rest of us. Completely mad, of course. A bit like you, Jack. Good luck. I hope you manage to get out of the place in one piece.'

McGregor walked away along the bridge towards the bright tunnel of rain-softened neon lights that marked the Ginza. He stopped. Came back. 'Was it all worth it?' he said. By the look on his face it was obvious that he did not think so.

Chapter 58

T he iron gates were closed and padlocked. He peered through the bars. Beyond the soft, white curtain of falling snow, the house was in darkness. There was a bellpush set into the stone wall. He tried it several times. No response.

He tried the side gate. Locked.

Damn. I've got to know if she is home.

A quick look around, then he climbed over the spiked gate. He bumped his mutilated hand painfully in steadying himself when he leaped down.

He made his way up the drive, snow and gravel crunching underfoot. He rang the front doorbell. There was a long silence. He was about to ring a second time when the porch light went on. The door opened.

Reiko looked half demented. Her face was dark with grief. There were shadows under her eyes like smudges of axle-grease. Her hair was awry. She was wearing a kimono that seemed to have been hurriedly dragged on. There was pathos in the way a slim shoulder was bare. And she was drunk.

She swayed on the doorstep staring at Ransome. Her face went through a series of strange kaleidoscopic changes as though her features, each acting independently, were trying to organise themselves into a suitable expression. Finally, she simply crumpled onto his shoulder and began to weep, wildly. 'He said you were dead. He said you were dead,' whispering it into his ear, over and over.

Ransome could feel her ribs. She was thin as a bird.

They lay on her bed together, Reiko clinging to Ransome as though he might vanish like a ghost at cock-crow. He told her what had happened to him. It sobered her with astonishing speed. She wept for him, knowing how much he had cared for Kaizei. She wept for his maimed finger, staring at it in disbelief, holding it against her lips as though she might repair it. She wept for her father.

The day after his suicide, when she was still reeling from the news, Shoji had told her about Ransome's death in the snow. She had dismissed the servants and locked herself in the house. The children had been taken off to a cousin's house by Akiko, their nursemaid.

Reiko said, 'I'm sorry about being drunk, but I couldn't think of any reason to go on.'

She was suddenly anxious. 'You are at terrible risk here. You must go. Shoji has taken over my father's interests. He comes and goes all the time as though he owns the place—and me. I hate him,' she said. 'He is responsible for my father's death.'

She told him about it. He had done the act in his office. A handgun.

'Why did he do it?' Ransome asked.

Reiko said simply, 'Disgrace. Betrayal.' She rose and went to a low lacquerwood box in the corner of the room. 'He left me a letter, explaining.' She came back and sat cross-legged, holding an envelope in her hand as though it were broken doll.

'He had always known about my uncle's war record, I told you that. But he says in this letter that you told him there was something else going on: something much worse.'

Reiko took the letter from the envelope. 'My father was a major contributor to my uncle's scientific research foundation for years. He thought the work was about food technology, something of vital importance to

Japan's exports. He contributed millions of yen. But he says here that my uncle lied to him. He says that he had never been told about "the real work"—whatever that is. What you told him apparently made him realise what was really going on.' She looked at Ransome curiously. 'What was it you told him?'

Ransome gave her the rest of it. He told her everything. When he finished, Reiko stared past him as though seeing the approach of some nightmarish creature. 'How horrible,' her voice no more than a whisper. 'My uncle did such things?' She looked at him. 'And Shoji?'

'He was part of it—and he's kept it going.'

'No wonder my father was so shamed.'

She handed the letter to Ransome. 'He left you this.'

Three pages covered in Japanese characters, typed in neat rows. Ransome stared at the impenetrable text. 'What is it?'

'A list of his brother's companies, now run by Shoji.'

'Did your father say anything about this in his letter?'

She shook her head. 'Just that you'd know what to do with it.'

Ransome said, 'It might help.' He thought he knew how. He must ring Uto.

She said, 'My father also wrote something else.'

Ransome looked at her. The pain was showing.

'I was to tell you that he knows of something which proves what you are saying is true.' She read from the letter: ' "Tell Mr Ransome that my nephew admitted to me that there have been many deaths. Always these have been covered up. Recently they had their worst accident. Several people died because of an experimental failure in a laboratory." '

'That's all?'

'Yes.'

Ransome felt a pulse beating in his head. 'Did he say where the laboratory was?'

She shook her head. Slowly she folded the letter and put it back in its envelope. 'Like my father,' she said, 'I feel tainted by all this.'

She was looking at him as though he were a stranger. Ransome thinking, how are we ever going to bridge this gulf?

'Can I use the phone?' The sooner Uto had this information, the better.

'Yes. There's one downstairs in the entrance hall.'

The house was silent. The lights were on in the lounge below, left burning when they had passed through.

He walked downstairs and through the sliding screen that led into the vast lounge, heading for the telephone.

Until he was halfway through the room, Ransome did not see him.

Caught in a pool of soft light, Shoji Takanichi was sitting on a divan staring over the top of a pair of half-glasses. There was a document in his hand and a file on the coffee table before him. He had obviously heard Ransome's footsteps on the stairs and had, perhaps, expected Reiko.

Ransome stopped in his tracks. Emotions crowded. Fear was part of it—the man scared him—but most of all it was rage. He felt it begin to erupt within him like molten lava.

Shoji was clearly astonished. He stood up. He took off his glasses and put them and the document down on top of the file.

'What good fortune, Mr Ransome,' he said. 'I thought you would have been intelligent enough to have left Japan by now.'

'You bastard!' Ransome said, hearing his own voice break with emotion. He had never felt such hatred as he did towards this man. 'We found Kaizei.'

Shoji shrugged.

'You killed him, you fucking animal.' He felt himself trembling.

Shoji made a dismissive hissing sound. 'I killed him? His own actions killed him, Mr Ransome. I told you what happens to traitors in this country.'

Since he had seen poor dead Kaizei earlier that day, Ransome had imagined a dozen violent scenarios involving his destruction of this evil man. Now, here he was—and alone. It was his chance for vengeance, yet, in this moment, he was unable to move.

'Have you come to steal more photographs, Mr Ransome?' Shoji said, his eyebrows rising like little wings. He looked like a fox who had just found a rabbit in a trap. He crossed the room and picked up a framed photograph from the top of the grand piano. 'Here, Mr Ransome,' proffering the photograph with a look of contempt on his face, 'perhaps you could manufacture some more lies with this.' He walked around behind the piano as though to use it as a barrier between them.

Ransome let out a shuddering breath. Suddenly he wanted to smash the man to a pulp with his fists. He should be made to feel something of the pain Kaizei must have felt. He moved towards Shoji.

At that moment, the man turned his back on him and reached upwards. Too late, Ransome saw what he was doing. The samurai sword hanging on the wall! He sprang forward knowing it was already hopeless.

The gleaming blade sang as Shoji dragged it from the black sheath. He turned to face Ransome, the edge glinting in the light. Only the width of the piano distanced them.

A single-frame image of the bloody walls in Eiko's flat came into Ransome's mind and was gone. His mouth dried. He looked around quickly, but there was nothing with which to defend himself.

Shoji raised the sword high above his head, holding it two-handed. The action was familiar. Ransome had seen it in a dozen Japanese films—the actor samurai Mifune about to fight a decisive personal battle. It was inevitably deadly, quick and bloody.

Shoji began to move around the piano, coming at him steadily. The man's arms were straight. The blade vertical.

Ransome backed across the room. The low, subdued lamplight in the room painted Shoji's face as a menacing mask. The bones of his face showed through the skin like a skull.

Circling backwards, warily, Ransome tried to keep well out of range, but the walls crowded in. The furniture seemed to be under his feet.

Blood on a doorhandle. Eiko's slashed face. He felt a growing sense of panic. The Lady had entered the room and was watching him being stalked.

Shoji moved forward with the deadly assurance of an experienced sword fighter.

A sideboard stopped Ransome's backward progress. He glanced behind him. With a great shriek, Shoji leaped and slashed downwards.

A desperate, instinctive sideways leap. The blade whistled like a stockwhip, missed Ransome by an inch. There was a crash. A line of priceless pots on the sideboard became dust.

Shoji regained his balance at once. His face was twisted with rage. He began to track Ransome once again. He skirted around the divan, coming fast.

Quickly Ransome stepped over the back of another divan and began to move along the long plate glass window that overlooked the garden. If he could make it to the screen door at the far end of the room, there might be a chance to get out into the passageway and through the front door.

Shoji guessed his intention. He traversed the room, corner to corner, cutting off the possible escape route.

Ransome found himself alongside a low wooden table upon which were more of the pottery collection. As he passed he grabbed a pot about the size of a man's head. Holding it by the rim, he hefted it.

Shoji stopped for a moment. His eyes gleamed in the light. He began to move forward once more, more cautiously now that Ransome was armed.

Ransome threw the pot overarm. Shoji managed to block it with the blade of his sword. The pot split in two and crashed behind him. Ransome grabbed and threw a second, smaller pot.

Shoji swayed. It glanced off his shoulder and smashed to smithereens on the wall ten feet behind him.

Even as Ransome picked up a third pot, Shoji screamed '*Hai!*' and launched himself through the air.

Ransome flung himself backwards. His heels caught on the bamboo display frame holding the ancient kimono. The blade whistled past his face. Shoji's vicious downward slash bit into the silk. Ransome hit the ground hard. As Shoji dragged the blade free of the enfolding silk, Ransome rolled frantically sideways, trying to regain his feet.

The blade reared again.

He dived headfirst over a low divan. The second stroke split the leather. A cloud of white goosedown filled the air.

Blood on walls. Blood on a sheet covering a body.

Ransome was on his feet and really frightened now, his flesh anticipating the bite of steel. The harsh breathing was partly his, partly his assailant's.

Shoji came on, closer and closer. The blade slashed once and a lampshade was split asunder; twice, pottery shattered; three times, a painted screen was cut in half. Shoji screamed with each stroke.

Unnerved, Ransome reached the grand piano, trying to put it between him and his death. As he drove into the gap between the piano and the wall, he snatched up a framed photograph and, without looking, slung it backhand. It sliced through the air. Shoji let out a cry of pain.

Ransome turned. The man was standing holding his forehead. He took his hand away and looked at it stupidly. A curtain of dark blood began to move down his brow and past his eyes.

Shoji seemed to lose his reason. His face screwed up with rage and he rushed around the piano at the run, the sword held high, screaming wildly.

Ransome picked up the piano stool and slung it. His pursuer saw it coming and propped. The heavy stool smashed harmlessly against the wall, bringing down the scabbard of the samurai sword.

Shoji came on, scenting blood.

Ransome went backwards around the piano, fast. The blade drove, angling down and across, right to left. With a splintering crash, Reiko's 200-year-old cello was sundered. The top half crashed against the piano, the bottom half remained in its stand.

Suddenly his heels caught the edge of a carpet. Ransome crashed down sickeningly on his back. Above him, the ornate ceiling, then, a moment later, Shoji's triumphant face filling the frame. Rising above him, the sword's blade gleaming red in the light.

Frantically, Ransome threw himself under the piano. The blade slashed down. There was a crashing chord as the honed steel sliced through the polished lid of the keyboard and through the keys, to embed itself in the wooden frame.

Ransome scrambled out from below.

Shoji was trying to wrest the blade free. He tugged, uselessly. The razor-sharp, laminated blade was half-buried in a wooden bearer. The man screeched with frustration.

Something erupted in Ransome. 'You bastard!' He smashed him sideways with his forearm. The blow caught Shoji across the chest. The force of it crashed the man sideways, hard against the plate glass window, leaving him a crumpled heap on the ground.

Ransome grabbed the handle of the sword. The blade was immobile, caught in the dense fibrous grip of the walnut timber. Come on, damn you! Ransome felt the veins in his head popping with the effort.

Shoji was on his hands and knees struggling to rise. Naked rage impelled him to his feet, blood streaming down his face.

The blade loosening.

Shoji rushing at him now.

Abruptly, it came free. Ransome swung round in triumph.

Shoji ran at him. Ransome smashed him away with another savage backhand blow. Shoji staggered back but retained his balance.

Ransome's rage turned cold. He tightened his grip on the long handle of the sword and raised the lethal blade high above his head.

At that instant, Shoji flinched, holding his hands up in front of his face. Suddenly he looked like a fragile, frightened man.

For an infinity their eyes locked. Part of Ransome said *do it!* Now he could avenge all the faceless hundreds who had died at the hands of this man's father.

Now he could avenge Kaizei, and Eiko, and old Aoyama, who had wanted to meet his maker with a clear conscience.

Now he could avenge the shadow dresser who had hidden from the world and ended up in the Emperor's moat, and the poor devil who had finished his life frozen in the bathroom of a cheap hotel.

Shoji's face betrayed him. Upon it, in quick succession, there appeared a complex sequence of emotions: hatred, fear, shame, humiliation. A sob escaped him. Slumping backwards onto his heels, he covered his face with his hands. He curled into a ball, his head against his knees.

Ransome lowered the sword. A moment before it had been so alive, so weightless and beautifully balanced that it seemed to have a life of its own. Now it felt like a dead thing in his hand.

'Why didn't you kill him?' Reiko said.

Ransome whirled around at the sound of her voice. She was standing by the sliding door, clutching her kimono about her, watching him. She looked exhausted and dishevelled. How long had she been there?

'Why?' Reiko questioned Ransome with bitter eyes. 'He's like his father—a monster.'

He did not answer her.

Suddenly she screamed something at Shoji. He did not reply, nor did he look at either of them.

Ransome walked to the door overlooking the garden. He found the catch and slid the plate glass sideways. A draft of icy air rushed in.

Out onto the terrace. Snow was still falling. The garden lights gleamed on the foot-deep covering that mantled the ground.

As hard as he could, Ransome threw the sword towards the darkness on the far side of the garden. It spun horizontally, like a glinting boomerang. The blade struck a stone lamp, knocking off its capping of snow. The hand-tempered steel rang like a bell. The sword disappeared into a drift of white.

He returned to the room and closed the door. Reiko had not moved.

Shoji was gone. From outside there came the sound of a car engine roaring, the skid of gravel, then silence.

Reiko's eyes blazed at Ransome: anger underlaid with something else, perhaps respect. 'Why? He would have killed you.'

'If there's any justice, which I doubt,' Ransome said, 'maybe the bastard will freeze in hell.'

Chapter 59

The lights in the computer science building at Tsukuba University burned all night. Asking the right question had taken time. It was 3.00 a.m. before Uto and the two computer experts from the Police Intelligence Unit made the first breakthrough.

Using the new Hoshino-designed parallel array computer, the PAX 128, they had begun with an exhaustive analysis of the Takanichi companies on the list supplied by his brother and passed on by the American journalist. Although they had identified many of the companies as potentially having laboratories, they had drawn a blank. The affairs of the Takanichi Group were extraordinarily complicated and the structures of the seventy-two companies wilfully obscure.

Accessing national taxation records, they established the names of all Takanichi Group personnel. They officially numbered 6400. The investigators crossed the file with Tokyo's official 'missing persons' report. There were over fourteen thousand names on the current register. It was the same most months and most years in Tokyo. There were thousands more missing citizens whose names were never reported, but they could only work with the information they had.

The PAX crunched the numbers effortlessly. The names of four men were thrown up. They were described variously as laboratory technicians, research chemists, or medical doctors. All had worked for one or other of the Takanichi companies; all four had been reported missing around the same date—within the past three weeks.

Searching back over six years' lists, the computer threw up the names of another seven Takanichi employees, all described as being involved in food technology work, all reported missing.

Another even more interesting connection was made. The name of the Takanichi employee reported missing most recently cross-checked with that of a man who had died a few days before in the infectious diseases hospital.

Uto had the crucial insight. The trigger was Reiko's father's information that there had been some recent laboratory accidents. From situation reports that had been vetted by the Intelligence Unit in the past weeks, he was aware of the serious quarantine crisis, a situation that was being kept under the tightest security.

At 4.00 a.m. Inspector Uto made a call to a high-ranking officer in the Health Department. He pulled prime ministerial authority to insist on names and details of all the victims from the quarantine island. These were processed. Another report of a death in quarantine cross-checked with someone recently reported missing.

Uto insisted on being given details of the diseases that had killed the men. This required personal clearance from the Minister. The information was phoned through within an hour.

He was told that an autopsy had been done on what was left of a man who had been found dead and whose body had been badly burned. Because the same virulent symptoms had been detected on the corpse as on the other victims, the body had been quarantined. Dental records had just thrown up the name of the man. It, too, cross-checked with a missing report concerning a Takanichi employee.

But, although it seemed to establish vital connections, in the end the analysis was a failure. Uto's colleagues tried many variables, but there seemed to be no vital common factor. None of the missing men were listed as having worked in the same Takanichi company. They came from various parts of Japan, although most were in the Tokyo area. The investigators were not able to tease out the one piece of information they so desperately sought: a clue to the location of the laboratory where the accidents might have taken place.

At dawn, deeply frustrated, Uto drove the thirty-seven miles from Science City back to Tokyo.

Chapter 60

From the direction of the riot, a short column of Buddhist monks together with a few umbrella-carrying civilians marched along the edge of the Imperial Palace gardens. Their drenched saffron clothes clung to them. Their banner was sodden with rain. From time to time they chanted in unison and one of their number rang a bell.

It's one solution, Ransome thought. Opt out. But he didn't feel like peace, nor Nirvana, nor chanting. He wanted to smash something.

There seemed to be thousands of helmeted police on both sides of the road. They ignored the monks.

Uto's driver had brought Ransome here from the safe house an hour before. They had sat in the car since.

Uto appeared from the glass-walled Ministry of Information building. Ransome watched him as he hurried across the courtyard, past the guard's office and into the street where the khaki, steel-meshed riot wagons were parked two-deep. He began to run, leaning into the downpour. The driver got out and held the door for him, and he slid in, streaming rain. The acrid bite of tear gas came into the car with him.

Uto's driver ran across to the shelter of the building.

'Any luck?'

Uto switched on the ignition. He shook his head, engaged the clutch and swung past the police barricades. He said, 'But I may know someone who can help us.'

Beyond the windscreen, Tokyo flowed past, a drenched

city painted in sombre greys and blacks. As he drove, Uto told Ransome about his night's work: the potential epidemic, the quarantining of the sick and dying and about the technicians who had died in laboratory accidents.

By the end of it, Ransome felt numb. 'What's the disease?'

Uto gunned across the traffic into another lane. 'No-one's saying; not directly; not even when I pull prime ministerial rank. It's been locked up tight by the health authorities. On the file it says the jurisdiction is exclusively with the Health Department. Officially, my unit is not supposed to get involved. Unofficially, I made a phone call. I was told that it's a totally new virus, part plague, part anthrax, like nothing they've ever come across before. They fear they may have a pandemic on their hands.'

Ransome stared blindly out the window, thinking: are all Shoji's claims true? His skin crawled at the thought of it. The image of the line of white arms pushed out through the judas holes of cell doors flashed through his mind.

'Christ,' Ransome said fervently, 'I hope you can stop this bastard.'

'He's gone to ground,' Uto said. 'I think he's waiting to see how the political situation is shaping. If his thugs win the battle of the streets, he'll reappear.'

'How is it shaping?'

'Badly. Police resources are stretched to the limit. The Prime Minister is seriously thinking of declaring martial law, but now there's even doubt about the loyalty of some sections of the defence forces.'

They passed a column of twenty armoured personnel carriers crowded with riot police heading back towards the inner city.

'I wonder whose side they're on?' Ransome said.

A muscle worked briefly in Uto's jaw.

* * *

The love hotel in Shinjuku was pure Tokyo kitsch. The triangular tower was a pencil-slim stack of capsules variegated in gold and blue. Each capsule had a circular window. A gold tent-roofed penthouse capped the bizarre structure. Uto double-parked in the narrow street and left a sign on his windscreen.

There were four men waiting in the foyer. One of them was the Elvis Presley clone from Ransome's abduction. He did not acknowledge Ransome but, instead, kept a wary eye on Uto as though he expected trouble at any moment.

The four rode up in the lift with them to the top floor. No-one spoke.

At the penthouse level foyer, the Presley clone knocked. The door clicked open. Uto and Ransome were ushered inside. Their escorts followed.

The man in the circular bed with the two naked young girls smiled at Ransome, his ugly face creasing up in surprise like a soft rubber ball. The single eyebrow hooked in query.

'Ah, Ransome-san,' he said.

Ihari, the younger. Frogface II.

Ransome nodded at him. He seemed less menacing without his clothes.

Ihari rose from the bed. In contrast to the ugliness of his face, the young man had a finely proportioned body with a flat muscular stomach. The Elvis Presley clone held open an embroidered gold kimono. Frogface pulled it on.

He turned towards Uto and bowed. Uto bowed back. Ihari invited them to sit on the white leather divan. He spoke to the girls in a harsh voice. They rolled off the bed and walked past Ransome and Uto, their doll faces set in an annoyed pout, their tiny pubescent breasts aimed at the world like bayonets.

Ihari dismissed his henchmen with a wave of his hand.

One of the girls came back carrying a pot of tea and some cups. She had put on some clothes: a micro mini and a T-shirt upon which was printed the legend 'Poccari Sweat'. She filled the cups and left.

Ihari sprawled on the end of the bed opposite them, affecting languor but his eyes were sharp.

Uto and he then spoke together in Japanese for several minutes. Uto made no attempt to translate. From time to time Ihari shook his head. It seemed clear that he was not interested in being cooperative.

Uto said something that caused Ihari to look directly at Ransome. He said in English, with a strong north-east American accent, 'Sorry we had to lean on you. We are business partners of Takanichi Shoji. We were asked to warn you off, so we did. It was nothing personal.' He turned his palms upwards to show his lack of malice.

Ransome shrugged. 'You would've killed me if you'd been asked.'

Frogface grinned. 'Sure we would.'

'Then fuck you too,' Ransome said.

Frogface laughed loudly.

Uto went on talking. His tone had grown sombre. After a time Ihari began to look uncomfortable. His face grew hard, the eyes troubled. Something Uto said seemed to upset him. He rose and walked about the room in silence, agitated as a new prisoner in a cell. He sat down again, leaned forward and began to talk intently to Uto.

Fifteen minutes later they left.

Back in the car, Uto said, 'Smart young man. An MBA from MIT. Likes to assist the police—if it doesn't cost.'

'Did he tell you what we need to know?' Ransome said.

Uto shrugged. 'I hope so.' He was concentrating hard, driving relentlessly through the nervous, rain-shy traffic. 'They've been working with Takanichi Shoji for years. They've made a lot of money together. They know more about him than he would like to believe.'

'Information as insurance,' Ransome suggested.

Uto nodded. 'He tells me that down at number four wharf at Kachi-doki there's a cargo loading for the Middle East. He's been organising the shipment for Shoji. The manifest will record automobiles and heavy industrial equipment, but the hidden cargo is weapons. Shoji told Ihari they were conventional weapons. When I told him what was happening, and that the weapons might be biological, he suddenly became quite helpful.'

Away to the left on the edge of Tokyo Bay, the chemical purity of a yellow column of smoke from a factory stack was being contaminated by an ice-grey mist.

'Strange people, the *yakuza*. Ihari's son said, "We Yakuza may be crooks, but we do have certain standards."' Uto laughed. He swung the car onto a ramp that plunged down into the cancerous city below.

* * *

Dusk.

A new industrial area of functional buildings, landscaped grounds and chain link fences. To the south, the glow of the city was gaining ascendancy over the dying winter daylight.

As Uto drove around the three-storey concrete building, Ransome shot pictures from out the car window. There was a high perimeter fence, the top strands laced with barbed wire. No lights showed. Within the grounds they saw no-one. The fourth wall of the processing factory, a cat's cradle of pipes and ducts painted in different primary colours, faced onto a muddy canal. A glutinous smear of green scum had captured the lock gates.

Uto cruised slowly back to the front. Huge Japanese characters were written in blue along the face of the building. For Ransome's benefit, he translated: 'Ukazi Fish.'

Was this the place? Ransome wondered. Was this where Shoji had experimented for the past years? Was this where his technicians had died? He looked at the featureless industrial building, feeling his tension grow.

The wire mesh gate gaped open. A glass-walled gate-keeper's hut no bigger than a telephone booth was unmanned. Uto drove through and stopped the car near the front entrance.

By the short flight of steps that led into the building two cars were parked: a black stretched limousine and a dark blue Datsun. 'Shoji?' Uto asked, squinting questioningly at Ransome.

Ransome said, 'Looks like his car,' thinking of poor, dead Kaizei, regretting now that he hadn't been able to summon up enough hatred to finish Shoji off when he'd had the chance.

They got out of the car. Carrying his camera, Ransome walked to the limousine. It was locked. He tried peering in through the black glass windows. No-one inside. He backed off and filmed a shot of the limousine in front of the building—the licence number and the company name in frame.

Uto was trying the door handle of the Datsun. It opened. He sat inside for a moment examining the contents of the glove box. He got out and closed the door quietly. 'Hire car,' he said, looking thoughtful. 'How many of them? I wonder.' He unbuttoned his jacket and drew out his pistol.

'You wouldn't have a spare, would you?' Ransome said.

Uto's eyes flickered. His hesitation was momentary. He went back to his car and unlocked the boot. From beside the spare wheel he pulled out a black plastic shopping bag. Inside, was a cloth parcel. He unwrapped it. 'You can handle one of these?' he said. The pistol was a black automatic.

'Yes.'

Uto released the clip, checked that it was loaded then punched the magazine back into the grip. He handed the pistol to Ransome, who shoved the gun in his jacket pocket, hitched up his camera harness and nodded to show he was ready.

There were lights on inside the small reception area. Through the glass walls they could see a desk and switchboard. The door was open. Their eyes met. Uto made a slight motion with his head and walked slowly inside.

Silence.

To one side there was a flight of stairs. Uto looked upwards briefly then passed the reception desk and followed a short passageway. Beyond a swinging door was a vast food processing hall that seemed to occupy the whole of the floor. Dim overnight lights gleamed on stainless steel processing machines and a warp and weave of conveyor belts.

Uto led back to the reception area, moving faster now. They went up the stairs quietly.

On the first landing, slumped in a sitting position against the wall, was the body of a man. A vivid patch of blood was showing against the expensive grey fabric of the double-breasted jacket.

The last time Ransome had seen the man was in a law office in Yokohama. Ransome remembered the smooth whitewash about Section 731, then the hatred on the arrogant vulpine face. Now there was a look of surprise upon it. Death had caught Section 731's apologist unprepared. Had it been Yonoi behind all the violence?

Uto was ignoring the body. He peered up the stairwell behind the foresight of his extended pistol.

Ransome put his lips close to the policeman's ear. He said, 'Yonoi. The lawyer from Yokohama. He was third in command at Harbin.'

Uto did not look at him, but his eyebrows rose as he processed the information.

Ransome framed a shot from a point on the wall about chest height, then panned down the red smear, stark

against the white wall, to dead Yonoi. He began shooting, thinking, so who the hell had come in the Datsun?

He swung round to film Uto as the policeman moved
upwards, keeping close to the wall, tracking him, holding
the shot as steady as possible.

Towards the top of the next flight of stairs there was a
second body. It was upside down. The bloodied head had
jammed against the iron bannister, preventing the dead
man falling all the way down to the landing.

'Recognise him?' Uto spoke quietly.

Ransome craned his head to look. The man was young.
Something familiar about him. The cropped hair was the
trigger.

'The police lieutenant who arrested me in Shinjuku.'

Uto nodded.

So that was how the *yakuza* had come to be in his cell.
Was it this one who had handed over Katie so that he
might meet his terrible end?

They were on the middle floor. Several glassed-in
offices faced them. Beyond, they could see a deserted
processing floor similar to the one below.

From somewhere above, Ransome caught a subtle
whiff of something burning. Up the stairs, Uto leading,
still being careful but moving fast.

At the top of the stairs there was a metal door with a
series of elaborate locks and bars. On the wall beside it,
bold in red, was the international sign for 'No Entry'. The
outward opening door was ajar. Uto went through.

Through the camera lens Ransome saw a long passageway that appeared to run the length of the building, on
one side a blank wall, on the other a series of doors, Uto
trying each one as he went. All locked. The smell of
burning was strong now.

Halfway along there was another notice: the same pro-
hibition sign together with lengthy instructions. Uto
could tell him later if it was significant. Ransome kept on

shooting. The sign filled the frame. In the bottom corner was a red death's head.

He turned and framed Uto, who had stopped by an open door. He was staring at something. He went through the door behind his gun. Ransome turned into the door after him, keeping him in shot, viewing over his shoulder.

Beyond Uto, at the far end of two long parallel stainless-steel benches, he saw a man, maybe forty feet away, out of focus. He was standing perfectly still, looking towards the camera. Ransome pulled focus. The blurred figure sharpened and became Shoji Takanichi.

Ransome looked up from his lens to take in the whole scene. Shoji stared at them in silence. Behind him was an open wall safe. By his feet was a metal rubbish bin with a thin column of smoke streaming upwards. Burning the evidence?

The laboratory was huge. Ice-blue and grey, steel and glass. It gleamed with a pristine cleanliness, a forest of pipettes, beakers, flasks and test tubes catching the shadowless white light. There were no windows. Into the left wall were set six heavily barred green doors framed by dials and gauges. Refrigerator units, Ransome guessed. All along the right-hand wall were ranged a line of silvery retorts, each big enough to hold a man, each connected with pipes to smaller tanks and gauges. Behind him, to his right, between the door and the wall, there were chest-high stacks of cages.

Rats. Black rats. Hundreds of them scuttling in their cages and making a low, excited, twittering sound that made his flesh crawl.

He pressed the camera trigger and began a slow 180-degree pan from right to left, taking in the whole scene. First the rat cages, the tall retorts, then Uto came into shot, his pistol extended, already halfway to Shoji, who seemed to be in a trance. Pivoting around slowly, slowly, past glass columns of green, red and yellow chemicals, past centrifuges, computers, the wall of refrigerator doors coming into shot now, dials and gauges.

Now reversing the pan, back to Uto. He was standing still now, something odd about his stance. He was putting his pistol down on the bench. He was raising his hands. What the hell? Ransome held the shot. A smiling face in big close-up crowded the edges of the frame.

'My left profile is better,' Cord said.

Chapter 61

Cold steel was pressing into the back of Ransome's neck. He dragged his eye from the lens and lowered the camera.

'Put the camera down on the bench,' Cord said. 'Slowly.'

Ransome obeyed. Cord watched as his man frisked Ransome, running expert hands over his body. Uto's spare pistol was dragged from his pocket.

'Goodness,' Cord said with mock disapproval, 'I thought journalists were supposed to be non-combatants.'

From the far end of the line of tanks, opposite Shoji, Cord's other henchman appeared—the Japanese. Shoji must have been able to see him all along; Uto, only later. In his hand the man held a small automatic machine pistol. Ransome guessed it was an Uzi; he had seen a couple of them in Kampuchea. Now the man could cover them both within a small arc.

The man who had searched him appeared to Ransome's left. He too had an automatic pistol. He must have come in from the passageway behind them. Maybe he had been behind them from the time they had entered the building?

The Caucasian walked behind Uto and lifted the policeman's pistol from the bench. He put it in his pocket. He raised his own weapon and, two-handed, smashed the stock down on the back of Uto's head. He went down with a cry and lay deathly still.

'You bastard,' Ransome said. He began to move towards Uto.

The man turned and smiled at Ransome. He had the innocuous face of an accountant. He was aiming directly at Ransome's navel.

'Wouldn't chance it, I were you,' Cord said. 'He likes firing that thing.'

Uto didn't move.

'Could be no-one else'll get hurt,' Cord said, 'we play it right.' Something approaching a smile was edging onto his face. He was nervous, but in charge. 'Since he doesn't want to die right here, Mr Takanichi has just agreed to stop burning his files and—how shall I put it?—"join forces" with us, allowing us to help him further develop his useful technology.'

Shoji was looking at Cord without expression. He dropped the file he held in his hand onto the bench.

Ransome said, 'He doesn't look all that keen on the idea.'

Cord laughed. 'He's embarrassed that he didn't think to tell us what he's been doing all these years.'

'How do you think you're going to get him to cooperate?'

'If he doesn't, he's got serious political problems.' Cord laughed. 'Imagine what the media would make of this set-up? Anyways, with something this big, you'd be surprised how many resources can be mustered to assist Mr Takanichi with his work.'

'Who are you, Cord? Who do you work for? You CIA?'

Cord smiled. 'Let's just say, Ransome, that I'm a God-fearin' patriot working for some Good Ol' Boys who are realistic enough to understand that might is what makes democracy great.'

Ransome felt despair overwhelm him. 'Nothing changes with you people, does it? Forty-five years ago some of your fellow realists did a grubby deal to use an obscene technology. Now you're at it again.'

'There is no deal, Ransome,' Cord said. 'We've raised our moral standards since 1946. This time,' smiling, 'we're stealing it.'

Ransome shook his head in disgust. 'Any idea what you're stealing?'

'Sure we know,' Cord said. 'Before he died, your friend Aoyama told us enough to excite our interest. At that moment, my orders changed. Up till then I was only supposed to make sure you didn't embarrass our main man here so's he could get on with making his political run. But seems like he was holding out on us, sneaky fellow.' He gestured around the laboratory. 'All this stuff—state of the art science— pity we can't just ship it out. But with Mr Takanichi's help, however reluctant,' grinning now, 'we can replicate this Stateside.'

'For Christ's sake Cord, it's a whole new disease he has developed, his own special little contribution to mankind. His father perfected it: a combination of pneumonic plague and anthrax virus with a few other nasty complications thrown in for good measure. Water-carried, air-carried, carried in the natural food chain, whatever you fancy. Affects everyone. Within two days you start rotting like a piece of overripe fruit. No known cure. And he's about to sell it.'

Cord's eyes were still bland, but some of the confidence was ebbing. 'What are you talking about?'

He had Cord's attention. 'Has he told you he's got a shipment of this stuff down on number four wharf, Kachi-doki docks? Dangerous shit. They've sealed off the area. Everybody's wearing masks and barrier clothing. By the time we left, they'd found fifty-eight cylinders hidden in a cargo of machine tools and cars. And guess where it's heading, Cord.'

Cord stared at him.

'The Middle East,' Ransome said.

Cord looked at Shoji. Shoji Takanichi said nothing.

'Yeah, there's gratitude for you, Cord. You keep his father's nose clean all these years and now Shoji flogs the stuff he didn't get round to telling you about to anyone who'll buy it. You don't believe me? Ask him, why don't you?'

Cord looked accusingly at Shoji.

Ransome said, 'He doesn't actually care who buys this shit. Do you, Mr Takanichi?'

Shoji met Ransome's eye silently. He did not change expression. After a moment, ignoring both men, he began stacking the files on the desk in front of him. He reached into the safe and pulled out several more.

Ransome said, 'Got a family, Cord? Got any kids?'

The American said nothing.

'Maybe one of your own sons will rot if ever someone starts to use this shit.' God, what's the point, he thought. It was useless.

'If it's that good,' Cord said, 'we've got to control it, don't we? Just as well we're going to have the benefit of Mr Takanichi's cooperation. Right now, he's leaving with us. You, unfortunately,' parodying regret, 'are not.'

Cord's Japanese gunman looked at him expectantly, waiting for the signal.

At that moment, Uto stirred. Cord immediately nodded to his man covering Shoji. The Caucasian moved nearer to the policeman, cocking his weapon.

Ransome thought, Oh Christ, not in cold blood. Keep him talking somehow. 'Did Shoji tell you there's just been an accident in this lab? It's probably infected.'

Cord said, 'Shut up!' He nodded to the Caucasian. He nodded towards Uto. 'Do it.'

Shoji reached in and took something else from the safe. He turned and shot the Caucasian in the back of the head. There was an exploding spray of scarlet.

By the time Shoji loosed off the next shot, Ransome was halfway to the floor, diving left.

From behind, a shriek of pain from Cord's Japanese. The explosive roar of a machine pistol. One side of the laboratory fragmenting: glass instruments exploding into dust, liquids spilling, the ceiling disintegrating in the upward arc of bullets. Overhead, shattered lights swinging wildly showered white sparks.

Ransome scrambled desperately to get out of the line of fire.

Shoji's third shot caught Cord in the face. Still trying to drag his pistol from under his arm, the big man cannoned backwards into the rats' cages. His legs collapsed under him. He sat down, heavily, dragging three complete stacks of cages with him. They came apart. Black rats spilled over him like treacle, squeaking shrilly as they fled their prisons.

Shoji fired another shot. Ransome dived straight over the Caucasian. A hot mist of blood from a flaring artery sprayed his face. He gasped in relief as he made cover around the end of the steel bench.

The rats spread, panic-stricken. He lashed out with his feet, kicking them away in disgust. Overhead, the sparks spluttered on, fizzing like catherine wheels. Somewhere liquid gurgled. There was a pungent reek of chemicals.

Ransome could hear the Caucasian dying, making small gagging sounds as he choked in his own blood. He peered around the bottom of the bench. The man's machine pistol was in view. It was two metres from Ransome, in the open but jammed half-under the man's body.

Beyond, Cord was a road for rats, struggling free of their broken cages, scampering down him and scattering in all directions. He was sprawled back among the cages, both hands covering his face. Blood was seeping through his fingers. His jacket hung open. His gun showed half-free from the shoulder holster.

Ransome rose to his knees and crawled to the far left side of the bench. A quick sighting look over the top of the bench and back. As Ransome ducked, a shot rico-cheted off the steel top. Shoji had been waiting for a target, pistol extended.

Ransome tried to steady his breathing. Think. Think! Could he get to Cord's weapon? He needed something to create a diversion. Glass flasks, half-a-dozen of them: in that moment looking over the benchtop he had glimpsed them, about halfway along.

Here we go.

Keeping low, he began moving along the bench with his back to the wall of refrigerators. Frantic rats moved before him, rushing through pools of liquid, scampering over broken glass. He would have to guess the distance. Five metres, seven. Stop.

He came up fast, reaching with his left hand. The flasks were a metre further than he had gauged. As he lunged to grab the nearest, Shoji came round the far end of the bench. An image of him, half-crouched, aiming two-handed.

Ransome kept on going upwards. A shot. Glass shat-tering into a curtain before him as he rolled over the top of the bench. Over and over, something gashing his leg. He crashed onto the floor of the centre aisle, scattering rats. Half on his feet, throwing himself forward. A second shot. The shelter of the bench, his breath tearing his chest, the smell of chemicals half choking him. But safe, the glass flask in his hand.

He looked at his weapon. Hefted it. Twice as big as a beer can, full of a pale liquid that might only be water. It might just buy him time to get to Cord's gun.

Cord lay still now among the empty cages. Dead? Ransome wondered. The butt of the pistol was tantalis-ingly visible.

A quick look. Shoji was back in front of the wall safe.

A shot, followed by a whining ricochet.

Ducking low, Ransome moved two metres to his left. He

set himself. A deep breath and he came up and lobbed
the flask in a sidearm, grenade-throwing action. A
glimpse of Shoji raising his weapon, then down again
counting one . . . two . . . as the flask flew. He heard it
smash on the far wall and flung himself across the open
gap.

Keep your eye on the ball, the coaches always said. As
he passed Cord he plucked the pistol cleanly from the
holster and was past the gap in one continuous motion,
diving behind the cover of the opposite bench.

The sound of a belated shot. A piece coming off the
ceiling. Another shot slammed into the door behind him,
high up.

From the far end of the laboratory there began a
strange keening sound.

A long moment later a third bullet clanged on the
casing of a dangling neon tube. It threw off a fizzing
shower of sparks. Ransome slipped off the safety catch,
counting the shots now. Four. Five. The thin blade of
sound moved up a register. What the hell is it? he
thought.

He moved to the right behind one of the huge silver
retorts. Cautiously, he looked around it.

Suddenly Shoji appeared above the bench, struggling
upright, his mouth agape. The high-pitched screaming
was coming from him. He lurched forward a few steps,
then fell, out of Ransome's sight. Gun in hand, Ransome
moved fast to the far end of the aisle.

He saw that the far wall and the surrounding steel
benches were blackened. From out of the wall safe a thick
tongue of flame flickered as from the door of a furnace.
The waste-paper basket in which Shoji had been burning
the documents was ablaze.

He saw Uto moving feebly as he tried to throw off the
dead weight of the Caucasian. And he saw Shoji, down
on his hands and knees, struggling to his feet.

With a terrible effort he made it, his face an amalgam of anguish and rage. He straightened. Staring straight ahead and holding his pistol in front of him two-handed, as though to make doubly sure of his next shot, he began walking towards Ransome, screaming. There was something odd about the space around him. He was haloed in a strange white light.

Jesus, Ransome thought, he's on fire.

Shoji kept on coming. He was opposite Uto now, not seeing him; seeing only Ransome, his eyes blazing with hatred. The weight of his pistol seemed too great for Shoji. He struggled to level it.

Ransome took aim.

The man's legs began to buckle. He fell sideways against the bench.

There was a muffled explosion.

The white light around Shoji had become a blue and green shroud. The man was a human torch. Along the full length of the benchtop a white flame began to run as though it were a fast fuse. Shoji bounced off the side of the bench and began a drunken downward spin. He fired into the ceiling as he fell.

Beakers and flasks began to explode like mortar shells. There was a blinding flash. Ransome was blown half off his feet by the blast.

Ransome flung the body of Cord's man off Uto. He dragged the policeman by his collar past the twisting, screaming shell that was Shoji, past the still figure that had been Cord.

There was a great roar as the first of the huge silver retorts blew. Deafened by the sound, Ransome wrenched at the laboratory door. Rats poured out through the door with him as he dragged Uto from the sear of flames into the passageway and back towards the entrance.

It was dark outside. As he came down the steps from the front entrance with Uto over his shoulder, the policeman said, 'Car radio,' his voice teetering on a knife-edge of agony.

Ransome opened the car door and awkwardly lowered Uto into the passenger seat. He felt himself trembling with exhaustion. How had the slightly-built Kaizei found the strength to run with him that day at Khe San?

Uto was bleeding from the mouth and nose. His eyes were rolling in his head, but nodding towards the two-way radio he said, 'The left-hand switch. Press it down.'

Ransome did so and handed him the mike. There was an electronic squawk, then Uto was talking. After a time he closed his eyes. 'They'll be here soon,' he said in a voice no louder than a sigh.

Ransome looked up at the top floor of the building. Black smoke and flickers of flame were beginning to show through the roof. He wondered what horrors were being carried up into Tokyo's night sky.

From time to time there were muffled roars as the chemicals exploded inside.

On the top floor, a window blew out like a firecracker. Dark smoke gushed outwards, twisting like a live thing. A salvo of brightly burning objects shot out. Rats—their shrill collective shriek a single contrapuntal note against the growling roar of the fire. Flaring like spent tracer bullets, they arched downwards onto the ground beneath the walls.

Someone appeared from the billowing smoke that filled the foyer. The man lurched forward through the door, barely managing to stay upright.

'Jesus Christ,' Ransome said.

Uto opened his eyes.

The figure was fire-blackened as though formed of tar. Smoke rose from the smouldering clothing.

Ransome felt nothing; not pity, not compassion. He saw again faces imprisoned in ice; heard the sound of wooden clubs on frozen flesh; saw the bland, unrepentant faces of those old men; saw dead Kaizei and the meat hook. Fire and ice. There was an irony to it.

Shoji paused on the top step, swaying. With a terrible effort, he came fully erect. For a long moment he stood as though summoning up reserves from somewhere deep within himself. He stepped forward into space. He crashed onto the steps headfirst and slid down. He lay with his arms spreadeagled like those of a man crucified upside down.

On the sharp winter air was borne the unmistakable stench of burning flesh.

Ransome turned. Uto had been watching him. He seemed about to say something, but a tide of pain flickered across his face. He closed his eyes.

Ransome got into the front seat and put his arm around him. 'You'll be alright, pal,' he said.

A few minutes later, he heard the wail of sirens.

Chapter 62

K aizei smiled that rakish smile of his, all creases and twisted teeth. The image froze. The legend 'For KT' appeared, superimposed over the freeze-frame, and was held.

Into Ransome's mind another, uglier image appeared. It was the same familiar face, but distorted by agony. He felt his skin shrink from the remembered cold of that bleak freezing chamber where his friend had met his end. He thrust the image away. He wanted to remember Kaizei at peace.

The face disintegrated into a coarse electronic screen of parallel lines and dots. The tape ran out. The video-recorder clicked off.

This week the world would learn about those old horrors and the more recent shameful acts. Martin Garrett had done his job brilliantly. Fourteen countries had bought the two-hour documentary.

What will people think? he wondered. What impact will it have? How will they deal with all the horror shown in it? Will it change them or will it be just another piece of history crowded out by commercials, something that happened to other people in another country far away? Now he was shot of it, it no longer seemed to matter.

He was aware of a depthless exhaustion. It had taken four grinding months of work, travel and frustration to piece it all together.

At first there had been the fear that he might have caught something fatal in Shoji's laboratory. Uto and he had been given a medical clearance only after ten days of strict quarantine. Uto had spent the first week in intensive care. There was a new steel plate in the back of his broken skull.

They learned that there had been a massive secret cleanup operation in the districts immediately surrounding the Tokyo laboratory. Uto had been transferred from the Police Intelligence Unit back to normal duties. Unofficially the policeman learned that Shoji's experimental team of scientists had been hunted down and 'neutralised', whatever that might mean. It was never explained. He also was told that all the relevant data had been destroyed. Neither he nor Ransome believed that.

Ransome had stayed on in Japan for a further six weeks completing Kaizei's work. The Japanese authorities had wanted him to go at once. Only the government's awareness of the harm the story would do to their opposition had made it possible. Ransome had been unable to elicit a single official comment from anyone in government about the matter of ongoing research on biological warfare.

Nothing about it appeared in the Japanese media after Shoji's death. When the documentary came out he knew that his story of the new biological weapon would be denied, and described as either fanciful, vindictive, or anti-Japanese.

The Prime Minister had made much of Takanichi Jurichiro's connection with the now-disgraced Section 731, and of Shoji's leadership of the extreme Right. This had helped him ride out the political upheaval. Only a month ago he had finally stepped down as leader, content to become the country's major power broker.

For Ransome there had been ten days in Washington working on aspects of the US involvement. Lloyd Brucchi and Julia Sumner had opened the right doors for him. He delivered his promise to Julia. It was she who broke his revelations about the American coverup in the *Washington Post*. It had caused acute embarrassment.

Right now, certain high officials in the State Department were pressing for a Senate inquiry into the mysterious organisation which had been running Cord. Early indications were that his had been a covert mission, not run by the CIA but from the basement of the White House and privately funded by extreme right-wing organisations.

The documentary, which he had called *Section 731 and Beyond*, was good, very good—the best thing he had done. But McGregor's question nagged away in his mind on its compulsive loop of regret: 'Was it all worth it?'

Had it been? Ransome walked out onto the roof garden. The fiery desert air from the inland had been carried over the coast by the easterly wind. It felt hot on his skin.

Reiko was standing with her back to him looking out over the ocean. She had not heard him come. Tonight she had decided that she could not bear to watch the tapes of the finished film.

Looking at her made him feel good. Since leaving Japan she had opened up like a flower. She had concentrated on settling the children into school and dealing with the conversion of the old San Diego ship chandler's warehouse he had bought overlooking the Pacific Ocean. In the past week she had begun giving cello lessons to a few of the graduate students of the university's department of music. In spite of the stresses engendered by his project, they were good together.

He crossed the wide terrace and gently put his arms around her.

She turned towards him, hugging him close. 'I'm sorry,' she said, 'I couldn't handle it.' From the beginning she had chosen not to be involved, but she had respected Ransome's need to finish what he had started. She had encouraged him with her affection and delight at being with him.

He shrugged. He knew that the subject caused her pain. Maybe, in time, she would be able to deal with it. 'Don't worry about it.'

Reiko said, 'The thing is, I think I *am* ready to see it now, but . . . This is silly, it's just that I'd like to see it alone. Do you mind?'

'Of course not,' he said, delighted that she wanted to confront it. 'Now?'

'Right now.'

With their arms around each other, they went back into the vast loft. She sat down, still holding his hand. She looked apprehensive.

He picked up the remote control. 'I'll just run it back for you,' he said, 'then leave you to it.'

The tape began to whirr backwards, backwards through all those frozen secrets, back through all those cathartic revelations and confessions to where the story had its grim beginnings on the icy wastes of Harbin.

He knelt down in front of her and kissed her softly. Her breath tasted sweet. 'Reiko, it's history. It has absolutely nothing to do with you. Okay?'

She tried to smile, but it didn't take.

'If you need me,' Ransome said, 'I'll be outside.'

The air was cooling, giving promise of some release from the heat. The moon glinted on the tips of rollers sliding in from the mysterious depths of the Pacific. From the beach below came the soft detonation of waves spending themselves on the white sand. From further out, the lighthouse blinked its seven-second warning signal.

He looked back at her, sitting staring at the blank screen, waiting for the tape to run all the way back. If you can handle this, he thought, we can make it. For the first time in a long while Ransome felt optimistic.

Afterword

This is a fiction, but one based on historical facts. The medical experimentation camp at Harbin in Manchuria did exist. It was the largest the world has ever known.

From 1937, the Japanese Army Biological Unit, Section 731, was manned by more than two thousand of Japan's most talented doctors who volunteered in order to conduct live experiments on prisoners of war.

Lieutenant General Shiro Ishii was in charge of the camp. His special brief was the development of biological weapons.

The records of Section 731 were completely erased to create a blank in history. Many members of the original Section 731 experimental medical teams now hold high office in Japan.